ELEANOR

MISS GRANBY'S SECRET

or
The Bastard of Pinsk

Eleanor Farjeon, born on February 13, 1881, in London, England, daughter of Benjamin and Maggie (Jefferson). Farjeon was a renowned English author, poet, playwright, journalist and broadcaster. Home-schooled, she began writing at the age of five and quickly gained recognition, particularly in children's literature. Her simplicity of style, combined with profound emotional depth, made her works accessible and enduring. She is perhaps best known for her hymn *Morning has Broken* which gained international acclaim thanks to the recording by Cat Stevens.

Throughout her career Farjeon maintained a close circle of literary friends and contributed to the World War II effort. She received numerous literary awards, including the Carnegie Medal in 1955, the Hans Christian Andersen Medal in 1956 for her novel *The Little Bookroom*, and the Regina Medal for children's literature in 1956. The Children's Book Circle present a prestigious annual Eleanor Farjeon Award.

Farjeon never married but had a contented 30-year relationship with George Earle, an English teacher. After his death in 1949, she befriended actor Denys Blakelock, who wrote a memoir: *Eleanor, Portrait of the Farjeon* (1966). She passed away in Hampstead, London on June 5, 1965, leaving behind a rich legacy of enchanting tales and timeless poetry.

SELECTED NOVELS BY ELEANOR FARJEON

Ladybrook (1931)

The Fair of St. James (1932)

Humming Bird (1936)

Miss Granby's Secret (1940)

Brave Old Woman (1941)

The Fair Venetian (1943)

Ariadne and the Bull (1945)

Love Affair (1947)

The Two Bouquets (1948)

ELEANOR FARJEON

MISS GRANBY'S SECRET

or
The Bastard of Pinsk

With an introduction
by Elizabeth Crawford

DEAN STREET PRESS

A Furrowed Middlebrow Book
FM97

Published by Dean Street Press 2024

First published in 1941 by Simon and Schuster

Cover by DSP

ISBN 978 1 915393 92 0

www.deanstreetpress.co.uk

INTRODUCTION

Of *Miss Granby's Secret* the *Liverpool Daily Post* (27 November 1940) commented, 'In this amusing book Miss Farjeon exercises once more the enviable gift which enables her to raise whole edifices on a foundation of cobwebs and moonshine'. And at no time was such an edifice more necessary as a protection from Real Life than in the Blitz winter of 1940. Indeed, as the publisher's note reveals, it was 'in a bomb shelter in London' that those cobwebs and moonshine were spun into this multi-storied, many-roomed, mansion of a tale. Dismiss, however, the image of a bomb shelter as a crowded Tube platform, for Eleanor Farjeon's was purpose-built, cosy and private, a few steps across the cobbled mews from her Hampstead cottage. It was here, with her companion George Earle, she settled down of an evening with 'blankets, eiderdowns and pillows, a table with books, writing materials, playing cards, aspirin, boiled sweets, torch and a little travelling clock' and conjured up the worlds of Adelaide Granby and of Stanislaw, the Bastard of Pinsk.

Remembered now principally as a prolific and successful writer of prose and verse tales for children, Eleanor Farjeon (1881-1965) was born to parents whose past lives might have seemed fanciful if met in a novel. Her father, Benjamin Farjeon (1838-1903), from an impoverished Jewish family in London's East End, Made Good in a peculiarly 19th-century manner. As a boy, with little education, he was a Fleet Street apprentice, a 'printer's devil', until, aged 17, lured to Australia by the Gold Rush. There he found no gold, but embarked on a new career as a newspaperman, eventually settling in New Zealand as manager of the *Otago Daily Times*. Impetuous, however, and determined to make his living as a novelist, in 1868 he returned to England, on the strength of kind, if lukewarm, encouragement from his hero, Charles Dickens. In London he became reacquainted a few years later with the famed American actor Joseph Jefferson, first met in New Zealand, and in 1877 married Jefferson's daughter, Margaret (1853-1933). Eleanor, their only daughter, was the second of four surviving children, a son dying shortly after her birth. By 1885 the family had moved to Hampstead, where, home-schooled by tutors and governesses, the children formed a close unit, Eleanor pairing with her elder brother Harry, and Joe with the youngest, Bertie.

In her attic bookroom Eleanor dreamed through her childhood and youth, writing all manner of stories, plays, and poems, her imagination stimulated by visits to all the new stage shows of the day, a privilege consequent on her family's theatrical connections. But, as she confessed in *A Nursery in the Nineties* (1935), 'I had no self-confidence, no foothold anywhere if it wasn't in my writing', while in *Morning Has Broken* (1986), a biography of her aunt, Annabel Farjeon comments that young Eleanor's 'thick, steel-rimmed spectacles, dark hair that would not keep in place, pallid thick-fleshed texture of her cheeks and awkward movements were not the attributes of a fairy princess or even a heroine'. It is, therefore, unsurprising to discover that TAR, a game of fantasy created with Harry, dominated Eleanor's life, allowing her to become whomsoever she wished.

Meanwhile, from his study several storeys below, Benjamin Farjeon sent out into the world nearly 60 novels, battling to maintain both his family and the status appropriate to a prosperous author. Alas, on his death he left little money, his tales of sentiment, of mystery, and of colonial derring-do already old-fashioned, and his young sons had no choice but begin earning their livings, stepping into the literary, theatrical, and musical worlds. Eleanor, however, remained, as was considered fitting, 'the daughter at home', still under the spell of TAR. That ended one day in 1910 when Harry decreed the game was over. As Eleanor wrote, 'I did not know that my life was about to begin when, pushed off the bright cloud of illusion, I fell through a vacuum and at last touched earth'. She was 29.

As she unravels *Miss Granby's Secret*, Pamela, Adelaide Granby's practical great-niece, comments, 'Aunt Addie's romance was like one of those Indian boxes that charmed in childhood; the green one contained a yellow, the yellow, a red, the red a blue, the blue a pink, and so on seemingly *ad infinitum*, till one reached the core, as tiny as a seed, which the nest had held like a secret, round which it had grown'. Similarly, with hindsight, it is possible to discern in Eleanor Farjeon's life the seed that in 1940 blossomed into *Miss Granby's Secret*, a seed first watered when in 1910 she 'at last touched earth'.

For it was only after the spell of TAR was broken that Eleanor emerged from the bosom of her family into a circle of Hampstead friends, among whom were some who, like Miss Granby's Pamela, were 'Young Fabians', members of the Fabian Society, espousing socialism and equal rights for men and women. It is known that Eleanor then quickly fell in love, an unrequited passion that pre-dated her well-known devotion to Edward Thomas, and it is with this first flowering of romantic feeling that Farjeon endows young Adelaide Granby. But whereas Adelaide pours her heart into *The Bastard of Pinsk*, Eleanor's feelings found expression in thirteen sonnets, eventually published as the opening sequence of *First and Second Love* (1949). Incidentally, many years after her death it was revealed that her secret attachment had been to Stacy Aumonier, a married member of the Hampstead circle, then a painter, two of whose watercolours were hanging on Eleanor's walls at the end of her life.

In *Miss Granby's Secret* young Adelaide Granby and the Tarletan Triplets are, as is the natural lot of heroines, beautiful, the latter with 'transparent complexions and sylph-like forms'. Moreover, like Miss Granby, the Tarletan Triplets 'share the romantic dreams which people the caverns of their ignorance'. In a similar manner 18-year-old Eleanor Farjeon's verse was so naively 'knowing' that it elicited the comment, 'Where did you get your knowledge from, young lady?' As the older Eleanor remarked, 'in the Nineties, when one was eighteen, one didn't know what sort of knowledge Mr X meant.' Over twenty years later she still retained this innocence, understanding, as her niece Annabel recounts, 'almost nothing of sex in theory and practice'. She was told by Eleanor 'that it was on a visit to Paris, sitting in the Luxembourg Gardens, that [George Earle] discovered this fact ...[and] explained, drawing in the sand at their feet diagrams of the male and female parts and how they worked with the tip of his stout British walking stick.' However, in the novel, Miss Granby, the author of 49 torrid romances, resolutely refuses Pamela's offer to educate her in this matter remarking, 'I always shocked my public. If I had known the facts of life, I couldn't have done it. I should have been much too coy. But fortunately, I had only my inklings'. Shortly after the 1920 visit to Paris, with facts now having replaced inklings, Eleanor and George 'sealed as true a marriage as could be without the benefit of clergy', the latter comment an allusion to the fact that Earle was married, though long separated.

In the inter-war years, while stories and poems for children streamed from her pen, along with, for much of that time, a lengthy rhyme each day for the Daily Herald, Eleanor published only one novel specifically for adults. In fact, her adult novels are little remarked and, although Annabel Farjeon includes *Miss Granby's Secret* in her bibliography, she makes no mention of it in the biography. Conversely, although *Brave Old Woman*, Eleanor's 1941 adult novel, is mentioned in the biography, it is omitted from the bibliography. *Brave Old Woman* drew on the life of Miss Newman, her erstwhile governess, the wartime atmosphere doubtless encouraging retrospection. Similarly, writing *Miss Granby's Secret* in the bomb shelter, perhaps reading sections aloud to George, Farjeon was moved to look back fondly on her young self, the Eleanor who had created romance in dreams and on paper.

For, stacked one inside the other, the Indian boxes of *Miss Granby's Secret* contain both Eleanors, the young daydreamer and the successful author. They can be found there along with both Adelaide Granbys, the youthful innocent and the novelist whose works were considered so shocking they were read behind the locked doors of the 'Doubleyou-Cee'; practical Pamela; raven-locked Stanislaw, carrot-haired Stanley Pinner, and, perhaps, a memory of Stacy Aumonier. Also included are the all-important governesses, Adelaide's romanticising Miss Linton, the Tarletan Triplets' sinister Madame Leroy, and a memory of Eleanor's own Miss Newman. In addition, we encounter a funeral, a will, a trunk, letters, a scrapbook, a diary (in two parts), Definitions, a full-length novel, letters, conversations, and a Query, transporting us from 1848 to 1932 by way of all manner of tribulation and coincidence, products of a peculiarly fertile and unfettered imagination.

Derbyshire is the county favoured as the setting of both outer and inner novels, with 'Braddon Hall' the mansion in which Count Stanislaw, the Bastard of Pinsk, stirs the blood of the Tarletan Triplets, and 'Pelham Place' the home of young Adelaide Granby, eventually inherited by Pamela. In these house names we can catch allusions to two very popular late-19th-century novelists, Mrs Braddon and Bulwer Lytton, the latter singled out by 'Aunt Addie' as favourite reading of her youth. Readers can enjoy teasing out other such references, although I dare say it will only be the exceptionally earnest Farjeon scholar who will recognise that '6 May', a date so crucial in Adelaide Granby's life, was also the birthday of Eleanor's much-loved brother, Harry.

Miss Granby's Secret was lauded in the *Tatler* (11 December 1940), as 'A rather lovely resurrection of all those taboos, those moral prohibitions, that conventional veneer which made the 'eighties and the 'nineties so outwardly strict, yet, at the same time, and perhaps as a consequence, made a love-affair something in the grand manner, more exciting, more romantic, and infinitely more memorable. Miss Farjeon has never written a more delicately humorous or more charmingly sentimental story. Only, I warn you, it is all a joke — a witty joke.' Thus, at Christmas 1940, with a vision of young love adorning its dust wrapper, *Miss Granby's Secret* offered an excellent distraction from the worries of war. Similarly, what 21st-century reader could resist a novel that, in the words of the *Liverpool Daily Post*, is 'elegant, gay, and a trifle improper'?

Elizabeth Crawford

CONTENTS

OLD MAN'S DARLING
(Autumn 193): Spring 1932)

Part One

MISS ADELAIDE GRANBY

Summer 1912

FOREWORD BY PAMELA LANG

My Aunt Addie died in 1912, at the age of seventy-nine. Her death received plenty of comment in the Press, though the paragraphs would have been still longer if she had died forty years earlier, in the bloom of her fame. This is what *The Times* said of her on July 3rd.

"We regret to announce the death from pneumonia of Miss Adelaide Granby, at her home in Sydenham, yesterday evening. Miss Granby will be a loss to her many readers, though it was a past generation that admired her most. She was born in Derbyshire in 1833; thirty years later the audacity of her first novel, Miss Ponsonby's Past, took London by storm. Her heyday was reached in the 'Seventies and 'Eighties, the sales of her best-known, often-reprinted work, The Purple Empress, reaching half a million copies. Miss Granby's style was not impeccable; she allowed herself a freedom of expression which was disconcerting to certain sections of the reading public, and was not above splitting an infinitive. But her novels were crowded with movement and incident, and she wrote with a zest that carried her, as well as her readers, away. One cannot doubt that she found enjoyment in the romances she turned out year after year. They amassed her a considerable fortune, out of which she endowed homes for Unfortunate Women and Stray Cats. Her indefatigable pen was busy to the last, and the proofs of the forty-ninth novel were beside her when she died. Her passing breaks another link with the past."

"The past indeed!" I hear Aunt Addie scoffing. "Fiddlesticks! I never belonged to the past, even when I wore ringlets. These chaps don't know what they're talking about.

An Advanced Woman: that is how Aunt Addie would have described herself. It is a pity she couldn't write her own obituary.

On July 5th *The Times* printed a letter from "A Correspondent". It was headed:

THE PASSING OF A ROMANTIC

A THACKERAY ANECDOTE

"Those to whom the death of Adelaide Granby means more than the end of a distinguished literary career may perhaps be forgiven for wishing to picture her to an age that rarely saw her. In her last years she suffered from delicate health, and went seldom abroad; but she welcomed all old friends in her seclusion, and nothing pleased her more than when young ones penetrated it. She had retained the incurably romantic heart of her own youth, as well as youth's gift of dwelling in delightful illusions—a gift which goes far to explain her popularity with two generations of readers. At the time when, as your notice says, 'she took London by storm' with her first novel, her success as a woman was no less than her success as a writer. Her attractive appearance, artless behaviour, naive wit, and personal charm were welcomed everywhere, and she formed friendships with most of the Victorian giants—'although dear Mr. Thackeray,' I have heard her say, 'allowed me but not my books into his house. I wondered why, but the only reason he gave was "I have daughters". I then expressed a wish that he would read them himself, and, making a comical face, he said in a big whisper: "I do!" "Oh, where?" I cried; "in your Club?" "Heaven forbid!" said the great man, and taking me by the elbow—"I read your books, dear Miss Granby, under the rose." "Oh!" I exclaimed, "how delightful! I had far rather my books were admitted into your rosary than into your house. May we meet there one evening and read one together, like Paolo and Francesca?" The proposal, Miss Granby added, left Mr. Thackeray rather bashful, and the affair, to use her own term, remained 'unconsummated'. Miss Granby's powers as a vivacious and unexpected conversationalist increased with her years, and she retained to the last the dancing eyes, fine

skin, and small exquisite hand for which young Miss Granby was as famous as for her pen. It was a surprise to all who knew her that she never married, but domesticity's loss was literature's gain.

"P. U. T."

The initials told me that the writer was Percival Upton Tennant, senior partner in Tennant & Tennant, the family solicitors. He was now over eighty, and left most of the work to Mr. Henry, his elderly son, but remained a constant visitor in Aunt Addie's house. His letter confirmed me in a suspicion that Mr. Percival would have preferred—how long ago?—literature's loss, and domesticity's gain. It was difficult to think of Aunt Addie married. She would have made a fascinating, but imperative, partner.

CONVERSATION WITH MY GREAT-AUNT ADDIE

To the end of her days she did not know the facts of life. I once offered to tell her. "No, my dear," said Aunt Addie, "I'd rather not."

"Don't you want to know?"

"Not till I stop writing novels," said Aunt Addie. "I think it would inhibit me."

"I should have thought it would have helped you."

"A little learning," said Aunt Addie winking. She had a drooping eyelid. It gave her left eye a permanently knowing look, for which she couldn't be held responsible. But it had a disconcerting habit of dropping suddenly, and then it seemed intentional. One could not be quite certain. Her right eye was as round and blue and candid as that of a wax doll. She flicked the suggestive eyelid up again, as far as it would go, without finishing the quotation.

"I don't see," I argued, "how a little of the facts of life can be dangerous to a writer."

"My theory is," said Aunt Addie, "that it had better be all or none."

I was quite ready to tell Aunt Addie all, and said so.

"Yes, I dare say," she said composedly. "But do you know all?"

I flattered myself I did. Wasn't I a Young Fabian? Aunt Addie looked at me with genuine interest.

"Does your mother know you've been to bed with a man?"

"Aunt Addie! Of course not!"

"You advanced young women don't tell your mammas everything then?"

"But Aunt Addie! I mean, of course, I haven't."

"Haven't?"

"Been."

"Been?"

"To—to bed with—"

"Dear me," said my aunt, "how you youngsters do jib at calling a spade a spade. Well, in that case, Pamela, how can you tell me all?"

"Oh well—" I said liberally. "There are such things as books."

"There always were," said Aunt Addie.

"I mean the sort of books that didn't even exist in your day, aunty. What we read now—"

"Tells you all? So did what I read. All I could take in, and turn to account."

"What did you read?"

"Byron. Mrs. Radcliffe. Bulwer. Tom Moore. The Classics."

"Oh, the Classics." I knew all about them. I had recently been invited to attend a local young women's debating society, got up by my nicer friends, daughters of the ladies my mother called on. Plays like *Mrs. Warren's Profession*, *The Cenci* and *Damaged Goods* (all accepted and dissected, in mixed company, by the daughters of women on whom my mother did not call) were taboo in that self-improving reading-circle; a touching group, whom such plays would have shocked, without their quite knowing what they were shocked about. Still, they yearned to be more open-minded than their mothers, and two of them admitted that they could see no harm in *The Vote*. The subject under discussion was: 'Do you believe in Platonic Love?' Finding that no one present, except myself, had read *The Republic*, I did not join that young ladies' debating society.

"Plato," I nodded.

"And Petronius," my aunt nodded back at me.

"Petronius?"

"Arbiter."

"Oh, yes! I think—I've heard of him. I've never sampled him yet."

"I found him very enlightening. Then, the Bible."

"Of course."

"Of course. Every word of it. All those begats."

"You couldn't have learned much from *them*."

"On the contrary. Padding is there for a purpose. Coating for the pill. And the pill, you know, so much pleasanter than the coating. It taught me in later life never to pad, but to model myself on the Apocrypha. The Elizabethans too."

"Oh, yes," I smiled. "'Julius Caesar' in class."

"Girls in my days had governesses at home. My second one leaned more to the Georgian romantics than to Shakespeare. My first did read 'The Quality of Mercy' with me. I read 'Tis pity she's a whore' by myself."

She pronounced it "wore", and I hesitated to correct her. Even the Sunday Theatre Society I had joined referred to this play lightly as "'Tis Pity". I contented myself with saying: "You covered some ground, then."

"Haven't you? I suppose you read Mr. H. G. Wells and the Smart Set. We read Mr. Richardson and *The Keepsake*. And every year we had *The Book of Beauty*. Lady Blessington was a *leetle* outside the pale, but nearly all her contributors were Barts or M.P.s, so my mamma knew the contents could not be deleterious. The book was allowed year by year on the parlour table, where the gold urn and angels on the cover looked very well. I was very fond of *The Book of Beauty*. And of things like the *Paston Letters*, and Memoirs. I used to read all the Memoirs I could lay my hands on."

I felt we had strayed far from the original point. Dusty, musty memoirs! I broke in eagerly.

"Memoirs don't really tell you *any*thing. I'm talking of scientific books, Aunt Addie. Forel, you know." (Hadn't I filched my brother's copy of Forel from behind the Boys' Own Papers on the top row of his bookshelves?)

"Dubois," murmured Aunt Addie.

"Dubois?"

"Eighteenth century. Rather old-fashioned perhaps. The Abbé Dubois."

"Oh, of course, the Abbé Dubois, you mean the man who taught Louis the Fifteenth things."

"He did indeed."

"I'm afraid I've never peeped into him, aunty."

"I daresay you never will now. Twenty-three, aren't you? He is eminently a writer to be peeped into in one's teens. My father's library was full of books like that. On the top shelves. At the back. Behind the sets of *Fraser's Magazine* and Bohn's Library."

"Well, they don't seem to have helped you much, Aunt Addie."

"Oh, yes, they did, they helped me enormously. I might never have written at all without their help. They teemed with delightful words."

Aunt Addie helped herself to a lilac cachou, to which she was addicted. "Pimps," she said.

"What?"

"Pimps. You've never heard of them perhaps?"

"Of course I have. A pimp is a—well—"

"A pandar," said Aunt Addie.

"Oh."

"And a pandar is a pimp. A little dictionary I kept by me for my spelling (which has always been shaky) told me *that* much. I don't want to know any more. It would spoil it. When I met my first pimp, I saw him as an elegant young fellow of fashion, rather like the Dresden china beau on one end of the mantelpiece; a trifle affected, but very pettable. Then I looked him up. Now pandar suggests something jungular and oriental. Between them they form, for me, a figure so romantic that I should hate to have it destroyed by your Mr. Forel."

"I don't think he even mentions them. Dr. Forel, aunty. He's a doctor."

"Worse and worse," said my aunt. "They are all iconoclasts."

"They tell you the *truth*, Aunt Addie. We aren't satisfied with subterfuges nowadays."

"You think yourself very advanced, don't you?"

"Well, yes. But I don't want to shock you."

My aunt bridled slightly. "I am quite incapable of being shocked, thank you, Pamela, and I know as well as you do what it is to be an advanced young woman. I scandalised my parents, and don't you forget it."

It was always understood that Aunt Addie had once experienced an unsuitable *grande passion*, on account of which she had never experienced another. She looked so like a wise doll, boasting of its past, that I couldn't help saying slily: "Scandalised them without knowing the facts of life, Aunt Addie?"

"Certainly, Pamela. Ignorance produces twice the scandals that knowledge does. Ignorance can be fluttered by a zephyr's whisper; it takes a Nor'-Wester to rouse up blasé old experience. I am sorry to disappoint you, my dear. I can see you are pining to tell me what your mamma has never told you. I won't have it. You shall not tell me all because you do not know all."

"You'd be surprised," I taunted her, "at what I know."

(More than Forel was hidden behind those *Boys' Own Papers*.)

"You'll be more surprised one day," said Aunt Addie, "after you're married, at what you thought you knew. And I'll bet you my best kid gloves you won't know all then. I don't see," she mused, "how any woman can know all who hasn't had an entanglement with a man of every colour."

"Good heavens, aunty!"

"Shocked?" said Aunt Addie pleasantly. "So sorry, dear, but I always shocked my public. That's how I made my name. If I had known the facts of life, I couldn't have done it. I should have been much too coy. But fortunately, I had only my inklings, so I have been able to run on to my forty-ninth novel unimpeded. It is my ambition to reach my Golden Jubilee publication. On the day I publish my fiftieth, I shall lay down my pen, and ask you to lend me Dr. Forel on The Sexual Question."

"Aunt Addie!"

"Well, child? Did you suppose I'd never heard of the man? I do read the literary supplements. But the critics, thank goodness, *are* coy. They never call a spade a spade, and treat authors who do with the discretion of attachés in the diplomatic service. So they are, in their way. They must choose their words, they mustn't upset the millions. They have their circulation to consider. They hint at this and that, but if one really wants to know what all the fuss is about, one must *buy* the books that Mudie's don't circulate. This Victoria Cross, and this young Mr. Lawrence! I decline to buy them, in order to learn the facts. Why should I, after years of resisting the temptation to send half a crown for the booklet, in plain wrapper, *What a Bride Should Know,* and *The Young Wife's Second Year*? I have always," said Aunt Addie, "put my own art first; I am not sure that I have been fascinated by anybody else's since I began to publish, except Miss Florence Barclay and Max. They really *do* understand the male and female heart."

"Max?"

"Beerbohm."

"Oh, the caricaturist."

"The *writer*. I should have been proud to have written *Zuleika Dobson* myself. That, and *The Rosary*."

I hadn't read either, and asked: "Are they much alike?"

"They both place love on its proper pinnacle. As I have always done, since I began to publish."

"How long ago was that, Aunt Addie?"

"Eighteen-sixty-three, and I've written one a year ever since then, and only changed my publisher twice. Mr. Thackeray turned down the one I submitted in 'sixty-two to Smith Elder. I used to twit him with it afterwards. 'Spare my grey hairs!' he begged good-humouredly; 'Miss Granby and Currer Bell will bring them with shame to the grave.' 'Don't mention me in one breath with that grim young woman,' I commanded. I really have no patience with those Brontës. A grievous trio! And what did they squeeze out of it? Not what *I* call revellers, though some might."

I wasn't attending much; while she ran on, I was making a calculation.

"So you didn't write your first novel till you were thirty?" (We started younger now, we clever ones.)

"I wrote my first novel," said Aunt Addie, "when I was sixteen. Perhaps my best novel. At all events, my favourite."

"And couldn't get it published for fifteen years?"

"It has never been published," said Aunt Addie.

"Why not?"

"It was too—"

"Shocking? Intimate?"

"Yes, that's it."

"Which?"

"Aren't they the same thing?" asked Aunt Addie, opening her china-blue right eye at me, more like a wax doll than ever. Then she winked the left. It was really very difficult to keep pace with what she knew or thought or meant. Advanced as I was, she often made me feel a step or two behind.

"What was the novel called, aunty?"

"I called it," said Aunt Addie lovingly, "*The Bastard of Pinsk*."

"Did you know what a—a bastard was?"

"I had read my Shakespeare."

"You *didn't* know what a bastard was!"

"That has always been the point."

"Do you know now, Aunt Addie?"

The left eyelid descended again, but this time very slowly. "We—well. To-day perhaps I should call it something else."

"What, for instance?"

"There is a word I've run into lately," said Aunt Addie, "and it also begins with a b. What it means I can only surmise. It sounds like a good solid Chaucerian word. Rugged. Yes, to-day I might call that novel of the 'forties *The Something Else of Pinsk*."

"But what, aunty? The *What Else*?"

"I am afraid," said Aunt Addie, "that if I tell you, you will go and look it up, and if it's not in the dictionary you will niggle among your Fabians until by hook or crook you've landed it. And then you'll be shocked. I heard a garage hand say it myself, but decided not to inquire. I did not want to offend his delicacy; and you had better not offend yours by inquiring, either."

She was quite right. I hadn't, in 1912, any acquaintance with that word. It does not offend my delicacy in 1932. It would have then. Aunt Addie pursued our talk to its last issue. "But me," she said, "it simply cannot shock, because, you see, I don't know what it means. That is why people kept a sofa-cushion handy while they read Ouida in the parlour with one ear on the door-knob; but when they read me, they went into the Doubleyou-Cee and locked the door."

Did Great-Aunt Addie know more than she implied?

Or was she masking her ignorance with an assumption of ignorance?

LAST WILL AND TESTAMENT

Aunt Addie died possessed of a considerable fortune. Her Last Will and Testament contained many clauses, but few surprises. A handsome sum was apportioned to literary pension funds, and she left the endowment for "The Adelaide Granby Gold Medal," to be awarded annually to the best work of romantic fiction in the English tongue written by any woman under twenty-five, to be judged by three male poets over sixty. It was especially devised "to encourage the growth of imagination in the young," and it appeared from a latter dealing with certain auxiliary clauses in the Foundation that my Aunt Addie considered five-and-twenty rather elderly for a woman—"It would have been thought so when I was a girl; but girls are so much younger now than they used to be. We attained to wisdom and experience before twenty, after marriage at eighteen. By twenty-five we were matrons and mothers in caps. But to-day woman is at a disadvantage, and takes much longer to learn what life is, so she may well continue to preserve a degree of youth at her quarter-century—and as for Romance, that is ageless."

The Adelaide Granby Medal had been designed for her, long before her death, by her favourite artist, Mr. Marcus Stone.

Her legacies included many public charities; children, birds, and cats, all, without knowing it, were a little happier for Aunt Addie's death. And some tender personal charities came to light, among them an annuity of two hundred pounds to "my dear old Governess, Alicia Mary Linton"—who turned out to be a bedridden dame of ninety, of whom we had never heard; her address was that of a comfortable Home for Gentlewomen in Surbiton.

The bulk of her fortune was divided without favouritism amongst her nephews and nieces, who benefited to an extent that allowed them to do things they had always wanted to long before they had ever expected to; for Aunt Addie, who had been very much loved by them all, cut up even warmer than they had counted on. She knew they were going to be both surprised and pleased, and she begged them not to subdue their expressions of pleasure, even while (she hoped) they regretted her a little. In an age when mourning had not gone out of fashion, she begged her female relatives not to go further than mauve or lavender, "unless purple was more becoming to their style of architecture; and I trust" (she added) "my heirs will lose no time in amusing themselves with what I am able to leave them. There is so much pleasure to be got out of the unexpected. While they repine, let them also rejoice. They will find that pleasure and sorrow can go harmoniously hand in hand." My parents at once abandoned their bicycles for a Panhard-Levassor. My Uncle Dick bought a week-end cottage in Surrey, and grew roses ten years sooner than he had hoped to. My Uncle Gerald said: "At last I can winter in Madeira." He fulfilled this ambition twice; then the Great War ended a habit he could not have kept up in any case, Madeira, as it turned out, being his synonym for Monte Carlo. In 1914 he was glad of a cushy job and salary in the Censor's Office, on the strength of his Continental vocabulary. My mother said: 'I told you so!" though she hadn't, and wondered what "dear Aunt Addie" would have had to say about it. I held the opinion that Aunt Addie would have delighted in a portion of her leavings being dissipated on anything so dashing as the Gaming Tables, which she had never seen in her life.

The sprightly old lady had never stopped gathering numbers of private friends and devotees, as well as professional acquaintances and admirers. She seemed to have forgotten none of them. Small sums and mementoes were lavished in a hundred directions; this part of the will must have been very trying to Tennant & Tennant, our solicitors as well as hers. Mr. Henry Tennant told us that she began by making out a list of some hundred names and an equal number of souvenirs, and spent hours in trying to pair them suitably. Just when she thought she had got it right, she would find herself left with Mr. Perry and her turquoise vinaigrette. Mr. Perry was her veterinary surgeon (whom she adored because he adored Mazeppa, her Maltese cat), and to him a vinaigrette, even a turquoise one, could only be considered "symbolically suitable". So then the old lady had to begin shifting the pieces on the board all over again," chuckled Tennant Junior. In the end Mr. Perry got the silver-mounted hoof of Bay Beauty, Aunt Addie's uncle's filly, placed in an Oaks before Victoria came to the throne; and the vinaigrette went to the unexpected child of Mr. and Mrs. Dancey's middle age. To this couple, her personal maid and her butler, long in her service, she left a little house in Muswell Hill, her aviary, Mazeppa, and a thousand pounds. All of her other servants had a year's salary.

To me, her only great-niece, she bequeathed Pelham Place (her girlhood's home near Matlock, which none of us had ever seen, and she herself not during my lifetime), five pounds a week for life in trust securities, a hundred pounds in cash, and "my yellow wooden trunk marked A. G. in brass nails. The key is on the ring in my walnut jewel case."

These came into my possession after the funeral, before which, in fact, the terms of her will were only hinted at.

LINES TO A******* G*****

If Adelaide Granby's will was not a surprise, her funeral was. Not even those nearest to her were prepared for the multitude of floral trophies that came to the house, or the bundles of letters arriving by every post. It fell to me to receive and attend to much of this part of it, for we were visiting Aunt Addie when she was taken ill, and stayed on to see everything through. Quite three-fifths of the writers and wreath-senders were strangers to me. As Aunt Addie's old life gathered its last wave, broke, and subsided, flowers were thrown up in a continuous stream, like spray from the disturbance created in time's ocean by her death. As for the letters, the postman delivered them in shoals five times a day. A week after each batch of acknowledgments had been shovelled by me into the local pillar-box, I could not have named one of these unknowns. Or yes, just one. Among the senders of tributes he stood out, represented by the biggest and most symbolic emblem in flowers I ever saw. On an urn of laurels, so large that it took two men to carry it up the steps to the front door, reposed a pillow of damask roses fringed with spirræa, and on the pillow lay, obliquely, a heart of pansies and forget-me-nots. The urn was surmounted by a crown of immortelles bound with purple silk ribbons, to one of whose streamers was attached a gilt-edged card, rather larger than that usually employed to bear the sender's sentiments. One side of the card was simply inscribed, in the most exquisite ornamental penmanship:

From Stanislaw

A weeping willow, beautifully executed, drooped its green tear-laden fronds above and about the tomb on which the words were written.

On the other side, in a painted floral frame, appeared in calligraphy so minute that it appeared to need a reading-glass, and so clear that it was visible to the naked eye, these

"LINES TO A******* G*****

When Death hath bereft thee of Breath and of Being
For those that remain to remember thee still,
One Heart will still beat for thee, hearing and seeing
The Voice and the Features that Time cannot kill.

For these were enshrined like the Bee's wing in amber
By Time turned immortal before we were old,
And the Lamp we then lit still illumes my Soul's Chamber
Where still thy Form dwells in a Halo of Gold.

These Eyes that beheld thee in Youth—in Youth only—
Preserved and preserve thee in Maidenhood's Flower!
Since a Lifetime without thee has never been lonely,
What is Death but a Figment devoid of his Power?

Belov'd One! Ah yes! Thou hast gone but before me!
Earth knows thee no more—but our Love was divine!—
And Death, when he claims me, can only restore me
To Heavens that always were thine, Love, and mine!

"Dear me," said my mother."

"Who was Stanislaw, mums?"

"I haven't the ghost of a notion. Fanny—" She turned to our housemaid who came over daily to help Mrs. Dancey, and was lingering at the door, drinking in the trophy with her eyes. "Ask your master to come here for a moment." When my father had joined us—"Read that," she said.

He did so, not troubling to suppress unseemly chuckles. "Who is this Stanislaw, Ned?"

"How the deuce should I know? Whoever he is, he's done the handsome by her."

"Ye—es," said my mother. "Eight guineas at least. But—" "It will want a coach to itself."

"That's just it—"

"It ought to ride on the coffin."

"Well, it can't," said my mother, rather tartly. "It would be most unsuitable. As it is, it makes things look as though he, and not we, was the Chief Mourner. I don't quite like it, Ned. The flowers painted on the card—passion-flowers, aren't they?"

"What's wrong with passion-flowers, old girl?"

"Nothing, of course, but—"

"Mums means, passion-flowers are suitable for a wedding, dad, but not for a funeral."

"Oh, she does? And what do you know about it?" My father pinched my twenty-three-year-old ear. My mother suppressed us both with one of her looks.

"If we knew who he was!" she complained. "But no address! And that ridiculous name! And those—peculiar words. What does he mean by 'the lamps they then lit,' and their being restored to 'heavens' that were theirs? What lamp? What sort of heavens? If he had just said heaven—but heavens in the plural might be—anything.

And 'one heart will still beat for thee'—as though none of ours are beating too. No, Ned, we can't have poor dear little Aunt Addie dwelling in a halo of gold in the soul's chamber of one who is a perfect stranger to all of us."

"He doesn't seem to have been a perfect stranger to her."

"'In youth only,'" said my mother quickly. "Tantamount to a stranger, one changes so. Who can the man be?"

"Ah, the old girl had her secrets like the rest of us."

"Ned—please. Jocosity is quite out of place. Besides—" She glanced at me, and frowned at my father.

"Now, mums! As if I didn't know!"

"Know, what?" asked my mother uncertainly. And then, afraid I should enlighten her, out of the depths of that Fabianism which she only saw steeped in sin, she smothered question and answer with: "You don't know who this Stanislaw is, at all events."

"I expect he was darling Aunt Addie's *Grande Passion*. She had one, didn't she?"

"Pamela! Really—I"

"Well, didn't she, dad?" I appealed to my broaderminded parent. 'I'm sure I've heard she did, and I hope it was true. It's too awful to think of dying without having had—oh, *everything* life can give you."

"You want a lot for your money, young woman, don't you?" My father pinched my ear again.

"Ned! This is not the place." My mother's eyes swept round the room, loaded with the offerings, sumptuous and humble, of those who had valued my great-aunt. She came back to that preposterous laurel urn. "I suppose," she hesitated, "we must let it go to-morrow with the rest."

"Why, of course we must, old girl. What are you thinking of? We mustn't break Stanislaw's heart."

"But it's well, almost vulgar."

"There's nothing to prevent the vulgar from mourning as well as the refined. Perhaps better, I shouldn't wonder. Vulgar or not, he seems to have acted like a gentleman."

"How?"

"We have his word for it"—my father glanced at the card—"that he preserved Addie's maidenhead—"

"*Maidenhood's flower*," amended my mother, hastily.

"Not quite the same thing, dear. Still, if you prefer. Mine is the more respectable version. Perhaps Stanislaw wasn't such a gentleman, after all."

"I've thought so all along."

Suddenly I said: "I don't think it's vulgar, mother. I think it's rather beautiful."

"It's very costly. But as for beautiful—" My mother's eyes roamed instinctively to our family tribute, a lyre of green palms, supported on a bed of pure white lilies—at least, they were pure white yesterday, but now a hint of brown tarnished the waxen edges here and there. It had cost three guineas, and bore all our three names on the card; I had insisted on paying my own guinea out of my recently granted dress allowance of twenty-six pounds per annum, though my father tried to undermine my hard-won independence in various generous ways.

My mother murmured: "Annie must give everything a good sprinkle to-night."

My father flicked one of the purple immortelles on top of the urn. "Those won't need it, at all events. Safe as houses. Keep longer than anything else in the room."

"Yes, I suppose so," agreed my mother, distastefully.

"That little wreath is just what overdoes it, to my thinking. I never did like immortelles, they collect the dust. So artificial. To me the whole thing's much too artificial. How Pamela can find it beautiful!"

But I did. Stanislaw's complicated symbolism seemed to come full circle with the simplicity of the wilting bunch of garden flowers brought in, first of any, by thirteen-year-old Ada Dancey. The honest cheerful child had companioned Aunt Addie constantly of late, proving herself an apt and common-sensible little nurse, and making a point of keeping, under the invalid's eye, a vase filled with the old-fashioned flowers she was fondest of. An hour after my great-aunt breathed her last, Ada had run redeyed into the garden and made a bunch of clove pinks, old man, Sweet William, and love-in-a-mist, tied it with her brown hair-ribbon, and left it by the bed, with a scribbled message: "For dear Miss Addie." That posy meant something, some spontaneous burst of feeling; and so, I felt, did Stanislaw's elaborate offering, though in his case it had to be left to the florist to carry it out. I fingered the "Lines to A*******
G*****" tenderly.

"Well, anyhow," said my mother energetically, "we can't leave *that* on."

"Why not, my dear?"

"But, mother, we must."

My mother ignored my protest. It is easier to answer a question than an emotion. "Why not? Because Aunt Adelaide was a *public figure*, and the journalists are pestering us enough as it is. To-morrow they'll go getting a list of all the people who sent flowers—all the really notable ones—and then, they'll find *this*! It would be just like the ha'penny papers to make headlines of it. I will not have Aunt Adelaide made a laughing-stock, if nothing worse, Ned, by this ridiculous Stanislaw, whoever he is. And I'm surprised at you, Pamela. I thought you new young women, clamouring for your votes and goodness knows what, had quite given up being soft and sentimental."

"Have your cake and eat it, my dear," smiled my father. "But if you insist on scolding Pammy for her public cries, and Stanislaw for his private sighs—where do you come in?"

"This is where I come in," said my mother. She reached for a pair of scissors on the piano, and snipped off the card.

"Don't tear it up," I said. "I'd like to keep it."

"What for?"

"In memory of Aunt Addie." I seemed to hear my great aunt saying silly: "So you modern young girls don't tell your mothers everything?" What hadn't she told her mother about Stanislaw?

"Oh, very well." My mother, having carried her point, gave over the card with a funny little indulgent smile. I was by way of being rather a problem to her, with my interest in woman's rights instead of man's. Perhaps she was thinking that a little good old-fashioned sentiment wasn't such a bad thing after all—in the right place.

"And the journalistic ghouls," observed my father, "prowling to-morrow night among the wreaths, will note only that Miss Adelaide Granby had one anonymous well-to-do admirer."

Well, they were able to note a little more than that, when they came to pause by that laurel urn, that red-rose pillow, that heartful of memories, that crown of immortelles. For next day, while strange men began to bear away the flowers, I found a moment to hide in Stanislaw's tribute a plain card, saying, in script as ornamental as I could make it:

From One Who Loved Her

But who he was I could not even imagine. It was as difficult to picture Stanislaw as an old, old man, as it was to picture Aunt Addie as a young, young girl.

MY YELLOW WOODEN TRUNK

"This is the one, miss," said Mrs. Dancey.

Soon after the reading of Aunt Addie's Will, and before the lengthy process of settling her monetary legacies had been completed, I was allowed possession of the yellow wooden trunk which formed a portion of my inheritance. Tennant & Tennant, my great-aunt's executors, had to know the nature of its contents, in case it contained articles for valuation. The younger member of the firm (our Mr. Tennant) asked me to meet him at the house one morning, and when Mrs. Dancey showed me into the morning-room, where he was going through Aunt Addie's little davenport, he asked me if I knew anything about the box in question.

"No," I said. "She never mentioned it to me."

But Mrs. Dancey knew all about it, it seemed.

"Miss Granby had it brought down to her by Dancey every year," she said. "Always the same day, June the twenty-fourth, in her bedroom. It had to be there before eleven o'clock, and I had to bring her her luncheon on a tray." She paused, and then said suddenly, as though it had been on her mind for years: "I don't suppose it matters now saying what it was."

"What what was, Mrs. Dancey?"

"Miss Granby's luncheon. It was always the same thing. A bowl of gruel."

"Do you mean," asked Mr. Tennant, "that Miss Granby lunched on gruel every day?"

"No, only on the twenty-fourth of June. And after I'd brought in the tray—"

"Go on, Mrs. Dancey."

"Well, it can't signify now. There's nobody sharper-witted for her age than my dear mistress was, but the first time it happened, dear me, I wondered if she was quite all there. Dancey, who was only a footman then, had been with her five years already when I came, and that first June, after he'd brought down the trunk and I'd done what she told me, I couldn't help being curious, and let my tongue run pretty free in the kitchen, till he said: 'That'll do from you, my girl, all book-writers have their funny sides, and it's not for us to talk about *out*side'. So, of course, I never did till now, and after that first time I took it for granted."

'What did you take for granted, Mrs. Dancey?"

"Oh, there, sir, I thought I'd told you. After I'd taken in Miss Granby's tray, she told me to put it down on the washstand, and take the key out of the door, and lock her in. And she wasn't to be disturbed on any account till dinner-time. Not for anything or anybody, she said, not if the Queen herself should come to call— only latterly, of course, she said the King. Then, when dinner was ready, I came and let her out. A very good dinner she always ordered for that day. That was the same, too. Duck and green peas and new potatoes, and cream trifle and strawberries, and a little glass of cherry brandy to finish off with; and always turbot and lobster sauce to begin with."

'Well, well!" said Mr. Tennant. "Did she have guests?"

"No, she sat down to it all by herself, to the last."

"Do you mean to tell me," said Mr. Tennant, "that this year, only five or six weeks ago—only three weeks before the old lady—"

He paused, as though he had seen a new light on Aunt Addie's death, which had been ascribed to pneumonia.

"Yes, sir," said Mrs. Dancey, 'latterly, of course, she hardly touched it, but when I entered her service you'd be surprised how she put it away."

"No wonder she was hungry after her prison diet."

"Famished is more like it, sir. She never touched a spoonful of the gruel. She-"

"Go on, Mrs. Dancey.

"She threw it out of the window, bowl and all."

"Really! How long did this go on for, do you say?"

"Thirty-one years I've been with her." Mrs. Dancey wiped her eyes. "I was six-and-twenty when I entered her service, and she would be, let me see, forty-eight or nine. Dancey said the maid before me had to do just the same, and when it really started who's to say?"

"Quite so." Mr. Tennant turned to me. "It's as well, Pamela, that Miss Granby's midsummer madness exhibited itself long before you were born, or we might have had to question the validity of her will. But your aunt, bless her, was eccentric for so many years, that this peculiarity may pass with the rest. And now suppose we go and find the box. One really can't help being rather curious. Will you know the key, Mrs. Dancey?" He had Aunt Addie's old walnut jewel case on the desk, and opened it for the housekeeper's inspection.

"That is the one, sir. Shall Dancey bring the trunk down?"

"No, don't bother, we'll go up. I have to examine the attics in any case."

We toiled to the top of the house. The back attic was rather dim and dusty, but very tidy. Its only light came from a narrow skylight inset in a niche between two angles of the roof. Around the walls were shelves lined with spare copies of Aunt Addie's novels, the earlier ones in three-volume form, and yellow-backs. These, growing scarce now, were sent as special compliments to her friends. Mr. Tennant took one at random from a shelf; the glazed cover depicted a woman, in the low-cut evening bodice of the 'eighties, kneeling on a rich Turkey carpet in a despairing attitude at the feet of a gentlemanly scoundrel in a crimson velvet smoking-jacket, who twirled his moustaches with an insolent smile. His unhappy victim embraced one of his amply trousered legs with her right arm, while, with her extended left, she proffered him the wedding-ring of which her hand was bare. Mr. Tennant read off the title, smilingly.

"'*Who Can Forgive Her?*' Ever read it, Pamela?"

"Not that one." I had, in fact, read very few of them.

He slipped it back in its place. "Prolific old dear, wasn't she?"

"She wrote forty-nine novels. She was writing her fiftieth."

"Yes, I've found the manuscript. Her publisher has been inquiring about it, but there are only three chapters, plus the title, so there's nothing to be done with it."

Alas for Aunt Addie's dreams of a Golden Jubilee! That fiftieth novel would never be published now. After the War, the *Cornhill* published the fragment of *A Modern Messalina* as a period curiosity, but at the time of her death it wasn't even that. Mr. Tennant made a rapid survey of the other contents of the attic. The floor space was occupied only with a few old chairs, and a small damaged table; some fenders and kitchen utensils were stacked in a corner. Besides these there were half a dozen boxes of various kinds—a dress-trunk crammed with old clothes, two empty cabin-trunks, a black leather Gladstone bag of appalling weight, and a modern light-weight suitcase, a big wicker basket full of blankets and curtains, and the yellow nail-studded box, three generations old.

"This is the one, miss."

As Mr. Tennant stooped to fit the key, Mrs. Dancey withdrew circumspectly.

"Knows her place, but must be itching to stay," said Mr. Tennant. "Not very much here, though, of instant interest. Papers mostly. Old stuff. Scrap albums." He lifted out the bundles carefully. There were quite a dozen albums, several filled with Christmas and birthday cards, named and dated in Aunt Addie's exquisite hand. They were mostly bound in padded silks, magenta, brown, and cherry coloured. There was a small box of very old-fashioned trinkets ("we needn't bother probate about those") and a thick corded blue satin sachet, stuffed with bits of lace. There was a brown paper parcel, neatly tied up ("Quite recently, look, she's used a sheet of paper with her publisher's label, and a postmark for last May"). My name was written on it.

"Well, that's your little lot," said Mr. Tennant, "but I shall have to know if there are any valuables in it." He balanced it on his hands. "It's a tidy weight. If it's banknotes, Pamela, I shall make you a proposal of marriage."

"I'll open it now, and put you to the test," I said airily, bending my face over the knot, in case I had flushed, for it was pleasant to joke easily on intimate topics with the other sex, even if there was a difference of forty years in your ages. We Young Fabians plumed ourselves on our freedom of speech and lack of embarrassment, but one still caught oneself getting rather red sometimes. However, the attic was dark, and the heat of the room on that July day excused anything.

"You're quite safe," I said, folding back the brown paper. "I'm not the catch of the season after all." For the parcel merely contained two more albums, handsome affairs, bound in pale tooled leather, with solid clasps and locks.

"And no keys," said Mr. Tennant.

"Here's a thick envelope though, addressed to me and marked *Private*. Perhaps the keys are inside." I opened the envelope, which had been placed between the albums. A rather bulky package came to light, and a letter written in Aunt Addie's fine hand. It was dated "June 20th, 1912," and began: "My dear Pamela."

I shook the long envelope. "No keys," I said. "Ought I to read the letter?"

"If it is private," said Mr. Tennant, "read it later by yourself. What's the package?"

I examined it. It was bound with pink ribbon, and sealed. On it was written:

My dear Stanislaw

"That's private too," I said, hoping there was no tremor in my voice.

"Yes, plainly the whole thing is for you to deal with, and not the probate officer. Well, if you unearth any bullion, let me know." Mr. Tennant got up and dusted his knees. "Phew! It's sweltering in here! Coming down?"

"I think, if you don't mind, I'd like to stay."

"No objection whatever," said Mr. Tennant. And he left me alone with Aunt Addie' s old wooden trunk in the attic, and one ray of speckled light filtering through the window. Enough for my purpose.

I read my letter first.

LETTER TO "MY GREAT-NIECE PAMELA LANG"

The Acacias
Sydenham Hill
June 20th, 1912

My Dear Pamela,

In bequeathing to you the things I treasure most, I bequeath to you a great part of myself, for whom I know you have a sincere affection—as I have for you. I have watched you for twenty-three years with much love, some amusement, and, latterly, a little anxiety. I have come to feel, my dear, that you need protecting. In my youth, girls were far too much protected; in yours, they are far too little. You are, I concede, much more instructed than we were— but, in my opinion, when instruction is applied all over the shop, without regard to growth and development, there can be rather too much of it. "A little learning is a dangerous thing" only when it cannot measure its own quantity, and thinks it has reached a goal. But a lot of knowledge, reaching its goal by a grasshopper's leap, is quite as dangerous. In both cases, there is ground to be travelled, and traversed. I have heard you lay claim to complete freedom, and discovered that by this you mean freedom of speech and thought, but not of action. Now I think (if you will excuse the vulgarisms), one should never jib at going the whole hog. Freedom of speech, in advance of experience, will lead you into saying some foolish things, while freedom of thought may run you, into irreparable errors—of which the greatest is the error of supposing that love is a matter for the scientists and doctors. And while you glory in knowing everything before you have lived anything, you may never discover those blissful sensations of ignorance which you have overleaped, which release one into a world of delights without limits (destroyed, at last, by knowledge, and seldom re-captured), and which, I assure you, are the very essence and poetry of a romantic passion. A passion without romance is not worth its salt. I had rather be taught passion by my lover than by my doctor any day—or do I mean any night?

Because I feel you are a child in material as well as sensational matters, I am tying up your little annuity in a way which will give you a certain degree of security during your years of inexperience, so that if you should come to grief in any way, through misplaced affections or rash speculation, you will not be thrown wholly on the mercies of a society that has never been very lenient to women who have taken a false step.

At the same time, I am leaving you a little legacy in cash, as I wish you to have an immediate chance of indulging yourself rather extravagantly. I cannot insist on your not putting it away in your post office savings book, but I hope you will prefer to gratify some wish of your own without thinking twice about it. Dress in the height of fashion for a season, or go to Bayreuth, or back a rank outsider in the Derby, or visit Persia, or buy a string of pearls or a pair of cheetahs (who, I believe, make very pleasant pets), or surprise the first beggar you meet by handing him a banknote for £100. Only it had better not be a banknote, they prefer cash. You cannot think what results may come from giving some poor outcast five gold sovereigns. It makes you feel for a moment like the Count of Monte Cristo. I know many a man with three thousand a year who has never succeeded in feeling at all like Monte Cristo.

Pelham Place. I have pondered long about my girlhood's home, the scene of my wildest ecstasies and my darkest griefs. When I am gone, it will mean nothing to anybody. For half a century it has meant to me everything that it was. Therefore, I have been careful not to revisit Derbyshire for fifty years. It is a pity to wantonly destroy the pleasures and the pains of memory. I say "the pains" deliberately, for as you come to know more of life and death, of love and hate, of sin and its opposite (see postscript!), you will find that life's pains are among its most inestimable gifts. Certain it is that one cannot exist forever in joyful ecstasy. The drop from the height to the depth is inevitable. Then follows the ecstasy of misery. The one thing to be dreaded and avoided, is the dead level. Anything is preferable to dullness. So, my dear child, since one cannot escape pain, since one must suffer grief, take this to heart: Revel in your grief.

This was once imparted to me by one who taught me much. I have never forgotten it.

In the new philosophy of your generation, you have, it appears to me, given up expectancy. In your determination to possess the present, you have ceased to be heirs to the future. We expected both happiness and unhappiness; we knew that love has a blissful ending, and life a tragic one. You young know-alls expect nothing of the sort. You think it can all be stated, cut-and-dried. Life must be green before you can cut and dry it. That is why smoking has never really appealed to me—one has never known the tobacco in the green. Wine, which one has known in the grape, is another thing. When you are ripe for excesses, I advise you to get tipsy. Over-smoking does not raise you to a height before the headache, but occasional inebriation is worth paying for. I hope with all my heart that your first love-affair will be with a Grape, and not with a Cigar. For affairs you will have; you cannot get off scot-free; tragedy and bliss must both be yours; and your books won't help you when (a) your lover clasps you to his throbbing bosom, or (b) expires under your streaming eyes. Our books, I think, did.

They taught us that life, rarely really happy, was almost absorbingly, passionately romantic. Inevitably one loved beneath or above one. Lords were enamoured of gypsies, who received in their fond bosoms the knife intended for their lover, and died, beautiful to the last, beneath an oak tree, henceforth dedicated to their memory. Or young gentlewomen, deprived of fortune by a parent's death, sank to the humiliating lot of a lady needlewoman, on which seduction (yes, seduction was not flinched from!) and starvation was their unescapable end. Damsels of Oriental persuasion with names like Zayda, cavaliers known to their nearest and dearest as Bertram, could come to no happy end— their names foredoomed them. And if we were not ourselves born lords or gypsies, sultanas or cavaliers, life's inequalities, presented to us harshly in the roseate glow of our first young emotion, made Juliets and Cleopatras of us all. The Facts of Life, my dear? At least, we did not gloss the Facts of Love. It is the ambition of numbers of nice girls nowadays to go on the stage. For what, if not for what we had, and they miss? We had no need of that second-hand experience. We lived it, not on the stage, but between four walls. All love-affairs were bedewed with tears, and purged with aching hearts; flowers withered all too soon; constancy must be tried; partings must be suffered; farewells are so much more heartrending than meetings, and sorrow's ecstasy can be indulged at greater length than that of happiness. There is a sort of bliss in pain which laughter knows not; so long as it is never, never sordid, so long as it is ever, ever noble, it is the fare the young heart loves to feed on. It gave us our private thrills, as a mere tale of domestic felicity could not. (I have always held Mr. Trollope inferior to Bulwer.) Domestic felicity, we were given to understand, would in time be ours, joy's climax for respectable young gentlewomen; the rest was the forbidden fruit we knew we must never taste. But we too read our books—and, vicariously, the juices of that fruit were sweet on our lips. That connubial love should also embody sweet and luscious emotions was what was never admitted to us, what we were never supposed to admit to ourselves. The story with the happy ending stopped at the first chaste kiss on the brow, or the cheek, or the hand. What wonder we took a deeper pleasure in the tragedy whose palpitating sorrows followed the too-close embrace? Welcome! Merely marks the end of the story; Adieu, adieu! Brings forth eternal tears.

As for the contents of this box, my dear, do what you like with them; but if you are tempted to consign them to the ashes, I ask this much: lock them up for another twenty years, and re-read them. Then, if you so decide, the auto-da-fé. My reason for this is, that I think your immediate feelings may be scandalized, or shocked at the very least. You were so eager to teach me those Facts of Life—and it may be I, in the end, who will initiate you, in the Facts of Fancy. They have been my compensation and my consolation for sixty-three years—since the day when the blackest and most shameful page in my life was torn from the book by a parent's inexorable hand. But for that, I should never have produced fifty romances. The first of them, penned in the extremity of my despair, is now in your hands. My present publisher may not be the man for it; he has been a little pernickety over my last three books. But I hope some more adventurous firm will do it—for at my moment of writing, I should be glad to think you would contrive to get it published, though at your moment of reading I do not imagine I shall care a damn. I have always wanted to write that word in full, and now I have.

Ever your affectionate
Adelaide Granby

P.S. *I am not quite sure what sin's opposite is. The obverse of every extreme should be extreme, and sin does not seem to have an opposite worthy of it. Virtue?—a negative quality, surely, redolent of monotony. Renunciation, perhaps? Yet the mere cancelling of a thing cannot be its opposite. Innocence? I have always feared the Garden of Eden must have become very dull, if it had lasted a little longer.

MY DEAR STANISLAW

The perusal of Aunt Addie's last letter to me took some time. It was closely written in her fine hand (she always used the old-fashioned Lady's Nib), and I read it carefully in my one ray of light, pausing often over its moral, or immoral, sentiments and exhortations to argue with her in thought: a common habit which unconsciously absorbs much of our time by day, and more of it by night, and in which we always get the best of it. Aunt Addie's ideas of love and conduct seemed to me, as usual, preposterous, while, irrationally, they only made one fonder of her. I longed to be sitting with her again in the morning-room, where she tolerated, without participating in, my cigarette smoking (as my mother never did), and to ask her, between my nonchalant, self-conscious puffs: "But, Aunt Addie! Have you ever tried a cigar? Have you ever been tipsy?" I imagined that disconcerting left eyelid descending in its ambiguous wink, which would make my airy smoke-rings seem like child's-play, and discount the cider on an empty stomach which had sent me heavily asleep among the bracken, during a cycling-party in mid-August but even while I made a bragging joke of it among my fellow free-thinkers, I had never dimly considered it as an orgy. "Occasional inebriation is worth paying for." I tried in vain to visualise Aunt Addie inebriated; I tried to picture her with a cigar between her lips, why, even the young men I knew didn't tackle them. Georges Sands? Miss Adelaide Granby, the well-known novelist, was not in the least like her French compatriot; she, at least, had never worn trousers.

"And how can you be sure of that, pray, Pamela?"

Well, I couldn't, of course. But it was improbable. The trouble was, Aunt Addie relished so many improbabilities, that it was difficult to decide just how improbable they were. I wished I had discussed Georges Sands with her. Was she an "advanced" woman, or a "fast" one?

"Is there any difference?"

My great-aunt's crisp clear tones inserted themselves into my mental argument.

"But of course there is, Aunt Addie! Fast women do things for self-indulgence, or—defiance. Advanced women act on principle."

"Never for sin?"

"Oh, calling things sin is such an old-fashioned idea."

"Then what becomes of the fun?"

"One doesn't do things for fun."

"Bosh!" said Aunt Addie.

This would never do! In life I had always found her finally unanswerable; now, in my mental reconstruction of her, I was allowing her her usual privilege. And, as usual, I knew the answers were to be found; but she would have none of them. I did her that much justice, anyhow. It made her presence almost actual, but I could not carry her quite as far as I wished. I longed to seize her delicate veined hands in mine, and startle a confession out of her: "Aunt Addie! What was your first love-affair 'with a grape'?" Would she have told me? Now she never would. My eyes fell on the fat envelope in my lap.

My dear Stanislaw

With eager fingers I broke the seal, and undid the ribbon. A medley of papers and envelopes fluttered loose. They may have been put into the envelope in some order, but not being pinned together were now "all everyhow". A few notes, and a quantity of poems, all in a script I recognised as that which had adorned Stanislaw's last tribute to my aunt. True, the script varied in ornamentation; in the verses it took twenty exquisite fantastic forms, the product of an era when penmanship was an art; but I was certain that the same penman, a master penman, had inscribed them. The notes were all in one style, and were written in violet ink. They revealed almost nothing; they were suggestive, where I desired them to be explicit; they said just enough to tickle, and no more.

Sleep well, my belovèd. Dare I ask you to meet me to-night behind Venus and Adonis? If hour and place be too remote for modesty, blame, but do not despise, your Stanislaw.

How many women are you? Three, at least! Sometimes so gay, sometimes so proud, and sometimes so unutterably tender. Adelaide! Adelaide!! And Adelaide!!! My Three Graces. I know not which of you I love the best.

To this note was attached a spray of what had once been three roses on one stem, now scentless and colourless.

If only Alicia can convey this to you! O the touch of your finger-tips in the cedar tree. Never, never forget your unhappy S.

I heard your three taps on the floor at midnight. I—Love—You! O my darling! Pray, pray be in the raspberry canes after luncheon. Your anger terrifies me. You must let me explain.

Stanislaw.

How beautiful you looked to-night, playing your harp! How beautifully you sang! I could hardly keep my eyes averted from you—I need not, thank heaven, my ears. I sat in my corner, apparently absorbed in my tedious duties, while choirs of angels floated round my head. And he sat, where I longed to be, at your side, drinking you in, and turning your music for you. How I hate Irishmen! Do not say you love them.

Your blissful, your tormented Stanislaw.

I have found one tiny lilac comfit left in the dear precious box. It shall stay there as long as I live, and when I am dying I will place it on the tip of my tongue.

I cannot, dare not, believe last night was true. I have dreamed of you and your gift of yourself till dawn. Can you find a moment to slip into the library after tea? I am now immersed in Addison and Steele—bring a volume of The Spectator with you, to cover your presence, in case we are disturbed. But I think we can depend on ten minutes alone—and until the ecstatic experience is repeated, I can neither rest, nor trust myself that it happened.

I cannot live without you—and I must. Farewell! God bless you.

Eternally your S.

All the notes were undated, excepting one: *Sleep well, my belovèd. At the foot of this was written in Aunt Addie's girlish hand: The Sixth of May, 1849. Let me never, never, never forget this night! I did not sleep a wink.*

Her writing, too, inscribed a folded paper:

His Hair!

Inside lay a jet-black curl, confined with a gold-brown strand from some other head. I knew that Aunt Adelaide had been famed for her silky gold-brown tresses.

A daguerreotype! In a leather case, lined with velvet, and a broken tinsel border. How eagerly I opened it, to decipher Stanislaw's features. But, if Stanislaw it was, time had faded him out of recognition. It was a full length portrait, in an oval, and as I turned the spotted silvery plate this way and that, all I could see was a pair of wide white trousers.

Frustrated, I turned my attention to the verses. There was a positive sheaf of them; and these, at least, bore dates.

May 6th 1861, May 6th 1854, May 6th 1883,

May 6th 1884, May 6th 1902, May 6th 1877—

No other day but the one Aunt Addie would never, never, never forget. Sorting them into order, I found they dated from 1850 to the present year; the last poem was sent for May 6th, 1912. Not a quarter of a year ago. The first, much more than half a century old, was inscribed:

A SUMMER'S NIGHT

It ran as follows:

Whene'er the moon her silver flood
Pours forth, as now, on yonder wood;
When fragrance from the linden trees,
Is mingled with the evening breeze:

Then sinks my heart into the tomb
Of Love now lost! Involved in gloom
The grave appears; and from the trees
No fragrance mingles with the breeze!

Departed spirit! Oft with you
This scene I've shared—the fragrance too:
Then, then how lovely was thy light,
O moon! And Nature's face, how bright!

The last was:

STANZAS TO A—

We met within a glorious pile,
Where many ancient things
Gave token to a vanished age
While our youth fledged its wing;
There where the summer's starry light
Most tremblingly did fall,
And broken shadows quivering lay
Beneath the ruined wall.

Oh! Ever be as thou wert then,
So kind and simple-minded,
Nor by the voice of-flattery
Let thy fresh heart be blinded.
For doubly great is she who stands
Upon the mound of Fame,
And can look back on her career
Without a flush of shame.

There be who say, as years roll on,
Our feelings lose their truth;
But still my spirit throbs for thee,
As in my earliest youth.
In spite of all philosophy,
Be mine this single lay,
To feel for thee to-morrow
As I did yesterday.

The one for 1863 ran:

LINES TO A—

The star of eve that shines when dews are weeping,
The glowing moss-rose hanging on the bough,
The swan upon the purple water sleeping,
Though beauteous all, were far less fair than thou.
Fair the comparisons; but yet remaineth
The charm for which no simile we find
'Mid birds and flowers which die, and star which paleth,
That master-charm of all—the gift of Mind.
When the bright eye grows dim, the light step faileth,

And faded is the fresh cheek's summer bloom,
That charm still lasts—its lustre never paleth
Till all that's mortal sleeps within the tomb.

At the foot of this, Aunt Addie had written: "Sent after I had published my first novel—but my bright eye wasn't as dim as all that." The comment had evidently been superscribed many years after the verses had been received, when her handwriting had already taken the character familiar to me. It reappeared here and there in comments on several of the pieces, springing off the quick tongue of her mind at some re-reading. In 1852, Stanislaw had sent her some lines in another language.

JE VOUDRAIS ÊTRE

Je voudrais être le nuage
Pour te préserver du soleil,
Je voudrais être ton image
Pour te sourire à ton reveil.

Je voudrais être la pervenche
Qui joue avec tes blonds cheveux,
Ou ton beau miroir qui se penche
Quand sur lui tu mires tes yeux.

Je voudrais être—

quite a number of other things: an angel with golden wings who kissed the rosy lips of his sweet treasure, while she slept: he wished to be one of those dreams whose illusions rock the dreamer in momentary bliss: a swallow, whose wing caressed her cheek, while his beak ravished one of her curls: he wished to be the shadow who followed wherever she went, the flower her glance lighted on, the desire her heart was set on:

Je voudrais, lyre harmonieuse,
Être ce que rêve ton coeur,
Et pour te rendre toute heureuse,
Je voudrais être . . . le bonheur!

Two queries had been appended to this by Aunt Addie; one in her girlish, the other in her adult, hand.

What is a pervenche?—Find out. A. G.

When on earth did S. begin to study French? He seems to have managed very well in the time!

In 1894 she received this, on the unforgettable day.

ANIMA MUNDI

ANIMA MUNDI—of thyself existing,
Without diversity or change to fear,
Say, has this life to which we cling persisting,
Part in communion with thy steadfast sphere?
Does thy serene eternity sublime
Embrace the slaves of Circumstance and Time?

Oh if we mourn, not because time is fleeting,
Not because life is short and some die young,
But because parting ever follows meeting;
And, while our hearts with constant loss are wrung,
Our minds are tossed in doubt from sea to sea,
Then may we claim community with thee.

We would erect some thought the world above,

And dwell in it for ever—we would make
Some moment of young Friendship or First-love
Into a dream, from which we would not wake;
We would contrast our action with repose,
Like the deep stream that widens as it flows.

If such things are within us—God is good—
And flight is destined for the callow wing,
And the high appetite implies the food,
And souls must reach the level whence they spring;
O Life of very Life! Set free our Powers,
Hasten the travail of the yearning hours.

"Very philosophical indeed!" was Aunt Adeline's postscript. "Verse Three would have sufficed, my dear Stanislaw."

Nothing else in the envelope seemed likely to throw much light on the affair; its contents were all of a piece with the laurel urn and dear Stanislaw's valedictory verses. I was glad I had kept that last poem, to complete the collection—but how I kicked myself for not having looked for the florist's name on the box, that I might pursue some inquiries as to its sender. But no! It hadn't, I remembered, arrived in a box, it had been borne, in unashamed nakedness, up the steps by staggering limbs, while the florist's van stood lightened in the road. It hadn't occurred to one to be curious before the van drove off.

I shook the envelope disconsolately. Nothing more fell out; but something was still wedged down the length of it. I drew out a folded letter, thin and rustling, marked in violet ink, in a large and rather untidy hand:

Very Private/ Read and Destroy AT ONCE!!

LETTER FROM "A. M. L."

Sweet Girl!

Fate is against us!

Not only *He* but I am to be torn from you. Oh, what have we done to deserve this?

Half an hour ago your Papa sent for me. I went to him, fortified by my intentions to intercede for you and S—, to upbraid him for his harsh treatment of you—oh, I was prepared to be eloquent! Words, tears, and looks should be my aids in your defence. I felt assured of victory. Picture my horror on finding *myself* accused of (to use his own expression) "*pandaring* to the *illicit affections* of his daughter and *an inferior.*"

I was dumb!—he stormed on. I found my tongue!—he silenced it. I protested to be allowed to defend and explain myself!—he confronted me with one of my own notes to S— telling him you would be in the Gothic Temple at the appointed hour. S—, dear, careless S—, must have dropped it in his room during his hasty packing. Faced with this indubitable evidence of complicity, words for the moment failed me; then, gathering my scattered wits: "*Tout comprendre—*" I began. He cut me short, and would not even listen. Indeed, the words meant to soothe, only augmented his violence. He employed a word not fit for a lady's ears to hear, or her hand to write.

"D— your Frenchifications!" he shouted, his face the hue of beetroot. "A little less French and a little more honest English best suits *this* house! G*d only knows what lessons you've been stuffing into my Addie's head along of your parleyvooing."

This, and much more that I am too agitated to recall, and would not repeat if I could. The upshot of it is, that I am to go to-morrow without seeing you. I shall try for an opportunity to push this under your door ere I depart. To-morrow, be assured, I will see dear S— in Matlock. His tears, his pallid features, as your father drove him away still wring my heart. What I feel for *you*, sweet girl, you know full well. What I feel for *him*—you shall never, never guess!

One last word. Suffering is to be the lot of all three. Do not let it defeat my Adeline! Rise supreme above it—and if, in so doing, you find grief clinging to you like the ivy, then *revel in your grief.* Strange advice, you say! But life, you know, is made up of *chiaroscuro.* Without the shades, the lights would lose their refulgence. While the ecstasy of joy is delayed and denied, let the ecstasy of sorrow be your cherished possession: the obverse of life's coin, the storm before the calm, the dark face of the moon.

When we shall meet again I do not know. But they cannot keep you incarcerated for ever. A few years hence you will attain womanhood. Spend these years in preparing to be an independent woman. Without this, one can be *nothing.* You know I am in advance of my times.

Farewell! If I can communicate with you again I will, I know not when or how.

Adieu! Adieu!

Forget not your

A.M.L.

The violet ink ceased to flow half-way down the fourth page. The rest of the sheet was filled with a pencilled scrawl in Aunt Addie's youthful script. What she had written was:

Turbot and Lobster Sauce
Duck and Green pease
Strawberries and cream or cream trifle
Cherry Brandy?

SCRAPBOOK

———————

That finished the available manuscripts. The scrapbooks and the two locked books remained. I picked futilely at the locks for a few moments, and was tempted to break them open then and there, but decided that I could not spend all day in the attic, and that it would be better to carry my possessions home than to injure the books in a fit of impatience. I did, however, glance with mild interest through one of the scrapbooks. It was a heterogeneous medley of print and pictures cut out of periodicals, engravings of Swiss and Oriental scenes, some Christmas cards and fashion plates, a disrespectful cartoon of Queen Victoria being wooed by Prince Albert, a programme of one of M. Jullien's concerts, and another of the Duke of Wellington's Funeral. Sundry naive pencil drawings punctuated these curiosities: "The Corner of the Yard from my Schoolroom window" (in the drawing-book mode of the times); "Bonny, my Favourite pony, and Fluff" (Bonny looked sadly over-eaten in his hind-quarters, and in need of oats to the fore, while it was difficult to tell if Fluff were feline or canine); and one page bore two bright little miniatures in body-colour—the top one, exhibiting a dome and a palm-tree on yellow sand, being labelled *Constanti-nople*, the bottom one, showing the same dome and a gondola on cobalt water, being *Venice*. On another were two or three paintings of "Ornaments from the China Cupboard"—a Chinese Teapot, a Chelsea Shepherdess, and a china patchbox decorated with little flowers, and the legend: "If you Love mee Lend mee not." Then, towards the end of the book came some surprises in the shape of paintings of astonishing accomplishment. There were pages of moths and butterflies, sprays of convolvulus, carnation, rose; the bloom on the wing and the dewdrop on the leaf were done with a perfection that, if technical execution ever can, amounted to genius. Most of them were signed "S. P."; but others, of inferior execution, and with evidences of expert touching up, bore the initials "A. G." Aunt Addie herself. A full-page water-colour of another kind was labelled: *The Picnic in Dovedale, June 3rd, 1849.* This, too, was from her hand, and had apparently been sketched on the spot, and stuck in the book afterwards. The picnic cloth was spread in a tree-shaded valley among the picturesque Derbyshire rocks and waters; around it sat the picnickers, seeming very far apart from one another, for the cloth was vastly out of perspective, in order to accommodate the feast. It seemed to be a feast of splendid proportions, mainly consisting of plates of fruit and decanters; there was also a recognisable game pie. The revellers were labelled with their initials. In the foreground you saw their ample backs and spreading skirts. "H. G." in a shawl must be Henrietta Granby (Mama); "J. W. G." (Papa) sat upright on one side of her, in a stove-pipe hat; on the other, "T. H." reclined in middle-aged profile, chiefly consisting of resplendent moustache. Farther round a little figure in sprigged cotton and a straw bonnet that concealed her features was ticketed "A. G."—the sketcher's self, done out of her head, I supposed. On the opposite margin of the tablecloth, "A. M. L." presided in magenta, dark-haired and dark-eyed; beyond her in the far corner a young male in a rather green suit and chestnut locks was simply labelled "S." His features were indeterminate. The whole sketch indeed was unfinished. In addition to pictures and cuttings, the book contained many samples of verse copied out by hand, two of the later ones being in an exquisite penmanship that quickened my heart. I recognised the style; it was that of the verses of the funeral trophy. No one but Stanislaw could have formed those characters. Another page was crowded with a copious extract in French—something by Lamartine—in the ungainly scrawl of the letter I had just read. It was signed: "Alicia Mary Linton." Of course! The old governess, whom Aunt Addie had remembered generously in her will. Very, very old now, but still living down in, where was it? Woking? Surbiton? Why, I could go and see her for myself. Perhaps I would. I put back the scattered contents of the trunk, sent for a cab, and bore my legacy home. There, after lunch, I examined it at more leisure, and to my delight found, tucked away in the sachet of old lace, two little keys of identical pattern. They fitted the locks of the books which had baffled me, and I had them both open in no time. Each had a carefully written title-page. One called itself, in unformed handwriting:

The Diary of Miss Adelaide Granby
of Pelham Place
Commenced August 3rd 1848

The other, in a script more elegant, bore the legend:

The Bastard of Pinsk

a novel

by

Miss Adelaide Granby

Commenced June 24th 1849

Aunt Addie's novel, written when she was sixteen! "Perhaps my best novel. At all events, my favourite." With a thrill of curiosity I turned the flyleaf.

"Look! Look! Oh, there he goes!"

"Oh, where?"

"Yonder! He is entering the chasm!"

I blinked my eyes. The writing was so minute, so close, so fine, that to read it for long at a time would cause me eye-strain. I ruffled the leaves of the thick little book with my thumb; twenty-six chapters or so, thousands of words of it. I caught a sentence here and there.

Lord Tarletan was a well-known lecher in London.

"Ah, women!" said the Grand-Duke tenderly.

Alas for youth, when it trusts its elders with its heart.

"If he had leapt into the jaws of H*ll I should not have turned back."

"Very heroic," I sneered, for I could scarce keep my temper,
"but do you never eat partridge?"

The Moujik found the governess still on the terrace. "Georgiana! Rash one! What were you going to do?" "Expiate my sin, Count Stanislaw."

"I prayed," said Caroline, faintly, "that you should be happy, though my heart should break."

Madame Leroy started and pointed her finger. "'Tis he" she cried. "The Bastard!"

This rapid survey at random, which had all the effect of to-day's "trailer" for next week's film-attraction, whetted my appetite; but I felt quite unequal to deciphering the novel for myself, and decided that, before I could act upon Aunt Addie's wishes, I must turn over the eye-aching task to a professional typist. A rising young journalist among my Fabian friends would tell me where to send it. I hoped I need not do the same with "Miss Adelaide Granby's Diary"; Aunt Addie, so recently living, might feel it desecrated her sense of privacy.

YOUNG LADY'S DIARY: 1848

––––––––––

The diary, I found, was in an altogether more childish, and therefore more legible, hand than the novel. It occupied only a part of the tooled leather book, a portion of which had been torn out of its covers. I shall not record it all; it was begun in August, 1848, and kept up more faithfully than those usually begun on January 1st. For some time the recordings were daily, and ran voluminously to ardent descriptions of the beauties of nature and the feelings they inspired in little Addie's breast. Summer's glories and the fading charms of autumn supplied useful exercises for a future novelist's pen. November roused less rapture in her, and events superseded scenery; but not a week went by without three or four pages filled.

August 3 1848.

Miss Linton says I ought to keep a diary for the sake of my writing. "Do you mean my handwriting?" I teazed, for the other day when Papa wanted a list of his latest box of books he had a fit of temper and said my handwriting would disgrace a cockchafer. I said I thought any cockchafer would feel set up if it could write half as well, and Papa said—"Don't answer back—I shall speak to Miss Linton about it—I expect my daughter to be brought up with the usual acomplishments—G*d knows I pay through the nose for them." My Mamma said, "Pray mind your tongue Mr. Granby, Miss Linton's French and Music are excellent."

"Her sketching and orthogriffy are lamentable," said Papa—"if she cannot improve herself and Adelaidc out she goes."

I burst into tears and I am affrayed I stamped my foot.

Papa said—"Go to your room this instant"—and I went.

Miss Linton replied: "No, my love, I do not mean your handwriting, I know it is my fault that it leaves much to be desired, but I am sure in spite of it you will be a writer. Even Shakspere was not held back by bad penmanshipp." "Do you think I shall write plays like his?" I asked. "I don't advise it," said my dear Governess, "for if you did I don't think your Papa would permitt you to associate with The Stage—but Novels like Mrs. Gore and Mrs. Radcliffe."

How wonderful that would be! Why should it not? I am writing this in my room, and the cedar tree—black as the tomb—taps on my windowpane. The sun is setting on the other side of the house and though I cannot see it the sky is sure to be a glorious mixture of Red and Purple, gold and silver clouds will come floating there like nights riding into battle or sirens swimming in a violet ocean. Ah me! When shall I realize my dreams? My Love! My Love!! My Love!!! What will you look like? Presently the Moon will rise o'er the cedar and fill me with beautiful longings.

Much of August was occupied with accounts of family jars, the Derbyshire landscape, and Miss Linton's influence, musical with a dash of French in it.

August 12.

Miss L— is teaching me the "Cascade de Roses" she plays so beautifully. I shall never manage the ripples with her elegance. I find the Harp easier than the Pianoforte when singing, but Miss L— says a Few Pieces on the Pianoforte are necessary to a young lady's outfit so I must persevere. To the Harp I am now learning to sing a very beautiful Trio called "Voga, Voga" in Italian, a Barcarola or WaterSong—of course I only sing one of the parts and I do not know what it means, but it fills me with feelings like moonlight. Miss L— speaks several languages with idiomatic proficiency and tells me how to say the Italien words, but thinks one foreign tongue enough at a time. In French I can now conjergate the Verb "Aimer" (to Love) all through. "To Kiss" is Baiser, but Miss L— says I must use this very carefully. "Why ?" I asked. "Not yet, my Love," she said, "I will tell you all one day, all

*you need now remember is Love's consermation lies in its First
Kiss." I did not like to ask her what consermation means. I must
find out. How sad that one does not like to display ignerence, it
keeps one from learning so many things and finding out is not
always verry easy. I shall consult the Dictioneries in the Libery.*

August 13.

*Consummation—the act of carrying to the utmost extent or
degree. Lat. Consummatio-Fr. Consomation.*

The utmost extent or degree-O my Love, thy first Kiss!

August 16.

*When finding the dictionery—which was not easy because the
libery is in a shocking muddle—I found a fassinating book by
Canova, his Life by himself. Miss L— says the Venus and Adonis in
the garden may be a copy of one of Canova's Chef D'Oeuvres—so
naturally I was eager to read about him, but he does not speak at
all about his statues, only about his marvellous lights of love. He
must have been as handsome and dashing as Lord Byron, from
whose works I have extracted nourishment for the exaltation of
my mind.*

August 28.

*The corn that was so full and ripe is cut. One day it stands
glowing in the kiss of the sun, the next it lies fallen on the fallow
field. Such, such is life! But take heart. The corn will grow again. It
is the little rabbits running I cannot bear.*

August 30.

Sir Terence Hogan came last night and spent the evening.

*He has a way of talking I cannot describe. He brought me a
satin fan with ivory sticks and an edging of lace, painted with
white and yellow flowers. I played him "Cascade de Roses" and
only made three mistakes. "What an acomplished young lady!" he
said at the end, "as acomplished as she is pretty." Papa said with*

one of his snorts "Ask her to write her name for you and you'll see
how far her acomplishments go." "I had far rather ask Miss
Adelaide to write my name," said Sir Terence which made me
laugh a good deal. "I am no good with a pen," I said "or a pencil
either I'm afraid." I fluttered my fan and smiled at him over the
edge like Lady Isabel in The Story of an Heiress. "Bejabers!" said
Sir Terence, "ladies can use some instruments without much
teaching. Miss Adelaide must come to my New Year's Ball. I won't
take nay." "Oh" said Mama "I think she is too young." 'Why Mama"
I said, "many a girl of my age is a mother in Italy." "Go to your
room at once, miss," said Papa to my mortification and surprize. I
all but stamped my foot at him, but looked haugty instead and
curtseyed to Sir Terence who was smiling broadly, and said
"Thank you, I am very fond of dancing" and went out of the room
in a dignified way waving my fan all the time.
My father is my very antipodes.

August 31.

Mamma said I must not say such things and Papa is annoyed
with me. Why must I not say such things if they are true? And so
they are. (See Lady Capulet.)

September 5.

He has kept up his annoyence for several days so I have kept a
good deal in my room reading and writing, and sat in the Gothic
Temple with Miss Linton. She has been relating her past to me. She
has been to Paris! She says she will reveal all to me in time. She
describes things so brightly I think I have been there myself. She
has loved and lost. But time and sorrow cannot undo her
faithfulness. "To love once is to love for ever," she said. "Fidelity is
Love's twin sister." How true! Oh when?

September 7.

Sir Terence rode up this morning and Papa sent for me. He was
all smiles again but why I do not know for it was not to him Sir
Terence brought the basket of roses and peaches. "Sweets to the
sweet," he said giving them to me. "You treat my little one better

than she deserves," said Papa. "Sure, that would be unpossible!"
said Sir Terence. I laughed and said "I wish you was my uncle." He
looked surprized and said "Why?" "Because then" I said "I could
hug you for the peaches." He looked more pleased now and said
"In that case I wish I was your uncle too." When he was gone Papa
pinched my ear and said, "You ought to mind that little tongue of
yours, however no harm's done, quite the contrary." So all is
chearful in the house again.

Cheerfulness and tearfulness waxed and waned by turns in
Pelham Place. During the next months various matters were
coming to a head. Miss Linton's shocking calligraphy was a sore
point; Mr. Granby, wanting a catalogue for his library, had
requested or commanded her to prepare one. The result brought
about a dreadful scene; but Miss Linton, promising to try again and
do better, stayed on, became Alicia to her pupil, and began to call
Addie Adeline. It was evident that she inflamed more and more
Addie's ambition to write, and fed her unborn romance. Addie
gained increasing mastery over spelling and phraseology, devoted
herself to dancing and music and French, and listened to endless
tales of Miss Linton in Paris. Her imagination supplied more than
Miss Linton told—who probably had little enough to tell. The
affection between the two was very great, but Addie's artless "pash"
for her governess had no hint in it of anything "peculiar." Her
surreptitious readings went on, and not even with Miss Linton did
she share what she found at the back on the top shelves. She was
always trying to find out the meanings of words she did not like to
ask about, and made some precious queer shots in the dark. "My
Love! My Love!" appeared at intervals in apostrophe, but had not
yet acquired an identity. It became plainer and plainer that Sir
Terence Hogan hoped to qualify for the part, Addie hadn't the
faintest inkling of it, and that Mr. and Mrs. Granby based their
hopes on it.

In December the New Year's Ball came up again, and Adelaide
was to be allowed to go!

December 3.

I have begged Alicia to work up my dancing with me. I am
determined not to disgrace myself by akwardness. Miss Linton is a

highly acomplished dancer. She says I have more gracefulness but she has more spiritedness. She has taught me the Polka which is easy and very amusing. Last night aftcr we had valsed she said she would dance me the Varsoviana that she had learnt in Paris. It is a Polish dance full of fire and languishment. It filled me full of feelings only to see her. I tried my hand, or rather my foot at it, but I shall never, never dance it like Alicia! Papa has promised me a beautiful ball-dress for New Year's Eve. My first! We have got The Ladies Gazette and Marna has even gone to the length of sending for the patterns in Le Bon Ton from Paris!! Among so many it is hard to choose, but Marna says those I think most handsome are too old for me. Little she knows how old I am at heart. I think about my ball dress day and night.

The discussions about the dress went on for days. The merits of silk, lace, and "illusion" were weighed, the trimmings (ribbons or rosebuds?), the colour (pearl? blushpink? sky-blue?), the shawl or scarf, the flowers for the hair.

"You must carry Sir Terence's fan." Mama was assured on *that* point.

White silk gauze and blonde lace was decided; a sash of green watered silk, and tiny festoons of leaves to catch up the three flounces round the crinoline; a wreath of leaves and white rosebuds on the hair. But who should make the dress?

December 9.

Alicia has discovered a needlewoman in Matlock, "a perfect treasure" she says. We are to have her in the house till the dress is done, and she will make Mama's at the same time.

Miss Spencer arrived, and the progress of the dresses was recorded with detailed enthusiasm. The lady needlewoman was kept hard at it, and just before Christmas the costumes were completed. Addie describes her green and white confection as "crisp and salacious to a degree"! Meanwhile, another flare-up over the wretched cataloge.

December 18.

Papa came into the sewing-room after luncheon and hurled Alicia's last list into the middle of the work. "If you want any waste paper for tacking, Miss Spencer," he shouted, "here it is!" He went out banging the door. Mama frowned, and dear Alicia went quite white. Miss Spencer, who was fitting me, looked sadly confused. I explained, "My papa is in a temper because he wants a neat cataloge of his library. If only Miss Linton wrote as fine as you stitch all would be well." "Oh dear!" said Miss Spencer, "if only he could have my brother."

It seemed that the needlewoman had a half-brother, much younger than herself, who had a "positive genius" for penmanship and brushwork. Although only sixteen years of age, he was becoming quite famous in Matlock, and had already been employed to write certificates of merit and congratulatory addresses. She hoped to article him on the strength of his gifts. Out of the ensuing talk the suggestion grew: Why should not Miss Spencer's half-brother make the catalogue? It is not clear who first propounded it seriously—Addie for Miss Linton's sake, Miss Linton for her own, Miss Spencer for her half-brother's, or Mrs. Granby for the sake of peace and quietness. But new ideas had to be instilled in Pelham Place with feminine tact. In their different ways, all the ladies went to work. Miss Spencer left some specimens of her brother's art accidentally about the place, not only delicate calligraphy, but enchanting paintings of horticulture and lepidoptera. The bait was taking when, on Christmas Eve, Addie developed measles. Sir Terence's ball came and went, and the gauze frock remained unworn. A disappointment for Addie; a bitterer one for her parents. Business carried Sir Terence off to Ireland. Dr. Baird pulled Addie through a sharp attack. Miss Linton nursed her devotedly. All thoughts of the catalogue were temporarily abandoned. But the invalid recovered, anxiety assuaged, and the edge of gratitude blunted, the vexed question reappeared on the horizon. Mrs. Granby took a firm line at once. "You know, Mr. Granby, that Miss Linton is incapable of it! Why do you only torment her and yourself? I'm sure we should leave her in peace after all she has done. If catalogue you must have, there's Miss What's-her-name's you-know-who-I-mean." In March, Miss Spencer's half-brother made his appearance in Pelham Place.

March 7 1849.

Miss Spencer's brother is come. Papa is quite delighted with him, he says he has never seen anything like his penmanship. He showed us his sketchbook this evening and you could almost brush the bloom off the grapes and the butterfly's wings. I have seldom seen Papa so good humoured, and while he is making the cataloge which will take several weeks, he is to improve my handwriting. It will be odd to learn of somebody my own age. Mama did not quite approve but Papa is determined on it and says Alicia can chaperone the lessons "and may get a bit of good out of them for herself," he said, "besides," he added, "we are giving the young fellow his keep and it won't cost us another penny." It is a pity about his hair, but Alicia says we will think of it as chestnut. He is very shy. Papa has put him in the little gunroom downstairs under my closet.

March 9.

We have decided to call him Stanislaw.

Here, to my disappointment, the diary gave out. The next sections had been torn away, leaving a thin thread or so dangling, and some blank pages at the end of the book. At some point in her life Aunt Addie had evidently resolved to destroy the written evidence of her Grand Passion of which I could not doubt Miss Spencer's halfbrother was the object. Terribly young-at the start. How long had it gone on under the roof of Pelham Place?—and how continued elsewhere? In what hour, in what fire, had Aunt Addie consumed her record of it? It was really too tantalising.

Then, disconsolately ruffling the last blank pages, I saw that one of them still bore some writing: a right-hand page, the few preceding it having also been uprooted, like those earlier. It looked as though she had made some entries at a later date, skipping certain pages, and, in tearing these out, inadvertently left the last.

"done wrong in the world's eyes. I know I have sinned woman's unforgiveable sin. Well, there have to be women like me in the world. To the end of my life I shall glory secretly in having broken

the bounds, and come to that knowledge which is hidden from my sex behind the altar. Oh Stanislaw! Though we never meet again, I will never forget that night of nights, no other man shall ever be admitted into the life of your Adeline!"

CONVERSATION WITH ALICIA
MARY LINTON

I was apt, and still am, to put off things I intend to do, that can be done at any time, in favour of immediate interests. But after reading Aunt Addie's incomplete diary, and dispatching the novel to my journalist friend, I got Miss Linton's address from Henry Tennant and paid my intended visit to Surbiton. Before doing so, I wrote to the Home for Decayed Gentlewomen (it called itself "Battledores Home of Rest"), to ask if Miss Linton could, and would, see the niece of her old friend Miss Adelaide Granby. I addressed my letter to the matron, in case Miss Linton was too decayed to write for herself. G. Norham, Matron, sent me an affable answer, saying that Miss Linton, though in fragile health, would be glad to see me any afternoon between 3.30 and 6 o'clock; there was an enclosure in a spidery hand, which ran: "Please come, dear Miss Lang, and be sure to give *dearest Adeline* my *fondest love.*"

"It's a long way to go," said my mother, who was inclined to negative other people's actions. "What are you going for?"

"Curiosity, mums." It was three parts the truth. I should have hated to own to one part of sentiment. I set out betimes, and arrived at "Battledores" soon after three. The Home of Rest was a large square mid-Victorian house, set in a cheerful garden, quite big enough to call itself "the grounds". There were cannon-balls on the stone gate-posts, and a gravel drive sweeping to the portico between solid bay windows. A remarkably pretty little maid opened the door. I asked for Miss Norham, and was shown in to her sanctum, the bay-windowed room on the right. I thought Miss Norham rather like the room; she was an ample lady with a square face, pleasant, but by no means soft grey eyes, and a touch of practised velvet in her voice.

"Miss Lang? So good of you to come such a long way in this heat. So very glad to see a niece of Miss Adelaide Granby. Such a loss! You must feel it even more than the rest of us."

"I was very fond of my great-aunt."

"She must have been a dear, kindness itself."

"Didn't you ever see her?"

"No, I am sorry to say."

I felt I ought to apologise for Aunt Addie. "She was in delicate health for years, you know."

"Yes, of course. She kept in touch after she arranged for Miss Linton's coming to us, and remembered us generously, most generously, on Pound Day and Christmas. We quite understood."

"Didn't she ever come to see Miss Linton?"

"No, and Miss Linton herself did not seem to expect it. In fact, I've never even heard her express the wish."

"She won't mind seeing me?"

"On the contrary, Miss Lang, she seemed very pleased."

"I'm afraid I'm early. It's difficult to judge, when you don't know the distance."

"There always has to be a first time, hasn't there? We say three-thirty to visitors, because the inmates always rest after lunch. It is a good rule for the old, and not a bad one for the middle-aged. One *you* won't need for a long time to come."

She said this so graciously that I felt youth slipping from me, and quickly hauled it back with schoolgirl slang. "Me? Oh, I'm full of beans!"

"So nice to see young things here once in a while. Now you've found your way, you mustn't desert us. I hope your dear Aunt did not suffer much?"

"It was all very sudden."

"A blessing for her, but of course a shock for you. I always say those left behind are those that feel it."

I bowed my head to this incontrovertible fact. Miss Norham glanced at the clock. There were so many things on the mantelpiece, that if the clock had not been large and square like her face it might have been overlooked.

"Just on half-past. I'll see if she is awake."

She left me alone with her photographs, knick-knacks, and numerous souvenirs. Her holidays had been spent in many places, and she was an indefatigable collector of "Goss-pots". Silver-framed photographs of affectionate women friends were legion; but place of honour was given to a picture post card signed "Yours sincerely Gabrielle Ray." I was back on the edge of my chair when Miss Norham returned.

"So sorry to have been so long. She was just waking up, and one mustn't be too sudden with them. We tidied her up for you. She's quite ready now. This way. You'll like her room, quite the nicest in the house, though too full of her funny old things, of course. Your dear aunt insisted on her having a nice large room."

I followed Miss Norham along a corridor, and, without mounting the broad staircase, was conducted to a pleasant room in the rear. Entering it was like stepping back sixty years. The curtains and furniture were those of the '50's, the ornaments earlier still. There was a bookcase filled with volumes in tooled calf, violet cloth, and watered silk. Even the outlook from the large windows did not disturb the effect. The garden was old-fashioned; one looked across formal flowerbeds to a shrubbery, set up against which, in full view of the four-poster bed, was a pseudo-classic plaster group of the kind that lent romance to "the grounds" of our grandparents.

"Venus and Adonis," whispered Miss Norham.

I stared at her, trying to recover the original of an echo.

"Miss Granby had it expressly sent down here all the way from her estates in Derbyshire, for Miss Linton's eightieth birthday, with instructions for it to be put where Miss Linton could see it. It was after she became bedridden, and Miss Granby no doubt thought she would like this reminder of a place they had once lived in together. So thoughtful."

That was it! "Meet me after supper behind Venus and Adonis, if hour and place be not too remote for modesty." Stanislaw's tremulous plea—but not to Miss Linton.

I turned to the bed, where Aunt Addie's old governess sat up looking at me. She was very, very old. Her thin hair, silver-grey stained with pale yellow, was dressed in ringlets and covered with an embroidered lawn cap like a baby's. Her hazel eyes swam in a face that looked too small for her features; her large aquiline nose was finely cut. Her hands, all blue veins and brittle finger-nails, lay outside the patchwork quilt that covered her bed. Her nightdress and bed-linen were of good quality. I sat down on the chair placed by the bed, and took one of the transparent hands in mine. She smiled at me vaguely and sweetly.

"Miss Alicia Linton?"

She nodded slightly.

"I am Pamela Lang, your old friend Adelaide Granby's niece, you know."

She nodded again, and murmured: "How you've changed."

"I am Miss Granby's niece," I repeated gently .

"Yes, yes. Beautiful gold-brown hair. Your hair is dark. Hair can be dyed," she said, with a sly smile. "Red hair can be dyed black."

Miss Norham patted her shoulder and said rather loudly:

"Miss Lang will stay and have tea with you, Miss Alicia. Is not that kind of her! I'm sending in something specially nice for you both." She bent down to say in my ear: "I will leave you alone!" and went out of the room.

As soon as the door closed Miss Linton' s frail fingers gripped mine.

"Prop me up higher, my dearest, they never prop me high enough. Is she quite gone? Are you sure? Now we can talk. Hush!" She put a mysterious finger to her lips. "They listen at keyholes."

"It's all right, Miss Alicia."

"Are we quite alone?"

"Nobody's in the room but you and me."

"Go and open the door rather suddenly."

I obeyed and returned.

"Nobody there."

"Nobody. Are you sure?"

"Quite sure, Miss Alicia."

"Then now we can talk." She fixed her swimming eyes on me impressively. I waited with interest for what was coming. "Adeline!" she whispered.

"I am Pamela, her niece."

"Yes, yes, you told me. Pamela. Now attend to me closely."

"Yes, Miss Alicia."

"Pamela! What do you think she will give us for tea?"

I swallowed my disappointment. "Something very nice, Miss Norham said."

"If it is toast I can't eat it. Buttered tea-cake, yes. Buttered toast, no. They always leave on the crusts. I've told them over and over and over again."

"If it is toast I'll cut the crust off for you."

"I won't eat it. It's too crunchy. Seed-cake. We have too much seed-cake. The seeds get under my plate. They don't mind a bit. I won't have seed-cake. Plum-cake is what I like."

I squeezed her hand. "Let's wait and see. I know it is going to be nice."

"Do you really think so?"

"Yes."

"What a dear girl! You aren't much like Adeline."

"Did you call Aunt Addie Adeline?"

"She was baptised Adelaide. Not so romantic as Adeline. I was baptised Alice. Alicia is very much prettier, isn't it?"

"Much prettier, Miss Alicia."

She gave a little sigh of relief. "I am glad you agree."

I tried to lead her gently back to the past. "Did you always change plain names for pretty ones?"

"Always. Why not? Life is drab. Then why not enhance it? Sorrow is frequent. One had better enjoy it. Imagination can do everything. I hope you have it."

"Well—not as much as Aunt Addie."

"She was a pearl. How is she? I never had another pupil like her. Limpid. She absorbed all I had to give her."

"You were very fond of each other, weren't you?"

"We adored each other. And we adored—"

She nodded and closed her eyes. Stroking her hand, I ventured to whisper: "Whom?"

"That's right," said Miss Linton. "The Accusative. So many don't. But then they aren't born writers like Adeline. I formed her style. It was my life's achievement. How is she?"

"Aunt Addie?"

"Adeline."

"Oh," I said rather feebly, "she's quite all right."

"On the surface, yes! She will never get over it."

I seized my chance. "Get over what, Miss Alicia?"

"Some wounds are too deep to heal."

"Was she—was she unhappy?"

"That father of hers!"

"He locked her in her bedroom, didn't he?"

"Locked who?" said Miss Alicia. "When is tea coming? They get later and later."

"Didn't Aunt Addie's father lock her in her room?" I paused, and added boldly: "Because of Stanislaw?"

Miss Alicia's fingers tightened over mine again. "Are you in love, Mamie?"

"Pamela."

"Are you in love?"

"Not yet," I smiled.

"How old are you?"

"Twenty-three."

"Good heavens! Do not tell me you are faithless!"

"To whom?"

"Your belovèd."

"But I haven't one, dear Miss Alicia."

She looked at me earnestly. "Have you never been in love?"

"I'm afraid not exactly."

"What do you mean by *exactly*? One is or one is not, one goes into it headlong, all or nothing. One sacrifices oneself. I'm slipping down." I propped her up again. "Don't leave it too long," she whispered, closing her eyes.

I was afraid of tiring her, and as she seemed to doze I took the chance to walk about the room. The mantelpiece was loaded with objects that did not become a craze till ten years later. Still, I preferred these funny china ornaments and glass paper-weights to Miss Norham's Gosspots, and was fascinated by an old toy, a painted alabaster cylinder that turned on a swivel, with an eye-hole in the top. You looked down, turning the cylinder, which displayed a magnified sequence of scenes: a view of Chatsworth, then an exciting grotto stuck over with seaweed and glistening bits of Blue John, then a river running through a gorge, then a garden made of artificial ferns and flowers, then a view of the Peak: Chatsworth again. On a round plush table lay a photograph album. I opened it, and saw pictures so remote in dress, expression, and attitude, that they might have been conceived on another star. One small carte de visite was of Aunt Addie at the age when Miss Linton must have been teaching her. An exquisite little person. We had a copy of the same photograph. Between two unfilled pages lay a painting of a passion-flower, with a purple emperor butterfly hovering over it, and a dewdrop poised on the lowest petal. It was inscribed:

"To Alicia, most Faithful of Friends from her devoted S. P."

Even without the ornamental script, I would have known this for Stanislaw's. That dewdrop was S. P.'s line of Apelles.

I wandered to the bookcase. Byron, of course, *Lallah Rookh* bound heavily in green and gold, and luxuriantly illustrated, a novel by Mrs. Gore, and *Eugene Aram*. And sets of *The Keepsake* and *The Book of Beauty*. I opened one of them, rich in romances and legends, poems and engravings—oh dear me! Here was a world from a star remoter still. At least the originals of those old photographs had once breathed. This world of high-flown sentiment never had. It had been expressly created for its age, an illusion imposed on the women of Aunt Addie's girlhood. A preposterous world!—when would we get the Vote?

I dwelt on the portrait of one who would have scorned it. She was sure of her all-conquering charms, this Miss Meyer, with her oval face set on a full swan neck, huge eyes, long nose, small curved lips, blue-black hair wreathed with pearls, round shoulder and bust swelling out of a lace bertha, taper fingers pressing rosebuds to her bosom, and an expression calm and discreetly alluring, as she posed in the angle of a marble terrace, a stone urn filled with foliage behind her, a sunset over a mountain-peak in the distance. A sheet of tissue paper protected Miss Meyer from contact with cold print on the page that faced her. I glanced at it—a description in verse of the picture:

LINES

ON

The Portrait of Miss Meyer

By Miss Power

The door opened, and the pretty young maid entered with a tea-tray which she set on an octagonal table near the bed. She smiled affectionately at its occupant.

"Miss Alicia's dozing," said the little maid.

"Never mind, just leave it there, I'll wake her gently. What's in the covered dish?"

"Teacake, miss." (Thank goodness!) "Miss Alicia doesn't like toast, so I do my best to bring her what she likes."

"I'm glad you're so kind to her."

"Yes, miss. She's kind to me. She likes me to sit with her when I've a moment. She wants to educate me, she says, only not hand-writing. She says she was never any good at it. But she knows the most wonderful tales, and she's teaching me poetry."

"That's very nice for you both."

"Yes, thank you, miss."

The little maid withdrew. I went to the tea-tray and re-settled the cups with a gentle clatter that achieved its object. Miss Alicia opened her eyes .

"Tea's here, Miss Alicia. And teacake not toast."

"They never on any account," whimpered Alicia Mary Linton, "send muffins."

So that was all one got out of "A. M. L.". I left without answers to a dozen questions. But attempts to pin down that old fluttering memory would have been in the nature of Third Degree. She must be spared, and my curiosity unsatisfied. I left, promising Miss Norham to come again soon. But I never did. I heard a week later that Miss Linton had passed away: "peacefully and painlessly," as Miss Norham informed me, in a letter perfectly phrased. She said in the course of it:

"Miss Linton made no disposition of her things. She seems to have no kin, and has left no will. As your aunt was so close to her, dear Miss Lang, and sent much of the furniture for her room, I feel it only right to mention this and ask your wishes. I should love to keep just one teeny memento of her, if I might, one of her little china ornaments perhaps. Before she died, she gave away some of her books. Please let me know what you think best about the remainder of her possessions."

After talking it over with my parents, I replied that I was sure she might keep any memento she wished, that I myself would love to have the photograph album and the alabaster peepshow, and that we were sure Aunt Addie would wish the furniture to remain in Miss Alicia's room for the benefit of the incoming old gentlewoman.

The album and peepshow arrived by return of post; and the following day I received a neat brown paper package containing the manuscript and typescript of Aunt Addie's novel, forwarded to me by my friend. He enclosed a note.

Dear Pammy,

Here's your great-aunt's masterpiece and Miss Muirhead's account. My genteel typist sometimes alleviates her drudgery by allowing herself to comment on her authors' scripts. (She is exceedingly impolite about my punctuation.) You may like to hear her acid comment in this instance. I suppose it's meant for a joke, but I call it myself in very bad taste. There was a loose sheet fell out, I do not know if a copy of this was required, however I have made one and clipped it to the cover where, if not wanted, it can easily be removed and destroyed, the sooner the better. I have corrected the spelling throughout. I should think it a breach of trust to read Miss Granby's novel before you do, but I admit I am not enough of a gentleman to have resisted glancing at the easily removable matter. A loose sheet indeed!

Pammy, Pammy! Why didn't you introduce me to your great-aunt?

HUGH.

Part Two

THE BASTARD OF PINSK

Summer 1849

Definitions: by a Young Gentlewoman

DEFINITIONS (at least I think so)

For Use in my Works of Fiction

GENTLEMEN

BASTARD	A very noble Hero of Royal Blood
PARAMOUR	The sort of Lover every Female dreams of
LECHER	A Man of the world
PIMP	An exquisite Young Gentleman of Fashion
PANDAR	A Sort of Pimp but probably more dashing, I daresay with wild or Tartar Blood in him

GENTLEWOMEN

LIGHT-OF-LOVE	The Star in a Lover's Firmament
PROSTITUTE	A sort of Female Substitute
MISTRESS	A superior Female Lover very Much Adored but not quite the Thing
ODALISQUE	A very Beautiful Woman carved in Stone in the East
WORE	One who has been worn by Life
LEMAN	A Particular Sweetheart though I confess she sounds rather sour!
DOXY	A Simple Country Wench, very free in the Dales

Definitions: by a Young Gentlewoman

OTHER THINGS

BROTHEL	A Place where Love boils over

WORDS USED BY GENTLEMAN BUT NOT BY LADIES

D*MN—D*MN*D	Never spell in full—write as D*mn or D—d or sometimes you may use Demm, demmy, demmit, or demmed
INF*RN*L	Not in full—stars, or initial and dash only, perhaps the final L to make all clear
H*LL	Never in full conversationally, for instance if a Lecher is saying "Go to it", but perhaps just once a Pandar might say it in full

WORDS USED BY GENTLEMEN THAT CAN BE WRITTEN IN FULL

DASH-DASHED-GREAT SCOTT-GOOD HEAVENS-GOOD GRACIOUS-GOOD LORD (but not GOOD GOD, though a Lady may say Dear God in an extremity) and

I think CURSE or CURSE IT

EXCLAMATORY ODSERVATIONS

OH! is more startled than AH !-but AH! is more feeling than OH!

The Bastard

Of

Pinsk

A Novel

by

Adelaide Granby

———

1849

Contents

Proem

———————

"Look, LOOK! Oh, there he goes!"

"Oh, where?"

"Yonder. He is entering the chasm."

"Ah, yes!"

"Ah, yes!"

"How well he sits his horse!"

"How handsome he is!"

"The morning wind tosses his raven locks. His eyes are as black as his hair. I knew it!"

"Nay, Adeline, they are blue! Blue as the midnight sky."

"You are wrong, Caroline, they are brown, brown as the chestnut's coat, fresh from the burr."

"Perhaps we are all of us wrong, dear Georgiana. They flash so one can hardly tell their colour."

"He will soon be riding under the wall below us. Then, if he looks up, we shall know."

"Oh me! If he looks up, we must bob down."

"Bob if you like, Caroline. I shall stay where I am."

"But Georgy! He will see you."

"Well, will that kill me?"

"How daring you are, Georgiana. It would kill me."

"Nonsense, Caro! Men's looks don't kill a girl. If they did. the world would soon fall into half."

"Dear Adeline, I don't mean, literally, *kill*. And yet, and yet, I feel—" (the fair speaker laid her hand on her gentle breast) "if I should meet his eyes, my heart would expire. Oh heavens, Georgy! He *is* looking up!"

It was too true! The rider on his snorting ebony stallion had reined up under the high castellated wall, from the top of which the three speakers had been watching his progress through the valley. Lifting at the same moment his hat and his pallid countenance, he bowed to the trio framed in roses and ivy in the Gothic opening overhead. His gesture was informed with the courtliest grace, while the faintest hint of a smile lent charm to the habitual melancholy of his brow, where the summer breeze still fondled his black curls. Oh, happy breeze!

His action had a different effect upon all three watchers.

Adeline's face glowed roseate as the sunset, Caroline's grew pale as death itself; Georgiana alone did not change colour, as, with a sudden impulse, she tore a cluster of roses from the crumbling arch and flung it to the rider! Unexpected as it was, the cavalier caught it deftly, and holding it aloft counted the blossoms on their single stem: One! Two!! And three!!! His wan smile brightened—white, radiant teeth supplemented the flashing of those eyes, now seen to be black as sloes—and, with an impulse as swift as Georgiana's, he pressed his lips upon each rose in turn, moving his eyes from girl to girl as he did so. Then, fastening the roses in his coat, he cantered on, and, crossing the bridge that spanned the cataract, was lost to sight in the glades of the woodland beyond.

The three girls stood transfixed, like maidens of ice, until the sound of his charger's hoofs rang no more on their ears. Only then did Adeline's slender arms fall from the waists of her sisters, and she hid her face in her hands—while Caroline, deprived of her support, drooped to the parapet.

"Georgiana! Rash girl! how could you?" murmured Adeline between her taper fingers.

Georgiana, though her cheeks now bloomed like damask roses,

stood her ground. "Why not? He knew we were there. He had seen us spying on him. It was—the merest courtesy to acknowledge him."

"A courtesy indeed! To throw an unknown flowers in a manner which would have been unbecoming *if you had been affianced to him*."

"Affianced! Ah," breathed Caroline, recovering slightly, "do you suppose he is married? disengaged?"

"How can one know?" sighed Adeline.

"One cannot," said Georgiana. "One can only surmise that one as handsome as he *must* be bound, in some way or other, to *somebody*. What woman could behold him—and not love?"

"While as for us," said Adeline sorrowfully, "we can never hope to meet him."

"If only we knew his name," murmured Caroline. "Who can he be?"

"Of this, at least, I am sure," said Adeline. "He is a bastard."

"What makes you so certain?" asked Georgiana eagerly.

"Everything! His dashing air, his flashing eye, his gallant bearing, and his noble mien. A hero of romance! Falconbridge himself is less all-conquering. Can you not *see* our unknown cavalier defying villainy and protecting frailty?" Stretching her yearning arms over the wall towards the sun-flecked shadows of the forest glade—"My hero!" she cried. "My bastard!"

And in their hearts her sisters echoed her cry: *"My bastard!"*

Chapter One

Introducing Lord Tarletan

The beautiful triplets, the Honourable Ladies Georgiana, Adeline, and Caroline Tarletan, were known all over Derbyshire as The Three Graces. Known at a distance, alas! For they attended no assemblies, and no balls were given for them at Braddon Hall, the most picturesque, the most sumptuous, the most envied mansion in England. Yet here the Three Graces were incarcerated like three pearls in one oyster-shell, and were seen abroad only during their carriage drives under the tutelage of their governess, Madame Leroy, an Argus[1] *sans peur et sans reproche*—as many a Derbyshire buck, who sought to bribe her, had discovered to his cost.

These beauties were the wards and heirs of their great uncle, Lord Tarletan of Braddon Hall and elsewhere. Lord Tarletan was a well-known lecher in London, where he enjoyed a wide and broad-minded acquaintance covering every class of society, from pimps to M.Ps. Nay, more! He has, in his day, frequented the Continent, where there is hardly a haunt with which he is not familiar. His Past covers many mansions. His Past? Say rather, his Pasts! And yet, by a series of deaths and whatnot, this man, to whom Life is an unsealed book, has in his care the fate of three girls so innocent they scarcely know Life is a book to be unsealed. And it amuses

1 Mem: Argos?—A.G.

Lord Tarletan to preserve them so. He has, if not an individual fondness for his great-nieces, an enjoyment (which almost amounts to tenderness) of the contrast these innocents supply to his spotted experience. This alone draws him back from time to time to Braddon Hall, which, in his boyhood, he had cause to detest. He sees in their prisoned youth his own over again, except that these feminine natures do not know they are imprisoned, and sing as sweetly as linnets in their cage. Or so he tells himself. *For what does any man know of the female heart?* Not even a Father suspects the rebellious passions to which it is a prey. How much less a Great-Uncle!

Lord Tarletan, then, continued to regard his wards as a pretty pastime, an occasional relief from the lurid joys of the metropolis. Let no rough hand brush the dewdrop from the rosebud's cheek until they are of marriageable age, when his plans for them are deep-laid and double-dyed.

The hour is fast approaching!

* * *

Lord Tarletan came into his title and vast fortune at the age of twenty-one. He had led his subdued and far-from-happy youth at Braddon Hall under the tight-fisted control of his stern father. He was, alas, a semi-orphan, and the tender ministrations of a mother, which might have soothed and instructed his chafed spirit, had been unknown to Roger since his third year. She had died at the turn of the century of a broken heart.[1] But even now, in 1849, at the advanced age of fifty-two, Lord Tarletan recalled a woman's delicate features, and her long loose silken curls shading a peach-like cheek, as she leant above his cradle, gazing at her babe with big, mournful blue eyes, swimming with unshed tears. Even now, she remained the one soft spot in a nature as hard as a rhinocerous. He detested his father, who allowed him neither the liberty nor the means to gratify a young man's natural whims. What wonder that Braddon Hall, coveted by many an heir to titles more famous but less affluent, was, to its headstrong heir, naught but a dungeon? He

1 Memo: Why? She had fallen in love with somebody, probably the gardener, and her husband would not let her.—A.G.

never learned to love it. Its constrictions had poisoned his budding years. What could he learn of Life, splendid, untrammelled Life, pent within the twelve square miles of parkland spread about and below the house on its wooded height? Its dales and groves, its chasms and cascades, its arcades and vistas, its lake, and its ruined temples (for no expense had been spared in laying it out)—these, he felt in his heart, were not the World. The people he consorted with daily, such as keepers and doxies, were not Society. True, not one of the latter but had received his surreptitious kiss, and borne him, in due course,[1] the prattling pledge of a love too light to merit any name but fancy. But he had read his Byron, and knew this was not all. His haughty imagination soared to richer delights. When he was nineteen his father acquired a new valet. Casimir Dubois had been recommended to the then Lord Tarletan by his friend and fellow peer, the Earl of P—, who, having caught the Frenchman seducing the Countess under a weeping ash, thought it best that they should part. He did so reluctantly, for Casimir was the best valet he had ever had, but—"These things will happen, my good man," he said.

"I quite understand, sir," said the valet discreetly.

"I knew you would. I have never found you deficient. How would you like to go to Braddon Hall, three counties away? There you would be free from all temptations. Lord Tarletan is a widower with one son."

"I am entirely in your hands," said Casimir Dubois.

"Very well. I will write you a testimonial at once, and you can go this very night. Delays are dangerous. Lord Tarletan is lavish, and will pay you what you will. Better you should not see the Countess again. It would only make her sad, and perhaps you too."

Casimir Dubois looked sad at once. But, like the crocodile, he concealed a cunning smile. This man was a viper of the deepest dye. Installed in Braddon Hall, he marked out the youthful heir as his next prey—little knowing that, at last, he had met more than his match!

For two years he made it his aim to gain an influence over Roger

---

1 Mem: ? Find out.—A.G.

Tarletan, awaiting his opportunity. Meanwhile, he instilled into the heir of Braddon Hall all his insidious knowledge of life and love.

"One day," he said, "you will be able to put all I tell you into practice."

"Not till my accursed father dies," said Roger, savagely.

"That may be much sooner than you think," said the valet. "After all, he is nearly fifty, and no man lives for ever."

The valet proved only too right. In the very hour when Roger attained his majority his father was found, purple in the face, dead in his bed! He who but yesterday had been the Hon. Roger at once assumed the title, the fortune, and the control of his affairs. His nature showed itself immediately. He spent the day of his father's death drinking champagne. Casimir encouraged him, amazed to find that no amount of tipple bemused that brain, as hard and clear as a diamond. He could support a carouse with the strongest head.

"To-morrow," said Lord Tarletan, "we go to Paris."

Chapter Two

Introducing Pauline la Reine

———————

In the summer of 1819, when Paris was recovering from the tarnished effects of the Little Corsican, and legitimate royalty gilded once more the Tuileries, Roger, Lord Tarletan, set foot for the first time in that dazzling city. Casimir Dubois accompanied him as his courier, and lost no time in teaching him how to make the best of his fabulous fortune. This man knew his Paris like a book, and his pupil proved only too apt. Under Casimir's guidance, Lord Tarletan took an *Hôtel* in the Champs-Élysées, engaged a staff of fifty or sixty servants, and furnished the already sumptuous apartments with everything that could add to their allurements. Cards and a baccarat-board,[1] green baize billiard-tables, coloured fountains in the vestibule, marble urns overflowing with fruits and flowers, a buffet always replenished with wines and confectionery, globes filled with goldfish and silverfish, satin couches fringed with silver and gold, and scented pastilles burning night and day in every room. In such surroundings he began to entertain lavishly, and ere long was plunged into the thick of the giddy whirl of the giddiest capital in Europe. Racing and gaming, dicing and dancing, feasting and opera-going left him little time for sleep. His appetite was insatiable, his vitality enormous. He amazed even Casimir, accustomed to all debauches, and none of the entertainments to

———————

1 Memo: Is it played on a board? Can I be thinking of Solitaire?—A.G

which he was bidden outrivalled Tarletan's in splendour. They frequently went on till after midnight.

"Upon my word, Lord Tarletan," Louis XVIII said to him more than once (for now he numbered royalty among his familiars), "your hospitality puts mine to the blush."

"Nonsense," said Tarletan lightly, "your Majesty's establishment is only just recovering from a family misfortune. Mine has as yet suffered no such reverse. Some more champagne before we ride in the Bois du Boulogne ?"

"Thank you," said the King. He lifted the golden bubbling glass, and sipped. "Delicious! Where do you get it? Yes, my dear Lord Tarletan, your establishment is almost perfect."

Lord Tarletan raised his brows. "Almost, Your Majesty? In what is my establishment lacking?"

"A mistress," smiled the King.

"Enough!" said the young roué. "It shall have one."

Yes! (thought Casimir, concealed behind a curtain). *In both senses of the word.* He decided then and there to supply her. He had no intention of letting his master slip through his fingers; an unknown woman would be his greatest danger—especially should Tarletan be tempted to make her his bride. *That*, at all costs, must be avoided. For wives have morals. Mistresses have none. Casimir Dubois knew where to find them.

The bird our unscrupulous Casimir had marked was no less than the humblest member of the Corps de Ballet at the Opera. While the master lolled in the boxes, ogling the Prima Donnas, the valet haunted the gallery applying his binoculars to some meaner tidbit. It did not take him long to spy, in the back row, a young person whose superb figure alone should have brought her to the fore. She had not precisely beauty, her nose was large and curved rather than small and straight, her lips thin rather than full, and she never smiled, or even simpered, like the rest of her companions. This no doubt put the dukes and bankers off when they rushed to the stage-door night after night, almost before the last chord had crashed through the house, each eager to claim his own and dispute her heatedly with any after-comer. But Casimir, looking further than a woman's neck and shoulders, saw, even at that distance, that this one teemed with fires, danced with abandon, and whetted the appetite.

After his eavesdropping, he lost no time in making his way to the stage-door like the rest, purchasing as he went a bag of cachoux. The performance over, the singers and dancers began to troop into the night, laughing and chattering as they compared their triumphs of the evening—their followers and *billets-doux*, their bon-bons, and their jewels. One by one they were borne away by the gentlemen waiting with coronetted cabriolets, to waste the hours till dawn in dancing, drinking, etc.

Last, and alone, came an opulent figure ill-concealed in a plain shawl. She alone had no velvet case of sapphires, no satin box of dragees, no shower of Parma violets, no scented note. Accustomed as she was to these neglects, she emerged on the now dark and empty street and was about to proceed as usual to her lodging, when a man-good heavens! Could it be?—yes, a man! Stepped from the shadows and laid a hand on her arm.

"Good evening, my beauty," he said.

The woman shook that bold hand from her wrist and cut short his fulsome compliments with a harsh laugh.

"Look closer, stranger! You'll find you are mistaken. If you seek Coralie Fleur-de-lys, or Dorine Delamere you are too late. Those beauties are already dancing unclad before the noblemen who are their fancies of an hour. Pauline la Reine is no man's beauty. Farewell."

"Not so fast," said Casimir. "I mistake you for nobody but yourself, my dear. I picked you out from afar as one who combines talent with character, a combination which may carry a woman farther than coral lips and alabaster brows."

"I would exchange them for them," said Pauline la Reine.

"You would be wrong. Put yourself in my hands and I will prove it."

"What do you mean? Who are you?"

"Call me Casimir. I shall call you Pauline."

"You presume. My name is—"

"La Reine. I know it. And you shall become one."

"A queen? I? You are mad. What does this mean? Somehow I do not trust you."

He offered her the cachoux. She took them, wondering, but suspicious still. Yet—these were the first gift she had ever received from a man at the stage-door, and she felt herself strangely affected by the incident. Not by the man—oh, no! She loved him not; nor, did she believe, did he love her. Yet that he was to influence her fate she could not doubt.

"You hesitate," said Casimir mockingly. "Do you think they are poisoned?"

She swept him contemptuously with her eyes, shrugged, selected a pastille from the bag, swallowed it—and lived!

"What do you want of me?" she asked at last.

"Take me to your room and I will tell you."

He offered her his arm. She bowed her head, submitted to destiny, and led him to the low quarter where, in the basement of a narrow, dingy house, she—lived? Let us say, existed. She lit a guttering candle, and let her strange companion drink his fill of the shabby surroundings in which she ate and slept. A table, a chair, a cracked mirror on the wall, a pallet with a shabby plush covering— no more. With a gesture of her arm superb as a queen's, she said: "I have nothing to offer you. You see all there is."

"No, not quite all," said the valet. "Let me see you."

She understood! She complied!

"Put them on again," said Casimir Dubois, "and we will converse."

Soon they were seated side by side on the couch.

"Pauline," began Casimir, "are you ambitious?"

"Like all my sex," said she.

"Would you exchange this foul tenement for a palace? This plain raiment for lace and gauze and pearls? This bare board for a perpetual banquet? This hard couch for the roseleaves of luxury?"

She asked: "Am I a woman?" He went on.

"Would you leave your place at the back of the scene to enjoy the footlights where men would pelt you nightly with diamonds and gold? Would you hear all Paris crying to all Paris: 'Have you seen La Reine? There is none to touch her!' "

Her thin cheek glowed, her rather narrow eyes glittered.

"Is there blood in my veins, is there breath in my body?" she demanded.

"I knew it! Listen, Pauline. I serve a wealthy master, an aristocrat of the first water—"

"His name!"

"Softly. Not yet. Suffice it, that any woman who enlists his interest can become what she will. There are no limits to his fortune or his power."

"Is he old and ugly?"

"He is young and passable."

"Well, what do you propose!?"

"That you should become his mistress."

"Very well."

"I will introduce you into his house—"

"To-night?"

"To-morrow night. He will be supping with the King. On his return he shall find you in his bedroom as a little surprise."

"You see what my clothes are like. I have no others."

"Pah as to that. To-morrow night you won't want any. Play your cards well, and in two days you will outshine all Paris."

"That is settled then. Good night, Mons. Casimir."

"Not so fast," said the valet. "There is one thing more. We have yet to arrange what I shall get out of it."

"Oh, I see."

"You cannot suppose," he said brutally, "that I am doing this for love of you."

"I am not a stupid woman, and I don't," she said.

"Nor do I suppose, my clever Pauline, that you are doing this for love of *me*."

"Well, I have only known you for an hour or so."

"Love needs but an instant to enslave his victims. You and I must be bound, not by love, but by interest."

Interest! The basest of human attributes! The most degrading bond that can unite two people. Yet Pauline did not hesitate. Once more she said: "Very well."

"To-morrow," said Casimir, "the bond shall be drawn up, bearing both our signatures. I will call for you at eleven o'clock and take you to the necessary place, where that shall be witnessed which will ensure your not playing me false. Then, with me at your elbow, you shall play for us both. You must give me half the jewels and money with which he enriches you. Is it agreed?"

"Agreed," said Pauline la Reine.

The following night, Lord Tarletan, returning from a gay time at the Louvre, entered his chamber in the highest spirits, and beheld, sleeping, apparently, outside the purple satin coverlet—a vision!

He started!—stared!—approached the couch—and touched her! She was no vision, she was flesh and blood. She stirred, stretched her marble arms, and opened her eyes.

They sinned.

Need one say more?[1]

---

1   Mem: Find out.—A.G.

Chapter Three

Exit Casimir

For a year things went as Casimir intended.

Lord Tarletan, revelling in his first mistress, lost no time in making himself the envy of the Parisian roués. There were, he knew, more radiant beauties in Paris, but none more richly formed for love's delight. He set himself to frame her as he would a picture; for such she was to him. Even at this age, Roger Tarletan was a man quite without tenderness; that the woman he had selected to share, *pro tem.*, his life had feelings of her own left him unaffected, except in so far as he could find them amusing. She was rather gloomy by nature, her sombre moods alternating with fits of frenzy that entertained him highly. No pet poodle she, performing tricks at his command; she was a panther—one to be controlled rather than tamed. While other fair ones babbled and were gay, no man had ever yet heard Pauline laugh, and rarely seen her smile. When she did permit those rigid lips to relax, their expression of mirth had in it something bitter, something saturnine, which made men shudder—and dream! Many a nobleman would gladly have exchanged his flaxen leman for Roger Tarletan's dark and incomprehensible mistress.

"Ah, my friend," said the Grand Duke Vladimir of Murmansk,

cousin to the then Czar, "what are her secrets? I would give ten thousand crowns to make them mine."

"With all the pleasure in life," said Roger, "when I am weary of her. Till then, I won't betray them to you. You'll enjoy them all the more, I can assure you."

Meanwhile, he arrayed her in the richest velvets and brocades, loaded her with gold jewellery encrusted with rubies, and discovering her to be a marvellous dancer, he installed her at the Opera House as *Prima Ballerina*, and spent a fortune in hiring Auber himself to write for her a ballet called *Fra Diavola*. Casimir had been right. That season all Paris was crying to all Paris:

"La Reine! She is incomparable! What, have you not yet seen Pauline la Reine? Believe me, she has never had her equal."

On the nights she danced the Opera House was full to suffocation. Noblemen in serried ranks stared at her through their opera-glasses from the boxes and the pit. Her fire, her frenzied transports, her reckless abandon, carried them all away. Only the ladies of Paris refused to go; on the nights their lords and masters patronised the Ballet they went somewhere else. It did not matter to Pauline la Reine. The theatre could hardly hold the gentlemen, who, the performance ended, pelted her with bijoux and Louis d'Ors, as she stood, panting, barely draped, before the curtain, bowing to the ground, and glowering in a way that enthralled and mystified them—for surely, if any woman in Paris had cause to smile, that woman was their idol, Pauline la Reine. But they could not see Casimir Dubois, hovering like a spider in the flies, to receive the loot from her hands and divide it equally.

One night, the Grand-Duke Vladimir leaped up in his regal box, wrenched from his chest the Diamond Star of Russia, and hurled it at her feet. The house acclaimed his action, the auditorium rang with vociferous shouts, and the royal gem was soon submerged in a Danae's shower of gold. Men tore the rings from their fingers, the jewelled studs from their bosoms, the gold fobs from their waists, to honour their idol, who, stooping swiftly, swept them into her diaphanous skirts, rewarding the donors with a display of limb beyond what even they expected of her. The shouts increased, men waved their cambric handkerchiefs and beaver hats, and, under cover of the tumult, Pauline, with unerring fingers, sifted out the priceless diamond star and thrust it into her corsage. Then, curtseying for the last time, she staggered, weighed down with gold, into the flies, and the arms of her accomplice.

"Well done, *ma belle*!" he hissed. "To your dressing-room, quick!"

He never allowed the partition to take place elsewhere. It behoved the valet to pocket his share before Lord Tarletan had set eyes on it. To-night the division took longer than usual. "A splendid bag, indeed!" he chuckled when at last the two heaps of gewgaws lay separated. "I am proud of you, Pauline!" And he laid a bold hand on her naked shoulder. Suddenly he started and peered closer. "But what is this?" he cried. His eye had caught the gleam of the Russian Star, too quickly thrust out of sight for perfect concealment. That bold hand became bolder; another moment and the Star, warm from her bosom, glittered on the valet's profaning palm. Pauline bit her lip and tapped her foot, annoyed.

"So!" cried Casimir, "*this* is how you carry out your bond, Pauline la Reine. This is how you keep the oath you swore! *This* is your notion of a division of the spoils."

"That Star," said Pauline coldly, "is no spoil. It is the highest honour a man could bestow on a woman."

"In that case," retorted Casimir, with a leer, "keep the honour, and welcome, as your share. I will take care of the diamonds."

She swept her arm wide upon the air. "Return it!" she cried, "or else—" She paused.

"Or else?" repeated her confederate. "Nay, between us there is no 'or else,' my dear." And he left the room with a triumphant look.

When Pauline regained the *Hôtel* in the Champs-Élysées Lord Tarletan was awaiting her with a splendid party, including the Grand-Duke Vladimir. At her appearance all the gentlemen stood up and clapped their hands, and, with a concerted action, filled their glasses with the juice of the grape, and raised them to her.

"Pauline!" they shouted.

Lord Tarletan tossed his down, filled up before any other glass was emptied, and raised it again—"And to our noble guest!" He turned to the Grand-Duke.

"But where, madame," he said, leading Pauline to her place between himself and Vladimir, "where is the Royal Insignia with which our guest chose to honour you to-night?"

Pauline took an iron resolution quickly. "My lord," she said, loud and clear for all to hear, "my lord, you have been deceived."

"By you?" Lord Tarletan shot a sharp glance from her to the Grand-Duke, who laughed and said:

"Alas, no! I am not the culprit."

"Nor I," said Pauline freezingly. "I am talking of something quite different. You have been deceived in Casimir Dubois, your valet."

"No man," said Tarletan, "is ever deceived in his valet, or ever deceives him. If you mean Casimir Dubois is a rogue and a rascal, I have known it for three years. What has he done now?"

"He has stolen the Diamond Star of Russia, my lord, and threatened to defame me if I did not say it was lost."

"I told you he was a villain," said Tarletan to Vladimir. "He shall be horsewhipped, and made to return the Star."

"Horsewhipped, certainly," said the Grand-Duke of Murmansk, "but as for returning the Star, he has sullied it by his touch, for La Reine and for myself. I shall get the Czar to change the Order, and, as soon as he does so, will send the first example to this lady."

And he bowed over Pauline's hand; as he raised his head their eyes met, and in his she read her destiny.

"Are you really going to horsewhip the fellow?" she asked Lord Tarletan.

"He shall bear the marks of it all his life," said Tarletan.

"I do not wish to be present," said Pauline. Turning her sombre gaze upon Vladimir—"Will you," she said, "walk with me in the grounds while it takes place?"

"Women are creatures of sensibility," said the Grand-Duke, and, offering her his arm, led her into the garden. As soon as they were out of earshot she gripped the arm on which she had been leaning.

"Have I mistaken you?" she muttered.

Royalty though he was, he wavered under her gaze.

"Would you indeed," she went on, "have liked to be the culprit?"

"Are you suggesting we should deceive Lord Tarletan?"

"I am."

"Say no more. I have always wanted to."

"Very well. Wait here. I must see to a little bundle, and write a letter."

"You need take nothing with you, and to wait to write a letter may be fatal."

"Oh, but I promise you I shall not be long. I do not like to go without a word."

"Ah, women!" said the Grand-Duke tenderly.

She vanished, and was with him in less than five minutes.

He was pleased to see that her hands were empty.

"You have waited to pack nothing, after all."

"Henceforth I rely on your generosity only."

"Then hey for Murmansk!" said Vladimir, embracing her.

*   *   *

And while a coach, bearing Imperial arms, dashed through the night towards the French border and another life, Casimir Dubois was writhing under the lash he had so well deserved.

"Take that! And that! And that!" cried Roger Tarletan.

"That, for a thief! That, for a would-be traducer! And that, you fool, for taking your young master for a fool! Why, I have seen through you from the very first. But men like me make use of their tools where they find them."

The valet cowered even more under his contempt than under his whip. "One day, my lord, I shall be even with you!" he muttered. "As for the woman you have called your mistress—"

"Don't waste your breath on lies," Tarletan cut him short. "Or even on the truth. The woman I have called my mistress is, at this moment, eloping with the Grand-Duke. The whole thing was arranged between us. I have my eye upon another morsel—and he, for some weeks past, has coveted mine. Noblesse oblige. To tell you the truth, I am sick to death of her."

The valet saw his power was gone indeed. With Tarletan reft of his interest in Pauline, what strings had he to pull? Gritting his teeth, he slunk into the night, and out of Lord Tarletan's life.

For ever? The ways of destiny are all too strange.

Chapter Four

Two Old Friends Meet Again!

With Lord Tarletan's career during the next thirty years, let us be comparatively brief.

Freed for ever from the need of a courier, he made the Grand Tour of Europe, continuing, in spite of every imbroglio, his bachelor course throughout. From time to time he dashed back to the banks of the Thames, for some restful amour in Kensington or Bayswater, then, all too quickly sated, re-tasted the wilder blisses of the Vistula, the Hellespont, and the Bosphorus. But Braddon Hall saw its master's face no more, until, in 1839, a lawyer's letter from London informed him that he had become, by a series of family deaths, the guardian of the Tarletan Triplets, his nearest of kin, and his heirs. To a man, still robust and lusty at forty-one, this was no welcome news. When the letter was brought him by a liveried flunkey he happened to be playing écarté with Louis Philippe, who was now his crony.

"Excuse me, sire," he said, laying down his hand. "This may be important."

"Read it, by all means," said his royal adversary, considering the trick while Tarletan ripped the seal and consumed the contents. At his lawyer's tidings, a black frown clouded his brow, and he cast the parchment from him with an oath. Meanwhile the King, taking advantage of his friend's ill-humour, brought off a clever coup and won the hand.

"That is another thousand francs," said the French ruler lightly. "Pardon me for saying so, but you don't seem pleased with the news from *Angleterre*."

"Would Your Majesty be pleased," demanded Lord Tarletan, "at hearing you were become responsible for three young children?"

"Your own?" asked the King, shuffling the cards with a well-practised hand.

"Not as it happens. A distant cousin's, but, curse him, he has died of the cholera."

"How old are the children?"

"Mr. Lodger, my lawyer, says they are six years of age."

"Apiece, or between them?"

"Apiece. They are triplets. Females. What can a vigorous bachelor do with such encumbrances?"

"You must place them under the care of the right woman."

Tarletan gave vent to a boisterous laugh. "That is precisely the sort of woman I have never known."

The King of France smiled and added up the score. "How much do I owe you all told?" asked Tarletan. "Let us say ten thousand francs. Will it ruin you?"

"Not yet," said Tarletan, pulling out his purse. "I have plenty left for the pursuit to-night."

"You mean Marianne Adorée."

"Is there anyone else? Since my arrival this morning, I hear of her on all sides."

"She is certainly the lady of the moment. All Paris is after her, and none can approach her."

"Why not?"

"She is guarded by a sort of female Gorgon."

"Well, Gorgons are not immune to honeysops." And Lord Tarletan spun a gold-piece skilfully.

"Ah, you will need a good deal more than one of those."

"L'Adorée is greedy, then?"

"No, on the contrary. She has Circassian blood in her veins, and loves for love's sake. She can resist nobody. But she knows her own weakness, so she has installed at her door a guardian to frustrate those who would storm her perfumed couch. This person squeezes from L'Adorée's wooers more Louis d'Ors than she would demand sous."

"And this gaoler, you say, is picked from the feminine ranks?"

"Yes, and Marianne allows her such handsome perquisites that she is not to be bribed."

"Pho-pho!" scoffed the English peer, winking an eye, "one may sometimes come a cropper with a *woman*, but I flatter myself I can always handle *women*."

His pockets weighed with gold, and he himself agog for a scented amour, Lord Tarletan wended his way that night to L'Adorée's dwelling, to be met upon the threshold by a tall, gaunt figure in rusty black garments, a ravaged visage, cold eyelids, and burning eyes.

Those eyes met his and wavered! The gloomy countenance blanched, the eyelids fell.

"By heaven," ejaculated Tarletan, "it is Pauline!"

"Roger—Lord Tarletan!" she muttered, off her guard.

"But what," he asked jovially, "are you doing here?"

She regained command of herself with a rapidity he could not but admire. "Serving another woman's beauty," she shrugged, "as, twenty years ago, my own was served."

"Those twenty years, Pauline, have dimmed your memory. Whatever you were, you were not beautiful."

"All the same, I had my hour."

"And it is over. Now it is this Adorée's turn. What is she like?"

"You will have to pay to find out."

"That is to be expected. You never found me wanting."

"I admit it."

"And how," asked Tarletan, "did your Grand-Duke treat you?"

"Like a goddess to start with, and a serf to end with."

"And after that?"

"Are you prepared to listen to me till daybreak?"

"Your adventures were numerous, then?"

"They were—and varied."

"Till at last you came to this. Do you like the post?"

"I, who have queened it in Paris in my day? I detest my post."

"Hum," said Lord Tarletan, thoughtfully, tapping his teeth.

"And yet," pursued Pauline, "it is better than the degradation I left for it."

"You had sunk to the very lowest, then?"

"You shall judge. Six months ago L'Adorée came from Circassia. The morning she drove through Paris all Paris acclaimed her. The streets were thronged as people poured out of their houses and shops to look at her; above the heads of the crowd men swarmed up the trees. An officer of high rank leapt off his horse and, dragging her coachman from the box, took the reins himself, and would have driven her then and there to his house, but that some young noblemen, carousing in the Place Vendôme, beset the vehicle and disputed the honour with him. That night, to make a long story short, she simply could not keep them off. Next day, seeing her danger, she sought, among the neediest, the most indigent, the most despised and ignored class of females in the city (need I say I refer to the class known as *lady needlewomen*)—Marianne Adorée sought for—what do you think?"

"I really can't guess."

"A respectable woman, Tarletan."

"And found—you!" Lord Tarletan threw back his head and roared with laughter.

"Look again," said, drily, she who had been La Reine.

He looked, and ceased to laugh. For it was true. In her neat, but dowdy, black garments, her hair tight-twisted into a knob at the back, her ornaments of jet, her once-opulent form reduced to decent spareness, every one of her thirty-eight years apparent in her face, her mien, her bearing, Pauline La Reine, La Diavola, the toast of Paris, looked the very essence of respectability. Lord

Tarletan, keeping his eyes fixed on that visage, continued to tap his teeth reflectively.

"How strangely you regard me," she said bitterly. "Is it as bad as all that?"

"No, Pauline, I begin to think it is as good as all that."

"I cannot think what you mean."

"Take me where we can talk in privacy."

She led her former lover to a small closet, and indicated an ottoman *à deux*. When they were seated: "Now," said she, "what have you to say to me?"

He unfolded his plan. It was nothing less than to remove her from Paris, and every form of life she had ever known, and install her in Derbyshire as the guardian and governess of the Tarletan Triplets. This strange resolve was made, not for his sake alone, but for that of the children. For already their innocence had begun to make its claims on his imagination. The vision of his dead cousin's charming infants—for charming he was sure they were, and innocent—waked in his breast the pulse which throbbed for his mother. If he could revive in them that memory of silken flaxen curls and sky-blue eyes, these tender maids would minister to, and amuse, a side of his nature that life had only touched once. Provided his three charges were not irksome, they might become a pleasure.

"Yes," he said to himself, "I will ensure their innocence; and who, for this purpose, so safe as a cast-off mistress?"

For it is only, Tarletan told himself, one that has known all who can preserve others from knowing anything. A pure and virtuous spinster would fill the girls' ears with warnings and their bosom with apprehensions. She would instruct them in dangers of which she herself was, in fact, ignorant. She would lead them to speculate in secret. No! Vice alone can perfectly guard Virtue, for Vice alone knows from what Virtue is to be guarded.

"Above all," added Lord Tarletan, "the guardian of these children must be one I can trust."

"And you think you can trust me?"

"Up to the hilt!"

She eyed him speculatively. "Even though I deceived you once?"

"But only once." He smiled in a way she did not understand. "You will not do it twice."

"What makes you so sure that I am born to be trusted?"

"I am sure, Pauline, you were born not to be trusted, but I am equally sure that everything you are, or have, or do is to be bought and sold. I am going to buy your trustworthiness, which, like your love of old, has its market price. Those ardent flames which consumed us in the past have long died down. Let neither of us pretend, and we shall understand each other very well."

She nodded, and for the first time, perhaps, these two strange natures really appreciated each other.

"Tell me what you propose," said Pauline La Reine. "Tell me what you make out of your attendance on L'Adorée. And don't exaggerate it by more than half."

"You shall have the truth." She named a sum which was double that she received.

"I will give you twice that amount for your complete allegiance," said Lord Tarletan.

"What does that comprise?"

"First, your withdrawal from Marianne's painted portals, leaving the way free for me to make my own bargain with her."

"And second?"

"Second, your guardianship of the iron gates of Braddon Hall."

"And the three young ladies inside them."

"Precisely so. I have already advised you as to their natures—"

"But you have never seen them."

"All English young ladies of six have the same natures. I require you to watch over and instruct them in a manner that will keep them as limpid at sixteen."

"And my credentials for this unaccustomed post?"

"I will invent them for you, and write your testimonials with my own hand. They shall be impeccable; I shall enjoy supplying you with a distinguished past. I shall represent you as the impoverished daughter of a noble house attached to Charles the Tenth. You have found no happiness in the present regime, brought about by sabotage and revolution; for years you have pined for nothing so much as a peaceful retreat in another land, which you can learn to love in place of that you have lost. England, above all, has always appealed to you, and the routine of English country life is your ideal."

"I shall be bored to death," said Pauline, shrugging.

"We must all pay a price for security, after having paid it too heavily for our pleasures."

"I shall not be much in character," said she.

"Were you in character as a *lady needlewoman*? No impersonation is beyond the power of La Reine, the Queen of the Footlights."

"And if I meet someone who remembers that name?"

"We will change it, to match your appearance. You shall be Pauline Leroy. Come, what do you say?"

"I say yes, of course."

Lord Tarletan emptied half his purse into her lap. "Go to Calais, at once, and fit yourself out. I need but one night to storm L'Adorée's defences. I shall join you soon, see you duly installed in Braddon Hall, and return to enjoy my conquest."

"Farewell, for a little while," said Pauline. "I shall go the back way."

Before she had reached that humble postern Roger Tarletan was knocking on Marianne's door. He heard a languorous voice bidding him enter. He entered.

*   *   *

The libertine asked the fair Circassian what she wanted for a present. Enjoying her liberty to embrace where she pleased, she twined her arms about him and said: "Your kisses." Even this hardened roué was impressed. Next day he presented her with a diamond *parure*, a carriage-and-four, and a *hôtel* in the Champs-Élysées, bade her a brief adieu, and went post-haste to Calais to join Pauline La Reine—or rather, as we must call her henceforth Leroy. To collect his legacy of the little triplets (who charmed him even more than he had imagined), to deposit them in Braddon Hall with their *gouvernante*, and to instruct his staff that the household and all its details were in the charge of Madame Leroy, who was henceforth to be obeyed in everything, took him the best part of a week. Then, all impatience, he returned to his inamorata.

By this time, L'Adorée, whose taste of liberty had gone to her head, had fallen into the arms of her new coachman, where Tarletan discovered her at two in the morning, clad only in her diamond necklace and bracelets. He stood for one moment, viewing them without comment; then, controlling by a superhuman effort the indignation surging in his breast, stooped over his fickle houri, tore from her neck and wrists the price of her shame—and was gone! The lovers shuddered between terror and relief. At least, they still lived. For awhile they lay there stupefied, dreading his footstep. But they heard it not. At last the man took courage to creep into his clothes and steal away.

On arriving at his modest lodging, he discovered his wife naked in her bed, adorned with diamonds on her neck and wrists. There were not two such *parures* in the whole of Paris. Stammeringly, he demanded an explanation; the woman, whose eyes were shining with ecstasy, told him that, should he insist on one, his life (she was to inform him) would not be worth the snuff of a tallow candle; but, if he asked no questions, he might sell bracelets and necklace and set up a livery stables. This always having been his ambition, he held his tongue. The earrings the woman retained; and on occasions when she had cause to doubt her husband's fidelity, she wore them all night, and forbade him to approach her. Which, for some reason, not clear to himself or her, brought him once more to her feet.

Farewell to them! They have no part in our story.

Chapter Five

As Handsome as Lucifer

———————

Ten years have flown by.

*   *   *

Let us now picture ourselves once more on the castellated parapet of Braddon Hall, where Georgiana, Adeline, and Caroline Tarletan, twined in the Gothic arch, watch the dark stranger vanishing in the vista.

At sixteen, the maidens are in the prime of their youth and beauty. All three are fair, all three have transparent complexions and sylph-like forms. Georgiana, the tallest, has chestnut hair and eyes; Adeline's tresses are golden-brown, and her hazel eyes are shot with golden lights; Caroline's locks are flaxen, and her eyes a translucent blue. The sisters' natures, like their appearance, differ, but within, as well as without, they have some things in common, and share the romantic dreams which people the caverns of their ignorance. Nothing has ever happened to the sisters. Braddon Park is their world—and what more can they want?

The gardens of Braddon are the loveliest in all England. The velvet lawns, the profuse shrubberies and ornamental trees brought from foreign parts, the acres of rose-walks, pleached alleys, and artificial waters, the sun-dials and statuary, the marble basins where silver fountains play, the ferny pools replete with rainbow-finned fishes, peacocks on every terrace, and a maze of trimmed box-hedge, furnish the eye with endless agreeable diversions. Beyond and around this cultured paradise stretches the seemingly illimitable park. Here, too, the craftsman's hand has been at work, so craftily that its art is unsuspected. But these umbrageous rides, where the spotted deer peep out, these little temples fallen into decay, these ruined towers that never have been whole, these sudden miniature ravines and chasms, these lilliput cataracts and tiny torrents, splashing down mossy crevices to the great lake—nay, even the lake itself is man's work improving nature's, as it were. The whole is an epitome of the universe. The loveliest of all the ruined temples, set in a grove of magnolias and acacias, stands on the northern extremity of the lake. Anyone seated there on a well-placed fallen pillar can behold, in the far-reaching watery glass, each variation of the heavens from sunrise to moonset. Æolian harps, hidden among high branches, tinkle unearthly music at the kiss of the passing zephyr, wafting the rapt onlooker to immortal spheres of emotion. Ah yes! Life is eternal, and love imperishable will come one day to her, as he comes to all, and these sensations, hardly to be borne alone, will be shared by another, and then—

And then?

Let not the dreamer lift her eyes from the bosom of the lake. For across the lake, facing the white marble fane, rises a black granite urn, that surmounts the Mausoleum of the Tarletans: a grim memorial, set among cypresses and weeping willows, of the transitory nature of happiness.

But for those who have never yet known happiness, and had it torn from them, that dark reminder has fewer terrors than for one who has given her all to love and lost it for ever! For they who know not life cannot know death. And so that temple remained the favourite haunt of the gentle Caroline; Georgiana preferred the highest bridge above the torrent, climbing intrepidly the narrow path on the rock, and gazing fearlessly into the foaming falls; while Adeline, dancing lightly across the arena of a copy of a famous Roman theatre, conjured up the gay scenes once enacted there, and thronged the stone seats with a richly-dressed company, and the earthen stage with a pageant of dancers and performing bears.

Yes, while the Tarletan Triplets had all this, what more could their hearts desire?

Oh, much, much more!

*   *   *

"Young ladies, what are you doing?"

The sisters started. The speaker was Madame Leroy. She had approached so noiselessly that they had not heard her step, or perhaps were too deeply immersed in their own sensations to be aware of anything till she spoke.

"Oh, Madame," cried Georgiana eagerly, "what a pity you did not come two minutes sooner! For then you would have seen him."

"Seen whom?" asked Madame Leroy.

"The mysterious Stranger," said Georgiana artlessly, for amongst their many ignorances was this, that anything in life needs to be hidden. Alas for youth when it trusts its elders with its heart!

"What do you know of this mysterious Stranger?"

"Nothing," said Adeline, "or he would be less mysterious."

"Is this the first time you have seen him?"

"Oh no," broke in Caroline, "we see him every day. For the past month he has ridden below the wall at eleven precisely, by the shadow on the sundial. He canters over the bridge into the forest. Sometimes he is followed by his servant, but to-day he was alone."

Madame Leroy knit her brows, but still spoke smoothly.

"Does he see you on the wall? Does he look up?"

"Not always," said Adeline, "but—" She dimpled with smiles. "He did to-day."

"Has he dared to address you?"

"Not once," sighed all three together.

"And what is this mysterious Stranger like?"

"He has jet-black hair and eyes," said Georgiana. "A marble brow," said Adeline.

"A melancholy air," said Caroline. "But when he smiles—!"

"Oh," said Madame Leroy, "he has smiled at you, then?"

"Yes," said Adeline, "to-day, when Georgiana threw him the roses."

"Ah," said Madame Leroy. "How came you to throw this Stranger roses, Georgiana?"

"I did it on impulse," said Georgiana, candidly."

"And what did the Stranger then?"

"He kissed the roses," Caroline said softly.

Adeline added: "He must be fond of flowers."

"That," said Madame Leroy, "is evident. And the servant, what is he like?"

"Very big and fat," said Adeline, "with a beard all over his cheeks, and bushy hair."

"He wears an olive habit, with black frogs," said Georgiana, "and a round shaggy cap of fur."

"His horse is heavy like himself," said Caroline, "but the Stranger's steed is an arrow, like himself. I think the Stranger has Spanish blood in his veins. He is like the Cid."

"Or Greek," said Adeline. "He reminds me of the Giaour."

"I am convinced," said Georgiana, "he is a Pole. To me he is the counterpart of Mazeppa. That is," she said, blushing, "His horse goes like the wind, but he, of course, is habited as he should be. In our opinion the Stranger is a—"

The word that trembled on her lips she did not utter. "A bastard," she would have said. And, for some reason she could not have explained, she thought she had better not. For if his royal birth was the Stranger's secret, what right had she to reveal it?

"Well," said Madame Leroy calmly, "the Stranger, in your three opinions is—"

"As handsome as Lucifer!" said Georgiana recklessly.

Adeline turned her head away; Caroline hung hers.

"In that case," said Madame Leroy, "I had better have a look at him for myself. It is time for your writing lesson. Come indoors."

And that, said Madame Leroy to herself, will be the end of it. Strangers who are as handsome as Lucifer must not be encouraged to ride in Braddon Park. But she was too clever to upbraid her three fair pupils. It was her business to keep them in Eden. Let them once suspect that serpents are also denizens of paradise and it would be the beginning of the end. Pauline Leroy, with age approaching fast, did not choose yet to end her affluent, if monotonous, circumstances. She had suffered too much from poverty in the past to risk a dismissal by failing her employer. How ruthless he could be she had cause to know. She thanked her stars that Lord Tarletan was from home. And yet, the existence she clung to was mere existence!—not life as Pauline la Reine had known it once. Sometimes the dead level of her days irked the once tempestuous woman sorely. However, she now dressed handsomely, if soberly, ate well, and slept luxuriously, and few though her subjects, was in a place of power. No, no, she must take no risks!

Communing thus with her thoughts, she led the way across the upper terrace, followed by the sisters, tenderly aglow. For them a monotony they had never suspected had been broken for this past month by the first flutterings of the wings of romance. For the first time their young breasts felt fascinating thrills. For all her watchfulness, Madame Leroy was not the Archangel Michael.

But next morning it was she and not her charges who leaned in the Gothic arch at eleven o'clock.

Chapter Six

An Adventurous Nature Seeking Its Ideal

─────────

And the next morning, at eleven precisely, Count Stanislaw cantered along the valley path under the ivied wall, where he had come to expect, as his daily right, that loveliest of spectacles, maidenhood in the bud, on the verge of blooming. He still wore on his breast the spray of roses thrown to him yesterday.

Nearing the angle of the wall, the turn of which would bring him into sight of anybody in the Gothic arch, he called to his servant, lumbering behind: "Kaspar! Follow yonder ride through the chestnut-copse. I made such good headway with my charmers yesterday that to-day I shall once more try my luck alone."

The bearded fellow chuckled rather coarsely. "You hope, no doubt, that having thrown their roses over the wall, the ladies are now ready to throw themselves."

"Or else, to permit me to climb up to them. In any case, your presence is not conducive to intimacy, it is enough to affright an Amazon, so do as I tell you."

The burly one grunted, but obeyed, and when he had disappeared among the chestnut fans, the Count spurred forward, chasing from his features the momentary gaiety that had enlivened them. With pale set look he turned the corner of the wall. It would seem to a watcher on the castellated heights that he was unaware of anything but his thoughts as he bent his head to the blossoms in the frill of his shirt.

Then, as one startled from a waking dream, he reined in his horse and permitted himself to look upward—to meet, not three rosy faces, but one dark one!

To say Count Stanislaw was surprised is to say too little. However, with admirable self-control, he raised his hat, bowed to the sombre figure in the arch, and would have passed on.

"Stop!" cried Madame Leroy.

He checked his steed and, keeping his head uncovered, allowed his rare smile to hover on his lips. Even at that distance, and at her age, Pauline Leroy could not deny its charm ; and, knowing men in and out from top to toe, admitted to herself the seduction of the tones that assailed her ear in excellent broken English.

"I am honoured and flattered by your ladyship's command."

"I am no ladyship, and you flatter yourself too soon," said Madame Leroy. "Are you aware that you are trespassing?"

"Trespassing? What does that mean?"

"It means that you are riding where you have no right to."

"I do not understand. The world is free."

"Not in England, sir," said Madame Leroy. "But I perceive from your accent that you are not English."

"No, madame. I am a Pole."

"From what province?"

"Pinsk."

"And even in Pinsk," said Madame Leroy, "do perfect strangers ride through private parks?"

"Is the park private? I took it for the countryside itself."

"The gates might have undeceived you."

"What gates? I have never seen them."

"Then how do you get in?"

"I put Kosciusko at the wall, madame."

"Kosciusko?"

"My horse." He patted his charger's neck. "He is named, of

course, after our national hero, and is as fiery as that patriot. Whenever he sees a wall he jumps over it."

"But the walls of Braddon Park are twelve foot high, with fosses on both sides!"

"That is nothing to us. We are used to overcoming obstacles. Whether a very high wall or a very strict lady." And the Stranger smiled so winningly at Pauline that, to her own astonishment, she felt disconcertingly pleased. This would never do! Concealing her momentary softening, she said harshly:

"Learn, sir, that trespassers on English private property are not allowed to disregard obstacles. What brought you to Derbyshire?"

"An adventurous nature, seeking its ideal."

"Invariably, it seems, in one direction."

"When one has, by great grace, found one's ideal, why look further?"

The young Pole's voice took on a still more singular sweetness.

"What have I done, madame, that deserves your censure? On the day after my arrival I set forth on my first ride, letting Kosciusko choose the direction. The clever fellow made straight for the open country; up hill and down dale we flew, leaping every fence and wall in our way. When he leapt one much higher than the rest I had only praise for his unquenchable spirit. It did not occur to me to say: 'Bad horse! Turn back!' If he had leapt me into the jaws of H*ll I should not have turned back—but he had leapt me into paradise! Such an enchanting place I had never beheld, such flowery grots, such noble foliage, such soul-stirring beauty of woodland and waterfall. I thought I must have died and gone to heaven—and when, as I rode, I saw above me three angelic faces, I was certain of it. Can you blame me if next day I came again—and next day—and the next?"

"Enough!" said Madame Leroy very severely. "I do blame you, very much indeed, for invading the sanctuary of three young English ladies. Now that you know such things are not permitted you will, if you are a gentleman, remove yourself from their neighbourhood as soon as possible."

The young man shook his head. "You ask too much."

"In that case, sir, I warn you that your next appearance here shall be greeted with horsewhips."

The Polish nobleman drew himself up haughtily and laid his hand on the hilt of the dagger in his belt. "And who," he demanded, eyes flashing, "will do the horsewhipping?"

"If necessary," said Madame Leroy, "I will do it myself."

His hand fell. "No man fights with a woman. Your word is my law. But at least explain why I must not be acquainted with your lovely daughters."

"Not my daughters—my pupils."

"I should have taken them for your daughters."

Once more, in spite of herself, Pauline Leroy felt her bosom throb as it had not for fifteen years. In that lurid past, which smouldered still in her veins, she knew this was a man she could have given her all to. So much the more must she guard her innocent charges from charms she knew to be past female resistance.

"Go, go!" she panted. "And never more dare to ride this way again. That is my last word. Go!"

He bowed till his raven curls mingled with Kosciusko's mane, and gathered the reins in his fine yet steely hand,

"Farewell, madame. Forgive me if you can, because when one is young one is full of folly."

So saying, he bowed once more and rode quickly away.

Madame Leroy stood staring after him. Yes, when one is young one is full of folly. She shuddered at the thought. What was this that possessed her? Why could she not be as angry with the trespasser as was her duty? An adventurous nature in search of his ideal. Those milk-and-water misses, what could he see in them? Once more she thanked her stars that Lord Tarletan was from home.

A step on the terrace made her turn her head.

It was Lord Tarletan!

Chapter Seven

News of Expected Guests

———————

"Well, Pauline," said Tarletan mockingly, "why do you start?"

In a moment she was mistress of herself. "If I started," she replied, "it was because you startled me. I supposed you to be in Cadiz or Buda-Pesth."

"Tut-tut! And I thought it was for joy at my return. You are wrong. For the past month I have been no farther away from you than London."

"I trust you have cause to congratulate yourself on whatever took and kept you there so long."

"I have," said Tarletan.

"Another successful love-affair?"

"Three," said he.

"Three all at once? I congratulate you."

"You are wrong again," said Lord Tarletan. "The three affairs in which I have been so successful concern, not myself, but my three charming wards."

Madame Leroy narrowed her eyes attentively. "You contemplate affiancing them so soon?"

"I contemplate marrying them off. They are affianced already."

"Affianced already!"

"Precisely, as members of royal families are frequently affianced without knowing it. Georgiana, Adeline, and Caroline have been promised to three exceedingly eligible bachelors for exactly ten years."

"You have been their guardian for exactly ten years!"

"And you their instructress for the same length of time."

"Do you mean to say you sought husbands for these children as soon as you set eyes on them?"

"Oh, sooner," corrected Lord Tarlctnn. "I made their husbands my object before I set eyes on them."

"Why so much haste?"

Tarletan smiled reminiscently. "Do you remember Marianne Adorée?"

"Perfectly. I have good reason to."

"I, Pauline, remember her for a very bad reason."

"What is it?"

"I practically ruined myself to set her up."

"But the Tarletan riches are fabulous!"

"Unfortunately. It would be so much better if they were a fact."

"I cannot believe you are impoverished."

"Nor am I. It is all a matter of ready cash. The Tarletan estates and possessions are almost priceless. Luckily for my heirs, they cannot be realized, for the revenues have only too often failed to meet my demands on them. That single night in Paris, ten years ago, they failed me. Among other things, I bought L'Adorée diamonds fit for an empress. The jeweller knew me and let me have them without a qualm when I said I was called to England and would settle up on my return. I did not let him suspect that I was at my wits' ends how to manage it this time! On the way to England I had an inspiration. The unknown infants should get me out of my pickle. All Almack's knew of the circumstances which had made three girls my heirs; these children would, in another ten years, be the pick of the matrimonial market, for whom every noble bachelor would vie. Three of the richest peers of my acquaintance had each a son in his early teens. I tackled their fathers singly, played them cunningly, concluded a bargain satisfactory to myself, and bound by legal deeds and documents, Georgiana to the Scottish James Dumbarton, Adeline to the Irish Terence Lorrequer, and Caroline to the English Percival Fawleigh."

Madame Leroy drank in this recital greedily. Apart from natural feminine curiosity in events of such interest she was cogitating rapidly how they might, perhaps, be turned to good account. But maintaining an appearance of indifference, she merely remarked:

"What sort of bargain did you consider satisfactory to yourself?"

"One that enabled me to pay the French jeweller and have plenty in hand for the next romantic adventure."

"I see. And why," demanded Madame Leroy, "do you come to break this news to me to-day?"

"Because," said Lord Tarletan, "the three young gentlemen are on their way here."

"Now!"

"At this moment."

"When will they arrive?"

"To-morrow, or the next day, or the next. It depends on their horses—and the young gentlemen. One can't always tell. They have seven counties to traverse, teeming with charms."

"And when they do come? What do you want me to do?"

"Entertain them, amuse them, make them at home here and see that before they leave they have won the girls' hearts."

"And what if the right young men don't fall in love with the right young ladies?"

"We'll have the names in the deed-polls altered, that's all. It is only important that one of each should fall in love with one of t'other. For all I can see, it doesn't matter which."

"And supposing none of them fall in love at all?"

"They must marry, all the same. The young fellows will fall in love when they ought fast enough—they know their slice of Tarletan depends on it."

"And what do you wish me to tell the young ladies?"

"Nothing at all, except that three visitors are being expected. Why d— me!" cried Lord Tarletan, "the fillies will fall head over ears in love at first sight. What do you think I've kept 'em so artless for? They've never spoke a word to a proper man in their lives. 'Pon my word, when I think of it, I'm almost tempted to stay and see the sport!"

"Why don't you?" asked Madame Leroy.

"You're too glib with your questions, madame," leered the man of the world. "You have your instructions, I've said my say, and I'm off."

"Without seeing your nieces?"

"Well, I had better take a peep at 'em. Where are they?"

"One moment." Madame Leroy laid a pale hand on his arm. "You have forgotten something."

"Oh no, my dear. You are going to ask me for money."

"I shall need a good deal if I am to do the thing properly."

"What do you do with all the money you squeeze out of me? You harpy, I believe you hoard it."

"Your table must be supplied. Your wards must be dressed."

"Very well, very well. No woman has ever called me a niggard yet."

This was true. Harsh, brutal, a loose-liver, he might be, but Roger Tarletan was ever open-handed. He loved not life on any other terms. To ensure this he resorted to many a trick to supplement Braddon's lavish, yet inadequate, revenues. His last trick, before leaving London in advance of them, had been to borrow from the three young suitors a sum more than sufficient for their entertainment. A moiety of this he now passed to Pauline. The rest he kept for a purpose of his own—a purpose in silken petticoats and blonde lace bonnet. But for this purpose he might indeed have stayed to "see the sport." He smiled with secret satisfaction as he counted out a hundred gold guineas into the "harpy's" palm. She, too, smiled secretly as she dropped them in her reticule—for what he had surmised jestingly was no less than the truth. For ten years now Pauline Leroy had hoarded her savings from the household expenses. Ten long dull years of boredom and—security! Some day they must come to an end. Even now she heard their knell ringing, as it were, from afar. But from the day Lord Tarletan had had a second use for her she had sworn never again to be cast penniless on a world that shows no lenience to women who have taken a false step.

Chapter Eight

The First Step in Deception

———————

Lord Tarletan found the Three Graces doing some intricate embroidery in the small saloon that opened on to the terrace. On seeing him the girls rose gracefully, and ran to encircle him with their arms. Pleased by their signs of affection, he caressed their curls and kissed them on the cheek, inquiring:

"Well, my pretty ones! And how have you employed yourselves since I saw you last?"

"Oh," smiled Caroline, "we have been very busy. I have committed three new poems to heart, Adeline has all but finished her bead cushion, Georgiana has executed a quite perfect water-colour sketch of the Mausoleum, and we have all learned a beautiful singing trio to our harps."

"Labours indeed!" Lord Tarletan shook his head as though wondering how delicate young ladies could support so much toil. "I hope you have enjoyed as well as employed yourself."

"Oh, more than usual, uncle!" cried Adeline rapturously.

"Such an exciting thing has happened lately!"

Before she could say more a violent fit of choking interrupted her—not hers but Madame Leroy's. The governess had followed her employer into the room, and now leaned, gasping for breath, on a mosaic table. Her pupils turned to her solicitously.

"Oh, madame, are you dying?" implored Caroline, clasping her hands, while Georgiana tendered her vinaigrette, and Adeline patted her gently on the back. During these ministrations, to their surprise, she pressed a rigid finger to her lips and fixed her dark eyes meaningly upon them. Then, sniffing at the aromatic salts—"A catch in the breath—it is nothing," she said in a loud voice; and, sinking it to a whisper—"Nothing, say nothing!"

They gazed at her, wondering if their ears had heard aright. What could she mean? Why should they say nothing? What had they to conceal?

"Now that we know Madame is not going to die," observed Lord Tarletan, "perhaps I may be told what is this exciting thing that has happened in my absence."

He was looking at Adeline, who had volunteered the information; but Georgiana caught the fleeting warning on Madame Leroy's features as she almost imperceptibly shook her head. Before Adeline could say a word her bolder sister cried impetuously:

"Dear Uncle, Floss has had a little family." Adeline's eyes became as round as saucers, and Caroline reddened.

"Very exciting indeed." Lord Tarletan smothered a yawn.

"At least, for Floss. Has she had kittens or puppies?" To tell the truth, he did not know whether Floss was a cat or a dog.

A musical trio of mirth rippled from the sisters' lips, and Adeline said, demurely:

"She has goats."

Lord Tarletan's bluff laughter made a bass quartet of it.

"Are you not longing to see them, Uncle?" asked Caroline.

He pinched her cheek. "Let us by all means pay our respects to Floss."

He strode through the tall French windows towards the quarters where the girls kept their pets, and they hung about him, chattering and plying him with questions. Adeline's surprise and Caroline's embarrassment had not escaped his notice, but he attributed these to the sensations roused in their maidenly breasts by Georgiana's frank statement of Floss's maternity. It was far otherwise. Their emotions were wholly due to Georgiana's suppression of the mysterious Stranger. Although they could not guess why, the sisters became aware, in the flush of a moment, that some things are better concealed. Georgiana, ever swifter to act than they, had not precisely told their uncle a fib, but she had committed a deception; and, by letting it pass, they had committed it with her. It was the first step! Not one of them, as they leaned over Floss's pen, where her litter of baby goats gambolled about her, would have dreamed of speaking now of their dear bastard. Perhaps Madame Leroy would explain later on why she had put her finger to her lips. Little they knew that this action was the first hiss of the serpent in their Eden.

But even young goats can soon lose interest for the polished lecher. Lord Tarletan yawned again, and led the way back to the terrace, saying:

"Well, my dears, I am glad to see you have so much to keep you from being dull."

"We are never that," said Adeline, "and now you are come we shall be less so than ever."

"A pity, then, that I am not able to stay."

"Oh, Uncle, you are not going?" cried Caroline.

"I must," he said. "But do not look so downcast. In a day or two you will have younger and livelier company than an old man."

"Who, sir?" asked Georgiana.

"Who, sir, who!" teased Tarletan. "What about a young man?" He found their astonished glances highly diverting.

"There *are* such things, you know—or if you do not, it is time you did." He saw the sisters exchange swift dimpling smiles. Not know, indeed! "Aha!" he went on, "I suspect your bosoms harbour more than your prayers. I'll say no more than this—should any young man turn up in the next few days, welcome him in and do your very best to make him happy."

"We will, we will!" they cried.

"That's my good girls. There is Madame Leroy beckoning from the window. I suppose it is time for your beadwork, or your sketching, or your music. I must be off. Remember my injunctions!"

"We will," they again assured him.

They watched him descend the winding steps which led from the terrace to the little postern outside which his horse awaited him on the valley road. They saw him swing himself into the saddle and canter away, and stood at the parapet waving their gauze scarves till he was out of sight. And if, in their mind's eye, they saw a coal-black charger instead of a bay one, if the figure in the saddle was alert with youth instead of bulky with age, who was to know?

Turning, they ran like thistledown into the house, trilling and pirouetting, they knew not why.

How radiant life had suddenly become!

Chapter Nine

The Accident!

———————

"Kaspar," cried Stanislaw, "I am in despair!"

It was the luncheon hour of that same day. While Tarletan and his nieces inspected the kids, the Count lay stretched on a sofa in his lodging, his hair disordered, his shirt undone at the throat, while his servant prepared his vodka at a sidetable.

"What is the matter?" asked the burly menial.

"Did you know that my three golden apples, my Hesperides, were guarded by a dragon, a female Ladon?"

"All young English ladies suffer under that disability."

"But it is monstrous!"

"You can't pluck golden apples for the asking. There are plenty of windfalls to be picked up for nothing."

"Speckled fruit!" said the Pole disdainfully. "I shall never have a palate for it again. Those divine girls have cured me of all women but themselves. But for them, Kaspar, the fever is incurable, and if I cannot allay it I shall die."

"Allay it—how?"

"You know as well as I do. By marriage."

"With all three?"

"With at least one."

"Which?"

"What does it signify? One is so splendid, one is so gay, one is so sweet, and all are so beautiful."

"Since you can marry one only you had better find out which it is you really prefer. Miss Adeline? Miss Caroline? Or Miss Georgiana?"

"Adorable syllables, even on your coarse lips! I don't know which is which, nor do I care. I shall marry one, and set up house with all three."

"H'm."

"Why not? A brother, as I shall become to two of them, may well have his sisters in his loving keeping. These girls are different from anything I've ever met before in Petersburg, in Paris, or in—"

"Pinsk ?" said the Moujik with a short rough laugh.

"Or in Pinsk," said his master coldly. "Bring me my vodka. It may clear my brain and help me to a plan, for somehow I must overcome this dragon's machinations."

Kaspar brought the tankard to his master.

"What is she like; this dragon?"

"She is terrible!" Stanislaw paused to take a long deep draught. "Imagine a pillar of jet, with a capital of chalk, in which glow two eyes as red-hot as the D*v*l's." Draining the tankard, he repeated: "Terrible!"

"She does not sound inviting."

"Inviting!" Plunged in torment as he was, Stanislaw could not restrain a wild burst of laughter. "She is a bunch of nettles, a rocky crag, a vulture ready to swoop—and not all my beaux yeux could transform her into a rose, a mossy bank, or a white dove. No, Kaspar, she is not to be got round. But somehow, somehow I must assail the fortress."

The Moujik refilled the tankard from the bowl and prepared the table for his master's luncheon. But Stanislaw either could not or would not eat. For three days he lay on the sofa, drinking vodka by the gallon, railing at fate, and apostrophizing the Three Graces, till

Kaspar feared for his reason. On the third evening, the Moujik administered a sleeping draught in the vodka, and when the young man lay pale and insensible went out on a secret mission. Not till the first ray of morning gilded his handsome features did Stanislaw stir. Languidly he raised his heavy lids, to see his servant standing over him.

"What hour is it?"

"Dawn."

"I have slept."

"All night."

"You drugged me?"

"To save your senses."

"For what? Ah, G*d! Had only that sleep been death! Drug me again, good fellow, and treble the dose."

"There is no need," said Kaspar phlegmatically. "While you slept, I have been making inquiries."

"And discovered, what?"

"That your three golden apples, who used to have a breathing-space from their studies at eleven in the morning, now have it at two o'clock in the afternoon."

"Is that all? C*nf*nd you!" cried Stanislaw, "what use is this to me?"

"Only," observed Kaspar, "that as the dragon thinks you ignorant of the change of time, she takes her own siesta in peace and quiet."

"Ah!" cried Stanislaw.

"And while she snores, the young ladies go every day to a certain arch upon a certain wall."

"Ah!" cried the Count again. "Where did you get this information?"

"At the West Gate, where the lodge-keeper's wife is a rose, a mossy bank, and a dove all rolled into one."

"Then this afternoon," said Stanislaw, "you suggest I should torment myself from afar by one more sight of my Hesperides ?"

"By your leave, I suggest a great deal more than that."

"What? Speak, in heaven's name! What?"

Sitting on the edge of his master's couch, the man divulged his plan.

That same afternoon, Georgiana, Adeline, and Caroline strolled listlessly to the archway from which they had seen their brief dream dawn and dwindle. The radiance of life had been extinguished almost as soon as felt. On the evening of their uncle's departure Madame Leroy announced the alteration in their daily programme. Why she had changed their hour of idleness from morning to afternoon they could not imagine. As she had been careful to avoid any appearance of censure, they did not attribute this change to him whose image haunted their sleeping and waking dreams. They only knew that the alteration in their habits had robbed life of its sweetness and savour. Their solace was to retrace their steps across the terrace, lean in the arch as in a happier hour, and conjure to their ears the sound of a horse's hoofs thudding down the valley, to their eyes the vision of a raven lock tossed across an alabaster brow. Communing thus with their thoughts, Adeline's lively face grew wistful, Caroline's blue eye was brimmed with tears, and Georgiana's fine bust heaved with a heavy sigh.

"Why do you sigh?" asked Adeline, sighing too. "I am thinking of him."

"And so am I."

"And I."

"We have not even a name to think of him by."

"Oh, Georgy, do you think he is thinking of us?"

"I hope not!" said Caroline, quickly.

"*Hope* not, fond girl!" cried Adeline in surprise, while Georgiana chimed: "How *can* you hope not?"

"For if," said Caroline, "he thinks of us as we now think of him—his heart is breaking."

So saying, she laid her head on Adeline's breast and wept freely, murmuring between her sobs: "Let my heart break, but let not his be hurt."

"Oh, it is true!" exclaimed Adeline in anguish. "Picture him riding every morn as usual, to find the archway empty! Let us pray that it means less than nothing to him. Women are reeds that can bear the weight of adverse winds, but men are oaks that crack under the storm."

"Yes!" agreed Georgiana on a deep note. "Rather death for all three of us than a momentary ache in his little finger!"

"Rather death for all three," whispered her sisters. And they clung in the archway, mingling their tears. Suddenly, with one movement, they lifted their heads, and three voices cried as one voice:

"Hark! Oh, hark!"

For below, still out of sight, the gallop of a horse became audible. The gallop? It sounded rather like a stampede! Who could it be but he? It must be he! But why such frantic haste?

As the rider rounded the angle of the wall, the reason was obvious. The gigantic stallion had broken loose from control. His eyeballs rolled and shot fire, his dilated nostril snorted, he was no longer the friend of man, but a wild beast bearing his owner to destruction. The Stranger's peril was imminent. Hatless, he swayed in the saddle, his hand grasped feebly the tangled reins that lay loose on the charger's neck, his feet had lost the stirrups. The three girls rose and shrieked—he cast one last look upward—a gleam of joy irradiated his agonised features—and in the next moment he was hurled from his seat, and fell, face downwards, prone on the velvet sward!

Before the girls could utter a second scream another figure galloped into view, and the Moujik, leaping from his horse, was kneeling by the Stranger's inanimate form.

"My master! My master!" he cried, wringing his hands.

He turned the limp body over and felt it carefully. "Ah, say not he is dead!" breathed Georgiana. The lips of her sisters were too dry for speech.

The servant looked up, and even in his distress removed the fur cap that covered his grey head. "Ladies, a thousand pardons," he stammered. "My master will never forgive himself for horrifying you with the sight of his accident."

"Will never forgive himself? Then," cried Georgiana eagerly, "he is not dead!"

"Not yet," said the Moujik.

Not yet? Ah Fate, be kind!

The man went on: "But he is insensible. Whether he has broken a rib or a leg, or dislocated a shoulder or an arm I cannot yet find out. If there were anywhere to carry him—"

"There is!" cried three young voices, ardently.

"You shall bring him in here," said Georgiana.

"We will send for our medical attendant," said Adeline.

"And nurse him back to health," said Caroline, "with our own hands."

"Wait! Wait till we come," commanded Georgiana.

The sisters disappeared from the Gothic arch, their quickly-tripping feet were heard on the steps that wound to the valley level, the little postern in the wall was unbolted and Georgiana, Adeline, and Caroline were kneeling on the turf beside the Stranger!

Oh heavens! How describe their emotions as, for the first time, they touched that pallid cheek, those hyacinth locks? Caroline fanned his brow with her cambric kerchief, Georgiana chafed his frigid hands in hers, and Adeline, greatly daring, laid her hand on the frill of his shirt. Turning her eyes towards her sisters, she said:

"He lives!"

"'Tis well," said Georgiana in trembling tones. "Man, raise him carefully, and follow us."

Before the Moujik could obey the Stranger stirred—his eyelids wavered—lifted—and three pairs of lovely eyes gazed into the jetty depths of his.

"Where am I?" he murmured. "Am I in Paradise?"

"No, sir," said Caroline, softly. "But do not speak, do not even try to think."

"I begin to recall," he said, speaking very faintly. "Kosciusko—!" His eyes turned to his horse, which, after throwing him, was grazing tranquilly near by.

"I'll take care of Kosciusko, sir," said the Moujik, with rough emotion. "The brute shall be shot for bringing you to this pass."

"My Kosciusko shot? He saved my life!" But he had spoken too energetically. Moistening his lips, he managed to say: "An adder raised its vile head in our path—the noble creature instantly trod on it—and then—no wonder he went mad! But for him—I must—have—died!"

His head fell back on Caroline's fair shoulder. He seemed to be dead indeed.

"Look to the horse," commanded Georgiana. "Follow the wall, and you will come to the stables. Tell the grooms what has happened, and say it is by our orders that that noble, never-to-be-overpraised steed be given the best oats in the granary."

The Moujik rose to his feet, caught Kosciusko by the rein, and hesitated. "My master?"

"Leave him to us. We will convey him in."

And they did! Those three fair nymphs, who had known till now the proximity of no man but a great-uncle, bore the Stranger up a hundred steep stairs! An almost superhuman strength was granted them, as Caroline cradled his head, Adeline his feet, and Georgiana supported his lifeless waist. At the end of the difficult journey, when they emerged exhausted from the scented shrubs which concealed the descent, they were met by no less than Madame Leroy herself. Puzzled by their delay, she had come in search of her pupils, where she thought she would find them—but the sight that met her eyes she had little expected. Startled out of her composure she cried sharply:

"Young ladies, what is the meaning of this?"

But in their concern for their dear, insensible burden they took her startled accents for an anxiety akin to their own; and as they deposited him on a seat, Georgiana panted:

"Madame, there has been a terrible accident."

"An adder stung his horse," explained Adeline, "who receiving the injury meant for his rider, could not help throwing him."

"He might have died," said Caroline, lingeringly relinquishing his head.

"And may yet," said Adeline, "if he is not well nursed."

"I see," said Madame Leroy, moved in spite of herself by the young man's pallor. "And who will nurse him?"

"I!"

"And I!"

"And I!"

"Have you considered what your uncle will say?"

"Uncle?" Adeline smiled joyfully. "Why, we are only carrying out his wishes. Did he not tell us to make welcome any young man who turned up in the next few days and do our very best to make him happy? Dear uncle! We will do our best indeed!"

"Our very best!" cried her sisters, radiantly.

"I see," said Madame Leroy.

With a strange dark surge of joy in her own bosom, she signalled to a passing gardener and gave him some hasty orders. Servants appeared to bear the corpse-like form to the terrace-room, where maids brought pillows and coverings, and Madame Leroy superintended the removal of the stranger's riding-boots, etc., etc. Who would nurse him back to strength and health? *I! I! And I!*

Silently Pauline Leroy echoed:

"And I!"

A shadow fell across her and the man on the couch. With that sense of doom which was ever pregnant within her, she turned—to meet the eyes of one strange to her, a rough greybearded man in a fur cap, who regarded her so intently that she felt uneasy.

"What do you here?" she asked.

"I have come to see if I can be of help."

"Who are you?"

"His servant."

"And your name?"

"Kaspar."

"I was not told. A bed shall be prepared."

"I sleep at his door."

"You prefer it?"

"It is the custom."

"Just as you wish. I will send you a pillow and blankets."

"I thank the lady. She is much too good." Madame Leroy withdrew, strangely disturbed. This man! Had he read her secret? He had looked at her as though he would penetrate her very soul— that is, if she had one. She knew this man was not to be her friend.

Chapter Ten

The Couch of Sickness

————————

And now began for the sisters a time of unexampled happiness. Too brief? But when time is merged in eternity, it is neither brief nor long-drawn-out. It is. One moment of perfect bliss becomes a lifetime—and what more can anyone ask than a lifetime of bliss? When Cimerian Darkness descends upon it, that which has been still is. Nothing can rend from the faithful heart the moment in which Love unveiled his eyes. I repeat, Nothing!

For two days and nights Stanislaw occupied the couch in the terrace saloon, tended and waited on by three, nay, four devoted hearts. The devotion of the sisters was easy to read; Pauline kept hers concealed. Bringing him, in her turn, peaches and grapes, soothing his brow with scented toilet waters, smoothing his pillow, she let no sign of her feelings emanate. She remained like a harsh Mother Superior in a dovecote of novices, who fluttered about and could not do enough for him. Now it was Adeline who came hovering like a butterfly, bearing a small knot of spicy flowers to refresh his nostrils. Now it was Georgiana, who entered like a cary-atid, bearing a syllabub. Or now he woke to find Caroline seated beside him, peeling black grapes with white finger-tips, and insinuating the juicy morsel between his parched lips. When he sought to thank them they laid their hands over his mouth and shook their heads.

"Not yet!" said Adeline. "You must not try to speak till you are better. What a shaking you had! Thank heaven no bones were broken."

"Something was wounded." His hand went to his heart.

"You mean—?" Adeline's candid eyes looked into his.

Smiling faintly, he murmured: "Kosciusko?"

"Don't speak! You've no need to worry. Kosciusko is well. We can't find a trace of the adder's sting. Is not that fortunatc?"

"Most," said Stanislaw.

"I thought I had commanded you to be silent! How are you feeling now?"

"Better, much better. I am always better when you are sitting beside me."

"Oh!" fluttered Adeline. "I think I hear Madame Leroy calling me." And she hastened away, all her delicious archness in commanding him turned in an instant to water by his words.

Her place was instantly seized by Georgiana.

"How flushed you are!" she exclaimed, wiping his forehead with a cambric towel. "What have you been doing? Has Adeline been making you talk? If so, I shall scold her."

"Do not. It is not her fault that I spoke."

"It must be. She has been asking you questions, I'm sure. Oh, do not shake your head so gallantly! Now, has she not been asking you questions?"

"Well, if she has—"

"There! What did I say? I shall certainly slap her if she does it again."

"Are you the oldest, then, of my sweet nurses?"

"No, we are triplets, born all together; there is not a pin to choose between us as to age."

"And *she* is Adeline. You are—?"

"Georgiana."

"And the third one is—?"

"Caroline."

"A name for an angel. Adeline is a fairy. But you, Georgiana, you—" He paused, and fixed his melting eyes on her. Pressing her hand to his cheek—"are a goddess," he whispered.

"Oh!" she gasped. "Is not that Madame Leroy calling for me?" Withdrawing her hand, the proud girl quitted him hurriedly.

But he was not long left lonely. Caroline soon appeared, with a book in her hand. She seated herself beside him, smiling serenely.

"I am going to read you one of my favourite poems," she said.

"What is its subject?"

"Death." Caroline opened her book at a page where lay the silk marker. "It must be very dull for you lying here with nothing to do."

"Nothing but taste sweet drinks and smell sweet flowers, nothing but watch angels floating about me. If heaven is dull, then I am—Caroline!"

She became a lily, then a rose, under his eyes. "Oh," she breathed. "You know my name?"

"I guessed it."

"How wonderful. You must have second sight."

"I have, when I am moved. And you?"

"I do not know. I have not thought about it. I am sure I could not guess your name."

"Try."

"Is it—? No! It could not be. Or—No! No name I can think of is—is—"

"Is what, dear Caroline?"

"Suitable," she said faintly. He had called her dear. Oh, had he called her dear?

"My name," he said, "is Stanislaw."

"Ah!"

"You sigh. Do you hate it?"

"No, oh, no. I—it is beautiful. But it is strange."

"Pronounce it, and it will not be so strange."

"It is not easy to pronounce."

"Yet try. Stanislaw. Say it. Stan—is—law."

"Stanislaw."

"Caroline!"

"Oh," she faltered, "I must leave you, I must go."

"But you have not read me my poem."

"Another time. Madame Leroy is calling."

Before he could detain her she had flown. But it could not have been Madame Leroy she had heard for that lady appeared at once from another quarter with a bowl and spoon on a tray.

"Eat it," she said briefly.

"What is it?"

"Gruel."

"I dislike it."

"In life one must swallow much that one dislikes. Come, eat it, it will do you good."

"And have you found, my stern gaoler, that the things you disliked in life have done you good?"

"No," she said."

"Then throw the gruel out of window, and tell me—"

"What?"

"Why I am one of the things in life you dislike."

"Have I said so?"

"Bah!"laughed the Count. "You must answer better than that, unless you wish me to take you for a stupid woman."

"It is not my concern what you take me for. My only concern is to see you cured—"

"Dear gaoler!"

"As quickly as possible—"

"Dearest gaoler!"

"So that you may go, and never return."

He sat up, agitated. "Yes! You do dislike me! Yet, I should be glad to do you good—if I could."

"Nothing and nobody can do me good. There is no good in life."

"Life must have treated you very harshly."

"It has."

"Tell me the story of your life."

"Not now. Not ever. Lie down."

"Then shall I tell you the story of mine?"

"When you are better. Lie down."

"When shall I be better?"

"Never, if you do not swallow your gruel."

"If I swallow it for my good will you consent to believe I wish for yours?"

"Oh, yes," she said, cynically, "I will consent to believe anything."

She offered him the spoon, but, putting the bowl to his lips, he swallowed the nauseous concoction at a gulp and fell back on his pillow.

"That is better," said she. "At last you lie down."

"Your treatment would take the heart out of anybody. It has taken the heart out of me. How dare you deprive me of my heart?"

"Release my hand!"

"I must see if my heart is in it," he laughed, impudently."

"Where your heart is I neither know nor care."

"Come, come, madame, confess you don't dislike me."

"Let my hand go!"

"Confess you like me a little."

"I neither like nor dislike you. You do not exist for me. Will you let go my hand? The young ladies are calling me."

"Everybody calls everybody in this place at the wrong moment. If I did not exist, how can I detain you?" He sprang to his feet and, tall woman though she was, towered over her. "Pauline, I swear you shall either dislike or like me!"

She smiled contemptuously. "You swear? I have heard so many men's oaths broken that yours will not weigh a hair in the scales of what I feel for you."

"What do you feel for me?"

She looked him up and down. "Nothing," she said. And before he could stop her she had wrenched her hand from his and left him.

He flung himself petulantly upon the couch, but turned his head as the light from the glass doors was darkened by the burly form of Kaspar.

"What is the matter with you?" asked the Moujik.

"Only that I have come as far as I can, lying down. It is time to stand up and assume a new position."

"Then you mean to get better?"

"From to-morrow morning." Stanislaw smiled with anticipation. "From to-morrow, Kaspar, they shall see a great change in me."

Chapter Eleven

The Margrave's Son

———————

That evening, after supper, Stanislaw found his sanctuary invaded. Instead of coming to him one by one, the sisters appeared together, each bearing a harp. Smiling, they grouped themselves before the window, where the sunset bathed their white forms in a roseate glow and turned their hair into a golden mist.

"Now," said Stanislaw, giving them smile for smile, "I know I am in heaven."

"You seem so much better," said Adeline, "that we think you can bear to hear us sing to you."

"And when I faint of rapture, what will you do?"

"Then I," said Madame Leroy, entering with a guitar, "will sing, and shudder you back to earth again."

She seated herself in the shadows and thrummed an exploratory bar or two.

"You play very skilfully, madame."

"Are you a good judge?"

"I am a passionate lover of music, and I play myself a little."

"Will you not now?" asked Georgiana, quickly.

"I would rather hear my angels, and my—" He paused, with his eyes on Pauline. "And my archangel."

"Skilfully changed!" said she. "Well, young ladies, begin!"

The girls rippled their harps; music rose and fell in the terrace saloon, as strings and voices combined in the lovely *Barcarola a tre Voci:* "Voga, voga, O Marinaro!" by Fabio Campana. Outside, the sun sank in a sea of amethyst and silver below the terrace, while in the Gothic arch hung the moon like a rosy pearl. Exquisite hour! Stanislaw lay entranced, his eyes fixed on the haloed trio whom sound and light made one.

As the last strain of melody died on the air he heaved a sigh—checked by the violent thrumming of the guitar. Madame Leroy broke into a strident song, accompanying her well-trained but unpleasing voice with skill. The song she sang was Alexander Heichhardt's passionate Polonaise: *"Are they meant but to deceive me, Those fond words that tell of love?"*

She sang it coldly, bitterly, without frenzy.

When it was ended Stanislaw made no comment. He was angry with her for deliberately wrecking his transports. But the sisters did not suspect her of any such purpose, and, accustomed to her harsh, though tutored, tones, supposed she had wished, like themselves, to give the invalid pleasure.

"Now, M. Stanislaw," said Adeline, "it is your turn."

He shook his head. "Not to-night. Comparisons, they say, are odious. Don't you agree, madame?" He turned his mocking eyes on Madame Leroy. She bit her lip, understanding that he had read her through and through. He addressed the girls again. "No, my angelic choir, I'll not sing to-night. Some other time, perhaps, when the air is less full of strains from supernatural spheres."

"It is only fair, however," said Georgiana, "that you should do something to entertain us, sir."

"Then shall I tell you the story of my life?"

"Oh do, pray, do!" they cried; and leaving their harps untenanted, they clustered on the floor about his couch.

"What do you say, madame?" he asked of the shadows.

"If you desire to tell your story, tell it."

"Desire!" he repeated sombrely. "Could any man desire to tell a tale like mine? But it is only right that my hostesses should know somewhat of the guest who, but for them, would have had no story to tell."

Propping his elbow on a pile of cushions, and his cheek on his hand, he gave his sole attention to the girls at his feet, and began his narration.

"Know, then, that I am a bastard."

The triplets caught and held their breath, exchanging looks, they said: "We knew, oh, we knew it!"

Their guest continued: "My royal father had, besides me, only one other child. A daughter, some three years younger than myself."

"Was she a bastard too?" asked Caroline.

"No," smiled Stanislaw. "That lot is not reserved for everyone."

"Foolish Caroline!" chided Georgiana. "You ought to know that girls are never bastards. A bastard is a monarch's noblest son."

Caroline blushed, abashed by her simple error.

"Go on, sir," said Adeline, fondling her sister's hand.

"Was your father's daughter very beautiful?"

"She was," said Stanislaw, "the most beautiful woman I ever beheld, until a month ago."

"And then," ventured Adeline, "you met one lovelier still?"

"Three," he answered boldly; and now three blushed instead of only one.

"Describe your sister," said a voice from the shadows.

"Can one describe beauty? She had blue-black hair, with a purple bloom on it, like the bloom on grapes. In her eyes the vesper-star appeared to shine. Her brow mocked the pearls that clustered mid the dim volume of her hair. Her looks were half frost, half flame. A simple robe of texture soft and light enveloped in its folds a polished form that seemed like a statue for Love's holiest shrine." He paused and sighed. "Have I described her?"

"Vividly!" cried Georgiana.

"I see her as plainly as if she stood before me," breathed Caroline.

"She must be the most beautiful woman on earth," mused Adeline.

"I used to think so." Stanislaw sighed again.

"What was this paragon's name?" asked the voice from the shadows.

"We called her Esmeralda. Ah, G*d! Even now I can scarcely utter that name and live!"

"Oh, did she die?" implored Caroline.

"I do not know." Stanislaw struggled with and mastered his emotion. "One day a distinguished foreigner visited my father's castle."

"You were reared in a castle?" came the voice from the shadows.

"Yes, in Pinsk."

"Indeed. Well, tell us more of this distinguished foreigner."

"He came," said Stanislaw, gloomily, "as an honoured guest. He left—dishonoured and dishonouring!"

"What did he do?" asked Adeline, wide-eyed with horror.

The young man's chin sank on his breast, and he murmured: "My sister."

"Ah, no!"

"Poor girl. She was not above the weaknesses of her sex. On the night of our guest's departure I heard her weeping in her chamber. I loved my sister above all earthly things. Her grief was my own. I sought and found her, bedewing her pillow with tears. I entreated her to tell me the cause of her grief—for long she resisted my prayers—I mingled my tears with hers—and at last she confessed that she had given our guest her all."[1] Stanislaw writhed on his couch. "I recoiled from her, my eyes starting from my head. 'What will you do?' she moaned. 'Pursue and kill him!' She clung to me 'No, brother, no! We loved—and I forgive him!' But I was mad! I rushed from the room, dragging her on her knees still clinging to me, till, exhausted, she fell at the door. Two loved —and one forgave. 'Twas not enough. Snatching my sword from my bedside, I hastened to the courtyard, calling to Kaspar to saddle Kosciusko— ha, ha! That horse had not his equal in Pinsk! Three hours after our guest had left us I was on his tracks—in two hours I had overtaken him—in two minutes he was writhing on the ground."

---

1 Mem: What is it? Find out.—A.G.

"What—what had you done?" whispered Georgiana. Caroline and Adelaide were as pale as death. Staring before him with eyes that saw a sight they could not see, the young man answered tonelessly:

"I had avenged my sister."

He paused, and no one spoke.

"When I returned to the castle she had flown. The place was in an uproar—we sought her in vain. I have not seen her from that day to this. My father, whom I had never before seen shaken out of composure, was like one distraught. He had no inkling of what had happened. I enlightened him. And when I told him what I had just done—"

"He fell on your neck," said the bitter voice in the shadows, "called you his dear, his noble bastard, and blessed you."

"No, madame," came the icy voice from the couch. "He *cursed* me."

"For avenging a sister?"

"For disembowelling a guest. 'As a man,' he said, 'I would have done the same; as a Margrave, it is my duty to banish you.'"

"As a Margrave!" repented the harsh voice from the shadows.

"Yes, madame."

"Your father is the Margrave of Pinsk?"

"Yes, madame."

"And then?" urged Adeline, breathlessly.

"He told me not to darken his doors again until I could bring to them a bride as pure as his dishonoured child had been. 'A daughter for a daughter,' were his words. But at the last he relented enough to embrace me and give me that which would enable me to subsist, and also that which would substantiate my position in the unknown society I must henceforth frequent. We embraced; and then, my horse and my moujik my only living links with the past and Pinsk, I left it—for ever."

Georgiana turned her glowing eyes upon him. "Say not for ever. Remember your father's condition."

"I do. But who would marry one with a tale like mine?" The young man buried his face in his hands and groaned.

A discordant twangling sounded from the shadows. Madame Leroy in rising had knocked her guitar on the floor.

"Young ladies," she observed, "it is long past your usual bedtime. Thank our guest for his entertainment, and retire."

But no word issued from the sisters' sweet pale lips. They glided from the room like wraiths in a trance. When they were gone, Pauline kneeled by the couch and obliged the youth to look at her.

"You are mad," she said, sternly, "to agitate yourself like this in your weak state. The telling of your story has been too much for you."

"I shall feel better now that it is told," he said, wearily. "I could not remain here under false pretences. Knowing both who and what I am, you may turn me adrift to-morrow, if you wish. But let me stay to-night to recover myself."

"I shall not turn you out," she said. "Why should I? Sleep well, Margrave's son!" He looked up with a grateful smile that almost won a smile from her forbidding features. Bending over him, she asked: "Do you resemble your father?"

He shook his head. "He was a taller and broader man than I, with ruddy hair and a nose like a balancing hawk."

"A father to be proud of," remarked Madame Leroy—and left the room, stepping carefully over the somnolent figure of Kaspar, stretched at the door.

Chapter Twelve

The Suitors

———————

Surprising! The next day, Count Stanislaw seemed almost completely recovered. Not so completely as to dispense with all ministrations, not so completely as not to need Georgiana's arm as she conducted him to the Gothic arch in which he had first beheld her and her sisters—not so completely as to require no repose in the ruined temple by the lake, where Caroline led him to point out the Mausoleum—not so completely as to refuse the cordial with which Adeline ran to revive him on his return, terrified lest his exertions had been too much for him. But sufficiently to become part of the household life, roaming hither and thither at will with this sister or that, opening up to them an endless vista of delightful days.

And while they strolled and sang, told tales, and recited their favourite verses the Fates were rapidly descending upon them in the guise of three young gentlemen, who had just ridden into the county. By no means ill-favoured young gentlemen, moreover, though they knew more about port and claret than that wine which pours out of a poet's brain. As they cantered they chipped each other, as young men will.

"Why so glum, Terry?" It was the Hon. Percival Fawleigh who spoke. "That's no face to go a-wooing with!"

"Faith, and I know it! But what the divil will I do if I don't cotton to Miss Adeline? She may have a long nose and a large foot, two things I never could abide in a woman."

"The de'il tak Miss Georgiana," said James Dumbarton, "if she hae a wide mouth and narrow shoulders."

"If Miss Caroline's waist be above eighteen inch," cried Percival Fawleigh, "I shall marry her first and then go to the d*v*l!"

"But should her waist measure nineteen," observed James, "you need not marry Miss Caroline, I suppose; nor you, Terry, Miss Adeline. But I, worse luck, maun wed with Miss Georgiana whether I like her or no."

"Why so?" asked Terence Lorrequer.

"Because only a fool throws away a sound investment, and no man likes to lose the funds he has sunk in a speculation."

"What, man!" ejaculated Terry. "Never tell me that the old Lord has milked you too?"

"Milked me? I should think so! Only three weeks ago he borrowed a cool ten thou, which I paid on sight of an agreement signed by my parent when I was too young to know anything about it."

"He did the same by me," said Terence, laughing. "And you, Percy?"

"There seemed to be no help for it. We are committed. After all, when the old boy dies, we shall be masters of fortunes; and the Triplets, beauties or no, are at least young."

"And simple. When we are mated, if we do not like them, we can return without difficulty to those three doxies whose rustic charms detained us in Leicestershire. Thank heavens," said the lively Irishman, "the doxies of Albion are as complaisant as they are prolific."

"In any case," added James, "they say the fishing at Braddon is unequalled in England, and scarce rivalled in Scotland. So we can enjoy ourselves all day, and only trouble to do a little courting in the evening."

Such was the mood in which these loose young bucks pressed forward towards their goal.

It was noon when the three horsemen, after cantering through the south gate of Braddon Park, came on an idyllic scene in a glade through which ran a tributary of the silver Brade. Under the spreading oak and chestnut boughs a fine cloth covered the sward, furnished with dishes of fruit and other dainties. Big jugs of milk held the four corners of the cloth against the breeze, which lightly ruffled the hair of those disposed about the Arcadian feast: three nymphs, as fair as Proserpine before her abduction, a presiding goddess dark as the Queen of the Underworld, and a manly form, seeming half-god half-mortal, sublimely handsome as the youthful Bacchus, yet as prey to the sorrows of human nature as Manfred. Behind him stood a broader, bulkier form—the Silenus, one might say, of this classic group. The four younger members were talking animatedly, the two elders seemed, as ever, on the watch. At the sound of the hoofs battering the turf, the mood of the picnickers broke like the surface of a lake into which a handful of pebbles has been cast. With one accord, they turned their heads to look up; with one accord, the three riders came to a standstill, and looked down. For a moment nine pairs of eyes met like strangers, ignorant of the destiny which wove them together.

Then the dark woman, rising, advanced and addressed the horsemen.

"If I am not mistaken," she observed, "you are the Hon. Percival Fawleigh, the Hon. Terence Lorrequer, and the Hon. James Dumbarton."

"Ye are no mistaken," said the last named; and Terence cried: "Why you must be a witch!"

"Not in the least," said Pauline, drily. "I am Madame Leroy, the governess of the three Misses Tarletan, and was warned by Lord Tarletan to expect you some days ago. Permit me to welcome you to Braddon Hall, and to introduce to you Lord Tarletan's great-nieces."

At her signal, the Triplets rose gracefully from the ground, and sank to it again, as each was named, like a curtseying swan.

"The Hon. Georgiana. The Hon. Adeline. The Hon. Caroline."

The gentlemen bowed, each eyeing his prospective bride with curiosity; and it must be owned that, at first sight, Terence found nothing wrong with Adeline's nose, James with Georgiana's mouth, or Percy with the span of Caroline's waist.

"And you, sirs?" asked Madame Leroy. "Which of you is which?"

They swung themselves from their saddles, and named themselves.

"I am Percy Fawleigh."

"And I, James Dumbarton."

"And I, Terence Lorrequer."

Renewed bows and curtsies.

"We are charmed to meet the ladies," said Percival, "of whom we have heard such flattering tales in London."

"In London, sir!" exclaimed Adeline. "What can they know of us there?"

The melodious, if melancholy, tones of Stanislaw answered her.

"The more cause have they to speak, to whom you are a mystery. One speaks no longer of that which one knows too well."

The three girls favoured him with wistful smiles; but the three gentlemen regarded the attractive speaker with some surprise, and James Dumbarton remarked:

"Lord Tarletan did not inform us that the young ladies had a brother."

"Oh, sir, this is no brother," cried Georgiana. "Heaven forbid! This is our guest, Count Stanislaw, Bastard of Pinsk, who is recovering under our roof from a serious accident."

"Then I trust he will soon be himself again," said Terry, "and able to pursue whatever pleasant course was interrupted by that same accident."

"I thank you," said Stanislaw, coldly. "Perhaps you will refresh yourselves after your long ride, and join our collation."

"I could do with a cup of wine," said Terry, more cordially.

"And I with a slice of game pie," said Percy, heartily.

"I never say na tae salmon," added James.

"Nor shall you now," laughed Adeline, "there being *no* salmon to evoke your *na*!"

"Nae salmon?" He stared at her with heavy disapproval.

"I wad not ca' it a collation wi'oot salmon."

"Will you drink a cup of milk?" asked Caroline, turning sweetly to Terence Lorrequer. "Only our uncle drinks wine in Braddon Hall, and he is absent."

"Faith," rejoined Terry, "but I'm thinking he has a butler in charge of the cellar's keys?"

Meanwhile, Georgiana was tendering Percy a plate of little cakes. "Do you not find game pie lies heavy at noon? Try this sugared one, with the pink dove on it."

The Hon. Percy, who had some remnants of manners, accepted the cake, and gave it to his horse.

"Gentlemen," said Madame Leroy, "come with me to the house. I will show you your rooms, and Lord Tarletan's rods and guns, while a meal is prepared for you more to your taste. Young ladies, resume your picnic."

The party separated. The three gentlemen went on to the house, wondering what sort of wedded life they would be expected to lead on cakes without the ale. The three girls sat again to their woodland feast, which seemed to have lost its charm. For, though they knew not why these visitors came, their coming had broken the trance in which they had existed from the moment Count Stanislaw slept beneath their roof. They wanted no other presence than his, for ever. This breath from the rude world—what would it bring?

Chapter Thirteen

Sporting and Courting

———————

For two days life at Braddon went on apparently little changed, yet oh, how different below the surface!

The young bloods from London were too gross in fibre to appreciate the delicacies of their prospective brides. They found the beautiful Triplets a trifle insipid for their town-bred tastes; but were nevertheless prepared to stick to the bargain, for the sake of the fortunes spent and to come. The girls, they believed, would make docile wives; but they found disconcerting the presence of the fascinating Polish Count, who completely engrossed the interest of the ladies. True, this left James free to fish, Percy to hunt, and Terry to shoot all day to their hearts' content; but Madame Leroy— another uncomfortable presence in the house—was ever at their elbows when they returned, urging them to set about their proposals. Her object was twofold: first, to accomplish her employer's instructions, and second, to rid herself of her rivals for Count Stanislaw's attention. He, meanwhile, was taking advantage of the sportsmen's absorption in their favourite pursuits to further himself in the affections of the sisters, for whom he felt an equal and increasing adoration. Not to him were their tender manners and young charms insipid! Sensitive, like the true romantic he was, he preferred the celestial arpeggio of the harp to the blare of trumpets and the clash of cymbals.

On the third morning, Stanislaw happened to be smoking his cigar on the terrace when Terence with his gun over his shoulder, Percival with his spurs upon his boots, and James with his salmon-rod in hand, crossed to the stairway which led to the valley. They exchanged curt nods with the young Pole, who watched their descent leaning upon the balustrade, where, in another moment, he found himself joined by Madame Leroy.

Presently he raised his head, to find her watching him as intently as he had been watching the departing sportsmen.

"Why have these gentlemen come?" he asked.

"A curious question for an uninvited guest," answered Pauline. "They have come because they were invited to come."

"By whom?"

"By Lord Tarletan, naturally."

"Then why is he not here?"

She asked, ironically: "Is Lord Tarletan accountable for his actions and movements to the stranger within his gates?"

"He is," said Stanislaw, with energy, "when the stranger has become as much a part of the place as the air that flows through it."

"Unfortunately, Lord Tarletan is ignorant of the fact."

"I wish he would return, that I might acquaint him with it."

"With what object?"

"That," said Stanislaw, "I should confide to him."

"And not to me?"

"No, because I find you still inimical."

(Inimical! She—to him!)

Madame Leroy shrugged her shoulders, and moved away. The Moujik, who had been lying, apparently asleep, on a bench in the sun, opened one eye, and observed her departing back.

"In your place," he said softly to his master, "I should begin to think of bringing matters to a head. From all I hear, Milord Tarletan is more likely to put a spoke in your carriage-wheel, than set it rolling in the direction of the church. As for the object of the young gentlemen's presence, that's quite apparent. You have only to put three and three together."

"Be silent!" cried Stanislaw, in agony. "Those three brutes, and my three Hesperides! It is not to be supported, even in thought."

"Last night, lingering by accident at a keyhole, I overheard the Hesperidean dragon rating the three brutes for dilatoriness. They consented, not too willingly, to make a move. That being so, I advise you to make up your mind as to your preference."

"I prefer all three."

"In that case, you had better elope with them to Turkey."

"Elope! But the very word is likely to shock them."

"Startle, not shock. A very different thing. Young ladies shrink from shock, but they love to be startled."

"That is true. A delicious tremor at a strange new thought—the planting of the seed. A still more delicious thrill in accepting the thought—the birth of the flower. And finally—"

"The plucking of the flower."

"The flowers."

"The flowers. Don't leave it too long."

"I feel you are right. Yes, Kaspar! I will begin to startle them—deliciously!"

That evening, in the retirement of his room, he spent an hour in penning three brief notes.

*   *   *

Meanwhile, the three sportsmen, spoken to seriously after supper by Madame Leroy, were preparing (with less enthusiasm) for the same campaign. Next morning, at the breakfast table, Stanislaw being absent (he took his in the bedroom now allotted to him, and rose late), James Dumbarton wiped his moustache, and said:

"Weel, Miss Georgiana, am I to be a solitary fisherman for ever?

I've a little trout-rod, fit for a lady's hand, that I should like tae teach ye how to cast."[1]

"Don't let them be having it all their own way, Miss Adeline," cried Terence. "Let you come out with me to-day, and if you have never known the ecstasy of winging your own bird, you shall before the sun sets."[2]

"Fishing and shooting are very well in their way," said Percy, "but for unmitigated sport, give me riding and hunting. Miss Caroline won't deny me the pleasure of her company, I'm sure."

The Triplets exchanged looks of consternation. Only last night, each had found under her pillow—how could it have got there, but by the ministration of the God of Love?—a scented note, inscribed in an exquisite hand. A certain hour—a certain spot—in each case different—had been implored by one to whom none of them would have refused her all. For the first time in their innocent lives, each sister kept a secret from the others. She, she alone, was the chosen confidante of the Bastard—and she did not dream of whispering the precious fact to those who had ever been her confidantes. Why? Because each tender note had ended thus:

"Tell no one!"

They heard, with sensations of woe, the suggestions which threatened what had promised to be a day in paradise, and ransacked their brains for some presentable excuse; but before they could find any, Madame Leroy was speaking for them composedly.

"My pupils are grateful to you, sirs, for your charming offers. Young ladies, go and exchange your morning gowns for more suitable attire."

How they longed to rebel! But the habit of obedience was too strong for them. With despair in their hearts, they went to their rooms and exchanged their muslins for such Amazonian raiment as befitted the day. Perhaps, they thought, they might seize a moment

---

1 Mem: I confess to not being very adept in dialects, and I myself find too much of them very tiresome, but perhaps a hint now and then from Sir ,Walter Scott and the poet, Robert Burns, will suffice to keep the reader in mind of James Dumbarton's nationality. Our surgeon, Dr. Baird, is also Scotch.-A.G.

2 Mem: The poet Moore is less instructive in this matter than the poet Burns, and I have to fall back on the peculiarities of speech in our neighbour Sir Terence Hogan, but they are very elusive. I wish it was not impolite to take notes in compnny.-A.G.

with Count Stanislaw to explain the disaster. But when they descended he was still not to be seen.

While the sisters were dressing for out-of-doors he had put in an appearance, all eagerness for the first glimpse of his loves, anticipating their blushes and downcast eyelids, their first shy signs of acquiescence in what can only be called an assignation. Instead of this, he encountered Madame Leroy, who asked him to perform some trifling errand which would remove him from the vicinity for an hour, and which, as a gentleman, he could not refuse to perform. When he returned the sextet had departed.

Surprised that the usual signs of life were wanting in the saloon and on the terrace, he delivered to the governess the skeins of green and purple Berlin wool, without which she could not, she said, complete the pelerine she was knitting for herself against the autumn airs. Having been duly thanked, he prepared to go in search of his three Hesperides, when she detained him by suggesting he should hold the wools while she wound them into balls.

"With pleasure, madame," he said, feeling the very reverse of that emotion. His first assignation (with Georgiana on the rustic bridge) was almost due. However, he thought, if this wool-winding takes too long I can always pretend exhaustion and retire.

Madame Leroy began on a leisurely ball.

"It is going to be a sultry day," she said. "I believe I feel thunder."

"There is, indeed," he agreed, "an ominous pressure in the atmosphere, and the place seems strangely silent."

"True," said she, "but that may be due to the absence of the young ladies."

"Their absence?" He cast a look through the tall windows, and swept the vacant terrace with his eyes. "But I suppose they will not be absent very long?"

"Oh, no. They are sure to be back by nightfall. If they are not, Mr. Lorrequer, Mr. Fawleigh, and Mr. Dumbarton will find I have a bone to pick with them."

"What can you mean by that?"

"Merely that the Misses Tarletan are enjoying a day's tête-a-tête with our three sportsmen. Pray, do not hold the wool so tight or it will snap. Yes," pursued Madame Leroy significantly, "one is only young once."

Count Stanislaw could hardly trust his ears. What! Georgiana, Adeline, Caroline had all deserted him for another cavalier, at the very moment when he was about to sound their tenderest feelings— and his own!—deserted him, without a single word acknowledging the billets-doux on which he had expended such exquisite care. Was this their answer? Then—he could mean nothing to them, after all! They did not respond. Or, if they had, once, shown symptoms of response, they had been lured away by the first bold advance made by the world upon their fragile defences. Gloom and desolation swallowed him up. The hands that held the detested purple skein trembled so violently that portions of it slipped off his fingers.

"Take care, sir," said Madame Leroy in her acid tones. "You are tangling the strands almost past redemption."

"Excuse me," he muttered. "I am suffering from an ague."

She considered him, and saw that he was indeed quivering in every fibre; and while consumed with rage that he should be so moved, she wondered if she had not gone too far.

"You had better go and rest in some shady spot," she advised; and, bowing low, he left her—to roam his favourite haunts until twilight, when the three couples returned to the house. All the young ladies were on the verge of tears, and, from the traces on their cheeks and eyelids, had been over the brink at least once in the course of the day. As for the young men, they joined forces hastily in the smoking-room, and indulged in language from which my pen must refrain.

"What sort of luck, Percy, did you enjoy?" asked Terence Lorrequer, his feelings sufficiently relieved.

"Never ask me more to go hunting *à deux*!" exclaimed the Englishman, filling a glass with Madeira. "Miss Caroline rides like a young Diana, and if one had nothing to do but look at her, one might want little else for the rest of one's life. Unluckily, that's not enough for a fellow. Of conversation she is totally devoid; a murmured Yes! or No! or Do you think so? is all I could get out of her, till we sighted our prey—and then one got a positive glut of tears! Not a deer, not a fox or a badger, not so much as a hare would she allow me to run to earth! I tried my best to argue with her—I expounded to her the beauties of the chase—in vain! She wept so copiously that I was obliged to attend to her—but curse me, if I ever hunt with her again. As for love-making, we never came within an ace of it."

"My case was much like yours," said Terence Lorrequer. "Miss Adeline appeared a veritable Calypso, and as we started out with our guns, I began to think I might even enjoy the day. She can chatter, too, brightly enough, though without innuendo, and for a time we did pretty well. Then we startled a covey of partridges— they flew up with the rattle of wings that is music to me—I raised my gun, prepared for a right and left, and—felt my wrist seized and jerked. My gun, deflected, sent its shot into the ground. And does my lady apologise? On the contrary. 'How dare you?' she cried. 'You would not hit and kill an innocent bird?' 'If you do that again,' I rejoined, thoroughly vexed, 'I shall hit and kill an innocent young woman.' 'If, by woman, you mean me,' she retorted, 'do so, and welcome! I would rather die than see a partridge fall.' 'Very heroic!' I sneered, for I could scarce keep my temper, 'but do you never eat partridge?' She cast me a look of scorn. 'I would never shoot one.' And so it went on all day. In the end, I've come home with an empty bag, and a courtship not even commenced. What was your fate, James?"

"As bad, or worse, than yours," growled the Scot. "Miss Georgiana looked the perfect Hypolita, and though she was rather silent, that's a fault on the right side. She cast her fly, too, very prettily, after a little instruction; but when she had hooked her trout, refused to play him. As soon as she understood what was wanted of her, she let the fish run away with her line, and escape. After that she declined to try to hook another; and when I told her to sit down and hold her tongue, she asked me why. 'Because,' I said, 'I want tae fill ma creel, and the fish dinna come whaur tongues are clackin'.' 'I'm glad to hear it!' says Miss Georgiana, and thereupon begins to recite aloud some interminable poem about an albatross that I thought would never end. If it did, she maun hae begun it all over again, but by then I was past knowing an albatross from a mayfly. I lost my temper, she burst into tears—and all I've got of it is a good day's sport lost. If it weren't for the guineas I'd ride home to-morrow."

"And so would I!" cried Terence.

"But we cannot go home unplighted," added Percy, sulkily. "Our fathers expect it of us, and, after all, a wife can be kept in her place."

"That's verra true," said James. "We'll abide by the contract. Let us make our proposals by letter to-night, demand our answers in the morning, and go—for, by the Lord, there's no attraction to keep us here."

"None!" laughed Terence.

"None whatever!" swore Percy.

No attraction, James Dumbarton? None, Terence Lorrequer and Percival Fawleigh? So lightly men speak, not dreaming Fate plays with them as a cat with a mouse. When they parted to make their evening toilets a thunderstorm was rolling up from the west—while from the south rolled a travelling-carriage, bearing that which was even more portentous.

Chapter Fourteen

Close, Close Was the Embrace!

———————

It is evening in the saloon and on the terrace. The company is assembled, moodily. Madame Leroy sits knitting her pelerine under a lamp; Georgiana, Adeline, and Caroline stand listlessly at the window, watching the sullen clouds of the oncoming storm. The three gentlemen have not yet left the table, where they have wined and dined heavily, to console themselves for their unfortunate day. On the terrace Stanislaw paces to and fro. The moujik is nowhere in view.

How the three longed to run to the troubled man, whose aspect was as wild as the thund'rous sky. A blood-red sun sunk under lurid clouds, the hills reverberated with muttered thunder that had not yet reached Braddon, and ever and anon a jagged flash of light rent the black dome of the sky like a tree of fire.

The sisters looked forlornly into the night, and trembled—for him, and for themselves.

"How restless he is," murmured Caroline.

"He looks feverish," said Adeline, "he will be ill again."

"He should be made to come in before it rains," said Georgiana. "A soaking might prove fatal."

"He does not look at us—he will not turn his eyes our way," whispered Caroline. "He was silent all through supper."

"Do you think he is angry with us?" asked Adeline.

"Why should he be?" But Georgiana thought he well might be. Instead of keeping the tryst he had pleaded for, had she not gone fishing with James Dumbarton? Adeline and Caroline were asking themselves the same question (substituting the names of Terence and Percival for that of James). They felt as though their happiness was doomed as though some unforgivable act of theirs had blemished them for ever in Stanislaw's eyes. For the first time in their lives each longed to be free from the presence of the others, so that she alone might seek the distracted pacer on the terrace, explain her conduct, and heal his mortal hurt. If (as each could not help hoping) that hurt had been dealt by her.

Presently the terrace began to be spotted with large drops of rain, born of the heat they did nothing to refresh. Soon they increased in force and number, drenching the raven hair of the man outside. Ever and anon he raised a hand to dash a dripping lock out of his eyes. Madame Leroy, a figure like Atropos, rose, with her black bone needles in her hand, and advanced to the window, which she threw wide open.

"Come in!" she cried in loud peremptory tones.

He cast a tortured look in her direction, but did not obey. A crash of thunder hurtled overhead. The girls shrank back with little shrieks of terror. The raincloud burst like the Deluge, and serpents of light with red forked tongues licked heaven from the zenith to the nadir. Fearless as another Boadicea, Madame Leroy strode into the pelting night and dragged the young man back to the shelter of the saloon.

"Strip off your coat and boots at once!" she ordered.

"Fetch me the rug from my chamber, Adeline! More pillows, Caroline! Georgiana, tell Martha to prepare a *tisane*"

Gladly they hastened away to do her bidding. It seemed as though sickness had given him back to them—a gentle relapse was not entirely unwelcome, if only he did not die. While Adeline and Caroline flew to the upper rooms, Georgiana descended to the kitchens, which she found in a state of bustle and excitement.

"What has occurred?" she asked, her hand to her heart. "An accident, miss! A catastrophe!" cried a dozen voices together.

"Catastrophe? Where? To whom? What sort of catastrophe?"

Charlotte, the cook, pushed aside the crowd of voluble domestics. "A coach has overturned on the valley road. William" (one of the grooms) "saw it happen from the lower terrace. The horses were plunging wildly, only Mr. Fawleigh happened to be looking from the dining-room window, and he and the other gentlemen ran out to help. The coachman's leg was damaged, but he managed to limp here, and there he sits."

Georgiana turned her eyes to the man, who, spattered with mud, was receiving the attentions of the chambermaids.

"Are you much hurt" she asked.

"Not to what I might be, but I'm afeard the lady and baby may be mortally wounded."

"A lady—and a baby!" exclaimed the horrified girl.

"To be sure, miss. She hired me in Matlock to bring them to Staleybridge. But this cursed storm (begging your pardon, miss) had something to say as to that. The horses took fright at the thunderbolt. There was no holding 'em. The Duchess won't see Staleybridge this many a day."

"A duchess? Good heavens!" cried Georgiana. "If she be dead!"

"I think I hear them coming into the hall," said Charlotte; and bustled up, followed by most of her fellow-servants. But Georgiana, swift as an oread on a moonlit hill, was in advance of them all.

She gained the hall just as Percival Fawleigh staggered through the great doors with a woman's form in his arms. Behind him came Terence Lorrequer, with a much smaller human burden; while James Dumbarton lugged a handsome dressing-case, marked with a coronet.

Percy, with aching arms, lowered his luxuriant charge to an oaken settle, and knelt, unwilling to relinquish it completely, keeping one arm passed under her noble shoulders, while Terence and James stood by, envying him his position, which allowed the ravishing head to droop on his bosom.

"Oh, is she dead?" whispered Georgiana.

Not so. She lived! She stirs—sighs—opens her eyes. Eyes wherein seemed to shine the vesper-star! From her bonnet, tumbled awry, escaped a cloud of blue-black hair. Hair with a purple bloom on it, like the bloom on grapes! Her cloak slipped from her polished neck and bust—her form seemed a statue for Love's holiest shrine!

Georgiana gazed upon her, like one stunned. Incredible! Yet true.

The beautiful stranger raised herself a little; her lustrous eyes travelled from face to face, then, as though recollection had burst upon her like a lightning-flash, she shrieked aloud:

"My child!"

"Here, madam, safe and sound!" cried Terence Lorrequer. He held towards her the tiny bundle he carried. Bursting into tears, she clasped it to her superb bosom.

At that moment, the door of the saloon opened abruptly, and Madame Leroy stood lowering on the threshold.

"What is all this?" she demanded. "Why, Georgiana, do you procrastinate, when—"

But Georgiana did not wait to hear her finish her sentence. Flying past her into the saloon, she flung herself on her knees by Stanislaw's couch, and cried:

"Rejoice, dear Count, rejoice! Your sister Esmeralda is arrived!"

*   *   *

Too astounded to speak, Stanislaw leapt to his feet. A thousand questions crowded in his eyes, but before one could form on his lips, the open door admitted the figure of the matchless woman and her child, attended by three very assiduous cavaliers. Madame Leroy brought up the rear. Caroline and Adeline, still hovering with pillows and coverings round the couch, were struck mute by the newcomer's lavish beauty. So vivid had been the Bastard's description, that they could not doubt this to be the sister he had left moaning on her knees, and never since seen till now.

As for Esmeralda, she seemed to turn rigid in the gentlemen's arms, as she exclaimed:

"Stanislaw! No, no, it cannot be!"

"It is!" affirmed Georgiana, eagerly. "Your brother, dear madam, and our honoured guest. Do not be so distressed. He has told us all—but, oh! To understand is to forgive." So saying, the impetuous girl swept the beautiful creature forward, and thrust the sister into the brother's arms.

Close, close was their embrace!

Georgiana surveyed them proudly, Adeline's face was radiant with joy, and sympathetic tears flowed down Caroline's cheeks.

Close, close was their embrace!

The three surprised sportsmen surveyed it with mingled feelings. Fain would they have enjoyed that brother's privilege—yet not the privilege of being her brother.

Close, close was their embrace!

Madame Leroy surveyed them narrowly. Only her eyes were alive in her sphinx-like face.

Close, close was the embrace! So close, that though seven pairs of eyes were pinned on them, they could not hear what murmured words the brother and the sister first exchanged. Too holy for other ears was that broken speech. At last the strained arms loosened, and Stanislaw lowered his kinswoman to the couch he had just vacated. Then, burying his face in her garments, he gasped:

"Esmeralda! Sister! Can you pardon me?"

"For what, my brother, must I pardon you?"

"For that night when I saw you last in our native Pinsk. For disregarding your prayers and tears—for following our father's flying guest—the man you had told me had dishonoured you—for pursuing him, and avenging you!"

"How?"

"I slashed him with my sabre."

"Fatally?"

"I left the dastard prone."

She regarded him intensely, with dilated eyes. "Have you," she asked, "betrayed our guest's name to our hostesses?"

"No, Esmeralda—for, at least, he was our guest. The Margrave our father was right to banish me."

"I never knew," said Esmeralda slowly, "what had become of you."

"The Margrave did not tell you? But I remember! When I returned to the castle, you had vanished. What had become of you I long to know."

She smiled, a sad yet brilliant smile. "Yes," she sighed.

"You were as ignorant of my fate as I of yours. We have much to tell each other."

Madame Leroy moved forward. "I too should like to hear it."

Esmeralda turned her limpid look on the governess. "You shall! You shall hear everything, dear madam. What can I deny to those who have succoured my brother—and myself?" Her eyes now dazzled the gentlemen grouped at the door. "They may ask anything of me they will. But just at this moment—" she rose with gracious dignity—"just at this moment, my infant has need of me."

"Come with us," said Caroline, blushing tenderly. "You shall have the room Queen Anne is said to have slept in. She was a mother, too."

"Thank you, sweet girl." And like a queen, attended by her damsels, Esmeralda moved serenely towards the door. The gentlemen drew aside, but she paused in front of them.

"May I be told," she asked in dulcet tones, "the names of my cavaliers and my preservers?"

"The Hon. Percival Fawleigh."

"The Hon. Terence Lorrequer."

"The Hon. James Dumbarton."

"Is every Englishman an Honourable? After this evening, I can well believe it."

"They may be for all I know and aught I care. But I," said James, "am a Scot."

"And I an Irishman!" cried Terence Lorrequer.

"I shall soon learn to differentiate," smiled Esmeralda. "And I shall begin by observing that all Englishmen are gallant, all Scotchmen leal, and all Irishmen irresistible."

"Do you like shooting?" cried Terence, impulsively.

"Do I like shooting! Many's the golden eagle I've brought down in Pinsk!"

"And fishing?" demanded James, jealously. "What," said Esmeralda, all aglow, "are there sturgeon in these English rivers too?"

"Sticklebacks!" exclaimed Percy. "You'll let me take you hunting, marm, now won't you?"

"Yes, yes! You and I will clear Braddon of its bears!"

A cold voice from the shadows. "You know, then, that you are in Braddon Hall?"

"My coachman pointed it out to me, madame, only two minutes before we were overturned. It belongs, he said, to a great nobleman, Milord Tartan."

"Tarletan."

"Excuse me, Tarletan. He is—" She threw an inquiring look around the room. "Abed?"

"In London," said Madame Leroy. "What is the matter? Are you about to faint?"

For Esmeralda had swayed a little. "No, no, madame, but I think I have sprained my ankle." She leaned on Georgiana, who passed an arm around her waist, and said: "Do not, madame, keep her standing with any more questions. I am sure her baby is—"

"Ah," said Pauline. "We must not forget her baby. So you are married, madame?" The two women faced each other unflinchingly.

"I am a widow." An expression of sublime sorrow bloomed on Esmeralda's handsome features. "My husband was the Archduke of Limoges. Our guest, my brother!" she turned swiftly to Stanislaw. "The man you thought you slew, but left half-dead. I need not blush to name him. I followed, found, and nursed him back to life. He bore me with him to Limoges, and there repaired the wrong that he had done me. Rid, Stanislaw, your soul of unnecessary remorse! Wash out the sense of guilt. You were—you *are*—no murderer!"

"Thank heaven!" cried the Triplets with one voice. They turned their joyful eyes upon the Bastard, who stood staring at his sister, struggling with emotions which kept him inarticulate.

"And the child?"

It was the Moujik who now spoke. Stepping from the shadows, he confronted Esmeralda, with a servile bow.

She gasped: "Kas—!"

"Kaspar, the Moujik. Has the royal lady forgotten her poor servant?"

"No—Kaspar—no! Only—" She passed her hand across her brow. "It is so strange to find you here like this."

"No stranger, my lady, for you than it is for us. So the child is the Archduke's daughter?"

"No, his son." And, like a Madonna, the beautiful Archduchess passed from the room with her infant at her bust.

*   *   *

The notes of proposal to the Tarletan Triplets were not penned that night. Instead, three young sportsmen burned the midnight oil, trying to compose elegies to the blessed state of widowhood, with very poor success. For Percy, James, and Terence, horse, rod, and gun were mightier than the pen.

Chapter Fifteen

Brother and Sister

For some reason best known to themselves, the three sportsmen loitered about next morning without attempting to make themselves scarce in their usual hasty fashion. What had mitigated their appetite for sport? At least it had not been impaired for food; they fell heartily on the toasted muffins, the broiled ham and eggs, the bloated herrings, bread-crumbed kidneys and black puddings, with which Braddon always supplied its morning guests; and with the puddings (fare for epicures without delicate stomachs) they partook, French fashion, of quantities of white wine. The young ladies trifled with their poached eggs and whiting, and sipped a little cacao, while the governess consumed a dish of devilled bones washed down with black coffee. Neither Esmeralda nor Stanislaw had appeared at the breakfast-table. It was made known by Madame Leroy, that though the Count could be pronounced on the highway to recovery, he had begged to be allowed to share his sister's tray in her room, she now having the role of honour as invalid.

"What's wrong with her leddyship?" asked James Dumbarton, lowering as though whatever was wrong with her was the fault of Madame Leroy.

"Has she taken a fever after her last night's exposure?" asked

Percy; while Terence in the same breath suggested that the shock of her overthrow had probably prostrated her.

Madame Leroy buttered a piece of toast before easing their anxiety. "The Archduchess," she then assured them, "appears to me to be a lady of inexhaustible vitality, and is suffering from nothing worse than a sprained foot. I have bandaged it very tightly, and later will assist her to dress. To-morrow I hope she will be fit to put her foot to the ground and resume her journey."

"'Twould be a peety to hurry her," muttered James.

"More haste less speed," agreed Percy.

"All the more so," ventured Caroline, timidly, "since her unexpected reunion with her brother. They must have much to say to each other."

"So it appears," said Madame Leroy, munching her toast, which crackled between her teeth.

In the handsome chamber allotted to Esmeralda, the brother and sister had been busy for an hour recounting their past experiences and expatiating on their present aspirations. To see them now, she reclining on her pillows nursing her infant, he seated by the bed, an interested onlooker, would have been to see two people who, whatever the agitations of their last parting, were now in a state of complete understanding with one another.

"Last night," Stanislaw was saying, helping himself to sautéed Cambridge sausages, "I dreamed you were attending at my wedding, in the capacity of bridesmaid."

"Hardly possible," smiled Esmeralda, "for a widow like myself." She laid aside the infant for a moment and, finishing her slip soles dressed with cream, she asked: "Who was the bride?"

"The Tarletan Triplets."

She laughed low and musically, resuming the infant. "A very improper dream! Yet who am I to say so? I dreamed of myself in the arms of our three cavaliers."

"Which of them do you fancy?"

"I cannot say until I know more of their positions and bank accounts."

"I am sorry to find my sister grown so mercenary."

"After marriage with an Archduke, dearest brother, I must be careful not to lower myself. What have you been able to learn of these Honourables?"

"Only that Percy is heir to an English Duke, James to a Highland laird, and Terence to some Irish heaven-knows-what."

"For the present I shall not favour any one of them above the others. It is useful to keep them dangling—but, to tell you the truth, I hope for higher game than *heirs*."

"I wish you luck, dear sister, with all my heart."

"I do not doubt it, since you will share any that may befall me." She reached out her white hand. "Moreover, I am prepared to act as matron of honour at any of your weddings."

He kissed her hand and pressed it to his heart.

"Ah, Esmeralda! If you knew how I burn to possess them!"

"I think I do. Have I not seen you burn more than once ere this? But remember, we are in England now, where marriage is a circumspect affair. My advice is, woo them for all you are worth to-day; make up your mind to-night, and elope with your choice to-morrow."

"To-morrow? Why so much haste?"

"Because I have a shrewd suspicion that Lord Tarletan will not remain long in town, and you had better be on your way before he returns."

"Nothing has been said about his return."

"I feel certain London will not hold him much longer."

She caressed and put down the infant, and adjusted her shawl.

"What makes you think so?"

"He will naturally wish to observe the progress of these three Honourables with his three wards."

"Ah, these Honourables!" Stanislaw struck his brow. "Spokes in my wheel! Yesterday they bore off my belovèds for the entire day."

"To-day they shall do nothing of the kind. They shall not even wish to. I will take care of that."

"What will you do?"

"I shall get up." The Archduchess put one rosy-toed foot out of bed, but withdrew it quickly as the door opened, and admitted Kaspar.

"What are you doing?" she asked imperiously. "Why do you enter my chamber without knocking?"

"A thousand pardons," said the servile moujik. "Doubtless in Limoges you learned to forget that in Pinsk the servants never stood on ceremony."

"I have not forgotten that you were always impudent," Esmeralda. answered, petulantly. "However, I shall not order you the knout."

She smiled as she said it, and was startled to see the man grow white with passion; the hairy growth on cheeks and chin could not muffle the gritting of his teeth. "Come, come," she said, lightly, "I was only joking."

"Of course. It is an upper class privilege. But don't joke too far, Madame the Archduchess—for even moujiks have feelings." He turned to his master. "I thought you should know," he said, "that the young gentlemen are kicking their heels on the terrace, that the young ladies have vanished into thin air, and that Madame Leroy looks like a vulture ready to pounce."

"Oh, Madame Leroy! Let her pounce. Not much harm in her. After all, she is only the governess."

"I should not underestimate her if I were you," said Kaspar. "She strikes me as a woman who knows how to play her cards, and when I crossed the terrace just now she was telling the young men they must finish their business out of hand, or she would feel obliged to communicate with Lord Tarletan."

"What did I say?" cried Esmeralda. "He is certain to come before long!"

"And," continued the moujik, addressing her, "it is *you* she fears. Anyone could see with half an eye how you went to the young men's heads last night."

"In that case," said Esmeralda, very briskly, "I had better set to on their hearts without further delay. Kaspar, find Madame Leroy, and request her, courteously, to aid me at her convenience in making my *toilette*. Do so, if possible, in the Honourables' hearing, and say I hope to enjoy the sun on the terrace at noon. While you, brother"—with a smile at Stanislaw—"make hay while that sun shines with the lovely young Tarletans."

"Who have vanished," sighed Stanislaw, "into thin air."

"At the precise spots appointed for yesterday's assignations," said Kaspar. "How know you this?" cried the lover, joyfully.

"Because I myself insinuated into each little ear that time and place were the same, though the day was different."

"Ah, Kaspar, how much I owe you!" cried Stanislaw.

"One of these days we will make up the account. Now I will go in search of Madame Leroy."

The Moujik found the governess still on the terrace, berating three very ill-humoured young gentlemen. Apologizing for his intrusion, he delivered Esmeralda's message. The brows of the young gentlemen cleared like magic, while Madame Leroy's became slightly overclouded. Obliged, however, to accept the situation, she answered frigidly: "I will go to the Archduchess at once."

"Pinsk is indebted to you," said the Moujik.

She paused a moment before she asked: "For what?"

"The care you bestow upon her daughters—and sons."

So humble were his tones that she could not be sure if the hair on his lips concealed a sneer or not.

Chapter Sixteen

Pink Kid Gloves

"Do you find the flies troublesome? May I employ this fan?"

"Is the sun in your eyes? Shall I open your parasol?"

"Are you feeling faint? Dare I refresh you with your vinaigrette?"

"The flies *are* a little over-attentive," admitted Esmeralda. "It would be most kind of Mr. Dumbarton to keep them off."

James seized the heart-shaped screen of pheasant feathers and plied it vigorously.

"The sun *is* somewhat overwhelming," agreed the Archduchess. "I should be grateful to Mr. Fawleigh for a touch of shade."

Up flew the standard of the little parasol, whose fringed dome Percy adjusted to her needs.

"A whiff of the vinaigrette from Mr. Lorrequer," confessed the beautiful invalid, "would help more than anything to restore me to myself."

At a touch from Terence the turquoise lid turned back, the stopper was removed, and the aromatic contents duly wafted beneath the most fascinating nostril in the world.

A *chaise longue* had been placed upon the terrace. Esmeralda, supported by several fancy-work cushions, reclined thereon, with a rich rug over the lower portion of her person. The sprained foot rested on a little bolster. Her *toilette* (from Storr and Mortimer) was perfect. A *capote* in tulle, ornamented with pink flowers, protected her complexion from the ardours of Phoebus. The gown of snowy *mousseline* had two flounces, run through with rose-pink ribbon, which emerged at two spots on the left as flat bows with streamers. A similar ribbon, but broader, encircled the waist; the transparent bodice, gathered in points to the throat, was fitted trimly over the corset which rose only to the bust, where the tantalising rose-white skin glowed softly through the shirrings of the muslin. Tiny puffed sleeves came barely below the shoulders; the charms of the rounded arms were displayed to the tapered wrists, where broad gold bracelets held in place the little pink kid gloves. A console placed to hand accommodated the fair invalid's dainty adjuncts: ivory-handled parasol, lace-flounced handkerchief, feather hand-screen, turquoise vinaigrette.

Beside the *chaise*, in a cradle that had rocked many a Tarletan, the infant slept, in readiness.

And about mother and child fluttered three attendant beaux, handling vinaigrette and parasol and fan as though such things as guns, rods, and hunting-horns did not exist.

"I am afraid," said Esmeralda, with her sweetest smile, "that I am spoiling a good day's sport for you gentlemen."

"Why, as to that, ma'am," offered James Dumbarton, "one canna go feeshing every day, after all; one might as well do something else for a change."

"What gallantry! Does Mr. Lorrequer echo that sentiment?" She dazzled the Irishman with her liquid orbs.

"Indade, and I do not! It is mighty poorly expressed. I say one can do nothing better on a bright summer day than abandon the chase for the sake of the charmer."

"Prettily said!" The little pink kid gloves applauded delicately. "But I dare say Mr. Fawleigh, who stands there so silent, is itching to be riding."

"Englishmen do not itch," said Percy, stiffly.

"What a fortunate race! In Pinsk we itch constantly for sport, for danger, for love. It is I who express myself poorly in your tongue. Should I have said, Mr. Fawleigh pants to be riding? Or do not Englishmen pant either?"

"They do," said Percy awkwardly, "with you at their side, ma'am."

"Bravo, Mr. Fawleigh! I thought only Frenchmen could turn compliments. Here's Kaspar. What can he want?"

The Moujik approached and addressed himself to Terence.

"Excuse me, sir, but Jack Turner" (the Head Keeper) "wishes to speak to you about a fox that was found shot yesterday in the park."

"Does the spalpeen think I did it?" shouted Terry.

"He did not say, sir. He simply gave me the message. As Terence bounded away Kaspar turned to James. "And you, sir, Henry Baynes" (the Bailiff) "would like to see you."

"What for? Does he think I've shot a salmon?"

"How do I know?" shrugged Kaspar. "I merely repeat his words."

"Verra weel." But James Dumbarton withdrew with a very bad grace.

"And who," asked Percy, "wants me?"

"None that I know of," said Kaspar, and retired.

"None that I know of!" echoed Esmeralda. "Ah, our good Moujik does not know everything." Her cheeks dimpled; she stretched out a little pink kid hand, which Percy grasped.

"Do *you*," he stammered, "want *me*?

"I want a friend."

He hesitated, cleared his throat, and said: "May I be that friend?"

"How can I say? What do we know of each other? Esmeralda of Limoges—who is she? A Margrave's daughter, the widow of an Archduke, the mother of an heir, the possessor of an estate of eighty thousand a year. That is all. And the Honourable Fawleigh, who is he?"

"Well, if it comes to that—" Percy did not usually expatiate on himself, but he felt some expansiveness was the lady's due. "The son of the Duke of Fawleigh, with a present estate of ten thousand, heir to five times that and three or four castles. A town house in Belgravia. Well known in Almacks. Can jump anything."

She smiled—and shook her head. "Having said so much, how much wiser are we? Friends *know* each other. Ah, Percy! I need a friend."

She seemed unaware that his name had escaped her lips. But it broke down the young Englishman's reserve. This time he cried, not tentative, but in earnest:

"Oh, let me be that friend!"

"Can you ?—and will you?"

"I will! I can! Anything!"

"Men, men. They swear so much. They swear so readily."

"Tell me what I can do!"

"But can I trust you?"

"I am an English gentleman."

"That is enough. When I asked: 'Can I trust you?' I did not mean: 'Can I trust your honour?' but 'Can I trust you not to misinterpret what it is I need of you?'"

She fixed her glowing gaze on Percy Fawleigh, who, roused in a way that surprised himself, exclaimed:

"My life! Ask for my life!"

She smiled and sighed. "Your life! Ah, yes. It would be simple if I asked you for *that*. A man is proud to offer his life for a lady. It is a gift noble enough to be asked for and conceded. It is the lesser demand which sounds ignoble, and seems to cast a shadow on the asker because it bestows no glory on the giver."

"But what? What sort of thing?"

"Money," she said.

"Oh—money." His voice was decidedly less ardent.

"Yes!" she cried passionately. "And now let us never speak of it again!"

"What!"

"Leave me."

"But, Duchess—"

"Archduchess. Leave me this instant."

"Esmeralda—"

"No, Percy, no. I read you in your voice. You did not ask yourself why I, with all my fortune, am, for the moment, in need of a little money. Your instant thought was: She is going to ask me for a trifling loan—how can I get out of it? Oh, easily! You do not have to try. I send you away."

"Esmeralda!"

"Go."

"You wrong me."

"Prove it."

"How much do you want?"

"Nothing, from one who cannot give without requiring an explanation."

"Unjust! I have never suggested an explanation."

"Of course not, when you had not even reached the point that might have justified it—in a usurer. Forget that I ever asked you, as a gentleman. I ask for nothing, and shall not explain anything."

"No gentleman would sink so low as to expect it. How much do you want?"

"Nothing at all—from you. Is not that Mr. Dumbarton returning?"

"To the d*v*l with Mr. Dumbarton! How much do you want?"

"I don't want anything. I only need it."

"A thousand? Two thousand?"

"Ten."

He turned towards the house. "Farewell, then, Percy."

"Nay, not farewell, Esmeralda, never farewell!"

"But you are leaving me, you are going—"

"To write you a cheque."

"My friend!"

The word—or the tone in which she uttered it—brought him back, to her feet. She held out a pink kid hand. He pressed his lips to the little hole in the palm and hastened away, so exalted that he hardly noticed the Scot who, as the Englishman vanished into the house, appeared from the side of the terrace. He was looking rather sulkier than usual, but brightened up on finding Esmeralda alone, and sat down by her couch, remarking:

"That Moujik of your brother's is a sumph."

"It describes him admirably. But what makes you say so?"

"Because when, after some trouble, I found the Baillie, he said he had sent me no such message at all."

"How strange. I wonder—" Here Esmeralda paused.

"You're wondering what?"

"Never mind. A woman's wonder is aroused by trifles. For instance, since last night I have wondered much about *you*."

"Have you indeed?" The Scot looked round, saw nobody in view, and ventured to pose an arm on the head of the *chaise*. This position gave him the advantage of being able to lean a little closer to his beautiful *vis-à-vis*. Breathing heavily, he managed to ask her:

"What?"

"What?"

"What have ye been wondering aboot me?"

"Oh!" She shook her head archly, with an alluring touch of embarrassment. "Do you want to put me to the blush? I defy you. I used to blush. Girls do. But rarely widows."

"Ay," said James, "but the Archduchess of Limoges is a rare widow."

His aptness surprised him, and produced from the pink gloves the plaudits he had envied Terence earlier.

"Such wit deserves a reward."

"May I name mine?"

"It depends on what it is. You might ask—much." She caressed her lips with the edge of her feathered fan.

James hesitated. "Tell me what you were wondering aboot me."

"Is that all? You're just a curious man, and nothing more? Well, as you will. I wondered, for one thing," she indicated the enormous cairngorms that clasped his tartan and adorned his finger, "how the son of a Scottish Laird came to possess such handsome jewellery. Are not Scotch Lairds notoriously poor?"

"Whence got you that idea?"

"I have heard that their estates are nothing but heather."

"Havers!" cried James. "My father's estate is worth a rental of eighty thousand to him."

"No more?" She laid a consoling pink hand upon his arm; pleased, though surprised, he ventured to cover it with a brawny one.

"Why, how much more would you have?"

"I? Not so much. I was not dreaming of asking you for eighty thousand."

James removed his hand.

"Only for ten," she said, indifferently.

"For ten? Ten—pounds!"

"Ten thousand."

His face grew purple.

She tossed back her curls, and laughed. "How you blush! Ought I? I know it is an almost ignoble request. But I really ask no more. I am not greedy. Pending my rents from Limoges, ten thousand will just suffice. I may have to impose myself on Braddon for some days—the servants must be suitably recompensed; and I should like to make the governess a little present. The coachman, too—I must make good his losses: his couch and horses, his cape, which was badly torn. Then there are the young ladies. The Margrave's guests invariably marked their visits by the gift to the daughter of the house of some rich gem." She played with the ruby pendants in her ears. "A pretty custom. There are three daughters here. Three pearl tiaras, perhaps. Still, ten thousand will do."

James rose to his feet.

"Dear friend! There is an inkpot in the saloon."

"And what if there is?"

"You are going to write me a cheque?"

"I am not," said James.

"You mean, you have the cash with you? Better still!"

"I have not. Ten thousand!" He paused. "And if I had—"

"Well, if you had?"

"I should stick to it," blurted James, very abruptly. She stared, as though her ears had not heard aright. Her hand flew to her heart, as one who had received a mortal wound. Then, her face burning with pride and scorn, she sprang up—only to utter a cry of pain.

"My foot!"

She staggered. James was forced to run and support her. She sank involuntarily into his arms, exclaiming: "Do not touch me!" She thrust at him with her little pink kid hands.

But the feeble effort was too much for her; she groaned with agony, and buried her face in his bosom. His arms tightened about her. She raised her eyes to his; those eyes flashed fire.

"My G*d! What brutes men are! They deny a woman a nothing, and take her all! The tiny pink gloves struck a tattoo on his heart. She burst into tears. Her agitation, exhibited at such close quarters, was contagious. He trembled with confusion, pride, pleasure, pain, with self-reproach—with love!

"My lady—"

"*Your* lady? Oh, never!"

"I say you shall be!"

"Release me, Mr. Dumbarton. Esmeralda *yours*? Out upon your dishonourable proposals!"

"Is it dishonourable to ask you to become the bride of eighty thousand a year?"

"A paltry eighty thousand? No doubt you would be delighted to tell your laird that you were wedded to the Limoges millions."

"Meellions!"

"As though love were a matter for barter and sale! Eighty thousand! What sort of establishment will Mrs. James Dumbarton enjoy? One in which a penurious husband will grudge her pin-money for those small compliments which society expects and exacts."

"But with the Limoges meellions," argued James, "ye wull na *need* pin-money."

She clasped her hands before her, and with heaving bosom, expanded nostrils, and fixed eye stood motionless, like some noble production from the divine chisel of Canova. "James," she said, and the syllable made his heart thump, "the man I elect for my spouse will possess all I am, all I have. I could not consent to be his without yielding him *everything*—person, and soul, and fortune. But he that values my fortune above my soul, shall never possess my person." She withdrew from his embrace, bit her cheek to control the agony of the movement, and leaned on the couch, with fluttering eyelids. "Go," she whispered.

"For why?"

"You should know why."

"I dinna."

"Because," she murmured, "I do not wish to despise where most I—"

"Whaur most ye—?"

"James, I implore you!"

"Esmeralda! Whaur most ye—?"

"Feel."

"But feel, what?"

"Spare me! Are you quite merciless?"

She paused, and cast a glance in the direction of the French windows. James followed her eyes, and beheld Percy Fawleigh emerging, envelope in hand. He waved it lightly, confidently; she put a pink kid finger to her lips, and wafted him a kiss.

James saw ravishing beauty and golden millions receding. He braced himself, and turned sharply on his heel.

"Where are you going?" cried she.

"Tae write you a cheque."

He brushed rudely past Percy Fawleigh in the doorway.

The Englishman, slightly ruffled, approached the lady, and dropped his plain sealed envelope in her lap. She fingered it tenderly.

"A love-letter, Percy?"

"I ventured to enclose a little line." He seized her hand.

"It asked—"

"Hush! Someone is coming!"

"It ventured to suggest—a closer acquaintance."

"Closer?"

"Much closer!"

"I understand. How weak we women are. Do not wait now—to-night—"

"To-night! When? Where?"

"I will send word. Go quickly. Let no one suspect what we are to each other."

He saw the wisdom of this, and bounded down the terrace staircase as Terence Lorrequer leapt from the rear of the house. He reached the couch like a greyhound coursing a rabbit.

"Blessed be the saints!" cried he. "I find ye alone. Was not that Percy Fawleigh just gone from you?"

"It was."

"Then he won't come back. And James is still absent. I have my lovely charmer to myself. Now was not I clever to be rid of them?"

"I don't understand."

"This was the way of it. I have a thousand things to say to you that can only be said when your two little ears are mine. But that stiff young Englishman and that dour Scot were resolved, I could see, to share you with me. The Lorrequers share their females with nobody!"

"Are you not proceeding rather fast?"

"The faster the better. While you were still in your room, I waylaid that Moujik of yours, and bribed him to fetch away James under some pretext, and me under some other."

"But why you?"

"That was the beauty of it. I wished you to be through with Mr. Fawleigh before I returned. For he is my strongest rival."

"Yet you left him the field to make his impression."

"So that I could return and efface it. He laughs best who laughs last."

"And what about Mr. Dumbarton's impression?"

"James? He can't make one to save the life of him." She began to laugh. "I love a woman who can see a joke."

"Yes, yes, but I am laughing at my joke, not yours."

"Laugh, then, and I'll be content with looking at you."

"Content with so little?" Her cheeks dimpled demurely. The next moment she was in the Irishman's arms, panting for breath against his amorous lips.

"Stay, stay!" She struggled, and managed to free her mouth. "You forget—I am a widow."

"Wrong, my angel! I have remembered it with satisfaction this thirteen hours. Are you long a widow?"

"A year."

"That's long enough. Where did the Archduke die?"

"In Greece."

"Of what?"

"Swimming the Hellespont."

"The black-hearted villain!"

"Why?"

"No man swims the Hellespont if a lady isn't in it."

"How do you know I was not in it?"

"Would any man swim the Hellespont for his wife?"

"You are right. She was a beautiful odalisque. Her name, Zayda. The Archduke was impulsive. He saw her on the other bank, and leapt."

"Bad cess to him![1] I am heartily glad he drowned."

"Terry." The pink kid gloves were laid on his shoulders. "He was the father of my sleeping infant."

"He did not deserve to be."

"He left us—penniless."

---

1 Mem: Ought I to write this cess? Ask Sir Terence.—A.G.

"Ah, that he were alive, so I could kill him!"

"My friend."

"You have none better."

"When the thunderstorm o'erturned my coach last night—"

"Thrice-blessed storm!"

"Do you know where I was going?"

"To Staleybridge."

"But you do not know why."

"Tell me."

"It was—to sell myself."

"Good G*d alive!"

"To one who shall be nameless. He knew my plight. He sent his insidious messengers to Limoges. Oh, Terence Lorrequer! Blame me if you must."

The hot-headed Irishman shook his fists at heaven. "Could you leave your sleeping infant to starve?" he shouted.

She wept.

He wiped away her tears with a hundred kisses.

When she could speak, she whispered: "He offered me ten thousand pounds."

"The spalpeen!" The Irishman tore his pocket-book from his breast; without stopping to think, he pulled out a wad of banknotes—ten of them! Each good for a thousand pounds. Showering them into the sleeping infant's crib—"There, poor innocent, there!" he cried aloud. "The price of thy mother's shame."

"Ah, Mr. Lorrequer!"

"And after all it is I who have paid—"

"The price of my shame?"

"Esmeralda! You mean—?"

"Ask me not what I mean. I am a woman of honour. I can pay a debt."

"To-night!"

"Terence!"

"The hour!"

"I will send you word."

"I cannot wait." She thought that he would seduce her then and there. He grasped her arm. She held up a pink kid hand.

"My infant needs me," she reminded him gently.

Irishman though he was, he was a gentleman. He withdrew. When James Dumbarton reappeared on the terrace, cheque in hand, mother and child were one. Averting his eyes, James laid the folded slip on the console, secured it with the turquoise vinaigrette, and passed behind the *chaise longue*. He only paused there long enough to mutter: "Tae-nicht?"

"To-night," she echoed.

"What time?"

"I will send you word."

Chapter Seventeen

Love Vignettes

NOON

High on the bridge above the cataract, stood Georgiana waiting for her love. This was the hour named in his treasured note. This was the place where, yesterday, he had waited in vain.

"Do not fail him," the Moujik had whispered. Fail him?

Never again! Though he came not in an hour, a day, a year, here would she wait till he, or his spirit, joined her.

She had not to wait a minute. Skirting the narrow ledge which ascended the face of the rock, she saw Count Stanislaw coming. The journey half made, he paused, pressing his hand to his side. Her heart turned to ice in her breast. What if he fell? Clear as a bell, her voice rang down to him.

"Count! Count Stanislaw! If you are giddy, do not attempt the ascent. Go back—or stay till I can come to you."

"No, Georgiana! It is I who come to you."

(Georgiana! Her name on his lips! Heaven opened above her.)

"But you are sadly out of breath."

"Say, out of heart."

"How can that be?"

"Yesterday—it was slain."

His voice had taken so melancholy a tone, that she could not form an answer. She stood stricken on the bridge, till the Bastard stood beside her.

"You," he said, "slew it."

The birds grew mute, the wind died out of the trees ; a mortal stillness enveloped the ravine. Only the rushing of the cataract spoke to their ears, and it did not speak of life.

Presently the proud girl's lips parted, and words issued forth; they seemed to be impelled from her by some spiritual force of which she was hardly aware.

"I have committed a sin. Then, do not spare me. If you have suffered, I have suffered too. Yesterday I thought I should enter Paradise hand in hand with one—to whom I have dealt a worse than mortal hurt. It is no excuse that I was compelled to do it. I should not have allowed myself to be compelled. I should have died first. It is not too late. Perhaps there will be forgiveness for me in heaven."

She swayed, and would have fallen—had not a manly arm encircled her waist.

"Georgiana! Rash one! What were you going to do?"

"Expiate my sin, Count Stanislaw."

"Noble, deluded girl! You have not sinned."

"Ah, but I have. I have wounded you to the quick."

"Not so!" He pressed her hand to his lips. "The wound proceeded from my own darker self. Alas! My Georgiana's pure, proud nature knows all too little of life, too little of man. We are wayward, we are cruel when we love."

"Love?" she whispered.

"Ay, love!" he repeated, passionately. "The slaves and tyrants of those we cherish most. Say not that you, the innocent, have sinned. What right had I to pen you that bold note—?"

"It is my dearest treasure; I would not have it unpenned for all the world."

"What right had I to steal like a thief to your room?"

"It was you who came and placed it in my bed?"

"What right had my lips to press the pillow that would press your check?"

"You kissed my pillow?"

"What right had I to ask—to hope—to expect—that you should feel for me what I feel for you?"

"Oh!" sighed Georgiana, so overcome, that had he not held her the cataract would have received her.

"None, Georgiana, none! I had no rights. You had, and exercised the right to reject that presumptuous letter, to show its mad writer, by absence and silence, your answer. And when I came to this hallowed spot at noon—and saw not the form that I looked for—when I waited, hour after hour, and heard not her footstep—what right had I to groan and beat my breast, and cry aloud: 'I am betrayed! Betrayed!' Echo gave back the hollow cry: '*Betrayed*!' 'Betrayed by Georgiana, whom I love!' '*You love!*' 'Who loves not me!' '*Not you!*' 'And nothing is left to Stanislaw, but to die!' The forest caves reverberated: '*Die!*' I tore off my coat—loosened my cravat—sent one last prayer for mercy speeding upward, and then, with my loved one's name on my lips, I—"

"No!" exclaimed Georgiana. "No, no, no!" For in his frenzy, the Pole had suited his action to the word, rent open his coat, ruffled his raven locks, and appeared about to fling himself into the miniature abyss. The Triplet clung to him with all her strength, fragile compared to his—yet it sufficed!

His anguish subsided into a bit of shuddering, and sinking on his knees—"Oh, Georgiana! I cannot live without you!" Her face, her very figure, filled with light.

"Then let us die together!"

"Or live together!"

He was on his feet again, his arms flung wide. She closed her eyes and crossed her hands on her bosom.

"Say what you mean, noble Bastard, for I am yours. You are my will, my master, and my law. If you bid me die, I will die. If live, I will live."

"Then live!" he whispered ardently. "Come away with me!"

"Away? Go from my home? Go from my sisters?"

"To-morrow, at midnight, I will have a carriage at the postern."

"A carriage—at midnight!"

"Be there, if you have the courage, cloaked and hooded,. and we will drive away, by night and day, over hill and dale, to Pinsk."

"To Pinsk!"

"There, in the great Cathedral in the city, lit by a thousand candles, surrounded by the populace and the peers, there while the organ music rolls to the fretted dome, there, my belovèd, I will make you my bride."

So still she stood, he knew not if she had heard him.

"Speak, Georgiana!"

"Stanislaw, I come!"

AFTERNOON

The shadows lengthened over the Roman amphitheatre (a replica *in petto* of one in Italy), where Adeline, whose tryst was at four o'clock, sat counting the minutes, She had sped to the spot engraved on her heart, although, when the Moujik muttered the word that thrilled it with joy, there were still five hours to wait ere the moment of rapture. But not again would she risk being severed from bliss; in the crumbling theatre only she deemed herself safe. Five hours spent waiting for Stanislaw would pass like five seconds—or if the time seemed long, 'twould be one long day-dream, replete with life's sweetest offering: expectation. Furnished with her thoughts, she sat in the shade of woodbine and eglantine, heedless of passing time. Nobody came. Only the bees hummed in the tendrilled bower, and butterflies frequented the wild rose. One, of more splendid attractions than the rest, caught her attention. It hung on a scented briar above her head., Two charming hands, as soft as summer cloud, cupped and imprisoned it! The fragile wings protested; Adeline laughed! Her light straw hat lay beside her on the grass. She slipped her handsome captive under its brim, and told herself she would only let him go when one more handsome came to capture her!—then blushed at the wanton thought, and lay back on the scented turf, to dream again—till she slept. How long, she did not know. She thought her butterfly had settled on her lips—opened her eyes—Count Stanislaw was leaning over her!

"Oh!" she cried, in soft bewilderment. "Has it escaped? Has it flown?"

"Of what are you speaking?"

"My butterfly."

"Is there a butterfly?"

"I am confused with sleep. I thought it brushed my lips."

"A dream, perhaps."

"We can soon see. It is, it was, there." She pointed to her hat; he stayed her hand.

"Nay, do not lift it, Adeline."

"Why not?"

"Would you destroy, or even confirm, a dream? What is more lovely than a dream uncaptured?"

"But some time—some time, must we not awake?"

"And when we do, the dream escapes for ever. Do not lift your hat yet."

"I will not," she promised, "till you bid me to." She smiled at him, and suddenly looked sad.

"What causes the shadow?" he asked tenderly.

"I have just remembered. As I sat here waiting, I wondered if you would be angry when you came."

"*I* Angry with *you*? How could you suppose it?"

"Because yesterday—"

"Yesterday is wiped out, sweet Adeline. Yesterday there was storm in the air, for everyone. To-day—" He swept his arm out, indicating the sun on the arena, the sky translucent, innocent of clouds.

"Oh, yes, it is happy, and I am too," she said.

"And I am too."

He took her hand in his. She blushed a little. Who would have thought the twining of fingers could be so sweet? To cover her confusion she inquired:

"What made you choose this theatre for our meeting?"

"I have often watched you here. I knew you loved it."

"But when," she said, amazed, "when did you watch me? You have only just begun to quit your couch."

"Oh, it was long before Braddon sheltered me. Sometimes, after those morning rides, which seem so distant I can scarcely recall them—"

"But I," said Adeline, "will never forget them."

"After those rides, taken that I might see you—"

"Me, and my sisters."

"You! *You*, Adeline!—I could not rest in my lodging. I returned to stroll in the park, more times than once; and so I came to know your favourite haunt. Hidden in this very bower, when you knew it not, I saw you dancing on the sward down there, dancing light as a butterfly. Your gauze scarf floated gracefully about you, the fortunate breeze played with your golden curls, you hovered and dipped, hovered and dipped again, and at last, as you sank to the ground, you raised your head and wafted a kiss from your hand—in my direction."

To raise her head now would have been beyond her powers. Adeline hung it. "I had not seen you."

"I wished, I hoped you had! To whom, if not to me, did you blow that kiss? Kisses are not blown into the air for nothing."

"Well, then, I confess, the kiss was blown to—somebody. I like to come here and imagine myself the dancer in this theatre—I people the seats with Roman lords and ladies, in gold and purple silks—and I dance for them."

"And there is one among the throng, one whom you dance for more than any other."

"How did you guess?" she murmured.

"The Emperor, perhaps."

"How did you guess?"

"His hair is black, and his eyes are black—"

"Count Stanislaw!"

"And it is to him the dancing butterfly wafts her kiss."

She hid her face in her hands.

She heard him say: "Let us look at your prisoner." She could neither move nor look. She heard him reach for her hat, lift it, and sigh. Oh, had the butterfly flown? Then, perhaps, as she slept, its wing had brushed her lips, and not, as she had begun to think—to hope—Oh heavens! What was she thinking? That he, Count Stanislaw—? Bold, shameful thought! She could never look him in the face again. But if the butterfly had not escaped, what else—who else—?

She waited breathlessly for him to speak. He said no word. She could bear the suspense no longer, and murmured through her fingers: "The butterfly—is it flown?"

"No, Adeline."

"It is—still there?"

"No, Adeline.,,

(What then?)

"It is dead," said Stanislaw.

Her hands dropped from her face. He knelt beside her, holding her hat inverted in his hand. Within it lay a lifeless Purple Emperor. She burst into tears. He took her in his arms.

"I am the most heartless creature alive," she wept.

"No, my sweet girl, but you do not know your power. Beauty has never known its power to slay."

"I did not mean to slay the butterfly."

"You did not mean to wound me yesterday. Yet wounded I was—and the butterfly is slain."

"I will never, never, never do so again!"

"Do you promise me, Adeline?"

"I promise you anything!"

His cheek pressed to hers was bathed with her flowing tears. "I shall claim that promise very soon," he whispered.

"Whenever you will."

"To-night!"

She looked at him, wondering. "What is it you will claim of me to-night?"

"Your faith and trust in me."

"You know they are yours."

"Prove it! To-morrow night, my Adeline, I must go."

"Go—where?"

"Away from Braddon."

"Ah, say not so!" she cried.

"Alas, it is true. My sister has brought me tidings of serious import. I am wanted in Pinsk, and nobody must suspect it."

"And yet you tell *me*."

"You have my faith and trust."

"I will deserve them."

"You have—my love!"

"Ah, that I can never deserve," she breathed, o'ercome.

"There is only one way to deserve love, Adeline, and that is to restore it."

She hid her face again.

"At midnight to-morrow," whispered Stanislaw in her ear, "there will be a travelling carriage at the postern."

"For you?"

"Must I go alone?"

She clung to him, as the ivy clings to the oak. "I cannot, cannot let you go alone."

"My Adeline! I knew you would not fail me. Be there, in cloak and hood and we will drive away, by flood and field, to Pinsk."

"To Pinsk!"

"There, in the Chapel Royal, lit by ten thousand candles, thronged with lords and ladies in purple and gold, I will claim the kiss you threw me when you knew it not."

"Stanislaw!"

"Or must your Purple Emperor die twice?"

"Oh, Stanislaw! I come!"

TWILIGHT

And Caroline, pure, pensive Caroline? From eleven o'clock till eight, the appointed hour, she sat in the ruined temple by the lake. A book bound in satin lay on the marble altar. Ever and anon her slender finger turned a gilt-edged page, and she conned some chosen verse she had copied there. But she knew them by heart, these verses chosen with unerring taste, and often her lips moved silently, while her eyes traversed the lake to the Mausoleum, whose reflection darkened the far side of the water. It was the time of water-lily and dragonfly. Wax cups with hearts of gold floated in scores upon their flat round leaves; above them shimmered and flashed slim shining bodies, like tiny streaks of blue and crimson fire. In the groves of ash and willow set round the lake birds choired all day.

Then the shadow of the broken column, upon whose fallen capital she was seated, became a black pointing finger on the grass. Day died. The blue and white water changed to amber and amethyst. The dragonflies folded up their gauzy wings, the lilies one by one closed up their buds. The thrush sang his last song, the nightingale her first. In the dream-like air of twilight, which robbed all things of their hues, and turned the maiden to the semblance of a ghost, one object in that scene grew ever more solid, ever more real: the tomb. Caroline knelt beside the altar, and prayed.

The bells of Braddon rang out eight o'clock.

She opened her eyes. She was no longer alone in the little temple. Beside her at the altar knelt the figure of one to whom she knelt in her heart. Black-garmented, beside the white-robed maid.

Their eyes met gravely, neither smiled nor faltered.

"Stanislaw."

"Caroline."

"Do you hear the bells?"

"I do."

"What do they say to you?"

"Stanislaw is deaf to their message till Caroline tells him what they say to her."

"They say to me many things. Sometimes they ring for joy, sometimes for grief."

"For which to-night?"

She was silent.

He asked: "What were you praying for just now?"

"Not for myself. For another."

"Whom?"

"You know."

Now he was silent. Strange! This gentle girl, the most timid of the three, gained in the starlight a serenity that awed him. She was like a white flower that blooms with the coming of night. He could almost believe a perfume issued from her. He could not pretend or prevaricate in her presence.

"Yes, Caroline, I know. You prayed for me."

"I did."

"But what you prayed I cannot dare to guess."

"I will tell you presently. You also prayed."

"I prayed—for myself. You see how different a man is from a woman."

"It was G*d who made him so, and I am glad."

"I prayed—that you did not hate me."

"How idle a prayer! Nothing could make me hate you."

"I prayed—that you should forgive me yesterday's injury."

"Yesterday's injury! It was mine, to you."

"Unwittingly committed. I injured by misinterpreting you and allowing you to see it. I need your pardon."

"I pardon you, then, although I hardly know why."

"I prayed—for something else."

"For what?"

"Your love."

She sat very still. He laid his head on her knee. Her hand caressed his hair. He knew not whether this was the ecstasy of earth or heaven. While her fingers lingered on his brow he heard her open the book upon the altar. As from a great distance her voice came to him.

> "'Say, what shall still this bounding heart,
> Bounding as boundless—strong and wild?—
> Or what shall heal each wounded part,
> With gentlest healings, soft and mild,
> And still this restless storm of breath?'
> DEATH!"

He turned his head on her knee that he might see her. Her face was shining with an unearthly light. He spoke under his breath.

"The poem you were going to read me on my sickbed." Her mild eyes dwelt on him as she proceeded:

> "What, what shall change my love for thee!
> The intensest love heart ever felt; What bound its deep infinity,
> And bid it have no power to melt,
> Scattering its dreams,—above,—beneath?'—
> DEATH!"

A shudder passed through his frame. "No more!" he cried. "No more! Thy love and death must not occupy the same breath! Would'st tell me of the intensest love heart ever felt, only to snatch it from me? Would'st confess thy bounding heart, and bid me lose it in infinity? No, no, dear Saint! Thou can'st not be so cruel!"

He flung himself, racked with sobs, upon her breast. She clasped him as a mother might her child—a sister, a brother—a wife, an erring husband!

"Hush, hush. Your prayer was answered, noble Bastard. It is true I love you. It is enough that I do. I can die, bereft."

"It is not enough!" he cried, impetuously; and then, imploringly: "Forgive my wildness. But why should you die—when you are not bereft?"

"Without your love," said Caroline, "I am."

"You have my love! My love is yours!" he vowed. "Heavenly angel! O not turn so pale or I shall think I hold a spirit in these arms. My Caroline, look up! Oh, Caroline, consent to live, for Stanislaw!"

The fair girl raised her head like a flower revived. "For Stanislaw, I will consent to anything."

They clung together, two castaways in a storm. Alone, they must succumb; their salvation lay in each other.

"I prayed," whispered Stanislaw, "the day would come when in some little wayside church in Pinsk we should kneel at another altar and pledge our plight."

"In Pinsk," she murmured, like one in a trance.

"Does the thought appal you?" he asked tenderly.

She threw back her head, the moon shone full on her white throat and dilated eyes, which looked beyond, not on him. He seemed to hold a sacrificial victim in his embrace.

"Yes, yes, it appals me, it is too much bliss! More bliss than mortal woman has a right to. I love, I am content to die for you. But *you*,—love *me!* Oh no, it is not possible!"

"It is true, my belovèd! Is the time not come for you to say what prayer you breathed at the altar?"

"I prayed," said Caroline, faintly, "that you should be happy, though my heart should break."

He folded her to his bosom. "If Caroline's heart break, how can I be happy? Only your happiness keeps my heart whole. My Caroline! the bells of Braddon were no knell, but joy bells. They did not ring for parting, but for union. Caroline, come with me!"·

"Wherever, whenever you will."

"To Pinsk, then, to-morrow night! Put on a hooded cloak, be at the postern; at midnight I shall have a carriage there. We two will drive o'er wood and water to my native land, and there, in some simple shrine, lit by one taper, we will be made one for life!"

"And for death," said Caroline.

Chapter Eighteen

La Polonaise!

———

(A Lesson in Deportment)

That night saw no gathering in the saloon. None of the young ladies put in an appearance. Each on her return to the house had pleaded a headache and gone to her room. Esmeralda and Pauline were the only ladies to grace the supper-table. Stanislaw, too, was absent; but the three sportsmen assisted the Archduchess and the governess at a sumptuous feast of turbot and lobster sauce, duck and green peas, cream trifle and strawberries. Even they had not their usual appetites; as for the ladies, they merely toyed with their plates, and as soon as the meal was over Esmeralda begged to be excused.

"What, not one little tot of cherry brandy?" tempted Percy.

"I feel a headache coming on," she said.

Madame Leroy remarked, apparently to the air, that headache seemed a universal ailment. Esmeralda suggested that they might all be suffering from the aftermath of the storm. Pauline said, possibly so. Esmeralda then retired, with a bow for the governess, and sweet pathetic smiles for the cavaliers, who, left alone, consoled themselves with the port. Pauline, disturbed by the shadow of coming events, went upstairs to the wing where the

Triplets occupied three chambers, side by side. She tried the handle of Georgiana's door. It turned—but the door did not yield. For the first time in her life, Georgiana had locked it. The doors of Adeline and Caroline gave the same result. Pauline was now really uneasy. Were the girls within? Was this a subterfuge? Stanislaw, where was he? Her mouth became a hard thin line across her face. She rattled a handle, calling sharply:

"Caroline!"

A faint rustling told her that the room was occupied.

Then Caroline's voice, muffled and drowsy, answered.

"Is it you, Madame Leroy?"

"Who else can it be? You have locked your door. Are you ill?"

"No, madame. But—but I had fallen asleep."

"Very well. I am sorry I disturbed you. Sleep again." Adeline's next. At the rattle of the handle, Adeline's voice ejaculated:

"Oh!"

"Adeline!"

"Who is there?"

"Madame Leroy. Why have you fastened your door?"

"Oh, I—I had a headache."

"Is it better?"

"Yes, a little. I—have gone to bed."

"I see. I hope your head will be quite well in the morning." Last, Georgiana's. For some time there was no response to the rattling. It was she, then, whom Count Stanislaw had decoyed! Pauline banged on the panels. She was ready in her fury to break the door down. But her salvo of blows brought forth a startled:

"Good heavens!"

"Georgiana!"

"Yes, madame?"

"Your door is locked."

"I suppose I must have done it."

"I suppose the same. Who else? Why did not you answer

me?"

"I—have only just waked up. I am sorry."

"It does not signify. Do you want anything?"

"Only to sleep."

"Good-night, then."

"Good-night, madame."

The governess prowled away, her suspicions unsatisfied.

Such a thing had never happened before. And although each girl was in her chamber—who knew if one of them was not alone?

She hastened feverishly to Stanislaw's room. The door was ajar. She peeped within—it was vacant. Indifferent to the dictates of decorum, in two strides Madame Leroy was beside his bed, dragging the pillows angrily from the bolster. His nightshirt, neatly folded, lay between them. So, all was well! He had not gone in to any of the young ladies. She clasped the garment to her chest—then dropped it, shuddering, remembering far-off hours when nightshirts played no part in shameful scenes. With a suppressed scream, she rent the longcloth in two.

"This will not do," she muttered. "These olden furies, are they not yet dead in me? I must, I will control them!"

She ransacked his drawers for another, folded the nightshirt between pillow and bolster, straightened the covers, and crept away, taking the torn shirt with her. At the head of the stairs she paused and held her breath. There were whispering voices in the well of the hall. Two men down there, in secret confabulation. She scrupled not to play the eavesdropper.

"To-morrow, you say, at midnight?"

"And you know where."

"For two?"

"For four."

"Are you quite deaf to reason? How do you suppose you can carry it off?"

"I shall depend on the inspiration of the moment."

"By trebling your stakes, you will probably lose all."

"I must take that risk. The thought of losing any is pure anguish."

"Better anguish than failure."

"Then desert me, like a rat. I can live and die alone!"

"No heroics, my dear master, I beg of you. I sha'n't desert you. You seem to have burned your boats, so we must make the best of it. After all—" (a chuckle that made the listener's blood run cold)— "it will come as a triple shock to the old Lord. I'll see to everything, and will be there to escort you."

"To heaven on earth!"

"Tcha-tcha!" said Kaspar.

Stanislaw bounded, noiseless as a shadow, up the stairs. Pauline shrank back in a convenient niche. He passed without seeing her. She feared his observation less than Kaspar's. The Count was compact of emotion—and emotion can be played on. The Moujik's calculating brutality was another matter. He must not know she had a single inkling of their scheming—for scheming they were. If only she knew the nature of the conspiracy she must circumvent. All she had gathered was that something, somewhere, would happen at midnight to-morrow. But what? And where? To-morrow she must watch, and watch, and watch. Oh, that she had a hundred eyes, like Argos![1]

*   *   *

In their rooms, the Triplets sat appalled at themselves.

They had lied to their governess! Their drowsy voices had been feigned. Not one of them was abed. Each had been occupied with the same thing, her preparations for the impending flight. Each had collected a little bundle of mementoes: some trinket of their mother's, a lock of her hair, their father's mourning rings, a faded flower bestowed by Stanislaw, a few sketches and book-markers executed by themselves, as well as sundry trifles for the journey, a flask of Hungary water, a scarf, a muff. Their cloaks and hoods were ready; all that remained was the penning of sundry notes.

---

1   Mem: Argus?—A.G.

One to their guardian, one to Madame Leroy, and two (poor innocents!) to each of their sisters. If treachery *could* dwell in those pure breasts, each Triplet felt she was betraying her two other selves. They, who had always shared every thought and feeling in common, were now on the eve of an act which disregarded the bond begun at birth. Nay, even *ere* birth![1] Large tears dropped on these notes, as they folded and sealed them.

"Adieu, dear Adeline and Caroline!"

"Good-bye to my Caroline and Georgiana!"

"Farewell, Georgiana! Adeline, farewell!"

*   *   *

The next day everyone appeared as usual, and tried to act as though nothing had happened—was about to happen. Yet all day long the sisters avoided one another. They felt they could not meet each other's eyes, while their minds went over and over again his words, tones, looks, at the tryst. (And she, she alone, was his chosen!) All day long the sportsmen sought points of quarrel; hitherto the best of friends, their bonhomie was now destroyed by the meanest of human passions: JEALOUSY. All day long Esmeralda, her foot still requiring support, lay on the terrace playing her beaux like trout, yet always with her eyes on the valley road, as though she expected something from that quarter. All day long Stanislaw, paler than ever and with brighter eyes, brooded and seemed not to see anyone near him. And all day long, Pauline Leroy watched first one and then another like a lynx. Her only regret was that she could not watch Kaspar, who kept his place in the servants' quarters, and was invisible all day. But the rest of the company should not escape her! To-night she would assemble them in the saloon, and keep them there, if need be, until midnight! The conspiracy, be what it might, should be foiled.

Esmeralda alone was aware of the lynx-eyed woman. She found a moment, before the evening meal, to utter a warning word to Stanislaw. He had joined her on the terrace, where she was employing the time with a water-colour in her sketchbook.

---

1 Mem: ? Find out.—A.G.

"Madame Leroy suspects," she said, plying her brush.

"Suspects who, suspects what?"

"Everything and everybody. And I must say your manner, dear brother, gives her good grounds. Don't look so overwrought, so pre-occupied. Behave as though there were other people in the world besides yourself. Devote yourself after supper to restoring a natural atmosphere, and let us all go to bed as though nothing were brewing."

"Easily said."

"And done."

"What do you suggest I shall do?"

"Only what you did before I came. A little music and singing, if you like."

"Yes, music will fill in the time as well as anything."

"Even dancing," suggested Esmeralda, with a peculiar smile.

"You know," he said coldly, "how much I detest it."

"How strange to detest what one does so very well. You need not look daggers at me! By no means dance, but do exert yourself. Make yourself agreeable, speak more, act a little. Hist! Our dragon approaches!" Esmeralda described an arc in the air with her fan, and cried: "What a delicious evening, dear Madame Leroy! Did you ever see such tints upon the firmament? If only one could paint with nature's hand!"

"You sketch, I see," Pauline said drily.

"A mere amateur."

"May one look? A pretty talent, and quite imaginative."

Esmeralda had depicted the sun setting over the rocky heights, on the peak of which stood a man with chestnut hair in an ermine cloak.

"Who is he?" asked the governess.

"The Archduke, my late husband." Esmeralda sighed.

"Think me sentimental if you will. I ever seek to recall him as he lived."

"I'm not surprised. He seems to have been a splendid figure of a man."

"He was six foot two. The sketch does not do him justice. I am more proficient at the pianoforte than with my pencil."

"Perhaps you will condescend to play for us to-night?"

"With pleasure," conceded Esmeralda, graciously. "We will have a little concert." And as the governess retired, she murmured: "You see how easy it is, dear Stanislaw?"

Madame Leroy was more than satisfied. 'A little concert' would just suit her book; it would keep them together, and could be prolonged indefinitely.

*   *   *

They repaired after supper to the music room, a long and beautiful *salle* running the depth of the house, with windows along one side. Large urns of alabaster stood against the panels between the windows. The walls of eggshell blue were painted with lyres and pastoral pipes, the ceiling with rosy clouds and singing cupids. Gilt chairs and sofas, placed against the walls, left the pink marble floor free for performers. At one end of the room, where hung a small musicians' gallery, a fresco exhibited the god Apollo, crowned with sunrays, resplendent and adored among his Muses; at the opposite end, beneath a sea-blue dome depicting Tritons blowing conches, an elegant pianoforte by Clementi occupied a dais. Glittering lustres, branching from the walls, twinkled upon keys and music-rack; three others, depending from the ceiling, lighted the length of the room, which could easily have held two hundred people. The nine distributed there to-night seemed lost to one another; the dainty gold chairs they sat on were little islands on the smooth pink sea of the floor. Madame Leroy had had all the candles lighted, and the alabaster urns loaded with blooms. Outside, the summer night gathered its stars.

"What a splendid *salle*!" exclaimed Terence. "illumined and decorated fit for a fête."

"We are about to enjoy a feast of music," explained Madame Leroy. "The Archduchess, an expert exponent of the pianoforte, is going to favour us with some specimens of her powers."

"Nay, but," cried Esmeralda, "I must not be the sole executant, madame! I shall insist on singers to smother my mistakes. The young ladies, I hear, are perfect nightingales; while you, madame—"

"I seldom sing now. I never did sing much. Singing was not my gift," said the governess.

"What was your gift? For I am sure you had one."

Madame Leroy shrugged her shoulders. "One might call it—deportment."

"Deportment! How charming—and how circumspect! When my programme and my performers fall short, madame, perhaps you will give us a lesson in deportment." With a languorous glance round the room, she then remarked: "Can any gentleman support a poor invalid to the instrument?"

Six manly arms were tendered on the spot. She selected Percy's, by good luck the nearest. Terence ran to open the piano, and James took a seat by the piano-stool, determined to turn the fair performer's music, though he could hardly tell a quaver from a breve. The Triplets were disposed about the room, and Pauline had taken a sofa. close to the door, where, occupied with completing her pelerine, she could keep the clock in view: a life-size representation of the god Hermes inventing the lyre. The tortoise-shell, duly placed against his torso, contained the clock-face. Madame Leroy had only one purpose to-night—to let nobody pass through the door till the hands pointed to twelve. Above all, Stanislaw, who leaned in the farthest window, inhaling the perfumed night.

Esmeralda sat down at the keyboard, tried the ivory notes with fingers whiter still, and glided into a rippling *Cascade de Roses.* She played to admiration. At the conclusion the gentlemen clapped their hands vigorously, and cried for more. She gave them Linter's *Mazurka Elégante, La Vistule*, then dashed into the Tarantella from *La Muette de Portici.* Her brilliant execution evoked plaudits yet more vociferous, which she stilled by beckoning to Georgiana, Adeline, and Caroline.

"I insist on my right to a little vocal refreshment," she smiled. "My brother says you sing trios enchantingly. What shall it be?"

The young ladies, each with an elopement in view, felt that their voices would stifle in their throats, but they were too well bred to excuse themselves. They chose a wistful melody by Spohr, and acquitted themselves better than they would have expected. There was that in Esmeralda's touch on the keyboard which put new life into everything she essayed. Now it was she who expressed her enthusiasm.

"My brother is right! You sing like little angels, do they not, gentlemen? I, alas, can only sing like a woman."

She began to warble an impassioned love-song, in French. She had a luscious contralto, which set the blood vibrating. Not only her male hearers responded to it. The Triplets, regrouped on a settee below the dais, throbbed as they had not known the heart *could* throb. They did not (and perhaps it was as well!) understand the words of the song, but the melody, infused with that pulsating voice, was enough. This, *this* was love indeed! This was to be their lot when midnight struck! The song brought Stanislaw across the floor. He leaned on the flower-stands nearest to his belovèds, his trembling fingers tormented rose, jasmine, and larkspur. At the close of the song, the marble tiles at his feet were strewn with bruised petals.

"Pray, gentlemen, show us now what Britain can do!" cried the Archduchess; and, despite their protests, drew from Percy a hunting-song, from Terence a ditty by Moore, and from James a Border Ballad that roused them all. All but one, by the door, with her eyes on the torso of Hermes. The rest were clustered round the piano-stool like bees round their queen. Waves of light and warmth flowed from Esmeralda; her confident gaiety, tinged with continental abandon, dissolved their feelings of stiffness and constraint. They had all forgotten her who alone took no part in their pleasurable mood.

"Come, Stanislaw," commanded his sister, imperiously. "We shall not allow you to be silent any longer. He sings distractingly, does he not?" She appealed to the girls.

"He has never yet let us hear him sing," said Adeline. "But he promised, one night, to do so."

"Then the time is come." Esmeralda beckoned to the Count, who approached, with glittering eyes.

"Must I?"

"You must! What shall it be? A serenade? A battlesong ?"

"I will sing this." He placed a sheet of music on the stand.

"A polonaise? Excellent! I shall think I am back in Pinsk."

Esmeralda flung herself into the wild and passionate rhythm, and down the length of the room, in glowing tones, rang the stirring notes of Reichhardt's masterpiece: *"Were they meant but to deceive me—?"*

He sang the words as Pauline Leroy had not sung them. Not harshly, stridently, but passionately, adoringly, jealously, with all the varied emotions of which the heart that loves and doubts is capable. He had intended to sing something addressed to the tender bosoms of the Triplets, who hung on his voice with parted lips and swimming eyes—and yet he knew he was not addressing them. His song was directed solely at Madame Leroy, remote from him at the far end of the room, a dragon at her post. Why had he chosen this song?—her song!—to-night?

> *"Are they meant but to deceive me,*
> *Those fond words that tell of love?"*

What was she feeling, the woman intent on her pelerine? Resentment at his choice?—or secret triumph?

> *"Though my heart would trust them gladly,*
> *Though belief alone is bliss—"*

Her expression gave no clue to her inner feelings; she kept her locked face on her hideous work, never once lifting her eyes in the singer's direction. She might have been deaf, for any sign she gave. The rest of his audience was completely carried away.

> *"All my inmost soul concealing,*
> *Shall I sternly answer 'no'?*

Or each secret wish revealing
Shall my words unfetter'd flow?
Ever ling'ring, never speaking,
How my thoughts shall I express?
For my heart if you are seeking,
Strive to find it by a guess!"

He flung out the line like a challenge, himself surprised at the meaning that thrilled his voice—the defiant invitation, the consuming longing, the reckless d*v*lry of the final outburst of *'Tra-la-la-la-las'!* He made them sound like laughter mocking its own mortal wound, and concluded by bounding into the centre of the room, and, clicking his heels, dancing the last bars of the accompaniment with a grace and spirit that prostrated the onlookers.

"By jove!" exclaimed Percy. "Is that how the Polonaise is done?"

"No, it is how the Polonaise is half-done! It needs a lady to complete the movement. Esmeralda!" He flourished a hand. "Show them how we dance the Polonaise in Pinsk."

She shook her glossy curls. "You forget my foot. I shall not dance the Polonaise this month. But here—" She smiled down on the Triplets—"are *three* ladies who should be apt pupils."

"Oh, no, we cannot," they murmured. "We do not know the steps," said Georgiana.

"I will not pretend," said the Count, "the steps are very easy; but ladies who dance at all will master them quickly." He looked encouragingly towards Adeline—she understood! And rose obedient to his gallant gesture. Esmeralda began to play the song again, stopping, repeating, while Stanislaw gave the lesson. How well he gave it! How gloriously he danced! It was impossible to falter or stumble. Adeline, graceful as a fond gazelle, followed him charmingly, but after a turn of the room sank on the settee, flushed from the unusual exertions demanded by the figures. Esmeralda played on. Stanislaw offered his hand to Caroline. She rose and came to it like a homing-pigeon. Once more the lesson, once more the docile pupil, once more the turn round the room, he executing the steps with unrestraint and precision, she floating sylph-like through the fiery figures. On reaching the settee she sank beside Adeline like a dove on its nest, while, scarcely waiting for his summoning hand, Georgiana glided to take Caroline's place. She had watched the two previous lessons, needed none, and went round the room with him in stately dignity, to be re-united glowing to her sisters.

"Bravo!" cried Esmeralda, playing ever more *forte*. "You will soon dance *La Polonaise* like Polish women."

"Not if they dance from now till Doomsday!" shouted Madame Leroy. Her voice brought the astounded company to their feet.

The governess had leapt like a maenad into their midst. She clutched her knitting-needles as though they were a sheaf of poisoned daggers. "Dance? They? *La Polonaise!*" She shook with frenzied laughter. "Come, dance the Polonaise with me, Count Stanislaw!"

"You!" he stammered. "Shall I teach you the steps?"

Her lips curled back in a derisive snarl. "Oh, no, my Count! It is *I* who will teach *you*—a lesson in deportment."

They faced each other on the marble floor. They danced—the Bastard of Pinsk and—Fra Diavola! The music on the dais rose to *fortissimo*. It might have been music rising from the Pit.

None present had ever seen or dreamed of such dancing. It was less dancing than unlicensed passion; it embodied all the moods of so-called love: coquetry and repulsion, defiance and entreaty, exultation and madness, mastery and subjugation, now of the man, and now of the woman. Superb exponent as Stanislaw proved himself, Pauline la Reine outdanced him. Terrifying were the postures of her body, her stampeding rhythm, her arms that now commanded, now despaired! Appalling were her frozen attitudes, appalling her molten movements like streaming metal! Her ugly features expressed allurements unknown to beauty, glare of the panther, glance of the petrified hare. The devoured and the devouring! Sometimes she crouched, while Stanislaw stamped around her like her conqueror, sometimes she towered like a flame and burned him up; now with abandoned gestures she lured him to her, now with a shriek abandoned herself to him, and flung herself like his thrall at his spurning feet. Then up again, in a mad chase round the wheeling room, now she the pursuer, now he! Her dark hair fell from its confining bands, in her frenzy she tore her bodice from her shoulders, ripped out the dress improver, and emerged to sight in her calico chemise! Hair, fingers, arms were turned to flickering serpents, eyes to coals of fire, lips flowers that scorched who sought them. The onlookers were fixed as though they looked on Medusa—Esmeralda alone played on like one possessed by the demonic force that poured from the woman or devil who danced in their midst.

At last, with the scream of the d*mn*d on Judgment Day, she hurled herself at Stanislaw: he seized her, elevated her, and fell with her, on one knee. Her gasping form, half-clad, lay prone across it.

The music stopped.

Nobody spoke or stirred.

A voice from the music-gallery broke the spell.

"And the reason of this exhibition?" asked Lord Tarletan.

Chapter Nineteen

Esmeralda Swoons

———————

If petrifaction can re-double itself, it did so now in several of those present.

The three young men were merely somewhat embarrassed. They had witnessed a performance of the sort they would have appreciated in so-called haunts of pleasure, but till tonight they had hardly considered Braddon in this light. Caught thus indulging themselves by Braddon's master, their feelings were those of schoolboys about to be whipped. It was scarcely a scene to be participated in by gentlemen who recommended themselves as suitors to pure young girls.

Those same young girls sat white and mute as snow. Their great-uncle's voice had whipped like the crack of doom across a nightmare. Bewildered thought and feeling seethed within them, as they sat, horrified yet enthralled during the dance. That their governess should be capable of these things! That, being capable, she should exhibit them! Stanislaw?—ah, him they did not blame. They saw him as the prey of a vile tarantula, an octopus strangling him with inky claws.[1] Fain, fain would they have flown to rescue him, but the life in their limbs was congealed. Now their guardian

———————

1 Mero: If not claws, what? Find out.—A.G.

had come, like a champion; yet a champion whose eyes they could not meet.

What were the feelings of the beautiful *pianiste*? She sat like a statue, with her back to the gallery. She had no doubt of the identity of its occupant, and whatever she felt, she did not turn her head.

On the floor, the dancers kept their rigid posture. They might have been a group in bronze or black marble. For both, the voice from the gallery spelled disaster. Their coalblack eyes gazed up and down at each other, and Stanislaw's pallid lips formed one word:

"Tarletan?"

Hers framed the answer:

"Tarletan!"

Even to their own ears question and answer were inaudible.

They heard Lord Tarletan's heavy descent of the staircase from the gallery. He advanced, taking his time, across the gleaming floor, and stopped a little distance from them. Then he spoke again.

"It seems we have been harbouring unsuspected talents in Braddon. Let me felicitate Madame Leroy on a performance that would have done credit to Parisien Opera in its palmiest days. But somewhat outside my requirements in a governess. Great-nieces, go to your rooms."

"No!" muttered Pauline. Her eyes sought desperately the tortoise clock; the hands had not long passed the hour of eleven. "No, no!" she muttered again.

"What may you mean by '*no, no, no*'?" sneered Tarletan. "Have you shown yourself a fit instructor of youth and innocence? Children!" His voice softened, but its dictate was unmistakable. "Do as I bid you. Go to your rooms and try to forget what you have seen to-night."

Silently they arose, only glad to go. They glided past the dancers on the floor, heads bowed and eyes cast down—those lowered lids allowed them, as they passed, to drop soft looks into the Bastard's orbs, and each look plainly said:

"*I will be there.*"

When the door closed on them Lord Tarletan's expression

changed. Dropping his heavy fist on Stanislaw's shoulder "And now, sir, who the deuce are you?" he thundered.

Stanislaw sprang to his feet, leaving Madame Leroy to fend for herself.

"No man, Lord Tarletan, addresses me so with impunity."

"Your path must be strewn with victims," scoffed Lord Tarletan. "What are you?"

"The Bastard of Pinsk!" said Stanislaw, haughtily.

Lord Tarletan raised his eyebrows. "Very distinguished."

He addressed himself for the first time to the Honourables. "A friend of yours, gentlemen?"

"We can hardly call him that," said Percy Fawleigh. "We found the fellow installed on our arrival."

"Hum! Perhaps he would like to explain his presence here."

Stanislaw drew himself up, but before he could speak a sobbing sigh from the piano arrested attention. The Archduchess was swaying on her stool. "My G*d, my foot!" she moaned.

"By gad!" cried Tarletan. "Whom may we have here?"

The sumptuous creature managed to rise from the stool and, supporting herself painfully on the keyboard, turned her lustrous eyes full upon Braddon's owner. Practised lecher though he was, he was knocked off his guard by those eyes. He devoured her with his, a slow, purposeful smile.

"Milord," she murmured, "pardon a second intruder."

"The Archduchess of Limoges," explained Percy Fawleigh.

"Indeed!"

"Sister," volunteered James, "to this gentleman."

"Indeed!"

"Whose coach," added Terence, "overturned at the gates one night and left the lady helpless, as you see."

"Indeed!"

"Yes, indeed," sighed Esmeralda, tottered forward and swooned.

Lord Tarletan was prompt to receive her. He waved back the gentlemen who had started forward, and ignored Count Stanislaw, who had done the same. "Do not trouble yourselves," he said. "It is the part of a good host to see to his guests." Pauline, creeping over the floor, plucked at his coat-tails. He shoved her back with his foot. "What, you are still there, are you? Retire, madame, and don't reappear till morning."

"Nay, Tarletan! Listen—"

"Silence!" he growled. Her slip of the tongue made him adamant to the despair in her eyes.

"You will regret it—"

"What I regret can be safely left to me."

"Midnight approaches—"

"Let it! I have always found it the pleasantest hour of the twenty-four. I wish you good night, Count Stanislaw!"

Stanislaw, nothing loth, made his bow and exit.

"Detain him!" gasped Pauline as he passed through the portal. Ignoring her, Tarletan addressed the sportsmen genially.

"Gentlemen, I will see you in the morning. You know how honoured I am to entertain you, but I have ridden far today, and the hour, according to our country notions, is late. I am sure you will be glad to seek your couches. At breakfast we will discuss things close to our hearts."

Bland though his voice was, again there was no eluding his meaning. The gentlemen were dismissed without appeal. Unwilling as they were to leave Esmeralda in the arms of one whose reputation in London was a by-word, good manners left them no alternative but to clear their throats, murmur "Good night"—and go.

"And as for you," said Tarletan to Pauline Leroy, "you will do the same."

She clambered to her feet. "And if I refuse?"

"I'll lock you in."

"You are acting like a fool—"

"Mind that tongue of yours! Do you think I don't know you of old?" He gripped her by the wrist. "By gad, I'll take no chances! I'll see you shut up safe before I—By the way, which room did you allocate to the Archduchess?"

"During your absence," said Pauline flatly, "yours."

"That answers very well."

Dragging one woman behind him and bearing the other, Lord Tarletan mounted the stairs. Madame Leroy protested and struggled in vain. She continued her efforts to warn him; he would not listen, and was too strong for her. Her scream, as he turned the key outside her door, which would have curdled most men's blood, merely made him smile. "The old Pauline," he chuckled. Slipping the key in his pocket, he bore his handsome burden into his bedchamber.

Chapter Twenty

News for Lord Tarletan

———————

No sooner had the bedroom door closed behind them than Esmeralda opened her eyes.

"As I thought," said Lord Tarletan. "There is no need then to lay you on the bed and apply burnt feathers."

"I hate the smell," said she, demurely, "and can very well sit up."

"And your foot—?"

"I dare say it would bear me at a pinch."

"You little odalisque!" said Tarletan, fondly.

"Good! Then you are not going to be angry with me."

"You deserve that I should be. Why the deuce did you come here?"

"To find my husband, of course."

"I was half-way to London from Paris."

"How was I to know? You never told me you were going to Paris. You went there on some lady's account, I suppose."

"Precisely." Lord Tarletan smiled good-humouredly.

"It is what I shall have to expect, though I did not expect it so soon. I shan't demean myself by asking her name."

"Look in your mirror."

"You went on my account?" She became vivacious. "Ah, now I shall ask questions."

"Presently, presently. I must ask some of my own. Why could you not curb yourself sufficiently to await me in London?"

"I had eaten my heart out for you long enough. I thought you were dallying here with your three wards. I was curious to see if they were really your wards. And I am rather tired of posing as your mistress. I want to be acknowledged as your wife."

"All in good time. At present it is impossible."

"Fie, Roger! Nothing is impossible."

"Imprudent, then. It would entirely upset my plans for the Triplets' marriages."

"I fail to understand, dear lord and master. You keep so many things from me."

"And you from me. What is this brother of yours you've sprung upon me? It's news to me that you have one."

"Stanislaw?" She laughed. "I confess I was astonished to find him here. I had not seen him for æons. His presence is an extraordinary coincidence."

"A deuced awkward one. You must get rid of him."

"Don't you like him?"

"Not at all."

"He's a very attractive fellow—"

"That's not in his favour."

"—and head over ears in love with your charming wards."

"What, all of 'em?"

"Why not? Don't men claim the prerogative of loving several ladies at once? Ladies, of course, though they may be adored simultaneously by several, bestow their affections on only one at a time."

"I hope so, I'm sure. These three young bucks were all making sheeps' eyes at you."

At this point the infant woke and cried in its cradle.

"What's that?" asked Lord Tarletan, sharply.

"Our infant."

"It's news to me that we have one."

"It happened in London," said Esmeralda, lightly, "while I was waiting for you to come back to me—from Paris." She lifted the weeping infant tenderly. "I have heard that when husbands err they are lured back to virtue, and filled with sensations of remorse, by this." She applied the fount of life.

"What is it?" asked Tarletan.

"A boy."

"That complicates matters."

"I don't see how. To me it simplifies matters. I insist on your acknowledging me, Roger—not for my own sake, for his. I do not mind being known to your friends as your mistress, but I object to my child being thought a—"[1]

Lord Tarletan stroked his chin. "Perhaps you would like to know why I went to Paris." He drew from his pocket a purple velvet case and laid it in her lap. She looked at it with interest and, let us admit, some greed.

"Open it for me," she said. "My hands are occupied."

He pressed the catch, raised the lid, and revealed a magnificent tiara in seed pearls.

"Heavens!" ejaculated Esmeralda. She quickly replaced the infant in its cradle, seized the treasure, and fitted it on her head. "How do I look? How do I look?"

"Like a queen." Lord Tarletan presented a looking-glass.

She was enchanted with what it showed her, and indeed nothing more all-conquering could be imagined than this superb creature, whose blue-black hair gained and gave lustre to its ornament.

"Demme if you don't take the shine out of all the women of the town," cried Tarletan. "Now say I never think of you, my dear."

She embraced him fondly. "For this I would forgive any infidelity. What did it cost you?"

"Thirty thousand pounds."

---

1 Mem: What is a child called that is born out of wedlock? Find out.
—A.G.

"But you were stone-broke when we quarrelled last. You hadn't even the price of a pair of carriage horses. Where did you get this money?"

"Borrowed it."

"From a usurer?"

"From the prospective bridegrooms of the Triplets."

Esmeralda stared at him. "Thirty thousand pounds?" She pealed with mirth. He pinched her cheek.

"All very fine, but those thousands will have to be repaid some time or other."

"How soon?"

"I hope not for a long time. They will get their money back after my death."

"And not before?"

"Unless," said Tarletan, shrewdly, "anything occurs to put them off marriage with my wards. In that case I should have to fork out during my lifetime, and that would put me in a pretty pickle."

"But why? I don't see why."

"Here's how it stands." He took her on his knee. Of all the women he had ever known this one most pleased him, had most sway over him. He had met her, four months earlier, in Almacks, where, as the widow of an affluent foreign nobleman, she had begun to dazzle London society. Esmeralda was far the handsomest lady of the season; her voluptuous charms, her talents, her richly varied character, and her reputed wealth, above all her refusal to cede, sans marriage, those favours Tarletan was wont to take for granted, had induced him to break his lifelong rule of celibacy and do, at fifty, what he had snapped his fingers at at twenty and thirty, and even at forty. In short, mad to possess, he had married her—on condition that this should be kept a secret till he gave her leave to divulge it. The rash act consummated, he woke from his temporary intoxication, and saw that, from the standpoint of the Triplets, he had made a *faux pas*. His contract with the bridegrooms' noble fathers, years ago, was made on the assumption that his great-nieces were his heirs. What if Esmeralda presented him with one? The sums he had received for what can only be called the sale of innocence would then be debts of honour which even he would feel obliged to discharge. There was but one thing for it. The contracts only actually stipulated marriage. Till the girls were safely wed, Esmeralda must pass as his mistress. The knot once safely tied, he would acknowledge her. Meanwhile, he would hurry things on with the Honourables: hence, his introduction of them to Braddon. His recent domestic felicity was not lacking in tempestuous moments. About this time, when he discovered that Esmeralda's person was her fortune, she charged him in return with stinginess. He gave her few presents, and those not of the costliest. His wedding gift was a parure in jet. She pined for pearls.

"What man in your position," she had argued, "would not give his mistress pearls? Only a husband fobs his wife off with jet. Pearls, Tarletan, pearls—or the world will suspect we are married!"

He saw that her argument was covetously framed, yet perceived a core of truth in it. Pearls she should have! He made his interviews with the suitors the occasion of, as Terence had put it, "milking" them for ten thousand apiece, and had repaired to Paris to his old friend the jeweller, who brought out his finest coronet. Its tiers of roses and lilies took apart, to be reformed as ornaments for neck, bust, and arms. With this Lord Tarletan hastened back to London, avid for the connubial reconciliation—and found his Esmeralda flown! Not dreaming she was on her way to Braddon, he set discreet inquiries afoot, and pending results, thought he could not do better than see how the gentlemen's suits were prospering.

"You see now," he concluded, "how vital it is that they should prosper, for I dare not acknowledge you before the world, until the knots are tied. After that, it is of no consequence."

"Won't they or their fathers insist on the return of the 'loans'," she asked, "when they find you are not only married, but have acquired an heir?"

"I hardly think so. Of course, they won't be pleased. But the terms of the contract were—marriage. At the time, the girls were my undisputed heirs, and the future fortunes of their husbands secure. Nobody thought, I least of all, that an old fellow nearing senility would be captured by a leman from Limoges. When it is known, the contracts will have been fulfilled and cancelled. The fathers may grumble a bit, but won't make a family scandal; while

the sons should be satisfied with gaining beautiful young brides—
and they will be satisfied, if you, my love, cease to distract them."

"Can I help it?" she asked, archly.

"Of course you can't; you distract all mankind; so tomorrow I
shall certainly remove you—and your brother with you. He stands
to defeat my plans as much as you do."

"By being, poor fellow, in love with your great-nieces?"

"By having fluttered their silly little hearts. I may be an old
man, my angel, but I have eyes."

"He would make a very good match for one of them."

"And who would buy off the disappointed suitor? No,
Esmeralda! If you really wish to appear before the world as Lady
Tarletan, your bastard of a brother must be got rid of. Not that
'Lady Tarletan' matters to me. A mistress is ever more diverting
than a wife."

"True, but after a time one likes to settle down. And I have not
only myself to think of, you know." Her eyes sought the lovely boy
asleep in the cradle.

"Well, make up your mind. Does your brother go, or stay?"

Esmeralda. put her arms round his neck again. "He shall depart
to-morrow."

"He is departing to-night!" cried Pauline, entering the room
without even knocking.

Lord Tarletan sprang to his feet. "What do you tell me?"

"That Count Stanislaw is on the point of eloping with the
Triplets."

Chapter Twenty-One.

The Moujik and the Governess

When her gaoler had locked her in and departed with her final shriek in his ears, Pauline's first impulse was to give way to unbridled fury. But after dashing certain china articles to the floor and tearing at curtains and covers with her teeth, she reflected that all perhaps was not yet lost, and took herself in hand. She flung cold water over her face and arms, smoothed her hair, put on another dress, and threw up her window. Her room was on the second floor; a sturdy creeper climbed the wall to her window-sill. That night had proved she had lost none of her agility. In a moment she was sitting on the sill, in another swinging earthward by the creeper. She had left her watch aloft, but it could not be much more than half-past eleven. What next? Silent as a bat, she flitted round the house. The windows of the music-room were still open, the candles shining. Nobody had come to extinguish them. She cast a wild look round the deserted scene of her triumph and degradation. Stanislaw, he only mattered! That he had felt equally with herself to-night the strange bond which had linked her with him at sight, she could not doubt. Where, where was Stanislaw?

Not in his room—that, she soon verified. It was in disorder, there were signs of hasty packing. He was going away then—at midnight, but where?—and how?

Down she sped again, hair streaming, into the starlit night. She skirted the terrace, looking over the parapet. Nobody visible—but stay! There, far below, outside the little postern, was, if not somebody, something. She heard the jingle of harness, the stamping of hooves. The moon slid out of a cloud. It was a carriage! As she looked, a man emerged from the interior, and went to the horses' heads. He stilled their champing and stamping. In spite of the coachman's cape and the long whip, she knew him: Kaspar!

She fled like a shadow down the terrace stairway. The postern was ajar; she thrust it open, not pausing to think if the act were imprudent or no. A muttered whisper from Kaspar: "Make less noise. You're cutting it rather fine. Are they coming?"

"Are who coming?" demanded Madame Leroy, in a cold, clear voice.

The Moujik wheeled on his heel. "You!" He caught his breath, then said, malignantly: "A pity you couldn't keep your finger out of this pie."

"A pity for you, no doubt."

"Oh, no, not for me."

"If for me, I do not need your pity. This carriage—it is to take the Count away?" The Moujik went on securing the horses' straps, without removing his eyes from her. She waited for his answer, and getting none, observed: "A very large carriage for one traveller." Last night's whispers flashed across her mind. "Not for two—for four." She took a step nearer the Moujik, clenching her fists. Her voice rose to a shout. "The Count—and the young ladies—but it is monstrous!"

"And why? Don't you think he is good enough for them?" The man came close, and muttered: "Assist him, and he will always be grateful to you. Foil him, and you will live to regret it."

"I do not want his gratitude!"

"Or his welfare? I assure you, with one of the young ladies in his pocket, both you and I could make something out of it."

"Are you proposing," Pauline asked icily, "that I unite in your nefarious schemes?"

"I don't see why not," said Kaspar. "Unless, of course," he added, insolently, "you have schemes of your own that are nearer to your heart."

If looks could slay, he would have fallen dead on the spot. But they cannot, and he did not.

"I shall not permit this to happen," said Madame Leroy.

"How will you stop it?"

She shrugged. Seething with rage, she purposely let herself appear merely annoyed. She was well aware that any show of action on her part would bring him to grips with her. In a grapple with a man of his build and strength, she must perforce be worsted. She allowed herself to stand, like one at a loss, with her back to the open postern. Choosing a moment when he was off his guard, she stepped backward into the staircase, and slammed the door. His sharp ejaculation came too late; he threw himself after her, only to hear the bolts shot, and her steps flying upwards. There was no time to be lost. With a coarse curse he threw discretion to the winds, and shouted:

"Stanislaw!"

"I am here!" The Count himself came hurrying down the road.

"Why did you take the long way round? I expected you by the staircase."

"When I reached the terrace I saw somebody prowling there, and chose the longer route."

"A thousand pities! We might have had a chance of stopping her. Where are the young ladies?"

"Are they not yet here?"

"No, and if they don't come quickly, the game is up," said Kaspar.

"What can you mean?"

"That d*v*l, Pauline Leroy, has smelled a rat."

"My G*d!" cried Stanislaw. "I will return and fetch the Triplets myself."

"If you'll take my advice, you'll drive away at once."

"I will not go without them!"

He tried the postern door, which refused to open. He set his shoulder to it—all in vain! What matter! 'Twould not be the first time he had climbed that perilous wall by way of the roses. High overhead towered the crumbling Gothic arch, where he had first beheld his trinity of angels. Regardless of thorns, he grasped his flowery ladder, and began to swing himself up.

"Madman!" growled Kaspar.

A debonair laugh was his answer.

*   *   *

Meanwhile, Pauline was panting her way back to Lord Tarletan's room. We will return with her, and join them at the moment after she had made her announcement.

Chapter Twenty-Two

Check!

"Eloping with the Triplets!" bawled Lord Tarletan. "By gad, this is too much!"

"There is not an instant to lose," urged Pauline.

"I'll horsewhip—I'll strangle the Bastard!" shouted the peer.

"No violence, Roger, please," said Esmeralda. She laid a calming hand upon his sleeve, and addressed Pauline. "Are you quite certain of your information?"

"Information? I have heard nothing; I have seen all. A travelling carriage waits on the valley road, big enough to hold a Pacha and his Purdah." She clutched at Tarletan's free hand. "Come! Come and stop them, before it is too late."

"You had better accompany us," said Tarletan to the Archduchess. "You are his sister, and perhaps if he is obstinate can bring him to reason."

Esmeralda had her own reasons for wishing to avoid an open scene. From of old she knew that in a crisis Stanislaw could not be trusted to keep his head; he was prone to act upon rash impulses, to his own discomfiture, and that of his associates. She shook her luxuriant curls.

"No, Roger, I cannot come."

"Why not?"

"I have my duties as a mother."

"Be quick about them, for I shall drag the scoundrel here."

Esmeralda bent o'er the cradle till the door was closed. As soon as she was alone, she jumped up, pulled open her drawers, and hastened to make a packet of her valuables. Keeping her tiara on her brow, she adorned her person with every gem she possessed, rings, bracelets, brooches, necklaces. The jet parure enhanced her snow-white skin. Into her bosom she thrust the money she had wheedled from her beaux; she filled her gold-mounted dressing-case with the arts of her toilet, with Lait d'Amandes, Ruban de Bruges, and crimson lipsalve! Nor did she hesitate to add such portable trifles of worth as she could find in the lavishly furnished bedroom. The next hour was likely to be a crucial one, and she felt it was as well to be prepared. She covered her glittering charms with a light but voluminous wrap.

Meanwhile, Lord Tarletan and Madame Leroy were making all haste to the terrace; and, furious though he was, Roger could not refrain from emitting a curt laugh.

"Strange, is it not, Pauline, to think that you and I combine to stop an abduction. Twenty-five years ago another coach, a grand-ducal coach, stood at my door to abduct another lady. You must have shivered lest I should appear to cry check! As perhaps my three little geese are shivering now. What are their sensations at this moment? You should be able to tell me."

Pauline rejoined to this: "The Archduchess addressed you as Roger."

"Well, that's my name."

"I call it very smart work."

"I never let the grass grow under my feet."

By this time they had crossed the little saloon, and emerged on the terrace. But they had no need to descend the stairs that led to the postern. At that moment, the moon coming out of a cloud shone full on the Gothic arch, and the figure of him they sought! He sat with one leg thrown over the crumbling parapet; his hands still grasped the vine that had pulled him up. Madame Leroy started, and pointed her finger.

"'Tis he!" she cried. "The Bastard!"

Too proud to fly, Stanislaw vaulted lightly down upon the terrace, and went to meet them.

"Well," he said, coolly, "what want you of the Bastard?"

"Your presence for ten minutes in my room," said Lord Tarletan.

"I fear I cannot comply immediately."

"Immediately, or not at all, I fancy."

"What do you mean, my lord?"

"You are about to leave us."

"Am I a prisoner? Cannot I go where I please?"

"But not take what you please, when you go." Stanislaw turned a shade paler. "You understand me, I see. I hope you have the grace to be ashamed of yourself."

"I am not ashamed of loving," said Stanislaw, proudly.

"A very fine sentiment, with thrice the force it would have in an ordinary lover. Unluckily for you, it won't sound quite so fine to two of the treasures you intend to purloin. But no matter. You are not going to purloin any of them. You are coming with me and Madame Leroy to explain yourself before I kick you out. My legs may not be so nimble as yours in the dance, but they have more weight behind them. And, if you refuse to come of your own free will you will, I think, find my arms too more powerful than yours."

"You have no need to use force," said Stanislaw. "I am prepared to offer you any explanation you choose to demand."

"And the Moujik!" said Pauline, urgently. "He must come, too."

"Why?" asked Lord Tarletan. "A Moujik can't be of any particular importance."

"He is no common moujik," insisted Pauline. "To leave him in charge of the coach down there is dangerous. Order him," she said, in a low, stern tone to Stanislaw, "order him to follow us to your sister's room."

Stanislaw was scribbling something in his notebook. He tore out the sheet, folded it, pierced it with a spray of roses—three roses—

and bestowed it in a corner of the arch. Then, leaning over the parapet, he called:

"Kaspar!"

"Sir?"

"When the young ladies come, tell them to look in the place where first I beheld them. Then, and not till then, return to the house, and present yourself in the Archduchess's room. No words! Be mute! For once, do as I say."

Before the Moujik could reply, either to protest or acquiesce, Stanislaw drew back out of sight, and said calmly to his captors:

"Shall we go?"

Chapter Twenty-Three

"Forget Not Stanislaw"

———————

Are they shadows, these hooded forms that steal by moonlight? The moth reflected in water could not be more silent. Eyes bent on the ground, they see and hear nothing around them. Oh, softly, softly! Lest some errant movement awake the pitiless world and heaven be lost. Each step is a peril, each breath is fraught with danger. Falteringly, timorously, the three converge to one spot. From afar they behold the coach that will bear them to bliss. He, he is there! Soon she will be in his arms. The tiny feet tread faster. The last steps flutter and are audible. Three little gasps of fear—three hoods fall back—and Adeline, Caroline and Georgiana, standing at a stone's throw from the patient horses, stare at each other in terror that evaporates in bewilderment.

"Caroline!"

"Georgiana!"

"Adeline!"

"Oh!" (All three now on a single breath.) "You have discovered my secret!"

A pause. In a low voice Georgiana says:

"What secret? I have discovered none; I have one."

"I too," says Caroline, faintly.

"And I," says Adeline. "Sisters! Forgive me for not confiding in you, but—but I am eloping with the Bastard."

"And I," says Georgiana.

"And I," says Caroline.

With a common movement they melt in each other's arms.

"We are one," says Caroline. "He loves us all," says Adeline.

"We have not betrayed one another," says Georgiana.. "He knew better than we that we are inseparable."

"He understands us as we do not understand ourselves," says Adeline.

And Caroline adds: "He awaits yonder. Let us go to him." Arms twined, they move as one towards the carriage. A man steps from its shadow—it is not he.

"I have a message for the ladies," says Kaspar.

"A message?" Three little hands fly to three hearts.

"From—*him*?"

"I am to bid you look in the place where my master first beheld you."

They cannot speak. Three appealing fingers are extended towards the coach. The Moujik throws open both doors and allows the moon to stream through its empty interior. He bows, and vanishes.

The place where he first beheld them? Well they know it! The postern is bolted, the stairway is denied them. After awhile three cloaked forms emerge from the terrace saloon, and, still linked, float across to the Gothic arch.

And there, where oft they sat and watched for him, there lies his message, pinned by three sister roses. It is Caroline who gives a rose to each. It is Adeline who unfolds the sacred paper. It is Georgiana who reads the words aloud:

"Fate is against us. Forget not.

STANISLAW.

Adieu! Adieu! Adieu!"

Three cloaks fall from three figures, clad in white. Three heads are bowed above three pallid blooms. Three voices sigh:

"Adieu! Adieu! Adieu!"

Chapter Twenty-Four

The Truth at Last

―――――――――

How different a scene was enacting in Lord Tarletan's bedroom!

Not tenderness, but wrath—not love, but hate the mood.

Count Stanislaw stood confronting his accusers; his glittering eye betrayed his rising excitement. Esmeralda noted it, and, though for the moment she played the watcher's part, she managed to let fall a low-voiced warning.

"Careful! Be careful what you say to them."

She said it under cover of a sister's solicitude, with an arm about him as she caressed his fevered brow. The bystanders did not hear—but neither did he. At least, he made no sign that he had done so.

Lord Tarletan stood, legs apart, and riding-whip in hand.

His face was the hue of beetroot; he had no intention of controlling himself, despite the presence of his wife and babe.

"Well, sir! I shall not ask you to give an account of yourself. Your dastardly intentions are known to me."

"Why then," countered Stanislaw, "have you brought me to my sister's room, in which your own presence requires some explanation?"

"If you are thinking," said Tarletan, insolently, "of calling me out to defend your sister's honour I may mention that this lady is my wife."

"Your wife!" Madame Leroy's exclamation told Lord Tarletan that he had made a slip of the tongue. Simultaneously, Stanislaw rounded on the Archduchess, whose eyes passed rapidly from one face to another.

"Esmeralda! Why have you concealed from me that Lord Tarletan is no stranger to you? Why have you pretended your coming here was an accident? Why, why did you not tell me that you—were married?"

She quickly made up her mind what course to take. "Why? Because, dearest brother, I, like you, was ready to waive all for love. My husband had reasons for concealing our union. Dear Roger! Now that you have divulged our secret, and the suitors will certainly throw your wards over, there is no longer any reason why my brother should not wed one of them."

"Never!" yelled Madame Leroy.

Lord Tarletan shrugged. "Why so much fuss, Pauline? The secret will go no farther than this room, and the marriages of my great-nieces will go forward."

"You can hardly expect me to agree to that," said the Bastard.

"You mean to levy blackmail, do you?"

"I mean to relieve at least one sweet innocent from an unwelcome match."

Lord Tarletan did some rapid thinking. "Well, it's my own fault, demmit, and I must swallow the consequences. With the cat out of the bag the game is up, as far as the three young Honourables are concerned; and if Count Stanislaw is good for thirty thousand pounds, he shall have which filly he fancies."

"Thirty thousand pounds!" Stanislaw knit his brow.

"Not a penny less. I shall need it to clear a delicate situation. Otherwise I must repudiate your sister's claims, though I shall be very happy to continue her as my mistress."

Stanislaw was too confused by the sudden demand to observe Esmeralda's signs.

"Thirty thousand pounds is a very large sum," he faltered.

"One, surely, within the scope of the Bastard of Pinsk. Your father, the Margrave, is known for a person of wealth. I can confide a great-niece to his son without qualms."

Pauline Leroy burst into hysterical mirth. "Do, do, my lord, by all means, and make yourself the laughing-stock of London."

"What are you driving at?" demanded Roger Tarletan.

"That, whoever this young gentleman may be, he is not the son of the Margrave of Pinsk."

"The woman is mad!" cried Esmeralda, hotly.

But something in Pauline's eye gave Roger pause. He gripped her wrist and barked:

"How do you know he is not the Margrave's son?"

"Because he has described the Margrave to me—a taller, broader man than he is himself, with ruddy hair and a nose like a balancing hawk. The Margrave—" Pauline paused, and when she spoke again gave emphasis to each word with malignant relish. "The Margrave of Pinsk is a head shorter than I am, he has canary hair and a nose like a prize porker."

Once more Lord Tarletan asked her: "How do you know?"

"I was his mistress," answered Pauline Leroy.

At that moment Kaspar the Moujik entered the room.

*   *   *

"Confute this woman!" cried Stanislaw.

"Yes, Kaspar," broke in Esmeralda, breathing rapidly. "Madame Leroy has just told a monstrous lie. Husband!" She clung adoringly to Lord Tarletan. "You cannot believe her! Look at her eye! It swims in venom. You cannot, cannot trust her."

"Not an inch," said Lord Tarletan. "I never have. But I have always known her sincere under two circumstances: one, where her private interests are concerned, the other when she is in a raging temper, as at present. I do not think she claims this mistress-ship without grounds; to my knowledge she has been the mistress of practically all the big guns in Europe. Why should the Margrave of

Pinsk get off scot free? Though her reasons for shouting it aloud elude me."

"They are only too obvious," said Esmeralda. "She has a passionate unrequited attachment to my brother, and cannot endure the thought of his union elsewhere."

"Is this so, Pauline?"

"Yes, Roger," she sneered. "I would rather see Count Stanislaw dead in his grave than thrown away on one of your milk-and-water great-nieces. From the moment I set eyes on him I knew him for mine. It matters not to me that he is an arrant impostor. Twenty years ago, when for some six brief but resplendent months I was the reigning influence in Pinsk, the Margrave was a sonless bachelor."

"And daughterless?"

"The Margrave had no off-spring of any description."

Stanislaw had been listening like one stunned. For the second time he appealed to the Moujik, a vast immovable figure in the doorway.

"Kaspar!" he cried. "Can you hear these things and say nothing? Give her the lie."

"Unfortunately, I can't. She is speaking the truth."

"But you have always brought me up believing that I was of noble Polish birth."

"What!" ejaculated Lord Tarletan, "you don't then claim to have been elevated in Pinsk?"

Stanislaw answered haughtily: "I do not, my lord. If I have dilated somewhat on my surroundings in the Margrave's court it was but a touch of embroidery on the fabric of truth. Those surroundings should have been mine. By accident they were not. That is all."

"Where were you brought up?" asked Lord Tarletan.

"In Paris," said Stanislaw, "in the home of one I called my foster-mother. From my earliest days Kaspar has been my attendant. It was he who told me the story of my birth, and supplied the details on which I have feasted in thought till they became the truth. I grew up believing that the Margrave, a prey to conspiracies, had had me smuggled out of the country in babyhood, with Kaspar to watch over and rear me in the tradition of my high-born race; in due course I was to return and take my rightful place."

"How meanwhile did you support yourself in Paris?" asked Lord Tarletan.

"I earned my living," said Stanislaw in a low voice.

"How?"

"I had a gift."

"What was it?"

"Dancing."

"You danced in the theatres?"

"Nothing so low as that. I taught dancing. I loathed, I knew it was beneath me; but I had to live. My dancing-classes were notorious in Paris."

"He was a genius!" cried Esmeralda, enthusiastically.

"And you, my love!" Tarletan turned upon her sharply. "Were you also smuggled out of Pinsk in babyhood?"

To avoid an answer, she busied herself with her infant's safety-pins. Once more maternal love gained her a respite. Stanislaw resumed.

"One thing alone supported me in my distasteful work, the thought that I had a margrave for a father. To-night's revelations have shaken me to the core. What, in G*d's name," he cried, addressing Kaspar, "was your purpose in feeding me with lies?" Suddenly, his face brightened. "But *are* they lies? My lord!" he cried, "if not the Bastard of Pinsk, it is certain that I am somebody else's bastard! A letter to say so was pinned to my swaddling-clothes, which I can produce if you will allow me to go to my room. And that I am irrefutably of noble birth, I have a further proof on my person at this moment."

"Perhaps you will condescend to show it to us."

"With pleasure. Behold!"

The young man ripped open coat, waistcoat, and shirt! There, on his white chest, gleamed a diamond ornament, a jewel shaped like a star, of fabulous worth.

"Would any who had not blue blood in his veins," he demanded, "be dowered with this?"

"By gad!" said Lord Tarletan. "The Star of the Russias! The Grand-Duke Vladimir's Star."

Pauline pounced on it like a female vulture. "Stolen from me, twenty-five years ago! Stanislaw!" she shouted, "how came you by this?"

"My foster-mother told me it had been used, instead of a safety-pin, to secure some portion of my infant outfit."

"What was your foster-mother's name?"

"Clarice Marat."

"My G*d!" exclaimed Pauline. "You are my son!"

Her exclamation numbed all present. (All but one.) Then:

"Surprise after surprise!" observed Lord Tarletan. "Are you certain of this, Pauline?"

"As certain as I am that I bore a son. Now, now I understand the mysterious bond that drew me to Count Stanislaw at sight. My son! My son!"

"What," said Lord Tarletan, "yours and Vladimir's?"

"No, Roger! Mine and yours."

"Egad," said Lord Tarletan. "How do you make that out?"

"Easily." The gloomy woman looked deep into the past.

"You remember the night in Paris when I left you?"

"I am not likely to forget it. It put ten thousand crowns in my pocket."

She did not understand him, and ignored this. "I had had a superlative triumph at the opera. Duke Vladimir had flung me the Russian Star. That scoundrel Casimir annexed it from me in the wings of the theatre. I returned to the hotel where you and I existed in glory and shame, and presided at the feast. Afterwards, the Grand-Duke of Murmansk paid me his intimate addresses. I consented to be his. Till then, I had resisted his lightest kiss; and the child, born that day, now concealed in Clarice's bedchamber, was yours. I thought it advisable to say nothing about it to you at the time; and when Vladimir suggested instant flight, and while you were engaged in horsewhipping the thief, I hastened to my room, confided the child to Clarice Marat's care, and penned a rapid note, declaring he was a bastard of noble birth, but naming no names. It was the utmost I could do on the spur of the moment for one whom I never expected to behold again. This done, I rejoined the Grand Duke, and drove away, to the lurid life of Murmansk. Our parting, in less than a year, was sequent to a visit of state from the Governor of Tomsk. But that is neither here nor there. I suppose," she concluded, "you were furious, Tarletan, when you discovered my flight."

"Not in the least," said Roger, airily. "The Grand Duke's infatuation for you was waxing while mine was waning. One night he let fall that he would give ten thousand crowns to make you his. I snapped it up; and, only too willing to provide a brilliant setting for your finale, arranged a gala night at the opera with a banquet to follow. Further, I had the Star made which Vladimir flung you from the box, with so much *éclat*."

"This Star!" Pauline's hand grasped the jewel on Stanislaw's breast. "But it is priceless! It must have cost you treble the ten thousand crowns you sold me for, like a brute."

"The Star, my shrewd Pauline, made by my staunch friend the jeweller, cost me just ten crowns. Not bad paste of its kind. But, if it was stolen from you, how came it to be securing our infant's napkin?"

A hollow groan burst from Stanislaw's pale lips. Rending the bauble from its chain, he hurled it to the ground and trampled on it. "False! False! The whole world is false!" He struck his brow.

"Not the whole world!" declared Pauline. "Your mother remains."

He thrust aside her outstretched hands. "My mother! A mother who, indifferent to what became of me, abandoned me to the night and her *femme-de-chambre!*"

"You were so tiny," she pleaded. "I knew not what you were to become, my son! Yet when we met I loved you at first sight. A mother's love, though I did not know it then, and mistook it for something else. Stanislaw!"

She fell on her knees at his feet. Again he repulsed her.

"Mother, I loathe you! You have destroyed my life. Your son—and his. I am not even a bastard!" The young man buried his face for shame in his hands. "Never let me look on my mother's face again."

"Stanislaw! No! You cannot treat me so! Everything I am and have are yours. My insane jealousy is assuaged; at least, none can compete with me as a mother—and, as a wife, you shall wed whom you please; a marriage that will content your heart and restore your position. Roger!" She turned to Lord Tarleton, who was surveying her transports with a certain amusement. "You have now every reason to foster our boy's desires."

Stanislaw's pallid features lit up with hope. "Yes, father known too late! At least you can no longer object to giving me my choice of the Triplets."

"None at all," yawned Lord Tarletan. "But the law of England may; for if you are my son you are their uncle."

Hope lost again! With a moan the unhappy lover sank on a chair and buried his head in his arms.

"Cheer up! All is not lost!"

It was the Moujik who spoke at last. All eyes were turned on him as he advanced into the room and laid his hand on Stanislaw's heaving shoulder.

"There is no reason," said Kaspar, "for this despair. If Lord Tarletan will listen to reason there is none why you should not become his great-nephew. For certain it is that you are not his son."

"He is!" cried Pauline Leroy. "The child whose clothes revealed my quickly-penned letter, the child who bore that Star upon his person is the son I bore—"

"To me!" said Kaspar the Moujik.

Tearing the web of matted hair from his face and head, divesting himself of his heavy padded coat, he stood revealed, slim, saturnine, and clean-shaven: Casimir Dubois!

*   *   *

"Upon my word!" said Lord Tarletan. "My courier!"

"Yes, my lord, your courier! Who has waited for this moment for twenty-five years. To-night I hold the cards in my hand I think. I told you I should get even with you some day."

Lord Tarletan flicked his horse-whip very lightly. Casimir flinched a trifle, but held his ground and ground his teeth. "Oh no, my lord!" he said between them. "Not twice in a lifetime!"

"I gave you enough for two on the first occasion. I shouldn't wonder if you still bear the marks on you."

"I have cherished them. They have helped me not to forget. Listen, my lord! And you, my wife and my son!"

"Whom do you mean by your wife?" asked Tarleton, sharply.

"She whom you used to know as Pauline la Reine; she whom I introduced to your establishment. But first, I struck a bargain with her. You remember, Pauline? One does not provide another man's mistresses for love; I meant to feather my nest, but I did not trust her. No ordinary contract would hold good with such a woman. I required a legal bond. Before I revealed your name I stipulated that she should become my wife. Look at her, my lord! She would like to deny it; she cannot. Here are the marriage lines." He pulled them from his pocket and held them at a safe distance from Pauline's claws. "She was my wife before she became your mistress; consequently, the son she bore was mine."

Stanislaw looked as though death would be welcome. "The son of a courier and a ballet-dancer!"

"You will get over that," said Casimir, "when you are heir to Braddon."

"So that's your price?" said Tarletan.

"For silence, yes. Otherwise I go straight to the Honourables and tell them to exact the penalty. How I have planned and plotted for this moment! That night, twenty-five years ago, when I slunk from your final lash, I saw a woman slipping out of the house. At first I thought it was Pauline la Reine. I followed her to an obscure quarter of the city, arrested her with a hand on her plump shoulder—she screamed and turned her head—'twas Clarice Marat! In her fright she let fall the little bundle she carried; I need not tell you what and who it was. I caught it before it struck the pavement, else to-night had been very different for all of us. I read Pauline's note and suddenly saw my way. I and Clarice would bring up the child between us. I would foster the story of his noble birth, add to it the proof of the royal Star, and provide my son with a blue-blooded father; the Margrave of Pinsk seemed very suitable, and sufficiently far removed not to interfere. Stanislaw proved an apt pupil; he drank in all I told him, and enlarged on it. Kaspar the Moujik gave him a highly-coloured picture of his father's court, told him romantic causes for his banishment, inflamed him with the glory that should be his. All the time I lay in wait for the hour when I might use him to humiliate you. I was not certain how; but I knew that a Polish Bastard would be a more powerful weapon in my hands than the son of myself and your cast-off mistress. When he was ripe enough I brought him to England—and for the first time learned that you had three wards. Here was my opportunity! If I could ally my progeny with your family his fortune and your humiliation would be complete. That is what I have aimed at, and that, my lord, will sate my lust for revenge. If you ask me, a mild one. The boy is presentable, the girls are willing and you will only have to repay ten thousand pounds to whichever of the suitors is disappointed. Otherwise you must fork out thirty thousand. And where will you get it?"

"Here!" said Esmeralda.

They had forgotten her. So still had she kept in the background during these revelations, that her curious part in the story had not yet been examined. Now she came forward, her light wrap dropping from her, arrayed like an empress in seed-pearl tiara, etc., to lay a packet of notes in Lord Tarletan's hand.

"Bless my soul!" he exclaimed. "What have we here?"

"The money you require," said Esmeralda, "in order to release yourself from the suitors, acknowledge me, and establish our infant as your legal heir."

"Where did this money come from?" asked Lord Tarletan.

"From the same source," she dimpled, "as that which provided me with my tiara."

"You witch! You odalisque!" said Tarletan fondly.

"Not so fast!" cried Pauline. "I do not care whether you are Roger's wife or his mistress! But I will not see my son cheated of his hopes!"

"Nor I, I assure you—Archduchess!" sneered Casimir.

"I too have a son," retorted Esmeralda, "whose rights I must ensure." She cast a meaning glance from Casimir to Stanislaw. "And when my husband here has given me my rightful place in the world's eye, who should benefit if not my brother and his father?"

"Hold hard!" said Lord Tarletan. "The time has come for my odalisque to explain herself. If this young man is your brother, the old one is your father, too. I don't relish the thought of Pauline as a mother-in-law, and rather suspect a flaw somewhere. Who are you?"

"Your wife."

"Whose child is that?"

"Yours."

"And this man"—he pointed to Stanislaw—"is, you say, your brother?"

"Yes." But this *Yes* came after a moment's hesitation. "The son of Casimir Dubois and Pauline la Reine is, you maintain, your brother?"

Esmeralda was silent.

"What have you to say to this, Pauline?" asked Lord Tarletan.

"That I never bore any child but one. The woman lies. She is a common adventuress."

"How dare you," cried Esmeralda, "miscall the Archduchess of Limoges?"

"But you are not," said Pauline, savouring each word, "the Archduchess of Limoges."

"How dare you say so?"

"You have painted the Archduke as a man six foot two in height. He was four foot eight. You have depicted him with chestnut hair. He was bald."

"How do you know?" demanded Esmeralda.

"I was his mistress," said Pauline la Reine .

The beautiful odalisque could find nothing to say. Casimir began to look uneasy. Stanislaw, prey to his emotions, seemed to have lost awareness of all present. Lord Tarletan, curious, and not unamused, appeared to be waiting for what came next.

It descended on him in a tirade from Pauline.

"You poor deluded dupe!" cried the virago. "Keep this shoddy thing you have made your wife! But uphold my son, bestow on him a bride and a handsome dower or to-morrow I will go to the suitors' fathers and they shall learn the truth. Your name will be branded in society. Women will draw their skirts aside as you pass. Men will refuse your hand at baccarat. You will be ruined, financially and socially. You will be dis-Almacked! And all because," she added, with taunting smiles, "in your dotage you departed from your lifelong rule of mistresses only!"

It seemed that she had won the day. Lord Tarletan tapped his teeth. Esmeralda and Casimir waited for him to speak. Their destinies hung on his words. But it was not he who spoke. A hollow voice, the voice of a ghost, broke the silence.

"Esmeralda is not his wife! She is his mistress!"

"Silent, be silent, fool!" hissed Casimir.

Stanislaw drew himself up to his full height. Whatever his birth, this man looked every inch a nobleman.

"I will not be silent! To-night has shattered my world to its foundations. All that I am—all that I thought I was—has fallen to pieces. All I hoped for is ruined, all I possess snatched from me. No longer a bastard, but a man of ignoble origin, one thing at least is left to me: my honour."

"If you cannot stop him," muttered Casimir to Pauline, "he will destroy us all."

She did not understand; Esmeralda did; and Stanislaw, catching his words, cried in accents of ice and fire:

"Be thou destroyed, thou who hast destroyed Stanislaw!" He turned his back on the trio and henceforth addressed himself solely to Roger Tarletan. "The woman you think you married is my wife. Her child, therefore, is my child. You know what I am; a base-born dancing-master. Esmeralda is an equally base-born milliner. Five years ago she came to my classes in Paris. 'Twas Kaspar, or rather Casimir, who brought her there, when I was at an age he thought ripe for instruction in those matters in which the Abbé Dubois (perhaps his ancestor!) instructed his royal pupil, the Fifteenth Louis. But one thing, Casimir had overlooked. Inculcating in me the seed of Margravian nobility, he implanted unwittingly an idea of chivalry which, had I been the Margrave's son, would have been my birthright. I loved Esmeralda at sight, and continued in this feeling for several months. Where I love, my lord, I am tender of my women. I marry them. I married her, behind the Moujik's back. Young as I was, I scorned to smirch even a Parisian milliner; how much less to-day would I have smirched the Tarletan Triplets. I lost sight of Esmeralda nearly four years ago, and what she has done since I will not ask. But you, at least, can feel free from embarrassment. Your lifelong rule holds good; you are still an unmarried bachelor, still no father. Your burdens are on my shoulders. I will carry them hence."

"What are you going to do?" screamed Pauline, despairingly.

"I am going into the night, out of your lives. I will have no part in my parents' nefarious schemes. I leave Lord Tarletan to pursue his own as he will. As for his wards—" Stanislaw put his hand to his throat and seemed for a moment unable to utter a word. "Sir, I have only one request to make. Leave my memory untarnished where it is most cherished. Never let the Triplets know I am not a bastard."

"I undertake," said Lord Tarletan huskily, "that they shall always believe you so."

"I am content. I go—into the night."

Chapter Twenty-Five

Adieu! Adieu! Adieu!

"Hark! Hark! He comes! He comes!"

"Kosciusko's hoofs! I would know them among a thousand."

"Can you see him?"

"No, but he can only have one rider."

The sisters leaned as one body through the arch; their silver call fell as one voice on the night.

"Stanislaw! Bastard of Pinsk! Look up! We are here!"

The mad gallop ceased. Far below they heard Kosciusko whinny as he pawed the turf. But the moon was behind a cloud, and all they could see was a deepening of the shadows in the valley, where the horse and his rider drew up at the foot of the wall.

"Who calls the Bastard of Pinsk ?"

Was it his voice? So harsh with sorrow, so remote it sounded it might have issued from another sphere.

"Who calls but Caroline—Adeline—Georgiana!"

"My belovèds! My Hesperides! My three!"

"Your note, your rose-pinned note, what does it mean?"

"What it says, that Stanislaw and the Triplets must part."

"But why, oh why?"

"Ask me no more. Fate has decreed against us. Some are not born to be happy. I am one of them."

"And we, three."

"Say not so, my lovely girls, you must be happy. You must tear this page from your lives, you must forget me."

Tenderly from aloft the answer was wafted, tenderly it floated to his ears.

"Forget not Stanislaw! Forget not Stanislaw!"

"We will never forget you," said Georgiana, clearly.

"Whatever fate has in store for us," said Adeline, "you are imprinted on our hearts for ever."

"And when we lie in the Mausoleum," said Caroline, "the imprint will still be there."

"So be it, then. Love shall not be denied. On my heart, when I die, three names will be engraved. We will meet beyond the grave."

"Beyond the grave."

Tears drowned their voices as they clung together.

No more came from below—yet the horse did not stir. But something stirred—the rose-vine on the wall. Oh, what, what was this? He was climbing to them, had reached them, his arms enfolded all three! His kiss, his dreamed-of kiss, was on their lips: on Georgiana's—Adeline's—Caroline's!

His encircling arms fell away, the rustling of the roses began again, Kosciusko whinnied anew, the harness jingled.

"Adieu! Adieu! Adieu!"

And then—the Mazeppa gallop into the night!

*   *   *

But in the Gothic arch the moon, emerging from her palace of clouds, lit three transfigured girls. Their eyes shone with love's highest ecstasy.

"Sisters," said Georgiana, "all is well. His child—may come at any moment now."

Chapter the Last

(a)

Dried Rose leaves

———————

It is not always so.

The Tarletan Triplets awaited their infants in vain. They pressed their roses in the Book of Beauty and hoped for many a year. And when hope waned they faded out of life.

Softly they sleep in the tomb beneath the willows.

Hush!

Chapter the Last

(b)

The Rose Re-blooms

It is not always so.

The infants never arrived. And time, who dims all things, covered the Bastard's image with a veil. He seemed to them one known only in a dream. A few years later London society knew no brighter adornments than Lady Caroline Fawleigh, Lady Adeline Lorrequer, and Lady Georgiana Dumbarton. They seemed content with their lot. Only those who have suffered can know the anguish of breaking hearts beneath fair smiles.

Chapter the Last

(c)

Dried Rose leaves

————————

It is not always so.

The Triplets were not destined to be mothers; nor were they ever wives.

Pauline and Casimir passed out of their lives. Lord Tarletan bore Esmeralda to Andalusia. The sisters lived on in Braddon, in spinsterhood, and dried their roseleaves in the Book of Beauty.

And once a year, at summer's zenith, when the moon shone bright and full on tomb and tower, an ancient dream took shape and body again. The sisters sat once more in the Gothic arch; once more the hooves of a horse seemed to beat the turf, the sound of a vanished voice rang once more on their ears, the roses' perfume was that of other years—and ah! Once more their lips felt the burning imprint of a kiss!

It was—it *is*—enough!

VISIT TO PELHAM PLACE

It would never do!

I would never have the face to submit this sort of thing to a publisher. Could Aunt Addie have re-read her "favourite novel" for years, that she should even expect it? I would blush to show it to my modern friends, with its dreadful assumption that babies could appear at any moment after the first kiss—in a few days or a few years! In later life, Aunt Addie, whatever she didn't know, must have known better than that. Yet she would "be glad to think that I could get it published". Really, Aunt Addie! Had you no care for your own reputation?

"Reputation, Pamela, is a very shifting quicksand. What engulfs you in one generation gives you a foothold in the next."

"But the style, Aunt Addie!"

"What's wrong with the style? The book is *teeming* with style."

"Of the wrong sort."

"What you think the right sort may be the wrong sort one day. I think the work shows considerable promise for such a young gell. If *you* had written anything like it at sixteen, I'd say you had the making of a novelist in you."

"Ah, Aunt Addie, I hadn't Miss Linton at my elbow to give me the lead."

"If Alicia Mary Linton thinks she is responsible for my gifts she's saying more than her prayers. Well, do as I say, put it away in a drawer for the time being, and come back to it later."

Disconcerting how Aunt Addie popped up in my mental

conversations. I was really rather tempted to stuff the thing in the kitchen fire, and write a word of apology to the typist who was the only living person besides myself who had set eyes on it. But in deference to Aunt Addie's wishes I locked it away, and merely sent a cheque for Miss Muirhead's account. My first disbursement out of my cash legacy.

As to my legacy in real estate—

"What is the landed proprietress going to do about Pelham Place?" asked my father.

"I don't know. I haven't thought. It would be rather fun to have a look at it."

"We might run up together in the automobile," said my father.

"When we get it," said my mother.

An exciting suggestion. Miss Norham had referred to Aunt Addie's "estates in Derbyshire". Was I really the possessor of estates?

The law takes its time. My mother did not see why Mr. Tennant could not pay out thousands of pounds at once, if not in every direction at least in ours. The Panhard-Levassor did not materialise till September. We had to get used to it in short country spins before we risked anything in the nature of more than half a day's journey. My father insisted on driving it himself. He was enthusiastic rather than expert. My mother reserved her enthusiasm till his should wane, and she could persuade him to engage a "shovver".

One fine soft morning in October we started. The caretaker at Pelham Place had been warned to expect us. My mother decided to remain at home. I sat by my father, and exercised self-control till we were clear of London traffic. After that I enjoyed myself, with only occasional qualms. My father took each peril blandly, as though it did not exist, and reproved me with: "If you're to drive with me in future, you must learn to stop squeaking."

We did the trip in two days, reaching Matlock in time for tea. Pelham Place was nine or ten miles farther on, in Crumbolt. I could not tell whether it was a rather large village or a rather small town. In effect, when you reached it, it was neither. Crumbolt lay high. The approach was romantic, along a rising road between rocky verdured hillsides, with a river rushing through a ravine on the left. An occasional small waterfall splashed down through the trees to increase the flow of the stream. The trees on the steeps grew almost from top to bottom, and the way in midsummer must have been richly gloomy. Just now it was at its best; the leaves had thinned and brightened, the face of the rock ahead glowed with tender lemon and salmon, strong red and gold, and a light mist softened the hard contours of the hills. Just before Crumbolt the road widened, and became dotted with houses and cottages. Their gardens rose behind them in terraces, their fronts faced the gorge with the river, audible but not visible, in its depths. I began to feel a sort of picturesque melancholy, a mood not usual to me. I rather enjoyed it, but knew from that moment that nothing would induce me to live in Crumbolt.

Things cleared a little near an inn and a post office. My father tooted his horn, and came to a standstill. A man came out of the inn.

"Pelham Place?" called my father. The man jerked his thumb over his shoulder, the way we had come.

"We've passed it," said my father. "I shall have to turn."

I shut my eyes during the process, and recited Kubla Khan to keep my mind off it. I was convinced we would be dashed to pieces in "caverns measureless to man" before we were done. However, the backing and tacking ended in time, and I felt us shooting downhill instead of up. I looked on the world again, and suggested: "Go slower, or we'll pass it a second time."

A woman trudged with a pram up the hill; I shouted: "Pelham Place?" as we came abreast. She pointed behind her. "Turning on your left." It was an opening in the hillside we hadn't noticed on the way up.

"Peter Pan will never do it, dad."

"He can have a shot at it."

"Oh, *please* don't try!"

"Well I can't leave him out on the road. It means going back to the inn."

"Then let's go back to the inn."

I dreaded getting stuck in that stony cleft, though this turn was worse than the other. I was surprised to find myself, fifteen minutes later, walking up a narrow way with my father, the Panhard-Levassor safe and sound at the "Trout and Fly".

The lane described a curve above the houses on the road, and came out on a plateau hidden from below by the lowest rank of trees. One could breathe here. Some way behind, the rocky hill-side rose again, but less ominously. A gate in a stone wall promised hope, and as we hesitated a nice old woman in a sun-bonnet opened it. She took us in at a glance, and called pleasantly: "Mr. Lang?"

"Good afternoon; Mrs. Chester, I suppose."

"Good afternoon, sir. Good afternoon, miss. You've had a long journey, but the kettle's boiling."

We passed through the gate. So this was my estate.

About an acre and a half of shrubs, flowers, vegetables, and weeds. Only near the house were the weeds not predominant. It was a two-storied grey stone house, neither large nor small, attractive nor unattractive. Nondescript. Perhaps the back had more to offer.

"Can't I ramble?" I whispered. "We've had our tea."

"Mustn't hurt her feelings," said my father.

We followed Mrs. Chester to the old-fashioned kitchen quarters, large and inconvenient, yet somehow comfortable. There was a good fire in the big kitchener, and the utensils on the high mantelpiece, and the meat-jack in the corner, shone like gold and silver. The dresser was filled with the remnants of dinner and tea services, in cheap but pleasing transfer patterns. The window had lace curtains, but the table was covered with a reversible red and purple cloth in a large clover-leaf pattern. The floor had oilcloth over the stone flags, and two or three gay rag rugs, littered with a puppy, three kittens, and several small children. Mrs. Chester shooed them all out, and made us sit down to the plates of food on the table, while she brewed our strong pot of tea.

"You didn't say if you'd be staying, sir. I got two rooms ready."

"We were not sure of our plans. By the way, Mrs. Chester, you must refer all questions to this young lady. She's the owner."

The old dame turned to me with a smile.

"Yes," I said, "We'll stay one night if it's no bother."

"No bother at all, miss. I've aired the beds and put in the hot bricks."

"How long have you been here, Mrs. Chester?"

"I was born in Crumbolt, miss."

"Then did you know Miss Granby?"

"Just as a girl. I was about fifteen when she went away. She'd be going on for thirty then."

"She was very pretty, wasn't she?"

"As pretty as a picture. I heard my mother say there'd be no chance for any other young lady round about till she did go."

"I wonder why she went."

Mrs. Chester smiled demurely. "They said 'twas on account of Sir Terence Hogan. A much older man than Miss Granby. She'd never said yea to any, and old Mr. Granby, who had a rare temper, was that put out for throwing away her last chance that it led, so my mother always thought, to her flouncing off. Miss Granby had a temper of her own."

"And she never came back again?"

"Not once to my knowledge. She was too busy bookwriting in London. We used to hear rare tales of her there, and often read pieces in the newspapers. Have a bit more ham, miss."

"No, thank you, I've had a splendid blow-out. I'd like to run round the grounds before it's too dark."

"I'm afraid you'll find them sorely untidy, miss. I can only keep a little bit going, with my son coming in to dig it now and again. They're his children you saw. Granny keeps an eye on them for him sometimes. Won't you refresh yourself before you go out? I can fetch a can of hot water to your room. I've given you the room that used to be Miss Granby's. I thought you'd like it."

"Thank you very much." But as I went upstairs, I found I wasn't liking anything particularly. My spirits sank as I washed my face and hands at the vast washstand in the room that had held Aunt Addie a prisoner. It was at the back of the house, and looked down on the main part of the garden. A cedar tree on the lawn darkened the window where she once stood pining for Stanislaw. It was a fairsized room, able to accommodate the heavy mahogany furniture of a later period than her girlhood. The wallpaper was later too. Nothing there spoke to me of her, or the emotions of her youth.

I went through the other rooms, all much of a character, characterless. Somebody who had inhabited them in the 'Seventies or 'Eighties must have refurnished them. I knew nothing of the house's later history, and was not inclined to ask. Pelham Place had meant something to Aunt Addie, and that was why she had never revisited it. Whatever it may have been, I doubted if it could have meant anything to her in its present aspect. She was right not to go back, if she had anything delicate or beautiful to preserve.

Downstairs I found my father immersed in the library.

"Extraordinary!" he said, without looking up.

"What?"

"The sort of thing old Granby collected round him. Must have been a man of peculiar tastes."

"What sort of tastes?"

My father looked up, shutting his book, but keeping a finger in place. "Not the sort of tastes one expects a young lady to understand."

"Meaning your daughter?"

"Fortunately most of these things are very dull, unless you do understand 'em."

"I don't consider myself deficient in intelligence. They're my books now, dad. If they engross you, I'll make you a present of them."

"Rubbish!" said my father. "I wouldn't have 'em in the house! What your mother would think! I was only just looking."

"I'm going to have a look at the garden."

"Run along then." My father opened the book at his page again. I laughed and slipped away, glad of the chance to explore the grounds alone. I had kept those inherited documents to myself, and after seeing the scrapbooks, bits of old lace, and odd trinkets, my

parents had expressed no curiosity. I went into the misty October
garden in search of an Aunt Addie I only knew; and in search of
Stanislaw.

The unkempt garden ran back on the level for about two
hundred yards, and what it had been like sixty years ago was past
recovery. It was now chiefly neglected grass and ornamental
shrubs, with the remnants of tiled flowerbeds round the border.
Neither there nor elsewhere a hint of raspberry canes. It was
beyond the shrubs that I made my small discoveries. Behind the
plantation the rocks began again, and "the grounds" began to take
steps up the hill-side. The shrubbery had been formed in a
semicircle, with its hollow enclosure hidden from the house. When
you entered it, you faced the ascent. It looked a very likely
rendezvous, and routing among the rank growths of ragwort and
hogweed that had taken possession, I found a square stone or
marble plinth sunk in the ground. It had evidently once supported
a statue—two statues perhaps. Those who had the labour of
removing Venus and Adonis ten years ago must have found it
impossible to uproot their base, and been only too willing to leave it
where it was. Aunt Addie wouldn't know; it must have cost her a
pretty penny anyhow. The first step uphill was flanked by pampas-
grass; on the second, about two feet higher up, a narrow terrace
stretched from side to side of the rocky boundaries. At one end was
a broken column, its capital fallen in the grass—or had it, from the
very first, been laid there? Roses, gone back to briar, sprawled
everywhere, making the ascent a thorny one. It now resolved itself
into an irregular spiral staircase in the rock, with pauses for effect
at suitable points. In one, where a trickle ran down between small
ferns, a rickety bridge took the place of the expected step; in
another a sundial stood in a sunny angle; a spidery, vine-clad
tunnel of "rustic" work led to another riot of pampas-grass,
through which one reached the summit. I found myself on the top
of a circular spur enclosed by a castellated battlement, and
crowned with a dilapidated erection which I recognised at once as
the "Gothic Temple." Seated within it, one looked down on the
cedar and the roof of the house, across to the ravine where the river
flowed. It was damp, and smelled dismally of decay. It would have
enchanted Caroline Tarletan, but not me. That was all the grounds

could offer me. A constricted little effort at romance. I clambered down to rejoin my father in the library. There were a lot of books, ill arranged on the shelves. Most of them had suffered from use and disuse, and intruders had pushed their way in among the natives; works of fiction such as *Soldiers Three, A Princess of Thule, Red as a Rose is She, The Channings,* and *The Lilac Sunbonnet.* These and their like were not of youthful Adelaide Granby's time. By the "Classics and Memoirs" I remained untempted; I found a set of Spectators on the high shelves, but neither Petronius nor the Abbé Dubois. I did, however, find something to interest me tucked away in a top corner. It was a manuscript book bound in brown morocco, with a label printed in gold letters: "CATALOGUE."

The first page announced more imposingly:

CATALOGUE

of the

LIBRARY

Of Mr. Jonathan William Granby Esquire

of

Pelham Place in the County of Derbyshire

1849

The rest of the book consisted of the orderly catalogue, beautifully, even exquisitely written by hand. The hand of Stanislaw.

I hopped off the little library steps and sat on them, turning its leaves. Here was Petronius, here the Dubois Memoirs. Whether they were somewhere up there behind the Fraser Magazines I did not care; the book that recorded them had a meaning for me, and I decided to keep it in Aunt Addie's trunk.

"What have you got hold of there?" asked my father, from the other end of the room. He had laid his salacious discoveries aside, and was examining the drawers of an early davenport.

"Nothing of any importance. Have you?"

"Only a few overlooked bills and letters."

I crossed the room and, leaning on his shoulder, turned over his small pile of finds. An undated invitation for a *Conversazione* in Matlock. Visiting cards, big and little, among them that of Sir Terence Hogan, "The Laurels." A black-edged letter of condolence on Mrs. Granby's death in 1854: a model letter, which the writer, a Mrs. Stratton, might have culled from a correspondence manual for ladies. A bill for the services of Dr. James Baird, dated September 30th, 1849. I wondered if Aunt Addie had pined, after fate frowned on her grand passion, and needed iron. The thought even flashed across me that perhaps she—One of my friends, in a predicament, had upset herself rather badly. But no; Aunt Addie couldn't have known anything about *that*, in *those* days. Iron—and endless lectures. Poor little Adelaide Granby.

"Dad," I said suddenly, "don't let's stay. Let's go back to Matlock."

"What's in the wind?" asked my father.

"Only that I can't bear it. I'm rather blue, and fearfully bored. It's not seven yet, and only ten miles to go. We could get there easily and put up at a nice bright hotel, and start back first thing in the morning."

"Not afraid to trust me in the dusk?"

"I'll risk it, dad."

"Disappointed with your property, young woman?"

"I suppose I am. I don't know what I expected. I needn't keep it, need I?"

"You can do what you like with it."

"I shall sell it, and give Mrs. Chester something, of course."

And this was what I did with Pelham Place.

Part Three

OLD MAN'S DARLING

Autumn 1931: Spring 1932

DANNY

The war brought to me, as to other women, emancipation. There weren't many of my nice young girl friends of 1912 who in 1918 did not believe in "The Vote"; it was only a few of their more womanly mothers who pleased their men by declaring: "I shan't use it!" The rest of us were learning to stand on our feet. I had never been allowed to drive my parents' Panhard, but before peace was signed I had driven all sorts of things in France. Now, at twenty-nine, I began to dance, flirt, and drink cocktails with the rest of the world, but was not satisfied to leave it at that. I wanted to do something, and qualified as a dentist. My mother was not too pleased.

"If you must do something, though I'm sure, Pam, I don't see why, couldn't you have chosen something a little less comic?"

"Most people don't consider dentistry a laughing matter, mums."

"Well, no daughter of mine shall ever stop my teeth. I'd sooner trust myself to a man than to fifty lady dentists."

"I quite agree. The idea of fifty little whizzy wheels in one's mouth all at once is pure hell."

"Pamela! Where *do* you pick up your language? In my young day—"

"Only gentlemen said it, mums. Ah, but we hadn't the vote then."

"If you think you can do everything men do because of the vote—"

"Not everything, mums. They still have their marital accomplishments."

"I give you up," said my mother.

"I'll stop your teeth yet!" I boasted.

But she died just before I was qualified to do so.

In 1927, when my father reached his grand climacteric, he had a stroke. Not a serious one, but the first days were disturbing and uncertain. I sent for Ada Dancey instantly.

Ada had done her first-aid course so efficiently during the war, that after it her career was marked out for her. She was then eighteen, and had shown from a child an aptitude for nursing. Now her parents used part of Aunt Addie's legacy on her training. She went through Guy's without wanting to run away once, and at twenty-eight was an experienced S.R.N., gay, good-humoured, warmhearted, and practical, not intellectual, but with the sickroom intelligence and instincts of a born nurse, very appetising to look at, and an incessant chatterer. Her volubility was her only fault; she laughed at it herself, and didn't mind being told to shut up. She just gurgled, hit her mouth with her hand, made a face, and started off again. This did not deter people who had once been nursed by her from asking for her again. We nicknamed her "The Babbling Brook." In her Co-op, of course, she was called *Danny*.

"Hello! And what have *you* been up to with yourself?" she demanded of my father cheerfully, and settled down to the job. "Don't worry," she told me that evening. "I'll have him walking in a fortnight."

She was as good as her word. I was deeply grateful to her, and after that never lost touch with her. She confided her affairs to me, and had plenty to confide. She was a restless creature with an appetite for change, veering from Co-op to Private and back again. When she had "a little bit of luck" she laid off, to her own detriment in her profession. She won twenty pounds on an outsider at Epsom, spent it on a week in Paris, and came back to help me as attendant in my practice. She stayed three months, during which she spent most of her leisure writing copiously to the Boulevard Raspail. I had to translate bits of the lavish replies.

"Oo, he *was* sweet!" she sighed and laughed in one breath.

The answers from Paris stopped, as though cut off with a knife.

"Off with the old love and on with the new, I suppose," said Danny. "That's life all over, isn't it! Well, you can't blame him, if I'm not on the spot."

But she fretted a little, and left me for an elderly patient who wanted her permanently. She stayed till the old woman died, had a good time on the fifty pounds she was left, and went back to the Co-op. She had been an orphan for years, and had long ago sold the little house in Muswell Hill, and "blued it."

"You only live once!" said Danny cheerfully.

She continued to run to me in her ups and downs, always laughed at her own "botherations," and never lost her zest and comely looks. Doctors fell for her.

"And me for them," said Danny, with a gurgle. She had a very pretty gurgle, between a breath and a ripple.

In 1931 it was down, not up, with her. Some years seem dogged by bad luck, and this was one. I had her down to my Surrey cottage for Whitsun.

"Oo, isn't this heaven!" said Danny, stretched out in the grass in her bathing-dress, her strong white arms clasped above her head. "Wouldn't I love a little bit of all right like this for my own!"

"What about the little bit of all right you sold in Muswell Hill?"

"Muswell Hill! Whoever wants to live in Muswell Hill? The country for mine, every time! I'm nuts on the country "

"And have no use for Paris, of course."

"There you go, pulling my leg. I've said Bong Jour to gay Paree. I'd like to settle down. Why doesn't some rich old man come along and make me his darling? That's what I'd like to be, an old man's darling."

"And chuck up nursing?"

"Nursing'll chuck up me one of these days. I could nurse my old man and cuddle him both at once. Oh, well, I expect something nice'll turn up soon. It's a long lane that has no silver lining."

I lost sight of her for the rest of the summer. Then, one Sunday, early in September, she popped in on me. One cannot help using these expressions of Danny. Other friends may come in, run in, or drop in; Danny popped. She was looking very attractive, in a brand-new rustcoloured suit and hat that set off her red-brown eyes and red-gold hair, and her creamy skin. She had good silk stockings to match on her pretty legs, rusty suede shoes, and up-to-date gloves and bag. Her powder smelt very nice.

"Hello, ducky!"

"Why, Danny! How smart you look. Where have you blown in from, and what's in the wind?"

She gurgled and winked. "Come up from King's Langley all the way on the bus. Lovely seat in front on top. It's my Sunday off. You'll have to come along and see me."

"See you where? Coffee?"

Danny had struck me at the late and leisurely breakfast I allowed myself on *my* Sunday off.

"Love some. Three lumps, please. Plenty, thanks."

"Toast? Honey?"

"Oo, thanks! Bus riding does make you peckish, doesn't it?" She crammed a square of toast, thickly spread, into her fresh red mouth. "Nice-looking woman you've got now who let me in."

"Nellie? She's as nice as she looks."

"Been with you long?"

"Four months. Come on, Danny, spill the beans. "What is it?"

"'Member what I said to you in the summer?"

"Good lord, Danny! As if I can remember *half* you said!"

"Yes, I do run on, don't I? I mean, what I said about being an Old Man's Darling?"

"You don't mean to say you *are* one!"

"Well, not exactly, p'raps, but you never know, do you? He's such a sweet old boy, too."

"How old?"

"Ninety-nine."

"Help!"

"Yes. Shouldn't have long to wait, should I, eh?"

"Is he a bachelor?"

"So he says. I tell him, if he is, he ought to be ashamed of himself, and it's high time he did the other thing. Only my joke, of course. He loves a joke. I expect I'll look after him till he pops off."

"Is he senile?"

"Not nearly as much as some lots younger. He's wonderful for his age. Wanders a little, that's natural, now and then, but very sweet, you know, and sometimes quite saucy. No, it's his heart and his age. He wants looking after, that's all. He's got plenty of dibs—a pension. He was awfully highly thought of in his job, and I only wish you could see some of his work, it would surprise you. I do his housekeeping, and some of the cooking, and mend him up, and cosset him, and cut his hair, and that. He's got the most beautiful hair, lots of it, white as snow. I make it shine like silver. 'Used to be *your* colour,' says my old boy, 'they called me carrots.' 'They'd get told off if they called *me* carrots,' I said. 'Ah,' he said, 'in my young days red hair wasn't much thought of. If anything it was held to be a slur. Titian didn't come into his own till Rossetti and Co.' That's how he goes on; half the time I don't know what he means. He pays me a good screw. We get on A1."

"How long have you been with him?"

"Seven weeks, but it seems more like seven years. I can say what I like to him; *he* doesn't mind. The other night—" she gurgled. "Really, I oughtn't, I can't think how it slipped out." I waited, sure it would slip out again. "He'd rung his bell—it rings into my room. I ran in in my nightie, and saw he'd had a bit of a turn. So I got his drops, and as I lifted him. I said it! I must have been half asleep."

"What did you say?"

"I said: 'Now then, you barstard, sit up!'" Danny's laugh was infectious.

"Did he mind?"

"Not him! It seemed to perk him up, if anything. Instead of smacking my you-know-what, he said: 'Adey, my Adey!' and put his arms round my neck and kissed me. Of course, one expects it. They all get amorous about three in the morning. But the way he did it, and his calling me by my name was what surprised me. He'd never done it before. I sat with him till I saw he was O.K., and he held my hand and kept mumbling all sorts of things I couldn't catch, but I knew quite well he wasn't thinking of me. You always know when they're dwelling in the past. Well, now, and what about you? Practice booming? Patients rolling up in their Royces? We'll have you in Harley Street before we're done. How's dad?"

After that we talked of people and things known to us both. Danny stayed to lunch, said gaily that she "had a date" for tea, and only after she left did I realise that she had not told me the name of her "sweet old boy," or the profession in which he was so highly thought of. It was of no consequence; she had left me her address, and I thought of him, if I thought of him at all, as Danny's present case.

I heard no more of her till Christmas, when she sent me a card, and I sent her some very pretty paste clips. Her letter of thanks contained the following:

"And now about something I know will interest you. We had a nice quiet day here, I did the dinner and trimmings all up to the mark, holly and mistletoe and all the rest of it. I had port wine, he had a very weak whisky, afterwards I kissed the old boy under the mistletoe in paper caps and all. You'd have laughed to see us. I got him early to bed, and then began opening my parcels. I really hadn't had time for up to then I'd been so busy. Your lovely gift you bet I was pleased with them! Tried them on my undies and hair etc before I got out my jewel box to tuck them away. Couldn't resist turning over my "treasures" (!) while I was about it, and before I'd put them back I heard my old boy's bell. I dashed in just as I was, and found him gasping. Expect the excitement had been a bit too much for him though of course I try not to let him overdo it, and he only had a mite of the breast and sprouts. However, I soon got him to rights again and now for what will interest you. When I ran in I happened to have hold of the vinegarette dear Miss Granby left me in her will you know the one with turquioses (spelling?!) in the top. I had it refilled once and when my old boy was feeling nice and comfy I said to cheer him up here's something pretty take a whiff at it. So he did and then he said Danny how come you by my mother's vinegarette? Come off it, I jollied him, it was left to me in a will. That is as may be says my old boy, but it is my mother's vinegarette all the same, if you lift the plain end you'll see the

writing in the lid. You remember its a double-ended one, and the lid without the turquio—(oh bother it all!) the plain end I never could get open, but he seemed a bit fussed so just to satisfy him I got some pliers and prised it up. Of course I thought he was wandering but sure enough inside the lid in ever such tiny writing was this Julia Pinner from her Devoted Husband April 15th 1832!. Why that's your birthday I said! Yes he said, my father gave it to my mother to celebrate the occasion. You'll be celebrating your hundredth birthday next year, I said. If I live to see it, he said. Of course you will, I said, don't talk such nonsense! I'll see he does too. What do you make of it all? Quite a mystery eh!"

What could I make of it except that, in some way, at some time, Mr. Pinner had crossed Aunt Addie's life.

Pinner?

It sent me doing what I hadn't done for ten years, pulling open drawers upstairs till I had routed out the typescript of Aunt Addie's novel.

The Bastard of Pinsk.

I laughed aloud. The vinaigrette presented at his birth—*had* Mr. Pinner been born in wedlock? I really must go down and see Danny's "case" one day soon. This week was full; next week fuller. I'd go as soon as I could.

I went on putting it off. I was living in 1932, when the interest 1832 held for those long dead was only occasionally stimulated among my own immediate affairs. The visit to King's Langley was postponed indefinitely, like the long letter to that old friend in Alberta which year after year never gets itself written.

But one result Danny's effusion did have. It set me re-reading that ridiculous story—why, Aunt Addie had asked me to do so "twenty years after." I found she was right. Much that had seemed to me trashy now tickled me. I was able to see it as a period piece. Perhaps some modern publisher would prove venturesome. I must see about it—soon. Back it went in its drawer.

To Danny I wrote: "I shall come along and see your Mr. Pinner. If you find out anything more, do let me know."

There matters rested till April 1932.

ALABASTER PEEPSHOW

In April I asked Nellie, my nice-looking maid, if she wouldn't like a little holiday.

"I'd for rather do the spring clean," said Nellie, putting my grape-fruit and coffee on the table.

I reached for the morning paper. "You keep the place clean as a pin, Nellie. I suppose you mean you want to give me hell and the house a thorough upheaval."

"I've been with you nearly ten months now, and it's not had what I call a turn-out since I came. The box-room!" She said it as Hercules might have said: "The Augean Stable!"

"I haven't looked at it since I moved in. Bother you, Nellie, why can't you leave me in peace?"

"I could do the box-room easy by myself, unless, of course, it's personal."

"No, I don't think so, just junk." I propped up the paper. "Do as you like about it. Dear me!"

"Is anything wrong, miss?"

"No, Nellie, nothing at all. Only somebody I know—know about, rather—is celebrating his centenary. I'd no idea it would be noticed in the papers. Do you remember Nurse Danny who came here last autumn?"

"The lively one with red hair? Yes, miss."

"It's her old patient. He seems to have been quite a person in his way."

"What did he do, miss?"

"Designed stamps, and banknotes, and all sorts of official things for the Government. He retired at seventy, in 1902. They say here that everybody is familiar with his work, though few with his name."

"What name, if one might ask, miss?"

"Mr. Stanley Pinner, of King's Langley. King George has sent him a telegram."

"Fancy that," said Nellie, and retired to arrange the Tatlers and Spheres in the waiting-room.

So that was Danny's "sweet old boy"—Aunt Addie's Stanislaw. The paragraph concentrated praise of his gifts into a few lines; his draughtsmanship was a miracle. He was the sort of penman who could have written Oberon's and Titania's marriage lines on the petal of a forget-me-not. No wonder he had inscribed so exquisitely those memorial lines to Aunt Addie twenty years ago, when he was only eighty.

"I mustn't miss him," I told myself. "I'll write a line to Danny to expect me on Sunday."

But that day, already full of patients, landed two extras on me, with urgent needs that demanded instant attention. My last case of the day suffered from nerves, and the work was trying; dentists' patients think they alone suffer, they don't dream how they wring it out of you. When at last I knocked off, the telephone rang: Hugh Vernon asking me to dine with him at Gennaro's and go along to Greta Garbo's latest.

"I'd love to but I'm dog-tired, Hugh."

"Buck you up."

"As long as you don't propose to me again."

"I'll behave as though you were my maiden aunt."

"I'll come then. I'm so fogged I was afraid I might cave in, if you made yourself a nuisance."

I had only time to wash and brush up, and the note to Danny never got written. Next day was Saturday; I couldn't descend on her at such short notice. I would suggest next Sunday to her, and picnic this week-end by myself in Surrey.

"Shall you want me, miss?" asked Nellie.

"No, it's only one night. I can camp in the cottage. You take a long Sunday off with your boy-friend."

"I haven't got one," said Nellie, grieving faintly.

I was on the point of telling her to set about getting one, when I caught the expression which said she had her memories. "One of these blasted one-life-one-love women," I thought, and realised how little I knew about her.

I returned refreshed on Sunday night, garaged the car, and let myself into the house. A supper-tray was set in the dining-room; all the usual paraphernalia, plus one. At first I thought it was a pot of preserves, then I recognised something I hadn't thought of for nearly fifteen years. Alicia Linton's alabaster peepshow.

"Where on earth has *that* come from?"

I held it under the electric light, and applied my eye. Chatsworth, Grotto, River in Gorge, Garden, The Peak, Chatsworth. What a gem of a toy! How my friends would adore it!—and ransack the Caledonian Market for another. I could hardly eat my supper for playing with it. I hadn't half appreciated it in 1912. But how had it cropped up now? Of course! Nellie had taken a long Sunday off in the box-room. I taxed her with it next morning when she appeared with the tea.

"Nellie, how dare you! You've been at all that junk."

"You said I might."

"Not on a Sunday. I told you to enjoy yourself."

"I did enjoy myself, miss. Oh, miss—I"

She pointed to the peepshow by my bed.

"Amusing old thing, isn't it?"

"Oh, miss—I know it! I never dreamed till I found it yesterday that you were Miss Alicia Linton's lady."

"Good gracious, Nellie! Did you know Alicia Linton?"

"I was in service at Battledores, miss, and when I found the toy I remembered you coming as plain as anything, though I never reckernised you when you engaged me."

"You don't mean to tell me you were the little maid there? The one Miss Linton was teaching poetry?"

"Yes, miss. Poor Miss Linton. She used to show me her things—many's the time we looked down that peep-hole together. I loved it. I remember you writing to ask for it afterwards. That's how I knew when I found it yesterday."

"If I'd known you loved it I wouldn't have asked for it."

"Oh, I shouldn't have had the face to ask for myself, and Miss Alicia had given me lots of her books. I wasn't without a keepsake of her."

Keepsake! "What books did she give you, Nellie?"

"Those beautiful ones in silk bindings with pictures of ladies and poetry and stories in them. She said: 'Now Miss Granby's gone I've no more use for them.'"

"She knew my great-aunt had died then? I couldn't be sure."

"Sometimes she did and sometimes she didn't seem to.

Of course she was very near the end herself, and sometimes talked as though Miss Granby was in the room, Adeline she called her. She took me for her sometimes. 'Remember, Adeline,' she said to me, 'fidelity is the twin sister of love.' I've never forgotten her saying it. Next moment she called me by my right name: 'Nellie, I want you to have my books,' she said, 'those in the first two shelves of the little bookcase. Remember me when you read them.' I didn't know if I rightly ought to take them, but she seemed set on it, and I thought, you can always put them back if she doesn't pass. But she did, two days later, and nobody said nothing, so I thought I could keep them. I take them with me wherever I go. I often have a read in them."

"Have you them here now?"

"Yes, miss. Would you like to have a look at them?"

"I'd adore to. Drat! There goes eight o'clock. I'll have to bunk. Isn't Mavis May coming at eight forty-five?"

"Yes, miss, because she has to be at the studios early."

"There's always a because. Turn on my bath."

I hopped out of bed, gulped down the headlines with my

breakfast, and went to attend to a speck in Miss May's pearly teeth, before she exposed them to the camera-man in *"Once Bit Twice Shy."* It wasn't till lunch that, opening my paper, I saw the announcement of Stanley Pinner's death—"peacefully in his sleep." I'd lost my last chance to discover—what?

"Blow!" I said. "And I might have seen him any time this six months. Pamela Lang, you're a b—procrastinator."

LINES TO MISS MEYER

I wrote a letter of confidence to Danny on the loss of her sweet old boy, and said I hoped I should see her soon. She replied in a few hasty lines; she felt the loss *dreadfully*, missed him *terribly*, though wouldn't have him back on any account, was up to her eyes, had lots to tell me, and would pop along and tell it as soon as she could, just now her hands were full for poor dear Mr. Pinner had left her the house, wasn't it sweet of him, and everything in it, only his old firm sending somebody to collect every scrap of paper and drawings to do with his old Government work, because if they got into the wrong hands something about forgeries which she didn't understand: "Don't look much like a forger, do I, eh?"

There was nothing to answer in this; I must abide Danny's time, hoping that among the lots she had to tell me would be a little bearing on Aunt Addie's past, which had turned up again so unexpectedly through Nellie Cunningham.

She had brought me a pile of *Keepsakes* and *Books of Beauty* to look at, and I found myself absurdly enthralled by them. Secure in The Vote I could enjoy these superlative ladies of the Nineteenth Century whose point of view had threatened our own so long. What poems, what stories they fed on! The scenes of the romances, so remote from life, were laid in Italy, Spain, the Orient; most of the verses had a dying fall—death haunts these flowers, this tree once sheltered friends that are no more. As for the pictured beauties of their age, recurring at intervals behind tissue paper, with an address to each in placid rhyme—if they were really like their steel-plate engravings, did they ever live? Their graces of person, temperament, and toilet, seemed to remove them from shadow of evil and touch of decay. Be smooth and lifeless, fair ones, they seemed to say, secure in transparent gauze and lustrous satin, pearls in your raven or your floss silk tresses, a rose or a dove upon your taper finger, those large calm eyes looking upward and outward from their oval settings, as though unconscious of the swelling charms so liberally indicated lower down. Here was one I dimly recognised—"Miss Meyer"; one I had lingered over in Miss Alicia's room while she dozed:

> *"The star of eve that shines when dews are weeping,*
> *The glowing moss-rose hanging on the bough,*
> *The swan upon the purple water sleeping—"*

Surely I dimly recognised the lines as well? Where had I met them before? A line further on brought recollection:

> *"That master-charm of all—the gift of Mind."*

The Gift of Mind! I was convinced that expression had occurred among the documents bequeathed to me by Aunt Addie.

I made a bee-line for the wooden trunk in the box-room; I hadn't unlocked it since I took my present house, or examined it for longer. I tumbled out the old diary, the packet of letters, the poems Stanislaw had addressed to her year after year. The one for 1863, the year when Aunt Addie's gifts of mind had resulted in her first publication, was a faithful transcript of the Lines to Miss Meyer. Oh, Stanislaw, Stanislaw!

Amused, I carried the papers down to my sanctum and began to compare them with the contents of the books dedicated to lovely woman. Almost every one of the verses sent was there, sometimes condensed, sometimes slightly adapted. Even *"Je voudrais être."* Stanislaw had not composed one of them.

"IF YOU LOVE MEE—"

It wasn't till Whitsun, when I repeated last year's invitation, that I saw Danny again. I heard her clear gay "Cooee!" at the gate, and met her half-way down the garden path. She was lugging a smart new suitcase in one hand, and in the other a hat-box to match, and a parcel. After the first greetings:

"Ouf!" she said. "I'm tired. I'd sooner nurse a case of double pneumonia than clear up after a death."

"Of course you would. You adore double pneumonia cases. I suppose you've found plenty to clear up in King's Langley."

"'Cumulation of years, ducky. Not but what he was very tidy, method in all things was his motto, but 'plenty'? You said it! I brought some bits along I knew would interest you. Poor old sweet, I miss him terribly." Her eyes filled. She brushed the tears away. "Can't think why he was so awful good to me."

"He was grateful, and jolly lucky to have you at the last."

"Well, nobody's kicked up a fuss any old how. Not that there's anybody *to*, as far as I know. He hadn't got a relative in the world, and left most of his little all to the Freemasons. I hadn't been with him six months when he said: 'You suit me, Adey, stick to me and I shan't forget you.' 'Go on,' I said, 'I don't want any corruption and bribery, I'll stick to you as long as you want me to.' 'That's all I ask,' he said, and next week he sent for his solicitor and said in my presence: 'I'm going to leave this very kind lady provided for, and I don't want it to be said I wasn't Compis-something-or-other, there's nobody with any claims on me now and I know my own mind.' The solicitor, such a nice man, a Mr. Bracknell, beautiful teeth, smiled at me and said: 'We'll see it's not put down to undue influence.' 'Well,' I said, 'I'm sure it's very good of Mr. Pinner, and more than I deserve.' But, of course, I never dreamed he'd leave me the house."

"What shall you do with it?"

"Sell it—or let it—run it as a nursing home, p'r'aps—oh, I dunno. It's much too big for me-all-alone. You'll have to advise me. Oh, but never mind that now, look what I've brought you." She began on the knot of the parcel she was carrying. While she was working at it I remarked:

"I'll always be sorry I never saw Mr. Pinner. I suppose you never found out any more about that vinaigrette."

"Not exactly. I tackled him about Miss Granby though. Damn this knot, I can't think what I was up to."

"Did he say he'd known her?"

"Course he did."

"Did he mind talking about her?"

"Not a bit. He rather seemed to enjoy it. You know how old people are."

"What did he say about her?"

"Well—there! I think it's coming now."

"Cut it, Danny."

"What, waste a good bit of string? Not much! String's one of my economies. I never got what I call a real good talk about her. He wandered off a bit, towards the end he often called me Addie instead of Adey, and once he called me Alicia—"

"That was the governess, Miss Linton."

"Oh—yeah? Held my hand awful tight and said: 'You'll help me, won't you, Alicia, you'll help me always, you're the only friend we've got in the world, you'll help me?' I told him not to worry, I'd always help him, but, of course, I wouldn't bother his poor old mind to explain what he meant. It was the same week he went. There's no doubt he was sweet on Miss Granby at one time."

"And she on him?"

"I 'spect so, though they quarrelled."

"What about?"

"He couldn't seem to remember. He chuckled and said she was as pretty as a picture in a tantrum—that was some months before he died. 'What did she get in a tantrum about?' I asked. He said: 'It's all so long ago, but I think she was not very kind to my mother.' That's got it!"

The string came free at last, and out of the parcel Danny took another in shabby brown paper, neatly tied and sealed, a book or two, and a few other oddments.

"These are some things I picked out here and there during the rummage. Thought you'd like something to remember the old boy by, though you never saw him, for Miss Granby's sake. Look, here's some of his work, I couldn't help keeping back one or two to show you, did you ever see anything so marvellous? These books, this big one's called *The Dresden Gallery*, I know you're fond of pictures, some awful pretty things in it and some a bit h'm—h'm! Here's Miss Addie's very first book in three vols, *Miss Ponsonby's Past*—I dipped into it, but the style's a bit too old-fashioned for me, give me *The Sheik* every time—oh, is gold-leaf any good to you? I found a whole packet he used for his work, and some of his fine instruments, buzz 'em away if they're no use to you. This funny old seal he used to seal things with, carnelian, isn't it? He told me he picked it up in a gutter in Matlock when he was a boy, and thought it a tremendous find. He was quite poor, you know. There's two photos of him I thought'd amuse you, one in his prime and one when he retired, and this quaint old china snuff-box, look what it says—'If you love me lend me not.' Nothing about not giving though, so there you are."

She tumbled her assortment of gifts on the table. I picked up the photographs. Mr. Pinner in the 'Seventies and his prime was a pleasant-looking man, with a fixed expression that was the photographer's, and features largely hidden by hair; in the costume of his time he looked, as do most old photographs of men not very distinguished, slightly comic. At seventy he was clean-shaven; a very sweet mouth had come to light again, and his eyes were both _ kind and humorous. He looked rather a darling, and I quite understood him as Danny's "sweet old boy."

"Thank you, Danny. I'm really delighted to have these. What's in the packet?"

"I dunno. It's marked 'Adelaide Georgiana Granby,' so I thought it would be more *your* affair than mine."

"You never even opened it? What self-restraint!"

"Well, all those seals look so sort of official, I didn't like to. That's the little lot, ducky. I'm dying for my tea."

"Nellie is bringing it out to the hammock by the pond."

"Oo, bliss! Got time to wash and that and change into a sunbathing?"

Off she went to her room, and I sat fingering the relics of Aunt Addie's lover. The photographs made me sigh and smile at once; it was hard to fit this face into a Grand Passion. But how little exteriors tell. Now Hugh Vernon, with his looks, might easily—but Hugh, like most of the men I knew, was incurably flippant; and that didn't fit. It wasn't a matter of looks. I picked up the little patch-box—it wasn't a snuff-box-with its painted forget-me-not posies and its motto: "If You Love Mee Lend Mee Not." I felt I had seen it before, but I couldn't think where, and supposed I had only seen other boxes like it. That shop opposite Leicester Square Tube Station was full of them.

I gathered my 'little lot' together again, and, exercising self-restraint, decided not to open the sealed parcel till Danny had gone to bed.

LETTER FROM ADELINE TO STANISLAW

The seals on the parcel were impressed with Stanislaw's youthful find, a crowned eagle and a motto in characters which I took to be Russian. It contained yet another packet, and an envelope. Inside the last was the early picture of Aunt Addie at sixteen, with her writing on the back: *To my Belovèd Stanislaw from Adeline.* Next, a folded pink silk tissue paper, containing a gold-brown curl. Last, a letter addressed in Alicia Linton's sprawling hand to "Mr. Stanley Pinner, 15, Caroline Crescent, Matlock." Alicia's writing always put one off, and before settling to it I opened the final parcel—or would it contain another? Aunt Addie's romance was like one of those Indian boxes that charmed me in childhood; the green one contained a yellow, the yellow a red, the red a blue, the blue a pink, and so on seemingly ad infinitum, till one reached the core, as tiny as a seed, which the nest had held like a secret, round which it had grown. No, no more parcels; a letter and some segments of manuscript. When I saw that I held in my hand what had been torn out of Adelaide Granby's diary, I felt that at last I had come to the seed in the nest.

The letter was also from her.

The Acacias,
Sydenham Hill.
April 14th 1902.

My Dear Stanislaw,

How long is it since I have written to you? Fruitless to try to remember. In twenty-four hours you will reach seventy, and escape me again by a year. I see you are about to retire from work. I congratulate but shall not emulate you. When I retire from work I shall not live. This year I publish my 39th, and hope I shall live to publish my 50th. But Victoria's death was a great blow to me. If she can't go on for ever, why should I? How immortal one is as long as one lives and breathes! And loves? Yes, and loves.

You never forget our Anniversary—nor do I. You always signalize it exquisitely. I never forget our parting day—do you? I have my own way of signalizing it. I re-create and re-live it in every detail, as though I were sixteen again, and you a year older. And so we are at heart; for my part I could swear in the witness-box that at heart I am every age I ever was. What is this thing called "old" age? Our outsides alter, and to the younger generation we are as faded as the pictures in our albums. It amuses me when I see them treating my wits gently, as though my self were fading like my skin. The longer I live the more certainly I know that while our outsides wither, something within is intact, not old, not young—something that is myself, yourself. And yet, you are going to "retire"! From what? From work?—that is to say, from life? What about love?

Did you know I kept a record of our love? It has been my habit, for more than fifty years, to solemnly read this record day by day when March comes round, and, till the end of June, re-live each recorded hour, and very much more. How could I have recorded each blissful moment, each moment of grief? There were too many of them! Each separate minute of first and only love is a world in itself; that is why three or four months become, in retrospect, an eternity, that is the advantage of "young" age over "old" age. Later on the years are a continuity—but then a single year was 365 days, each day was 24 hours, each hour 60 minutes—and every one of those minutes held its meaning. No wonder the first half of life seems, so long, the last half so short.

Those minutes of joy and pain are recorded indelibly on my heart—therefore I send you on your retirement from life love's record in ink. I need it no more. Women's memories, Alicia once said, last longer than men's. When yours are fading, refresh them with the enclosed.

For ever your devoted

Adeline

P.S. No need to reply. I know the Sixth of May will bring me another beautiful poem from your pen.

YOUNG LADY'S DIARY: 1849

———————

March 10.

I had my first writing lesson to-day in the libery. It seems I hold my pen entirely wrong. Stanislaw showed me how to place my fingers, and then Alicia said he must place hers. At the end of the lesson he said to me: "I think you will write better in time"—and to Alicia: "I am afraid it is too late for you to make a good pen-woman, your style is formed, your hand is set, you should have begun earlier."

"Indeed!" said she, "I am not yet old enough to be your Grandmother!"

This made him turn pink, he flushes very easily, having a delicate skin. His hands are too delicate, but very steady, and when he is working or teaching he becomes absorbed and forgets to be shy.

Later on Alicia said to me: "How old do I seem to you? Does 27 seem very old?"

I said: "About as old as Lady Capulet because she was just double Juliet's age."

"Yes," said Alicia, "I suppose so, yet I have never thought of myself as old as her."

"You are a model of wisdom and experienced cunning," I pointed out, "and look at your past and all you have gone through."

"I have not told you nearly all," said Alicia.

"No," I said, "but I can well imagine it."

She looked unhappy, so I put my arms round her neck and said: "We will not speak about your past, whatever it was you are my dearest friend."

"Your dearest *female* friend," she said meaningly, meaning Stanislaw I suppose, but I can hardly call him a friend yet, and I think he is too shy to become one.

I am practising my new writing in my diary, and think this page shows an improvement already.

March 12.

S— paid Alicia particular attention to-day, and made her do certain stroaks again and again till she got quite cross at last and said she would not have her handwriting tampered with. "I am what I am," she said, "and it is a part of me. You must not try to teach your *grandmother* to suck eggs." She went out of the room after that, and S— looked quite cast down. I said: "You must not mind her, it is her age. It must be very sad to grow old."

"I do not like hurting people," said Stanislaw. "I am afraid she is offended."

"It comes of being sensitive. It is better to be sensitive than stupid."

"Are you sensitive?" he asked.

"Do you think I am stupid?" I teazed.

He blushed and answered: "No, I think you are clever and—" He did not go on, so I asked: "And what?"

"And kind," he said, after thinking.

"Oh," I said, "I am by no means always kind, I can assure you. I have my Papa's temper."

"I cannot imagine you in a temper," said Stanislaw—so I stamped my foot at him and cried: "I *hate* people without imagination!"

He looked so startled that I could not forbear to burst out laughing, on which he laughed too.

"You see, I can!" I triumphed.

"Well then, you must teach me to have more imagination while I teach you to write better."

"I wish," I said, "you would also teach me to sketch; I thought the painting Miss Spencer showed us most beautiful."

"I will teach you anything you like," said Stanislaw.

March 13.

I have kept him to his word. I brought my scrapbook to the lesson to-day and showed him my attempts. Alicia sat in a corner and did some woolwork. Stanislaw looked at everything carefully and asked if I had living models for Bonny and Fluff, and I said partly but they would not stand still enough, so I finished them off from memory. Stanislaw said it was better for beginners to have models than imagination, with a little smile, and I told him I had done the china ornaments from the things in our cabinet. I ran and fetched them so that he could see how close I had copied the patterns.

"The flowers and colours are nicely done," he said, "but I think the shepherdess is a little beyond you, and the drawing of the teapot and the box—well, I must show you a little about perspective." He picked up the patchbox and said:

"How very pretty."

"That did not come out of the china closet," I said, "it is mine. I keep my lilac cachoux in it."

He read the motto: "If You Love Mee Lend Mee Not"—then drawing my scrapbook to him copied it there in its fine script with all its flourishes exact to the life.

"Oh!" I said. "If only I could do it like that!"

"Was this a present to you?" he asked in a low voice.

"Yes, from my Godmama."

He said again that it was very pretty, and then we went to our writing. At the end of the lesson, when we rose to leave him, he said to Alicia who had not spoken a word: "I hope you have forgiven me for yesterday."

Alicia answered: "*Tout comprendre*—you know the rest."

"I am afraid I don't," he said.

"Do you not speak French?"

"No, not a word."

"Well then," she said, "in plain English, all is not only forgiven but forgotten."

March 19.

Papa said too many lessons and too little cataloge, so we have not done quite so much this past week, but I practice by myself, and have done more music with Alicia. I heard her singing a wonderful passionate song—"Are they meant but to deceive me?"—which I had not heard from her before; she says it is a sort of Polonaise, full of foreign feelings, which she had not felt since she was in Paris. I asked if she had the music and she said, Yes, and I said I would like to learn it. She said, "You would never sing it as it should be sung," which put me out a little, and I said well anyhow I would like to try, for I have found one can imitate feelings even if one does not have them.

March 20.

To-day Stanislaw said: "I never seem to see you now."

I said: "It is because the cataloge does not get on fast enough." "I will sit up at night," he said, "and leave more time for the lessons during the day."

"It will try you eyes to work long hours by lamplight."

"I shall not mind that," he said, "it is a pity to interrupt the lessons, now you are getting on better." I felt myself blush with pleasure.

"I am glad you think I will do you credit," I said, "but I should be sorry if you hurt your eyes."

"You are always kind," said Stanislaw.

I wonder what colour his eyes are. One does not like to stare.

March 21.

We are busy again, and Papa has praised Stanislaw to Mama for his diligence, so he is satisfied with the progress of the cataloge. But I wish he would not speak of him as "Young Carrots." I asked S— how long he thought the cataloge would take, and he said chearfully "O a very long time."

March 22.

To-day Alicia beckoned me to her room. I knew by her air of mystery she had something of extreme importance to tell me. "See," she said, "what I have just picked up." She shewed me a carnelian seal, carved with an eagle and a crown, and some foreign letters even she did not understand, although she speaks several tongues with idiomatic proficiency. "Where did you pick it up?" I asked. She hesitated, and then said: "In the gunroom."

"Do you mean," I asked, "in Stanislaw's bedroom?"

"I had gone to leave him the poems of Lamartine—I think I shall offer to teach him French—I knocked—he made no answer—I entered—he was not there! I had put down the book and was about to leave, when I saw this on the window-ledge. I picked it up carelessly—and then, I understood!" "Understood what?" I asked. "He is of noble birth. I have felt it from the first!' said Alicia.

I was nearly overwhelmed by the revelation. "But Miss Spencer is only a lady needlewoman."

"She is but his half-sister."

"They have the same mother."

"But not the same father, dearest. Oh, this crown proclaims the truth!"

Stanislaw the son of a King! I was dazzled and overjoyed.

"Let us impress the seal," I said, all eagerness.

We made several impressions, but the motto defied us. They were not even like ordinary characters. Alicia said they must be Hebrew or Greek or Sanskrit or Polish or Russian. I said there were no Sanskrit or Hebrew Kings now, and she said the motto was much more likely to be in Slavonic.

"I shall ask Stanislaw what tongue it is in," I said.

"Never, never!" said Alicia, earnestly. "He must not know we have probed his Secret. He will divulge it himself in his own hour. I will replace this where I found it, and he will not even know that we suspect."

His Secret! How wonderful! To think we have a Faulconbridge under our roof! Already I regard him with new eyes.

March 25.

The weather has turned fine and very mild. It was warm enough to-day to sit in the Gothic Temple. I said to Stanislaw, bring the paints and sketching-block, we will sketch in the open from nature. He had not ventured to explore the garden, so I had the pleasure of shewing him its beauties. He had thought it ended at the shrubbery behind the cedar, and was surprized when I led him through the laurel maze into the Grove of Venus and Adonis. He stood looking at them without a word. I told him who they were and he said: "I have heard of Venus."

"But not of Adonis?"

"No, I don't think so. Who was he?"

"One she loved," I explained. "Have you not read Shakspere?"

He shook his head and blushed. "I am afraid I have read very little. Your father's libery is an education in itself, full of things I never heard of. Was Venus and Adonis one of Shakspere's plays?"

"No," I said, "it is a very beautiful poem. Venus woos Adonis but he will none of her and dies and she mourns." He said nothing to this. "Look," I said pointing, "the wild violets are out. I brought them in from the woods because I think they are Shakspere's favourite flower—he says 'Violets dim but sweeter than Cytherea's breath'—Cytherea is another name for Venus."

I picked a few and he helped me, and then I led him up the rocky path to the terrace. He was interested in the column and I told him the fallen capital was one of my favourite seats when I wanted to ponder.

"What do you ponder about?" asked Stanislaw.

"All manner of things," I said. "Things I could not possibly repeat to anybody."

I felt myself growing red; and so did he. He said: "Is this where you want to sit and sketch to-day?"

"Oh no," I said, "I have more surprizes in store for you."

I led him on a bit more up the path till we came to the turn at the bridge. "Now," I said, "we are coming to something very dangerous!"

"If it is pricipitous," he said anxiously, "I have no head for heights."

"If you feel giddy I will hold your hand." I took his hand and went on tiptoe round the corner, pretending we were on the verge of great perils, and when we reached the bridge I cried: "Take care!"

"Is this it?" asked Stanislaw. I burst out laughing. He stopped midway with his hand on the rustic railing, and said:

"I never know how to take you."

"Do not fall over and be dashed to pieces!" I implored.

"What would you do if I did?"

"I should not dash in to save you, if that's what you mean. Ladies do not save gentlemen. I would bury you in a marble tomb, and hang a wreath of willow there once a year."

"Only willow?"

"Well no, to begin with you should have a laurel urn, and a pillow of roses, and a crown of immortelles. Is that enough to satisfy you?"

"It sounds almost worth dying for," said Stanislaw, and we laughed.

Suddenly I dropped his hand and flew ahead of him and hid in the pampas jungle, and when I heard him coming I pretended to be a panther and a snake. Then suddenly I felt I had been dreadfully silly, he looked at me so, and I explained: "When I was little I always played at being a panther in this spot"—which was not true, but I said it to cover my confusion, otherwise I would have gone on feeling ashamed for ever.

At last we reached the Temple and set out the paints, and he shewed me how to draw the composition and lay on the wash, and then do fine brush-strokes on the foliage. He was very quiet and assiduous, and I felt how wonderful it was to be taught painting by a Bastard. I did not do any more silly things on the way down. At the bottom he asked if he might have the violets to paint, and I gave them to him.

March 27.

Papa called me to him and said he had a message for me from Sir Terence Hogan in Ireland. He had written on St. Patrick's Day and sent me a sprig of the true Irish Shamrock. "Tell little Addie it is to bring luck to the receiver and the sender." "I hope it may," I said. "Write and tell him so," said Papa, "now that you are beginning to write a hand fit to be seen."

I penned a few lines to go inside Papa's, and then I penned another for I had determined to share my luck with Stanislaw. I divided my green luck into two and stole down with his half to the little gunroom which they have partly cleared to take his bed, and left it under his pillow with my note: "The true Irish Shamrock that brings happiness and good fortune to the giver and the receiver."

March 28.

I crept early to the libery to put back the Life of Ninon de L'Enclos and find another, and there was Stanislaw with his head on his arms on the table, fast asleep! I was much amazed to find him there before six o'clock, and did not know quite what to do. I stood on the little ladder and pushed Ninon back behind the Bohns where I found her, and just because I wished to be careful was clumsy, and one or two of the Bohns fell with a clatter. Stanislaw jumped up with an exclamatory sound and stood rubbing his eyes and staring at me as though he could not believe them. I put my finger to my lips.

"What have you come for?" he asked in a whisper.

"I am finding a book to read," I whispered back. "I often do before the maids are about." I got down from the ladder and came to him saying: "What are you doing here at this time of morning? Why have you risen so early?"

"I have not been to bed at all," he said. "I have been working."

"At the cataloge? All night!"

"I dozed now and then. I wanted plenty of time so that we could finish your sketch to-day."

"You will make yourself ill," I said as severely as I could in an undertone, for we still talked in whispers. "You must go to bed at once, if only to get an hour or two before breakfast."

He looked at me with, I thought, tears in his eyes.

"Never has anybody been as kind to me as you are."

I did not know what to reply, but he looked so pale and tired I took his hand and we stood for a little while not even whispering. Then I said: "Go to bed now, and look under your pillow."

When I got back to my room I found I had two Bohns in my arm which I did not want. Bohns in my arm! How silly! It sounds like old Nanny who when she was tired use to say:

"I've got a bone in my leg."

Still March 28.

I went to the Gothic Temple and waited for Stanislaw. When he came we began to sketch without saying much. Presently with his eyes on the sketch he said: "Thank you."

"Did you find it?"

"Yes."

"Did you like it?"

"Yes."

"I hope it will bring you luck and happiness."

He said: "It has—I have them."

Then we applied ourselves to the picture again. The scene from the Temple is very picturesque, with its tree-grown rock rising above the river. It seems to want a figure to express it, a wild and gloomy figure in a cloak. I would like to paint a man there wrapped in thought like someone in Byron, but figures are not easy. I thought I might ask S— if I could draw him from life, but I would change the colour of his hair and make it raven. Alicia and I are agreed we wish it were. While I was thinking all this he had been very quiet, and when I looked round he had fallen asleep again. He looked so tired I would not waken him. His hair is very soft although so ruddy.

March 29.

This afternoon I met him in the hall as he was coming down the stairs and I was below. I could not resist dropping a curtsey and saying: "Good day to Your Highness!" He stopped and looked upset, and did not answer. Then he came on down, and said in a low voice: "Miss Adelaide, I beg you not to address me so."

"Why not?" He hesitated and then said: "It seems to mark the difference in class between us, and I cannot bear it." I felt abashed and knew I had committed an indiscretion.

When I told this to Alicia she nodded her head. "His wishes must be respected," she said.

"I suppose they must," I said rather petulantly.

She reproved me. "You should be glad he does not wish emphasized the difference of birth. In his generosity he does not wish you to feel beneath him."

In spite of what I know him to be, I do not. When you have seen someone asleep and weary, you do not.

April 1.

I made an April Fool of Stanislaw, catching him nicely. I saw him crossing the lawn and ran behind the cedar and climbed to the second bough, screaming: "The rat! the rat!" Stanislaw ran like the wind, whistling to Fluff, and calling:

"Don't be frightened, Miss Granby! Find him, Fluff! At him, good dog!" He shouted, Fluff barked, and I laughed till I nearly fell out of the tree. He thought I had the histyricks which made me laugh the more. Alarmed, he climbed to wear I was and suported me. I wiped my eyes and got out: "April Fool!" He stared, and turned quite white, and clutched me harder. I said: "There's no need to hold me as tight as that." He shook so he needed me to hold him, I thought, and I felt quite sorry for him when he said "Forgive me!" and scrambled down all of a tremble. His eyes are hazel, but they are very bright.

April 3.

How radiant is life in springtime! It is the loveliest spring I ever saw. There was never such a rainbow as the one to-day.

April 6.

Last night we had some music in the parlour. This morning I asked Stanislaw if he liked music, and he said he had stood in the garden listening to all we played and sang. I asked why he did not come in, and he said he thought my Mama might not wish it.

I said to Mama: "Why should not the Librarian sit in the parlour after supper? Papa often likes the libery to himself in the evenings and the little gunroom has no elbow-room, but he could go on copying his lists at the table in the corner, and it would save lamp-oil."

Mama praised me for my economy, and said there would be no harm in it.

April 7.

I played both the Pianoforte and the Harp last night, and sang Duetts with Alicia. If I cannot yet write with execution at least my musical execution is tolerable. Papa while smoaking his cigar outside looked in at the window and aplauded his "little nightingale." S— sat very busy in his corner and said nothing and nobody took any notice of him.

April 10.

I made Alicia lure him into the garden to hear the Cuckoo.

Then I called: "Cuckoo!" from the shrubbery. S— said: "Is it not earlier than usual this year?" I climbed up Venus so that I could be seen over the laurestinus and called "Cuckoo!"again. He looked up and saw me and smiled. "She is a dreadful teaze," he said to Alicia.

April 14.

S— told me it would be his birthday to-morrow.

I said: "Then you will be a whole year older than me, though to-day we are of an age."

He gave a little laugh and said: "You aren't very good at arithmetic either."

"What do you mean by either?" I asked. "At writing or arithmetic," he said.

"But is not my handwriting improveing?"

"Certainly it is better than it was."

"But still very bad you think?" I tossed my head.

He looked at me anxiously. "Are you going to be cross?"

"Why should you think so?"

"Because," he said, "I never know which of the Three you are going to be."

"What can you mean, 'The Three'?"

"The Three Graces, the Three Hesperides, the Three—"

"Furies?"

"Well, perhaps."

"What a compliment!" I turned away.

"Now you *are* cross. Please don't, Miss Adelaide, for I cannot bear it."

I turned back again. "Well then I won't, if you can explain your *Three* to me."

He said rather shyly: "I think of you as Three."

"But I am only one, whether Fury, Grace, or Hesperid."

"No," said Stanislaw, "you are three at the very least. Sometimes so gentle, sometimes so gay, sometimes so spirited."

"And which do you prefer?"

"I—" He stopped, then stammered: "I like them all."

"In that case, none of them can be cross with you."

We were picking daffodils in the field behind the Trout and Fly. I am to do them for my next painting in my scrapbook. Stanislaw paints as beautifully as Raphael and writes better than Shakspere (handwriting I mean). I am glad he will be older than me to-morrow.

"Let then the Woman take—" (See Twelfth Night!)

April 15.

I wished Stanislaw "Many Happy Returns of the Day" and gave him for a preasant my little china patchbox, because he had thought it pretty. He did not want to take it. I said he must, to remember me by. "And," I said, "you must never never lend it to anybody. If you love mee lend mee not."

"I will keep it as long as I live," said Stanislaw.

To-night, during the music, he left the room. When I went up to bed he was waiting for me in the passage. He said:

"Miss Adelaide!" and seemed unable to go on. I waited, then he said: "I hope you will accept this from me." He gave me a most beautiful silver-mounted vinigrette with a crown of turgioses round the smelling end. "It belonged to my Mother," he said.

"Oh," I said, "I cannot possibly."

"Please do," he said, "to remember me by."

"But it is your birthday, not mine."—

"I think," said Stanislaw, "people should give preasants on their birthday as well as receive them when they have been happy."

"Have you?"

"Yes, never so happy."

"Well," I said, "I ought not but I will accept your Mother's Vine-grette and keep it as long as I live." He looked as though he was going to cry and I ran quickly upstairs.

It is a most beautiful thing. It must have been given to her by her Regal Husband.

April 16.

I asked Stanislaw if he had read so little how he came to know the Classics so well. "How well do you mean?" he asked.

"The Three Graces, the three Hesperides."

"I found them in your Father's Lempriere."

"And thought them just like me?"

"It is a great privilege to have so many books, I feel I must make the most of my time here."

"The cataloge is not nearly done?" I asked.

"O no it is still a matter of many weeks. It is not only the copying, it is the clasification. I have not yet begun on the book itself for that must be without a blemish, and there are thousands of books, all in a great muddle."

"That makes it much harder?"

"Of course."

I asked him if he had yet read the story of Penelope's web.

No, he said, what was it? I fobbed him off with saying it was not so very particular, but now I shall know what to do. I shall get up early and muddle the books he sorted and clasifyed the day before!

"You will be quite learned when you do," I said.

"More learned than I was I hope," he said.

"Do you like Lamartine ?"

"I cannot seem to manage French at all. I do not think I have a gift for languages."

"Miss Linton would be very glad to teach you."

"I am afraid I have not enough time."

After a moment's pause I said: "Shall I read Lamartine with you?"

"O!" he cried eagerly, "would you?"

"I am afraid," I said, "you have not enough time."

April 17.

I said to Alicia I thought it strange that my Father should have more books than Stanislaw's, he having read so little till he came here. "You must remember," said Alicia, "people like him are brought up with accomplishments rather than learning." I am reading the Plumpton Letters. There is a very curous tale of an elderly Husband who for curous reasons had to let his Wife seem to be his Mistress.

April 19.

The first cuckoo!

I called S— to hear it. He asked: "Are you crying wolf?" "No," I teazed "only Cuckoo!"

The next bird to listen for is the nightingale. S— says he has never heard one.

April 23.

William Shakspere's birthday. I told Stanislaw and said: "We will not write or sketch to-day, we will sit in the shrubbery and I will read you Venus and Adonis."

I read it all through to him while Alicia sat and did her embroidery. At the end I asked: "Do you like it?" He did not seem able to answer. I looked at him and saw he was very pale. I said: "What I cannot understand is how he could resist her." "No," said Stanislaw in a low voice.

Alicia then said: "Some people do not know how to seize their chances." After a moment she said: "I have no more purple wool, I must go and find some"—and she went away.

I did not seem to know what to say or he either, but after a while I said: "I am sorry you did not like the poem."

"I do," he said, "and I thank you for reading it to me."

"I like reading poetry, aloud and to myself." I looked up at the statue. "Poor Venus," I said.

"Why ?"

"For being repulsed."

"Poor Adonis," said Stanislaw, "for being so insensible and missing his chance."

"Oh then," I smiled, "you would not repulse her when she showed you her—"

Suddenly I felt myself growing scarlet, and Stanislaw was as scarlet as I felt. I said hastily: "I must help Alicia find the purple wool," and I ran away.

April 28.

We have hardly spoken to one another for days. I suppose it is all over. Our friendship I mean. O life, you are very hard and very cruel.

May 1.

We went out to see the maying. The children were plaiting their ribbons round the Maypole set up in the Trout and Fly's field. Old Mr. Chester fiddled for them. They called to me: "Miss Addie, come and dance!" so I took a ribbon and Alicia another and then I made S— take the one next to mine. He muddled it at first, which got us all laughing, but soon learned the right movement, and we danced till the ribbons were plaited. Then Mrs. Archer asked us to come in for our May-cakes and beer (but I had cowslip wine and S— asked for milk) and we had them in the field while the children sang their May-song. The cowslip wine quite went to my head, a very little of anything makes me lively, and I teazed everybody as I did before. Hannah Brownrigg was the May-Queen and looked very pretty and proud though her wreath was askew.

Without anything said, all is easy again.

May 3.

The cuckoo was late, the nightingales are early. Last night I thought I heard them over the hill and opened my window, and heard them practicing. I went and tapped on the floor of my closet and heard S— stir, then I opened the closet window and looked down and saw him looking up. "The nightingales," I said, and we listened together.

May 4.

I asked Stanislaw his opinion of nightingales. Alicia, who had also heard them, cried exstatically "They were divine!" S— said "I

am afraid I was disappointed." Alicia said: "Have you no soul?" I
told him they would be better later on, at first they only try a few of
their notes, just broken calls and trills. I said: "They are beginners
like me." Then we went on with the lesson.

May 5.

To-day Papa examined me on my progress and is very pleased
with it. He also expressed himself pleased with my latest paintings.
I did not tell him Stanislaw did the dewdrop.

"Now I shall be able to boast to Sir Terence of my daughter's
accomplishments," said Papa.

"When he comes back from Ireland," I said.

"He is back and is dining with us this evening. We might have a
little music afterwards in that pretty voice of yours. What have you
learned lately?"

I said I would sing "Sweetly the Nightingale" by Mr. Sphor. Its
beauty and tenderness carry me away,

"Believe me if all those endearing young charms!" trolled Papa.
"Give Sir Terence that. It will be a compliment to him as an
Irishman and as a—"

"As a what, Papa?"

"As a dear old uncle, eh?" Papa pinched my ear, a way he has
when he is pleased.

Later.

Sir Terence has gone. He was very agreeable, and pleasant to
Stanislaw too, although he thinks him an Inferior. But I know
better! His voice and manners are those of one, not merely of gentle
but of noble birth! I guard his Secret, yet his every look proclaims
it. He sat writing in his corner during the music. I sang "Sweetly
the Nightingale" for him alone, but he would not once look round.
Sir Terence sat near me turning the music-sheets, too soon or too
late, but fortunately I had my notes by heart. A beautiful night! The
nightingales sang again and we went out on to the lawn to listen to
them. Mama called "Take your shawl" and S— brought it out to me,
and Sir Terence took it from him and put it round me. I hoped S—

would stay but he went in again at once. The nightingales sang better than they have done yet. Sir Terence said: "Pooh! I don't think much of um!" "Then I don't think much of your ear for music!" I said. "I have an excellent ear, Miss Addie," he said, "and the proof is that the nightingales in the trees give me no joy after the nightingale in the parlour."

"Well then I forgive you," I said, and asked him if he knew Boccaccio's beautiful tale about a nightingale. He said he only knew Hans Anderson's, and I said: "That is just a fairytale, I prefer tales about real men and women."

"Then one day, Addie, I shall tell you one," he said. His voice was rather husky, and thinking he had taken cold I said: "I think we had better go in now." I meant to ask Stanislaw why he had been so sulky, but when we got inside he had gone to bed. I shall pick a quarrel with him for it to-morrow.

May 6 or 7.

I do not know if it is after midnight. I do not know if I am awake or dreaming, in heaven or on earth. O my love! My love! My love! One moment of bliss is the fulfilment of a lifetime. I love him with an intensity bordering on extatic worship. I did not know feelings could be like this. To-night Life has reached its apex. I am no longer a maiden I am a woman. All, all has been revealed to me. O my love!

May 7.

I feel as though I was still in a dream. Papa, Mama, Alicia do not seem to be real. I hear them speak to me, I even touch them, yet I myself seem to be somewhere else. My body is in the room with them, but *I* am in Realms I flew to last night in Stanislaw's arms. He had—yes, I must write the truth!—*sulked* all day and avoided me. At first I was amused, then cross with him, and then I found I could not, *could* not bear it. I went to my room in tears—and found a message from him under my pillow! Written in his beautiful hand. It ran:

"Dare I ask you to meet me to-night behind Venus and Adonis?

If hour and place be too remote for modesty, blame, but do not despise, your Stanislaw."

Under my pillow! How could it have got there but by the ministration of the G*d of Love? Unless Stanislaw himself—oh had he dared? I shuddered to think what, had he been seen, he would have suffered at Papa's hands. The horsewhip at least.

It was warm and cloudy last night, no nightingales. I did not know what time Stanislaw hoped for me—or how long he would hope. Sudden terror turned me cold lest he had ceased to hope! I was quite in a panic. Everything seemed to depend on my reaching him on wings, without the delay of another single instant. Feverishly I wrapped my shawl round me, and ran. The house was silent and my sandals made almost no sound. I found myself out in the garden scarcely knowing I was there—I ran to the shrubbery—it was so dark I could scarcely see, and my eyes were flowing with tears. I thought I had lost him for ever. Then his arms were round me—and it was I who was lost! We did not say anything to explain, reproach, forgive. Only—my love!—my dear!—and sweetheart, and I love you. At least, he said these things. He may remember better than I what I said, for what he said I shall never never forget. We trembled so that neither of us could stand up, and presently we were in the grass at the base of Venus and Adonis, and he was saying: "Addie, my beautiful Addie!" and "Sweetheart!" and "Dear Love" again and again—all little broken things like the nightingales practicing. So far he had only clasped me and stroked my hair and pressed his cheek to my head and kissed my eyes—I was in utter heavenly confusion—and then, O then he made me lean back in the grass and leaned over me and gasped "Addie! Addie! I must!"—and I knew I should not let him, but he did. I thought I would swoon for terror and happiness. Presently I was crying and so was he, and he kept on saying Forgive, forgive, forgive me! And I could not speak, but pressed him to me and forgave him, if not in words. I hardly remember leaving his arms, I was in my room again, throbbing all over, I seemed to be in them still. I seem to be in them still.

If I could remember more I would write it down. I have written all I remember so that in time to come I may read it every year on the Sixth of May and have it all again.

O what have we done?

May 14.

I have been too languid to write for a week. Mama has threatened to send for Dr. Baird. I tell her I am all right, only a little upset with the Spring. She has given me sulphur and Epsom Salts which I detest. I try to seem as usual, but I only live for moments with Stanislaw and he seems to avoid me. Only sometimes when we are alone for a moment we hastily take each other's hands unable to speak, and drop them when the door opens.

I am waiting.

May 17.

Nothing has happened.

May 18.

What am I to do? I would consult Alicia but do not know how to begin.

May 19.

Alicia herself gave me the opening to-day. I was sitting reading, or trying to read, in my room. The book was opened at the sad tale of "The Abandoned Orphan" from which I had hoped to learn when to expect, but my tears were falling too fast for me to read, and anyhow I know the tale by heart and it does not exactly explain.

Alicia came in and said: "Dearest, why do you weep? You have been mopey for days and your Mama is getting worried. What is the matter? What has happened? Tell your friend." She put her arm round me so that I could hide my face and speak.

"Alicia," I whispered, "how soon after you have given yourself to a man?"

"Good G*d!" said Alicia. "Have you given yourself to Stanislaw?"

I confessed I had. I said: "It was too sweet to resist. It happened before I knew."

"I know," she said. She made me look at her and said very earnestly: "I cannot blame you. If he had asked me, and I had not been pledged to fidelity, I would have done the same in spite of my age." Her tears mingled with mine.

I said consolingly: "Ninon de l'Enclos fell in love with her son when she was sixty."

"I am not sixty," she said, "and Stanislaw is not my son."

"How soon, Alicia," I asked again, "shall I bear his child?"

She did not reply for a moment, then she said: "I must warn you, Adeline, it does not always happen."

This took me by surprise. "Are you sure?" I said.

"Quite sure. It is as well to be prepared."

I suppose I ought to have felt a mother's grief, but I must own my feelings were rather those of relief. I repeated—"But if it should, Alicia?"

Instead of answering she asked me: "Do you love Stanislaw truly, Adeline?"

"I love him with all my heart."

"With absolute fidelity?"

"Yes, Alicia."

"You will never give yourself to another man?"

"I could not!" I cried.

"Then whatever happens I am your friend to the bitter end," she swore, "and if your child is born I will adopt it, though it should cast a slur upon my name."

Noble, noble Alicia!

But I think I would rather have my child for myself.

May 20.

My talk with Alicia has eased my mind, and surely after all this time nothing will happen. I woke up quite lighthearted, and laughed at a joke Papa made at breakfast. He and Mama seemed pleased, and Papa said: "That's more like my Addie." "I told you," said Mama, "it was nothing but the Spring."

"Well," said Papa, "if we have got back our spirits we must begin to—"

Mama coughed behind her hand, the sort of cough you do not take a linctus for.

May 21.

I had it out with Stanislaw in the libery. I went in to take back the Grammont Memoirs, and found him, as I knew I would, alone. I put the book back in its place and came and stood behind him with my hands on his shoulders, and said: "Darling." His left hand went up to clasp mine.

"Addie," he said without turning his head.

"Look at me, Stanislaw, or are you ashamed of me?"

"I am ashamed of myself."

"That's nonsense," I said, "I love you, and I won't have you ashamed of the man I love."

He turned then, and said: "Oh Addie, I must not let you talk like that, though it fills me with rapture."

"Why should not we be filled with rapture while we can?" I asked.

He said in a low voice: "You know what I am."

"Yes, I know there is a difference in our stations. Does it make any difference to our love?"

"None to mine, none to mine!" he cried.

"I love to hear you say it so generously."

"Oh Addie, it is you who are generous."

"For loving you? But that is a thing I can't help."

"Do you," he whispered, "do you really love me?"

"I love you with all my heart, with all my fidelity. I will never give myself to another man."

He pressed my hand to his lips. "I don't know what I ought to say or do. I have been thinking I ought to go back to Matlock."

"And break my heart?" I said. "Stanislaw, how cruel, how heartless you are! I would die before I broke yours, but there, it seems you haven't a heart to break."

"I haven't, for it is yours."

"You have, for you have mine." Then I said a line of Sir Philip Sidney's most beautiful song—"My truelove hath my heart and I have his."

Stanislaw said: "It seems too much to be true."

"It is perfectly true."

"Are you better, Addie?"

"Only if you are good to me."

"Oh heavens, I will be!"

"Then shall we finish the sketch at the Gothic Temple?"

He sprang up. "Yes, yes, how many days have we not wasted!"

"We will not waste another single one." This happiness will go on for ever and ever.

May 25.

All the days are beautiful ones now. We have hiding places for our notes to each other, and at night I tap signals on the floor of my closet, while Stanislaw stands on his bed with a long stick. One tap means "Yes," two "No." Other taps are questions and answers—"Do you love me?" "I love you." "Are you happy?" "Good morning," and "Good Night," and "Dream of me."

May 26.

What is against our union? Why should not Stanislaw declare himself? He may have his reasons for reticence about his birth, but love overrules all things.

May 27.

Papa is arranging a picnic party at Dovedale, a long day with an early start and luncheon by the water. We are all to go, and Sir Terence Hogan too. It came up when Sir Terence dropped in last night for "a sup of music." I sang my new song, the Reichhardt Polonaise: "Are they meant but to deceive me, Those fond words that tell of love?"

"Indade and they are not, then, Addie!" said Sir Terence, who, as usual, sat beside me turning the pages. Stanislaw of course had to stay in his corner. I found a note from him later under my pillow. He is jealous of Sir Terence—the very idea! My "old uncle"!

I have just tapped "I love you, dream of me" on the floor so I hope he will stop being so stupid, and I hope I shall sit by him during one of the long drives to Dovedale, going or coming. Coming back, perhaps, with the sun setting softly in the west.

May 28.

Stanislaw said it was not only Sir Terence but my choice of song that made him uneasy last night. "If you sing for me alone, Addie, how could you choose such words to sing? Do you think I would or could deceive you?"

I answered, "You may have secrets you do not tell even me."

He must have understood for he looked quite taken aback, and said in a low voice: "You sting me to the quick. Of what can you suspect me?"

I longed to speak of his father, but lacked the courage, and only said: "Of nothing, and I will not sing the song you do not like."

May 30.

The picnic has been fixed for the Third of June. Alicia and I are having new summer frocks. We went in to Matlock to be fitted by Miss Spencer. She was pleased when Alicia told her S— was getting on so nicely at Pelham Place.

"He writes as if he is happy," said Miss Spencer. "I'm glad, because he has not always been." Then she caught herself up and bit her lips as if she had said more than she meant. I couldn't help it, and blurted out: "Who is his father?"

She put a lot of pins in her mouth, and mumbled a little and her face got a dark red. So I said: "I'm sorry—is he dead?"

"No," said Miss Spencer, "he is—abroad."

Then she went on pinning us very busily, and Alicia and I exchanged glances over her head.

Abroad! Yes! In Russia, or Greece, or Poland!

June 1.

I have told Stanislaw we will watch our chance to slip away after the collation and enjoy the beauties of nature together. "I shall take my paints and block for an excuse," I said, "and if I am questioned they will serve as a cover."

June 2.

The dresses have come! They are most beautiful—Alicia's a sort of deep damask, and mine a striped muslin patterned with tiny leaves. I pray it will be a fine day.

June 4.

I could not write anything yesterday, terrible yesterday! Even if there had been time at the end of the day I was much too upset and excited. It began with my being divided from Stanislaw, when Sir Terence, who called early in his dogcart, insisted that I drive with him. However, we all set out and almost arrived together, Sir Terence keeping his lively stepper back. He was very gay and said he felt a boy again. We talked a great deal of nonsense, and he said: "Addie, your high spirits are very seductive. You're a seductive little lady altogether. Are yez ever serious?"

"Oh yes," I said, "I can be solemn on occasion."

"I'm glad to hear it, for I've something solemn to tell ye."

"Oh, not on such a sunny day!" I said, which made him laugh.

"I promise you 'twill not overcast the sunshine."

"Well," I said thoughtlessly, "keep it till after luncheon, when I shall be fortified."

"Agreed!" he cried smartly, and I remembered too late that after luncheon I must make my escape to Stanislaw. I turned the subject, so that it should not seem too firmly fixed, and said how dashed I had been about the New Year's Eve Ball—"I had a beautiful dress for it," I told him, "and I have never yet worn it even once."

"That's aisily remedied," said Sir Terence. "I'll give you a Midsummer Eve Ball instead."

I was delighted and cried: "Is it a promise?"

"Su're it is, if you promise to wear that beautiful new dress and take the shine out of every other pair of eyes in the room."

"Oh I shall count the days," I said in a glow.

We arrived in Dovedale at last, and while they spread the cloth I got out my paints to depict the festive scene.

Beautiful Dovedale! Never shall I tire of thy beauties!

I had to arrange things a little in my picture, as I could not sit in it myself and paint at the same time. I made a tolerably good composition, and washed in the sky and grass by the time they were ready. Once I called Stanislaw to me, on the pretext of consulting him on a point of art, but he muttered: "Do you intend to drive with him all the way back?" and before I could answer, either to scold or re-assure, Sir Terence came up "to observe the progress of the masterpiece," and said I had his check waistcoat "to the life." As Stanislaw moved away, Sir Terence said in a sort of loud undertone—"I hope ye've a nice bright vermilion in your box, Addie!" and winked and pointed with his thumb at dear S—'s head, and in case he had overheard I said rather loud—"I have a very beautiful madder brown"—and I think that was when I began to be upset with Sir Terence and S— and everybody else. When we took our seats on the grass, they had put me by Sir Terence far from Stanislaw, and I was annoyed by Sir Terence's jollity and Stanislaw's downcast looks, against reason, I thought, for had I not promised him a lover's tryst? I own I felt a little out with Stanislaw, for after all if he will not reveal himself he cannot expect other people's consideration, though he has all my love.

The food was sumptious, Mama and Charlotte had outdone themselves, and Sir Terence had brought a bottle of cherry brandy for "the Ladies." It came out with a flourish at the end of the feast, as a surprise.

Mama said: "How kind and thoughtful, she doted on it," when Sir Terence poured her out a glass, but when he poured one for me Papa said:

"Not for my Addie in the heat of the day."

"What, not just one little tot?" persuaded Sir Terence.

"She's better without it," said Papa, "but Miss Linton won't say no." And he passed my glass to Alicia. He was thinking of the

Christmas party four years ago when I crept down out of bed to the supper-table and sipped all the last drops in the port-wine glasses after the company had gone to the parlour. Then I danced on the table, and they heard me, and I was whipped. I felt so vexed at being treated still like a child, that when Sir Terence poured the glasses for the gentlemen I seized his in one hand and Papa's in the other and drank them both quickly before anyone could stop me. Never have I tasted anything so delicious! It made me feel swimming and excited, my feelings rose up in a mixture. Cherry Brandy is very like love in its effect on a person. I wonder if other people have found it so! Sir Terence roared with laughter, Papa looked furious, there were exclamations from Mama and Alicia, and I saw Stanislaw looking rather aghast, but I felt full of courage and past minding. I jumped up crying: "If I am to be treated like a baby I will not stay to dessert, I'll go back to bed!"—and I ran away laughing rather loudly. I heard Sir Terence call "Miss Addie, plaze!" but I would not stop, I felt angry with everybody in the world and quite reckless. I ran so fast that nobody could catch me, all I wanted to do was to get out of their sight and hide, and upset them. At the stepping-stones I pulled off my shoes and stockings and hopped barefoot through the stream to the further glade, and then I heard Stanislaw splashing after me, and to my surprise I found I was crying with rage.

"Go, go!" I heard myself saying.

He seized my hands. "Addie! Adeline! Pray compose yourself!"

I stamped my foot. "You had better take your own advice," I said. "You've been discomposed ever since we set out. Was it my fault I had to drive in the dogcart—Sir Terence is our guest. Was it my fault he called your hair vermilion, yet you've done nothing but sulk at me across the tablecloth."

"Addie, be just! I have done nothing to offend you. I could not help being cast down, or what happened just now. Sweetheart, dear little Addie, you are excited, but listen—I love you as I never loved you before."

"Will you tell my papa so?"

"It will end all if I do."

"Will you tell my Papa so?" I stamped my foot at each word.

"Yes, if you insist upon it." He was as pale as death. All my violent anger turned to love. I threw my arms round his neck crying: "My belovèd! My bastard!"

There, it was out! I thought he would fold me to him. Instead, he stared as he had done when I drunk the brandy. He stammered—"Your—Have I misunderstood you?"

"No," I said fondly, "you are my belovèd, and why should I not say so?"

"You are always generous," he said, pressing my hand, still with his startled look, "but—"

"But what?"

"Did you not—?" He seemed unable to proceed.

"Whatever I did," I said rather cruelly, "I don't see why you should turn vermilion to the roots of your hair!"

He dropped my hands. "If I do blush, it is with good cause."

My anger left me, I felt fond again, my feelings seemed to go and come in waves. I put my arms round him and said:

"Dear bastard! Tell your Adeline."

"Good G*d!" he cried. "Again!"

"Again—what? I don't know what you mean."

"I am glad to hear it. We will drop the subject."

"We will do nothing of the sort! I want to know your meaning. You keep too much from me. I will not let a shadow of misunderstanding come between us. Why should you be glad if I am deficient in knowledge?"

"Some sorts of knowledge are—unsuitable," was the best he could say.

"Unsuitable? To whom? For what?"

"For you to utter and for me to hear."

I asked haughtily: "What have I said that can possibly sully your ears?"

"You have called me—"

"My belovèd and—"

"Well," he broke in, looking very uncomfortable, "it is not true."

"Not true! Oh!" I shook him and sprang away from him. "Speak for yourself, false man! Your belovèd I may not be, but mine you shall be until I cease to breathe. Go!"

"Adeline!"

"I said, go. Are you deaf? Leave me alone, sir, with my eternal love and everlasting grief." I burst into angry tears. He endeavoured to assuage them with his handkerchief, but I pushed him away. "Why waste your ministration on one you hate?"

"I do not, could not hate you, Adeline. I worship and adore you."

"Is it true?"

"Yes, darling. Only—"

"Only what? I worship and adore you without any 'onlies.' Only what?"

"You must not insult my mother."

"Your mother!" I stared at him in astonishment. "How has she come into it? I never so much as mentioned your mother, Stanislaw."

He muttered something about implication, and I cut him short saying: "You are simply inventing a pretext to pick a quarrel! And why should you do so, only you do not love me! Why should you do so, only you want to be rid of me! Why should you do so, only —" I was unable to conjure up a third "only," so I stood tapping my foot and shooting scorn at him.

"I cannot quarrel with you," said Stanislaw. "I could not if I tried. But at least you should know that there are some words a nice young lady does not permit herself to say."

"In that case I am not a nice young lady. I never will be. I shall always say what I choose, when I choose, where I choose! Why not? And what have I said that makes me a nasty young lady?"

"You have called me—" He would not say it! Would not own to it. I said it calmly for him.

"A bastard. Yes. You do not mean to tell me you are not one?" Such baseness made me clutch my heart, while the tears rained down my face. I dashed my hand across my swimming orbs, and tried to control my shaking voice, as I said—"How I despise you,

Stanislaw! I am doomed to love you always, but I have ceased to honour you."

"In heaven's name, why?" he cried.

"For denying your birth, the thing that will bridge the gap when my father comes to hear of it."

"He must never come to hear of it!" shouted Stanislaw.

"Oh," I retorted furious with him, "don't flatter yourself that I shall tell him now! Oh no! It might make him urge me to smile on you, it might send him suing to you cap in hand, and that"—I stamped again—"would never do!"

"Addie, I simply cannot grasp what you mean."

"Not even for my sake, not even to me alone, will you own the truth?"

"Even for your sake," he said in an exasperated way, "I will not be a bastard!"

If he was scarlet before, he now was crimson. He began to stammer all sorts of apologies, and attempts at explanations of I don't know what. I would not listen. I stuffed my fingers in my ears. I got excited again, and cannot describe what followed, but there was a terrible quarrel. I told him I had discovered his and his father's Secret, and he seemed about to faint—I excused him of being ashamed of me, and said if he loved me he ought to tell Papa, I really cannot remember all I said and all he replied, but it ended in my crying that I would have no more to do with him, and I was going to Sir Terence's Midsummer Ball, where no doubt I should find better bastards than he and marry one of them. Of course, I did not mean a word of it, it was all the cherry brandy; but now I am calmer I still cannot understand why, if he adores me as he says he does, he refuses to reveal the secret that would remove all obstacles from our path.

I found myself presently wandering about alone, and was met by Alicia, very agitated.

"You have given us a terrible upset," she said. "Have you seen Stanislaw?"

I think I said I had not.

"You are not telling the truth, dearest," said Alicia.. "Where is he?"

I said I didn't know or care.

"They are waiting to go back—they must not leave the drive too late because of the horses. Adelaide, you really will have to come."

Her calling me Adelaide made me uneasy. I asked: "Are they very annoyed?"

"To say the least of it, your Papa and Mama were highly distressed, shall I say, but Sir Terence with extreme good humour has pacified them. He takes the blame on himself for encouraging you to partake, and will not hear of your being scolded for it. Mr. Granby has promised to say no more about it. You are to drive home with Sir Terence, your Papa and Mama will come in one of the carriages, and I will find Stanislaw and come with him and the paraphernalia in the other. He has—" she asked—"been with you, Adeline?"

I hung my head. "Do they know that?" I asked.

"No, I alone suspected. Dearest! What has happened?"

"Don't ask me, Alicia. I fear he is playing with me." I burst into tears.

"Hush, hush! Impossible." She looked very worried. "Dry your eyes. We must not loiter now. Your Papa thinks you have been sleeping it off, and are ashamed to put in an appearance. It is no worse than that, so come along."

My hand is too tired to write further, and my head is heavy with crying and I know not what. Papa and Mama were as good as their word, and except for Papa's—"So here you are at last, miss!" nothing was said. Sir Terence was kindness itself all the way home. The last ten miles I was asleep against his shoulder, and could hardly wake to stumble up to bed. I have stayed in my room all day.

All is over between me and Stanislaw.

June 12.

We are sad friends again. We made it up in the raspberry canes, but it is not as it was. I cannot deny there is a cloud between us. He keeps trying to explain things—what seems to upset him most is that he uttered aloud to me the word that should make us happy; I have told him to forget he ever said it, and I will too, and never, never refer to it again, since he wishes it so. Once he talked hesitatingly of his father, but I stopped him, saying his father was nothing to me, I did not care what he was, it was Stanislaw I loved. And so I do, but there is a shadow between us. How true it is that the Course of True Love never did Run Smooth.

I have released him from his promise to tell Papa.

June 14.

To comfort myself I have begun looking over my balldress. It needs taking in; I must have fallen away. Mama was both proud and worried that I shall appear at the ball in a 17-inch waist.

"Is my little girl pining about anything?" she asked. "Tell Mamma."

I am sure I am going into a decline, but I said cheerfully: "Of course not, Mamma. I am looking forward to the St. John's Eve Dance"

"So is Sir Terence," she said. "You know he is giving it specially to please you?"

"Yes, Mamma." I did not tell her I had almost asked him to.

"It is flattering," she said, "when a gentleman is ready to do things to please such a young lady."

"And such an old gentleman too," I said.

June 16.

I have been describing my dress to Stanislaw. "Don't," he said. "To hear you speak of it makes me unhappy."

"Pray, why?"

"Because others will dance with you and I shall not."

"Listen, Stanislaw, you shall dance with me, and in my balldress too."

"How, Adeline?"

"I will dress early and slip into the garden on Midsummer Eve, and we will dance for Venus and Adonis. Now, will that please you?"

"Everything you are and do and say pleases me, Addie."

"No, not quite everything," I sighed. "But never mind that. I am resolved henceforth only to be happy with you."

"Oh Addie!" he said. "Addie!" He opened his arms—but I have been careful after my escape, and only let him kiss my hand or cheek. I shook my head and said gently: "Not again."

"Do you mean never again?" he asked wistfully.

"Stanislaw," I said, "I have escaped a great danger. Would you imperil me twice?"

"I don't know what you mean," said Stanislaw.

June 18.

To-day S— said: "I wish that ball was over."

"Do you not want me to enjoy myself?"

"I have a strange uneasy feeling about it."

"Alicia calls that having a premonition. Now I have a premonition that something remarkable will happen that night."

"At the ball, where I am not?"

"Perhaps before or after the ball, where you are."

June 21.

Alicia said to me to-day: "You and S— ought to be more careful."

"What do you mean?"

"You are too often together and have nothing to show for it. And the cataloge lags sadly. Your Mama said to-day, 'When is that young man going to be done with it? He has been here more than three months.' I made the best of it, and pointed out that the cataloge of a big libery takes a very long time, that at the British Museum would take years, and said Mr. Granby found S— useful in so many other ways. 'What ways for example?' she asked. 'Such as making up the accounts, cleaning the guns, and Miss Adelaide's lessons.' 'I haven't seen much sign of lessons lately, and Addie has become very subject to moods. I wonder!' Mrs. Granby did not tell me what she wondered, but I am afraid I have more than a suspicion."

"Oh, bother your suspicions, Alicia! I am feeling particularly happy just now, and here you come upsetting me with 'suspicions'!"

"Well, be a little more prudent, that is all."

"Boo!" I said.

Midsummer Eve.

Why, oh why did I not heed Alicia's warning? What has happened to-night is incredible! I know not if I am more furious or more wretched. All that Juliet Capulet suffered Adelaide Granby suffers in excelsior!

To begin at the beginning of this frantic night.

I went early to my room to make my toilet. I knew Mama would want Alicia to help her, and made the excuse that I needed her help first.

"When you are ready," said Mama, "sit perfectly still with a sheet over your dress. My little girl must make her entrance as fresh as a daisy."

When every detail had been attended to, Alicia sat me on the ottoman. "You look a dream of youthful loveliness," she said. "Do you feel nervous?"

"What about?"

"Your first ball—all the people."

"Oh no! I am going to enjoy myself."

"In that case I'm sure you will. Ah the confidence of youth! Settle your skirts. Now to obliterate you!" She drew the sheet around me.

"Oh Alicia! It might be my winding-sheet."

"What a dreadful thing to say! Your Mama is calling. I must leave my sweet one."

No sooner was she gone than up I sprang. Down dropped my shroud, the butterfly emerged from the crystallis, and began to softly float down the stairs. Nobody was about on the upper floor, but in the hall I met Annie carrying a tray. She nearly dropped it.

"Oh miss, how you startled me! Oh miss, how beautiful!"

"Do you like it, Annie?"

"I never saw anything so beautiful! How good of you to come and show yourself."

She seemed unable to tear herself away, and time was precious, so I said: "I am going into the garden to find a rose"—and went in search of Stanislaw.

It was a fine warm evening, there has been no rain for a week, so the grass was dry. I was not afraid of staining my satin sandals, and tiptoed over the lawn to the shrubbery. Stanislaw was already there. When he saw me his breath was taken away. He could not speak. I ran to him, my scarf fluttering.

"Will Your Highness be pleased to honour me with a dance?" I sank in a low curtsey, and as I rose took his hands. He seemed too bewildered to say anything, but as I placed his hands where they should be he whispered: "Oh Addie, you are so beautiful!" Then we danced.

He is not very proficient, but I shewed him the steps and he did better; however, he was pretty soon out of breath, so I made him sit on Adonis, and danced the Varsoviana alone, humming Reichhardt's tune, but not the words he could not bear to hear me sing. I ended on another deep curtsey at his feet, and as I rose he opened his arms to me—I threw caution to the winds, gave him my lips again, and sank upon his bosom. He kissed me again and again—oh the bliss of it!

And that was how Papa found us.

Do not ask me, my diary, what ensued. The air was full of sounds, angry ones from Papa, and gasps from us. I may have whimpered, and Stanislaw tried to speak, but any words of ours were drowned in Papa's shoutings. He bawled something about— "So this is your rose-gathering!" and ordered Stanislaw to his room while he dragged me away. A flounce of my dress was torn and trailed behind me. This spoiling of my beautiful balldress annoyed me so that I forgot my fright, and when we reached the libery I had some of my spirit back. I was still trembling but determined to face it out, and declare my love if I die for it. While Papa banged the door I leaned on the table where my belovèd S— has so often sat pen in hand, and got my breath.

Papa then strode to me and said with a glare: "Annie informed me you were in the garden gathering roses, and what do I find? Perhaps you will tell me what has been going on in this house behind my back."

I took my courage in my hands to confess the truth. "Papa," I said, "my dear S— has seduced me."

"Good G*d!" my father cried, "it cannot be true!"

I would not deny my love for all a parent's ire.

"It *is* true!" I said.

"You don't know what you are saying."

"I know quite well and am not ashamed of it."

"When—" (he seemed to choak) "when did this happen?"

"It is happening all the time."

"Go to your room!" shouted Papa.

Mama came to the door in her handsome gown, and I saw Alicia's agitated face behind her. Mama said—"Good heavens, Mr. Granby, the servants can hear you. What is happening. *Adelaide!* look at your dress!" She burst into tears.

I cried out: "D*mn my dress!" while Papa, quite out of himself, shouted: "Mrs. Granby, your daughter is a b*tch!"

I stamped my foot at him, quite furious. "You sully your tongue, Papa, with such expressions."

Mama was gasping something about the carriage—and Sir Terence—and the ball—and the hour—but Papa drowned her with— "No ball for anyone in this house to-night! Our daughter has been seduced by that carrot-pated bastard!"

So he has known all the time!

I heard Mama shriek, and made one last appeal to him.

"Papa," I cried, "have you forgotten what love is? Do you not remember the day you seduced Mama?"

"Up to your room this instant!" shouted Papa.

I saw Mama collapse on the settee, and Alicia flutter about her, as Papa drove me before him, up the stairs. As I passed Alicia she cast me a despairing inquiring glance, but of course I could tell her nothing.

My Papa is unreasonably upset. If a young lady may be seductive, why may she not also be seduced?

Papa does not seem to know the meaning of words, and uses quite unmentionable ones himself.

He has locked me in!

It is intolerable, I will not bear it!

It is ten o'clock. Nobody has come near me. I shall not go to bed. I shall sit up all night. If Stanislaw comes for me I will fly with him to the ends of the earth. I have missed the ball.

Awful sounds are going on in the little gunroom. The floor is too thick to hear what they are saying. I have stamped as hard as I could, tapping the taps that mean—"I love you! I love you!"

It is nearly eleven. The sounds stopped half an hour ago. Oh what is happening?

Alicia has been to my door. I knew her scratch. She put her mouth to the keyhole.

"Adeline!"

"Alicia!"

"Stanislaw is gone. Your Papa has sent him away."

"Did he horsewhip him?"

"All but. Not quite."

"Where has he gone?"

"Back to Matlock."

"Did they drive him?"

"Your Papa said he could go on Shanks's mare."

"How brutal! He cannot carry his trunk all that way."

"It will be sent after him. Your Papa stood over him while he packed it."

"Did you see him?"

"Only a glimpse. No chance to get in a word."

"What did he look like?"

"I think he had been crying."

"Oh Alicia, intercede for us!"

"Dearest, I will."

The flowers of my life have bloomed away, the dreams of my youth are dreamed out.

A letter from Alicia, pushed under my door. Oh heavens! Papa is sending her off too. She goes to-morrow. I am alone in the house of mine enemy. Cimerian darkness falls on me. What shall I do? I will write a novel.

It is one o'clock! I have begun my novel. At least, I have written the name of it. I have called it

THE BASTARD OF PINSK

in Stanislaw's memory. It shall enshrine all I have gone through in these three months. The ardours of literature will ease my heart and perhaps prevent me from dying, as I should like to do. I have written the title-page as gracefully as I can, for Stanislaw's sake. Oh my love, my love!

I have been asleep. Grey light is coming through the window—something is tapping at the window.

It was he! He has come and gone. Oh darling darling darling. I went to the window, and he was in the cedar tree. I opened the window, and he came as far along the bough as it would bear him. I said: "Oh take care, you will fall."

"Oh Addie," he said, "if only I could touch you."

I stretched out my hand and he stretched out his and our fingertips just touched. "Stanislaw," I said, "what did Papa do to you?"

"Nothing but be very very angry. I think I did convince him that no real harm had been done. I could not blame him for shouting at me. I have presumed too far. But oh I loved you so much, Addie, it was hard to remember my station."

"Say the word," I said, "and I will fly with you."

"Oh Addie, I must not. Dearest, how could we marry?"

I said sadly: "Does your station then come between us?"

He nodded and I wept.

"Don't, Addie," he implored, "remember we are really too young to be married."

"You may be," I sobbed, "but I am not."

"Oh Addie, will they marry you to Sir Terence?"

I could not help laughing at that among my sobs. "Don't be ridiculous, that old man!" I said.

"Laugh or cry, Addie, don't do both. You will get histyrical."

I controlled my emotions and said: "Listen Stanislaw, listen darling Stanislaw. I will not marry Sir Terence or anybody. I will not marry anyone but you, and if I can't be married to you I will die a spinster, I swear it."

"You must not, I have no right to expect it."

"I swear it!"

"I swear too."

"Alicia is being sent away as well," I said. "I am losing both of you, but you need not lose each other. Alicia loves you, all in vain, and will be your friend. Perhaps we shall all be together again one day."

"Perhaps," he said. But we only said "perhaps" to comfort each other. A knell in our hearts tells us both—*All is ended.*

It was quite light now, nearly five o'clock, and I said: "The servants will be about soon, if they find you it will be dreadful. Goodbye."

"Goodbye, Addie. Oh Addie, how beautiful you are in your balldress. How beautiful you looked when you ran into the shrubbery last evening. I will never forget how you look and talk and feel, or how your hair smells. I am your lover always, always, Addie. Oh Addie, if only I could kiss your lips again."

"Last night—you kissed them last night for the second time. And now I shall await—"

I could not go on.

"What, darling, what have you and I to await? Nothing, nothing now." He began to cry. It dried my tears to see him. To comfort him I got the scissors and cut off a curl of my hair, and tied it, and just managed to reach it to him. "Now you can always feel and smell it," I said. He kissed it and put it inside his shirt.

"Now one of yours," I said, but alas, the scissors dropped to the grass, and I heard noises in the house. "Oh, you must go," I said. "Send me one somehow. Put it in an envelope for Alicia and drop it in the letterbox, and perhaps she can get it to me before she goes."

"I haven't an envelope," said Stanislaw.

I fetched him one and asked: "Have you a pencil?"

"Yes."

"Disguise your handwriting. Goodbye, Stanislaw."

"Goodbye, Addie."

"Goodbye! Goodbye!"

He went.

Parting is Such Sweet Sorrow.

June 24.

I went to bed after Stanislaw had gone and cried and slept by turns for hours. When I woke up I was still a prisoner. I don't think anybody has come in while I slept, because there was an envelope on the floor. On it was written: "Farewell! A. L. M."

Inside, I felt as I opened it, Stanislaw's hair!

How joyfully I took out the paper 'twas folded in! On this she had written: "His Hair—as we always wished it!"

I took out the lock of his hair. She had dyed it black. I could have slapped Alicia.

At one o'clock Mama came in. She was very chilly in her manner.

"You are to stay in your room till you have begged Papa's pardon."

I said: "I think Papa ought to beg my pardon."

"Then you will stay in your room."

They brought me gruel for lunch, which they know I detest. I threw it out of the window, basin and all.

Nobody has come near me since then.

I stand at my window and touch the cedar bough he climbed to last night—nay, this morning!—and gaze mournfully in the direction of Matlock as well as I can, because it is to the north-east and my window looks north-west. O if I were a bird! Or if mine were the curious case of the young lady the Hon. Grantley F. Berkeley writes about in his fassinating description of Bourne Mouth in one of my old Books of Beauty. I will copy it here for my consolation.

"A young lady, a very nice young lady, addicted to too tight lacing, heedless of the public caution given in the daily journals as to the effects of undue pressure, walked in a high wind on the cliffs. She was snapped like a tender flower—her bosom and her bonnet flew away to sea, while all beneath remained upon the cliff, the little feet stamping with anger on the heather. At that moment up came a down-looking gentleman; he heard a cry of distress, and he saw the usual extent of a female figure generally acknowledged by his eyes stamping apparently in grief. He offered his services, he asked what he could do; he listened to no purpose for a reply, and he offered his arm. A kick from one of the little feet made him look up for farther explanation, and he saw in the distance the bosom and bonnet flying away, while the hands which should have taken his proffered assistance were kissing adieus, or vainly stretched out towards the remnants left upon the native land. It was the first time that gentleman ever looked up; he has by this event been confirmed in melancholy, and never will look up again!"

I cannot write down this sad tale without tears—the down-looking gentleman so like my Stanislaw, now, perhaps, confirmed in melancholy—the vainly stretched out hands kissing adieu—ah! Could I but escape so to my Stanislaw I would tightlace till I could not draw a breath. As for the part that would be left behind, if he had my bosom he would not want anything else.

Three o'clock. I have pulled my bellrope, but nobody comes. Will they leave me here to starve? I am fearfully bored. I shall begin my novel.

It is no use, I cannot write, I am ravenous. I have pulled and pulled my bellrope. I wish I had not thrown my gruel out of the window. For my consolation, I will jot down a list of my favourite dishes and imagine I am eating them.

It has only made it worse. I will think of my novel. Adeline—Georgiana—Caroline. (Caroline Crescent, No. 15—he lives there!) Those are the names I have chosen for my heroines, perhaps I should say for my Heroine.

I shall pull my bell-rope without stopping till somebody comes.

"Stop it, Adelaide!"

"Not till I've had something to eat."

"Do you know you have been a very wicked girl?"

"No, Mama, I do not. I know I am hungry." She seemed to hesitate, then said: "Sir Terence is below. He has called to inquire the reason of our absence last night."

"And I suppose Papa shouted it to the housetops."

"Papa has told him as much as is advisable. Sir Terence had naturally supposed you were ill."

"Dear old Sir Terry! *He* wouldn't starve a person."

"Sir Terence is very kind, much kinder, Adelaide, than you deserve." She paused, and then said: "He would like to see you."

"Oh, then *he* isn't cross!"

"Wash your face," said Mama, "and go to the morning room."

"Is Papa there?"

"No, Sir Terence will see you alone."

I washed my face and hands and went to the morning room. He was sitting on the sofa. I sat down by him and said: "They are treating me abominably."

"Poor little Addie," he said, so kindly that I began to cry. "Aisy, now, aisy," he said, and took me on his knee. "So little Addie is in the throes of her first fancy."

"And my last!" I sobbed. "And they are starving me to death, except for gruel, which they know I detest."

"So do I," said Sir Terence. "Suppose you come and dine with me this evening?"

"Will Papa be there?"

"Just you and your Mama. No gruel! You shall have whatever you fancy."

"Duck and green peas?"

"My own favourite choice."

I tried to remember my list. "And lobster sauce?"

"Lobster sauce all by itself!" said Sir Terence.

"No, stupid, with turbot." Then I begged his pardon for calling him stupid, but he laughed and said he liked it very well, and no doubt he *was* stupid where very young ladies were concerned. "What after the duck?"

"Cream Trifle—and strawberries."

"Miss Addie is an epicure, I see. Anything else?"

"Yes," I said boldly, "a tot of cherry brandy."

At that he threw back his head and roared with laughter.

Then he wiped his eyes and talked to me kinder than anybody ever has. He said I was very young and he knew what it was to be unhappy at my age, and I must not think I would be sad for ever. He said he would do everything in his power to make me cheerful again, and would not worry me till I was older.

"Why should you worry me then?" I asked in surprize.

He did not answer me, but patted my hand and said: "Sure what a little girl it is!"

I sighed: "I am older than Juliet, and my heart is broken."

"'Twill mend, darlint," said Sir Terence.

Mend? Ah, no! My heart will never mend. Sir Terence does not know Life as I do. He does not dream of the Ordeal before me. He said he must go back and order that dinner, and Mama would bring me presently. I said: "And if I die of starvation first?" So he rang the bell, and when Annie came he said: "Bring me a loaf and butter and the honeyjar." Annie stared and said: "For you, sir?"

"Yes," said Sir Terence, "I'm dying of starvation, but not a word to a soul!" When Annie brought the things on a tray he cut me slice after slice till I was satisfied, and he said it looked rather bad for the lobster sauce, but I said I had room for lobster sauce at any time.

"That's a comfort anyhow," said Sir Terence, and went away, and I came back to my room, and made myself tidy and put on my new muslin, and have filled in the time of waiting with my diary.

To-night I shall sit up and begin my novel, while I await the coming of Stanislaw's child.

I know I have

*　　　*　　　*

The diary broke off abruptly, but I knew that when I routed out the remainder to-morrow, the connection would be complete.

NOTE BY "S.P."

————————

Attached by a clip to the last sheet of the diary was a note in Stanley Pinner's delightful writing.

The Eighteenth of April, 1892.

"An extraordinary document to read at my age! It is really time things were explained to Adelaide; but what would be the use? She never would attend to explanations. Ought I at least to assure her that I have absolutely no grounds for supposing myself to be a father by her or by anybody else? Dear thing! She had better remain as she is. I should be sorry to disturb any illusions she still takes pleasure in, even to clear my name as a young man. As an old one what does it matter? She has always steadfastly refused to meet me again, so I suppose she has some image of me she desires to preserve. I shall therefore leave things precisely as they are, thank her in suitable terms, such as will, I trust, please her, and when Alicia sends me her annual selection for the 'Anniversary' will copy and post it as usual on May 5th."

LETTER FROM ALICIA TO STANISLAW

———————

THE LAST thing left to examine was Miss Linton's letter. It was dated vaguely:

August, 1894

My Dearest Friend,

I have been very ill and our belovèd Adeline is getting me into some pleasant Home she knows of. How infinitely good she is to me! I was *intensely distressed* this year to fail, for the first time, to choose you a poem for May from my little hoard, I was much too feeble and all I could do was to get somebody to post you one of the "B.B." so that you could select something suitable for the occasion. I am sure you exerted *good taste*, though I *flatter myself* I have a more unerring taste in Literature, while you were *ever my superior* with brush and pen.

I am terrified of failing our darling who, as you know, has depended *from the first* on the Annual Reminder of your Anniversary, ever since I instituted it. In my severe illness a horrid thought has struck me—what if I should die before either of you? I probably shall—my age was ever a sore point with me—now it matters not. But when I am deceased, how will you manage? I shall endeavour to bequeath you my books, but in case of accidents, *look up the Keepsakes* in the British Museum. At the point of Death (from whose bourne I have safely returned *pro tem D.V.!*) one cannot repel certain thoughts in the small hours, and, it occurring to me one night that Adeline *might* predecease you (for though your junior the Scythe reaps where it will!) I employed myself by composing some Memorial Verses which would beautifully fit your case and Adeline's. Keep them by you and use *in case of need*. Not, I trust and pray, for many a day.

Are you enjoying your retirement, dear Friend? Think of me, as I now go into mine.

Eternally yours,
Alicia Mary Linton

Accompanying this were some untidily written verses—the first I ever saw in Stanislaw's perfect hand:

"When Death hath bereft thee of Breath and of Being—"

STANISLAW'S FATHER

As I laid down Miss Linton's letter, I heard sounds on the stairs, and called: "Danny?"

She peeped through my door, with the biscuit barrel from the dining-room in her hand. "False hunger!" she said cheerfully. "I suffer from it dreadfully and thought I'd go down to steal a biccy. Not in bed yet?"

"No, I've been reading the things you brought along."

"Any revelations, eh?" She advanced into the room.

"Thousands, Danny! There's only one thing left I'd like to know. I suppose Mr. Pinner never mentioned his father to you."

Danny laughed. "Oh, yes he did, only a little while before he popped off. It came up on his hundredth birthday. He was tickled to death at all the fussation about him in the papers and the praise of his cleverness and all the rest of it, and I caught him chuckling softly to himself. 'What's the joke?' I said. 'It'd surprise 'em, Adey,' he said, 'to know they're praising the son of a forger, wouldn't it?' 'Go on!' I said, 'you the son of a forger!' 'I am,' he said. 'My dad was quite as clever a penman as I am, but they sent him to Botany Bay for it, while his son gets a wire from the King! I used to be terribly ashamed of it, and never mentioned my dad if I could help it. Funny how things don't matter when you're a hundred that broke your heart when you were in your teens.'"

"I wonder if Aunt Addie knew," I said.

QUERY BY PAMELA LANG

What *did* Aunt Addie know?

Of course, she had been playing a game with herself all her life. Not only because it had paid her to—though it had; so she had no temptation to end it. Adelaide Granby had her wits about her. She may have been right in believing that anything interfering with the self-hypnosis by which she not only earned her living, but enjoyed her life, would be fatal to her powers of carrying on.

Carrying on! The darling old hypocrite! She had "revelled" in the idea of carrying on—but she had never carried on to the extent she hinted. Did she really diddle herself into thinking she had?

How much did Aunt Addie know?

How much did she feel?

FURROWED MIDDLEBROW

*titles available in paperback only

Printed in Great Britain
by Amazon

50615825R00188